Tales Out of Innsmouth

New Stories of the Children of Dagon

More Titles from Chaosium

Call of Cthulhu® Fiction

Encyclopedia Cthulhiana, 2nd Ed.
The Azathoth Cycle
The Cthulhu Cycle
Cthulhu's Heirs
The Disciples of Cthulhu, 2nd Ed.
The Dunwich Cycle
The Hastur Cycle, 2nd Ed.
The Innsmouth Cycle
The Ithaqua Cycle
Made in Goatswood
The Necronomicon
Nightmare's Disciple
The Nyarlathotep Cycle
The Shub-Niggurath Cycle
Singers of Strange Songs
Robert Bloch's Mysteries of the Worm
Lin Carter's The Xothic Legend Cycle
Lord Dunsany's The Complete Pegana
Henry Kuttner's The Book of Iod
Joseph S. Pulver's Nightmare's Disciple
Richard Tierney's Scroll of Thoth

Call of Cthulhu® Fiction

Tales Out of Innsmouth

New Stories of the Children of Dagon

SCOTT DAVID ANIOLOWSKI
PETER H. CANNON
PIERRE COMTOIS
JOHN S. GLASBY
C. J. HENDERSON
H. P. LOVECRAFT
GREGORY LUCE
BRIAN MCNAUGHTON
GARY MYERS
STANLEY C. SARGENT
ANN K. SCHWADER
FRANKLYN SEARIGHT

SELECTED AND EDITED BY ROBERT M. PRICE
COVER ART BY H. E. FASSL
INTERIOR ART BY DAVE CARSON

A Chaosium Book
1999

Tales Out of Innsmouth is published by Chaosium Inc.

Cover and interior layout by Shannon Appel. Copyediting by Janice Sellers. Proofreading by James Naureckas. Data mechanic Iggy Lombardy. Project, additional editorial Lynn Willis.

Please address questions and comments concerning this book, as well as requests for free notices of Chaosium publications, by mail to Chaosium, Inc., 950-A 56th Street, Oakland CA 94608-3136, U.S.A. For a current listing, visit our web page at:

http://www.chaosium.com

This book is printed on 100% acid-free paper which includes at least 20% post-consumer waste.

FIRST EDITION

10 9 8 7 6 5 4 3 2 1

Chaosium Publication 6024. Published in September, 1999.

ISBN 1-56882-127-1

Printed in Canada.

Contents

Dedication

To Ricoh Browning,
the Creature from the Black Lagoon

The One That Got Away

Narratologists, among whose eager acolytes I count myself, make a couple of distinctions which I think will aid us in understanding a nagging hint of fundamental *wrongness* in the narration of "The Shadow over Innsmouth." The first distinction is that, in a first-person narrative, between the *narrating I* and the *narrated I*. Since the operating assumption in such a story is that the narrator recounts his own adventure at some distance from the events, the narrating I has hindsight perspective that the narrated I, the remembered I in the narrated scene, did not have at the time. The narrating I has since learned of motivations and actions on the part of other characters that he did not know at the time so, if he wishes, he may, as a typical omniscient narrator, share with the reader the thoughts of the antagonists or information he did not know at the time about events transpiring elsewhere while, as the narrated I, he was busy fighting for his life. Yet if he wishes to create suspense and narrative tension by withholding information from the reader, he may do so without seeming as arbitrary as an omniscient third-person narrator who ostensibly has no reason to withhold part of the facts. With the first-person narrator the arbitrariness is less likely to be noticed, because it is easy for the narrative focus to slip from the perspective of the omniscient narrating I to the contemporary limitations of the narrated I. Since both are "I", the transition is liable to go unnoticed. But, as we will see, this trick can be pushed only so far before the reader cannot help noticing.

The second distinction is that between the *story* (the sequence of fictive events), the *narrative* or discourse (the actual telling of the tale, full of flashbacks, anticipations, alternations between scene and summary, alternating viewpoints, and other devices for manipulating the reader's reception of the facts), and the *narration*, or the scene of writing, the implied circumstances under which the narrator writes. Lovecraft himself carefully distinguishes the first and the second in his essay "Notes on Writing Weird Fiction": "Prepare a synopsis or scenario of events in the order of their absolute **occurrence**—not in the order of their narration. [Then] prepare a second synopsis . . . in order of **narration** (not actual occurrence) . . . with . . . changing perspective, stresses, and climax."

In "The Statement of Randolph Carter", for example, Carter is the narrator, while Lovecraft is the author. The story is the series of events in which Warren discovers the papyrus, persuades Carter to assist him, both go to the cemetery, Warren goes in, Carter feeds out the wire, waits, hears the terrible revelation, flees, and is caught and interrogated by the police. The narrative reshuffles these events, beginning at the end of the story, Carter already being questioned, and ending with the voice from beneath. The scene of narration is Carter swearing out his official statement in the matter of the disappearance of Harley Warren. The narrating I is the nervous man at the police station, fearing that they will never believe his story, while the narrated I is the hapless stooge of Warren.

In "The Shadow over Innsmouth" the narrator is Robert Olmstead (according to HPL's notes), who is recounting his remarkable experiences while on a trip east to investigate genealogical and architectural matters. The narrating I is Olmstead back in Cleveland, Ohio, some years later, while the narrated I is the venturer into Innsmouth who finds it much harder to get out than to get in. The story is a long one, beginning implicitly with the ancient conflicts between the Deep Ones and the lost Old Ones, the bargains struck by the Deep Ones with the islanders, Obed Marsh's visit, the introduction of Dagonism to Innsmouth, the riots and isolation of the town, the graduation of Olmstead, his conversation with the Arkham ticket agent, his visit to the library, his naive pilgrimage into Innsmouth, his discussion with the grocery boy and with Zadok Allen, his uneasy night and escape from the Gilman House, the pursuit, the exit from Innsmouth, his return home, the Federal attack upon Innsmouth, his further genealogical researches with terrible discoveries, his dreams, his suicide plans, the writing of the narrative, the implied liberation of his cousin, his trip to Innsmouth, and his descent from Devil Reef. The narrative discourse is the elaborate series of flashbacks within flashbacks within flashbacks ("analepses"), plus a final anticipation ("prolepsis"), all couched in the characteristically Lovecraftian narrative voice of shock, fright, and distaste.

None of this comes as much of a surprise. Literary critical theory would seem merely to be a tool for grasping the obvious. But if we press on further these tools will help us diagnose the problem of which we are dimly aware. It is this: By the end of the tale, we are made to realize that there must be a vast and plumbless chasm, like that off of Devil Reef, yawning between the narrating I and the narrated I. The narrated I was horrified at all he discovered in the seat of his unsuspected ancestors. But by the time he has come to set down the tale, he has undergone a total change in perspective, rejoicing in the imminent prospect of sprouting ichthyic gills and sporting under the sea in an octopus' garden. We should expect, in such a case, to be able to detect in the narrative an ironic distance between the narrating I and the poor unsuspecting narrated I. But we do not. Rather, it is all too clear that the narrating I shares in full the loathing and revulsion for all that he narrates. If anything, his hindsight seems to have increased his distaste for the earlier developments in the story which had before seemed innocent enough.

Granted, there are two or three cosmetic half-sentences meant, in retrospect, to count as hints of what was to come, but these only accentuate the inconsistency since they clash with the retrospective tone of the whole narrative. We should at least be able to go back and reinterpret a number of double-entendres, recognizable as such only in retrospective, but I can only discover one pretty mild one ("It was the end, for whatever remains to me of life on the surface of this earth, of every vestige of mental peace").

The problem is a lack of coherence in the implied scene of narration. Apparently we are to imagine poor Olmstead undecided between his familiar "landlubber's" perspective and his new fishy outlook until the actual telling of the tale itself decides him. But there is no discernible transition; what we read till the point of his astonishing confession in no way prepares us for the change. Indeed, so great has been the accumulation of distaste, disgust, and horror that we should surely expect him to end by telling us he will now shoot himself. Ask yourself if the account of Innsmouth you have just read would incline you to a second, more sympathetic look at the place!

Of course there is a good reason that it does not: Lovecraft means to shock us with the abruptness of the final reversal (much like Bloch's reversal at the ends of "Yours Truly, Jack the Ripper" and *Psycho II*). But if author Lovecraft has plenty of motivation, narrator Olmstead does not. Every twist wrought by the author from behind the scenes must be disguised and concealed by some plausible motive on the narrator's level, just as Joe Sargent hides his plans for capturing Olmstead behind a plausible story that his rattletrap bus has at last succumbed. The drastic alteration of narrative perspective in the twinkling of an eye makes sense in terms of the author's scene of writing, but none at all in terms of the narrator's scene of writing.

"The Rats in the Walls" is narrowly rescued from the same inconsistency by the simple fact of the narrator's having only temporarily lapsed into the consciousness of his ancestral memory ("I'll learn ye how to gust!"), awakening forgetful of this momentary transformation a short time later. By the time he sits down to pen the story, he has returned to his accustomed mentality.

The omniscient third-person narrator always has the privilege of temporarily confining himself to the limitations of any character's perspective, narrating perhaps in free indirect speech, in the idiom of the character, yet without constantly quoting him, with the result that much information unavailable to that character is withheld from the reader (such withholding is a "paralipsis") for a surprise revelation (such a retrospective filling-in is a "paralepsis") at the end. The third-person narrator is but a thin mask for the all-manipulating author. But the first-person narrator is himself something more of a character, the latter-day counterpart of the protagonist, his own earlier self; this kind of narrator has fewer options, since as an implicit character he requires motivations from within the story even to be telling his story. He must have narrative motivation for telling it as he does. So we must ask why Olmstead (not Lovecraft) would want to hold his big surprise till the end.

This becomes especially problematic since he has done nothing to mitigate the drastically negative picture of Innsmouth he has given the reader. Indeed, he explicitly tells the reader he is going to give him a much more shocking impression than the news media have conveyed already. Now why would Olmstead write such a narrative if he has since taken the antipodal view of the matter? We can imagine him writing the account, as he anticipates early on, to sort out his conflicting feelings, but this is not what happens. We never see a hint of mixed feelings. The account is unrelentingly negative till the last few paragraphs. If, between sentences, some great but unreported enlightenment, or supplanting of personality *à la* "The Shadow Out of Time", has occurred, would not the new enlightened persona see to it that the manuscript we are reading was destroyed? To preserve such an account, including the revelation that the Deep Ones yet lurk undiminished below, would be but to invite another Federal submarine assault more devastating than the first. This is the kind of cheat, sooner or later fraying the fabric of the work, that confirms Käte Hamburger's contention (in *The Logic of Literature*) that first-person narrative is more a matter of pseudepigraphy than of fiction proper. But, look, what do you want from a fish story?

* * *

The same challenge of narration Lovecraft faced in "The Shadow over Innsmouth", namely, how to coax the reader along as if sharing his horror and mystification even though the narrator, like the actual author, knows the full revelation already, comes back like a ghost to haunt any latter-day raconteur who seeks to spin a good yarn of Innsmouth, and there have been many. For now what can remain unguessed? One is going to have to try something altogether different. A naive narrator, gradually discovering the secrets the seasoned Lovecraftian reader already knows (and that the author knows that the reader knows) is likely to come across as just parodic. There had better be some twist thrown in. Or one might have the narrator himself aware of Lovecraft's tale of Innsmouth but discover there was a factual basis to it. Then the suspense can center on the question of just how far that factual basis extended. Or one might take the Deep Ones as granted and try to do something with their culture, like HPL did with the people of K'n-yan in "The Mound." All these strategies and more have been attempted, many successfully. All the growing number of Innsmouth stories attest to two things: the fecundity of the original Lovecraftian concept and the imagination of the nightmare saraband of scribes who tell the tales. You will read a whole netful of new ones here.

— Robert M. Price

About "The Weird Shadow over Innsmouth"

The Lovecraft stories that survive only in the form of unrevised first drafts (*The Case of Charles Dexter Ward* and *The Dream-Quest of Unknown Kadath*) are so good that it almost surprises us to remember that Lovecraft labored long and hard over most of his fiction. For instance, the familiar text of "The Shadow over Innsmouth" was by no means Lovecraft's first attempt at this tale. By chance he happened to retain a few fragments of an earlier, discarded draft, along with a set of notes on how the story would have run. What is left is more tantalizing than satisfying, but it does show that "The Shadow over Innsmouth" had itself transformed, evolved, and undergone a "change" on its way to becoming the version familiar to us. Though the notes and the fragmentary text have been published before (in *Something about Cats and Other Pieces*, Arkham House, 1949), what follows is brand new.

John Glasby has dwelt in Innsmouth so long in his imagination that he practically has Innsmouth salt water in his blood. What he has done here is to start afresh from the fragmentary draft and outline and write the story Lovecraft might have written had he stuck to it! It is strangely familiar yet different. You are in a parallel world. You think you know what must happen next, but quickly you learn not to bet on it. Glasby also manages quite nicely to tie up a dangling loose end: Is the Waite connection between "The Shadow over Innsmouth" and "The Thing on the Doorstep" purely tangential? Or mustn't there have lurked an untold tale waiting to be told?

If the title has a familiar ring, it isn't just because of its close similarity to "The Shadow over Innsmouth." No, Glasby has borrowed the title from the retitling used for the 1944 Bartholomew House paperback collection *The Weird Shadow over Innsmouth and Other Stories of the Supernatural*.

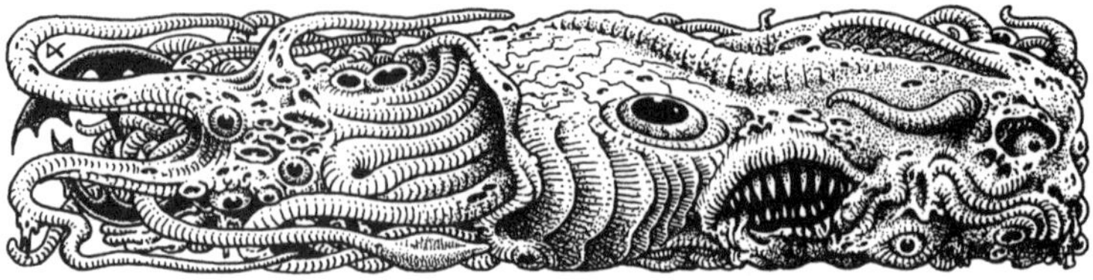

The Weird Shadow over Innsmouth

by H. P. Lovecraft and John Glasby

It was not by chance that I visited Innsmouth, although to the best of my knowledge it is not mentioned in any gazetteer, nor marked upon any map of Massachusetts. While it may be true that certain things I saw and heard two years ago during the summer of 1927 may be put down to either an overwrought imagination or pure myth and superstition, subsequent events and the testimony of Professor Derby of Miskatonic University lead me to the inescapable conclusion that the horror I encountered there was real. It is true that many of the occurrences which followed my flight from terror-haunted Innsmouth were either ignored by the papers or deliberately suppressed, and perhaps it would be better if they were to remain so.

Yet, if only for the sake of my sanity, I must put on record everything which led up to the Federal investigation of that ancient seaport, despite the fact that much of the evidence was destroyed by the fire which swept through most of the supposedly empty houses along the decayed waterfront which faces Devil Reef. As to the truth behind the whispered rumours that several torpedoes were launched into the deeps off that fearful reef, I can say nothing. The authorities refuse to admit to such an incident and all of my inquiries have been met with evasiveness or utter denial.

My name is Robert Olmstead. I was born and reared in Cleveland, where my family moved from Arkham in 1868. That there were many curious rumours associated with my family, especially on my mother's side, was common knowledge in Cleveland, although I was aware of little of this until my eighteenth year. Having obtained a junior post with the *Cleveland Advertiser*, I naturally had access to old copies of the newspaper and spent most of my lunch hours perusing these ancient records. It was this, more than any other thing, which stimulated my early interest in colonial times, particularly where such information related to my family tree.

It was here that I came across a reference to my maternal grandmother, Eliza Orne Williamson, whose inexplicable disappearance in 1914 has never been satisfactorily explained. I was only eight years old at the time and the explanation given me by my parents was that she had returned to Arkham, from whence her family had moved. The newspapers of that time were filled with news of European matters which were soon to lead to the outbreak of the Great War, but a couple of small paragraphs on one of the inside pages had been written concerning Eliza and these I found puzzling in the extreme.

How much of what was written was mere supposition on the part of the journalist it was impossible to tell, but the account differed completely from that which I had believed for ten years.

In essence, it stated that my grandmother had left the family home on the morning of September 23, 1914 with the intention of purchasing groceries from the store only a short distance away. That she never arrived there was a matter of record, attested by the store-owner and his assistant. Two independent witnesses, however, had testified that they had seen her being approached by two odd individuals who, after conversing with her for a short time, had accompanied her into one of the numerous alleys in the neighbourhood. From that moment on, no further knowledge of her whereabouts had come to light despite desultory police inquiries.

Looking back in retrospect, I considered it odd that neither of my parents had appeared unduly concerned by her vanishment at the time and, had it not been for the sworn statements of the two witnesses, I feel certain the authorities would not have been brought into the matter.

My mother, too, suffered from some strange malady in the two years prior to her death; one which the physicians were unable to treat or identify. It showed itself mainly in unnatural changes to her facial features and the texture of her skin. At times the fixed, staring expression in her bulging eyes, together with progressive changes in the shape of her skull, would positively frighten me. Following a period of perplexed debate, the doctors concluded that the illness was linked to some inherent disease, almost certainly of foreign origin. At the time, I saw no reason to disagree with their diagnosis but now, knowing as I do far more of my maternal lineage, I begin to wonder.

What hideous urge prompted me to delve further into my lineage, I do not know. Before this I had been quite content to accept what I had been told, but knowing something of the rumours concerning ancient Arkham, with its spectral tales of witchcraft during the seventeenth century, I proceeded to hunt out as many of the old records as I could to discover any link between my family and that town.

The newspaper files yielded little more and accordingly I transferred my search to the library. Yet even here, I was initially disappointed. There were brief references to the notorious witchcraft trials but nothing relating to my family. Either they had not resided there at the time in question or they had not been involved. Despairing of finding anything, I was on the point of giving up the search until such time as I might have an opportunity of visiting Arkham myself when, one afternoon, I became aware that I was being watched by an aged man in clerical garb seated at one of the nearby tables.

I naturally assumed that his interest in me was merely one of idle curiosity, but presently I got the impression it was something more than this and when I sat back in my chair, laying down my pen, he immediately rose and walked over, introducing himself as Father Conlan of the Holy Trinity Church. His eyes held a speculative expression and his next words indicated that he had taken more than a passing interest in me, for he inquired politely why I was so interested in the history of ancient Arkham.

As he seated himself opposite me, I told him of the curious happenings surrounding my mother and grandmother, that our family had originated in Arkham, and that I was hoping to discover more about the place and, in particular, where they had fitted into the community.

He listened in silence until I had finished and it was then that he said something which struck me as being distinctly odd.

"If you will forgive me, young man, it is my belief that you are looking in the wrong place."

Astonished, I asked what he meant by that remark. It seemed highly singular that a Catholic priest should have any interest in ancient witchcraft.

"Ah," he continued, "then you've never heard of Innsmouth. Well, I don't wonder. It isn't the sort of place anyone hears of, but things have happened there which may be of interest to you."

He continued to scrutinize me closely as if searching my face for something he half expected to see there. After a while, I began to feel oddly uncomfortable under his gaze and pressed him to go on.

For the next twenty minutes I sat entranced with a growing sense of excitement as he spoke of a colleague of his, a fellow priest who had lived most of his life in Innsmouth.

This Father Iwanicki had gone to Innsmouth more than forty years before to minister to the handful of Poles who dwelt along the southern fringes of the town. These folk were all gone now, packing up their meagre possessions and fleeing from some form of persecution, the nature of which was so extreme that several had been killed or had vanished overnight in circumstances which, though highly suspicious, were never talked about.

Now Father Iwanicki lived there alone and for some peculiar reason, possibly because he knew too much, he was kept under constant surveillance and Father Conlan doubted if he would ever get out of Innsmouth alive. There were, however, a few outsiders in the town who worked there but lived outside in Rowley or Ipswich and, with their connivance, he had managed to smuggle out certain old papers, these having eventually reached my informant. It was these which he considered I should read, although he warned me they contained details of certain events in the past history of the town which I would find very hard to believe.

By now my interest had been fully aroused and I readily agreed to accompany him to see these documents for myself.

Leaving the library, I accompanied him along a maze of narrow streets, finally emerging into a small square which I had never seen before. On one side stood the imposing Catholic church and next to it a smaller building situated within the grounds. Unlocking the door, Father Conlan led the way inside, ushering me into a small parlour. Once I had seated myself, he crossed the room to a small bureau, returning with a bundle of papers and a couple of large notebooks which he placed carefully on the table in front of me.

It was quite dark inside the small room with the tiny square windows letting in only a little daylight, and my host brought an oil lamp which he lit and placed beside me so that by its flickering yellow light I was able to examine the papers. Most of these I found were very old, some dating back more than a century: official documents written in faded black ink and pertaining to Innsmouth as it had been in an era long gone by. Of the names mentioned therein, those which cropped up most frequently were Marsh, Gilman, Waite, and Eliot. These families, my informant revealed, had been, and still were, the richest and most influential in the town.

After skimming through the papers I turned my attention to the two hard-backed notebooks, expecting them to be more modern than the documents. In this surmise I was mistaken, for both appeared to be almost as ancient as the papers, the pages yellowed and brittle. In places they were stained as if by sea water, rendering parts of them virtually indecipherable. The first was labelled *Ye Journal & Notes of Jedediah Allen, b. 1802*, while the second was similarly entitled *Ye Journal of Zadok Allen, b. 1831.*

There was clearly no time for me to read through them in their entirety especially since, as I have already said, portions of the spidery scripts were so affected by age and water that a minute inspection would be necessary to make any sense of them.

When I made to return them to my host, however, he thrust them back at me, intimating that I was to take them and study them at my leisure.

There was, he averred, much in them which I would find of great interest, and seemed exceptionally eager that someone else should become aware of this dark knowledge.

Thanking him profusely, I returned home, taking them up to my room, where I placed them carefully in one of the cupboards, for I felt a strange reluctance about allowing anyone else to peruse them. There had never been any hint of abnormality about my father's side of the family and I had sensed a curious emotion of relief on his part when my mother had died, almost as if there had been some dark and sinister secret which had been buried and forgotten with her. I certainly harboured no wish to reawaken any old feelings now that she was dead.

Over the following three months I spent all of my free time going through the papers and notebooks, struggling to decipher those passages where time and salt water had taken their inevitable toll, finding myself gradually held fast in a web of utter horror.

If what was written there was true, and many of the statements undoubtedly corroborated each other to the extent that I was forced to accept their veracity, then something unutterably evil had visited Innsmouth over a century earlier: something so awful that the town had shut itself off from the outside world almost completely.

Whether that evil still lingered down the years I had no way of telling, but the odd thing about my reading of those records was that they stirred some deep emotion within me, an urge to determine for myself what conditions were now like in Innsmouth; to seek out the truth behind certain veiled hints written on those blasphemous yellowed pages.

Certainly the narrative which emerged during my reading was such that a number of rational explanations could be advanced to explain it: the exaggerations of simple superstitious fisherfolk who saw evil in everything they did not understand; purposeful misinterpretation of the facts from motives of greed or jealousy; or maybe it was nothing less than the stark, unembellished truth! Piece by piece, I painstakingly succeeded in putting together that which follows: Much of the weird shadow which lay over Innsmouth undoubtedly stemmed from events shortly after the war of 1812. Prior to that, Innsmouth had been a great seaport, famed for its shipbuilding, a highly prosperous place which almost attained the status of a city. Fishing was a major occupation in those days and there was also much trade with the East Indies. During the war and for a number of years afterward, profit was gained from privateering, a lucrative, if dubious, trade carried on by a certain Obed Marsh and the Gilman family.

During the third decade of the nineteenth century there began a decline in the town's fortunes. Trade was bad, and, with a scarcity of fish off the coast, even this once-profitable industry declined. Only Obed Marsh's affairs continued to prosper. His three ships, the *Sumatra Queen*, *Columba*, and *Hetty*, regularly plied between Innsmouth and the South Pacific. It was about this time that whispered rumours concerning the cargoes Marsh's ships brought back from their voyaging began to circulate, chiefly in the taverns near the waterfront. Much of the unloading was carried out by his own men and consisted of bales of silk, tea, and other commodities common with such trade. What disturbed many of the townsfolk, however, were reports of nocturnal visits to the harbour on nights when there was no moon, always with Captain Marsh in attendance, when wooden boxes of considerable size were carried ashore and taken surreptitiously to the big mansion. Nightly wanderers told of seeing the unmistakable figure of Marsh, accompanied by Matt Eliot, his first mate, and three other crew members, making their way along the narrow alleys, bearing this cargo in a manner which suggested they had no wish to be seen.

It was also noted that at each sailing several crew members failed to return for the next voyage, even though Marsh's pay was the highest of all the ship owners in Innsmouth. Had these nightly incursions been simply a case of smuggling, the rumours would all have died down within a very short time, for this was a common practice along this stretch of coast and certainly not one to be frowned upon by the townsfolk of Innsmouth.

In time Obed Marsh grew to be feared, for the whispered insinuations now took a decidedly more sinister turn. His outspoken criticism of the various religious denominations brought him into open conflict with several ministers. Some claimed he was in league with Satan and that this alone was the source of his increasing wealth.

One of those who kept a constant watch on Obed's activities during this period was Jedediah Allen, whose own wealth and standing in the community had suffered much during the recession. On what grounds he blamed much of this on Marsh was not made clear in his own, often rambling, account. At first, he merely took to frequenting the waterfront whenever any of Marsh's ships was due in dock, secreting himself in the upper storey of one of the nearby warehouses from which it was possible to observe each vessel closely, even during the hours of darkness.

A staunch member of the Baptist Church, it was he who first spoke out against Marsh, even before the latter came out strongly against all Christian denominations. Initially few people listened to his suggestions that Marsh had sold his soul to the Devil in return for power and riches, believing that this show of antagonism stemmed merely from his hatred of the man and his, perhaps ill-founded, belief that Marsh had been directly responsible for his misfortunes.

But his often wild stories were soon to gain more definite credence in Innsmouth as Marsh's oratory against Christianity gained in volubility and vociferation. Then, at some time in the late 1820's, the Marsh Refinery was built from an older building which used to stand on the site near the river, and it soon became clear that a large quantity of gold was being imported into the town. Reports as to the origin of this precious metal were varied depending upon the informant. The general theory was that Obed Marsh had stumbled upon a pirate hoard on Devil Reef, the low black rock situated about a mile and a half offshore. Certainly it was widely known that at times when there was no moon, he would row out to Devil Reef and spend some considerable time there before returning. Although its position was well charted and parts of the reef were clearly visible even when the tide was high, most vessels avoided the spot because of its bad reputation.

On this particular matter the Reverend Joseph Wallingham spoke out openly from the pulpit, urging his congregation to have nothing to do with those who worshipped worldly riches at the peril of their own souls, a direct reference to Marsh. His sermon brought an immediate response. Now Marsh publickly sneered at those who followed the Christian faith, regardless of denomination, which had brought them to the indigence they now suffered. Instead, he avowed, they should turn their backs on God and follow his example. He swore he had met with some form of pagan worship among the islanders of the Southern Pacific, which could provide them all with everything they desired. This, he declared, was how he had succeeded in prospering while everyone else had seen their fortunes vanish.

Such a violent denunciation of the church caused him to be ostracized by the general population. Naturally, he was well aware of the indignation and fear with which he was widely regarded, but such was his nature that he disregarded it completely, continuing to go about his business as if nothing had been said against him.

Most people would have been content either to ignore him or to work, albeit reluctantly, for him, had no further incidents of an outrageous nature occurred. Much of the time he was absent on the long voyages to the East Indies, often for more than a year at a time. Of what he discovered in these remote, out-of-the-way regions, little is on record. The tales of the first mate, Matt Eliot, told mostly when he was drunk, are so preposterous that it is not surprising they were initially put down to a wild imagination.

Eliot would talk of an unnamed island in the South Pacific lying to the east of Othaheite which they had come across some years before and which they visited every time they made a voyage to the region. Here, Eliot claimed, the natives worshipped some heathen sea-god whose servants provided them with more fish than they needed, together with strange trinkets made of some strange kind of gold, sometimes set with precious stones. Eliot's talk of a smaller volcanic island on which were strange, incredibly ancient ruins, statues, and carvings found more acceptance than his mumbled hints of devils bringing riches from the sea, for even at that time it was well known that paganism was widespread in these tropical regions.

What brought things to a head, however, was when Obed transported a number of these natives back to Innsmouth. Here, we have direct evidence provided by Jedediah Allen, who persisted in keeping watch on Marsh and his queer cargoes. It transpired that Allen had been disappointed on previous occasions, for there had been a sudden cessation in Obed's nocturnal visits to his ships and it seemed that the importation of whatever was contained in those wooden crates had stopped. It was then he remembered the small cove a little way to the north which had been much used during the smuggling days. An underground tunnel was reputed to lead from the cove into the heart of Innsmouth. On this occasion, he secreted himself close to the beach near the cove. Nothing had happened on the first two nights but, undaunted, he had returned to keep a third watch.

Shortly after midnight, he had observed a small party moving along the beach from the direction of the harbour. Apparently the men considered themselves safe from prying eyes, for they carried lanterns by whose pale light Allen was able to identify Obed Marsh, Matt Eliot, and four crewmen from the *Sumatra Queen*. It was, however, the appearance of the others which sent a shiver of nameless dread through him and almost made him cry out. That they were natives brought back from that terrible island, he did not doubt. Yet even in the dim light cast by the bobbing lanterns, he saw enough to recognize that there was something inhuman about them, although distance and dimness were such as to make it impossible for him to say what it was.

Trembling and shaking, he had lain there and watched as the party disappeared into the cove below him. Not until a full half hour had passed was he able to pull himself to his feet and stagger back into town where he told no one of what he had witnessed.

Meanwhile, Obed Marsh had begun his campaign against the churches in Innsmouth, whose pastors were now the only people to speak out openly against his pagan oratory. Had these men been listened to and strong action taken by the populace, it is possible that the ensuing madness might have been averted and the shadow over Innsmouth lifted. But by now, Obed Marsh had established himself as the only real force in town. A number of churchmen unaccountably disappeared during the next two years, their churches were closed, and those of their congregations who did not follow the ways of Marsh also vanished or were driven out of town by various means.

The year 1846 saw the real turning point in the history of Innsmouth. That year a terrible epidemic struck the town. Men, women, and children died in their hundreds and the small number of physicians seemed unable to halt its course. It was inevitable that it should be attributed to some foreign disease, and when Jedediah Allen finally spoke out concerning what he had seen that night above the cove, even the doctors were adamant that the cause of the affliction was due to natives which Marsh had brought from unknown parts in the South Pacific. When other townsfolk came forward to state that they had also witnessed odd-looking foreigners in the vicinity of the waterfront and, on occasion, seen them swimming towards the harbour from the direction of Devil Reef, Obed Marsh and a number of his men were arrested and thrown in gaol on a charge of illegally bringing unidentified aliens ashore, the claim being that these had been landed on Devil Reef, from whence they had been forced to swim for the safety of the mainland.

That such seemed to be the case was made amply clear during the days which followed Marsh's arrest. Riots broke out between those who had thrown in their lot with Obed and the ordinary citizens of Innsmouth. The first entries made by Zadok Allen, a youth of fifteen at the time, substantiated his father's statements, since it appears that, at the time, neither was aware that the other was making these permanent records of these extraordinary events. That Obed's forces had a large number of foreign natives on their side may be accepted on the basis of the previous evidence, but the outside authorities who later entered the town dismissed as hysterical exaggeration the wild talk of other things which appeared in their hundreds from the sea. There was very little upon which the authorities could base any firm conclusions, and the loss of so many people was finally attributed to the epidemic. Marsh had meanwhile been released from gaol and now took over undisputed command of the town, enforcing his beliefs upon virtually everyone.

The Esoteric Order of Dagon was established under his leadership and at the same time he took a second wife. The ceremony was performed in secret and at no time did anyone in Innsmouth see this wife. Who—or *what*—this wife really was, neither narrator was able to say, although rumours were rife during the years preceding the Civil War. Most intimated that she was a native woman whom Obed had brought back from one of his voyages, but other hearsay claimed that she was something else, since the sight of the natives was fairly commonplace around the town. In general, it was believed that she was a foreigner who had suffered grievously from the contagion which had raged through the community and had been hideously disfigured by it. Whatever the explanation, Obed kept her locked away out of sight.

There followed a hiatus in Zadok's account covering the period when he served during the Civil War, and on the resumption of his notes it was clear that he had grave reservations about returning to Innsmouth. So many terrifying and inexplicable things had happened there that he fully intended to settle someplace well away from the town. His narratives suggested that what finally brought him back were the letters he received informing him that things were now much better, that the old ways had changed.

The probability that Obed Marsh had curtailed his activities while government recruitmen were in town may have led to this supposition. Following their departure things went back to being as bad as before. Trade fell off; industries closed down with the exception of the Marsh Refinery

Company. Fishing declined since, although the numbers of fish off the coast were still phenomenally high, the price dropped and they became more difficult to sell. More and more houses emptied and were left to decay into ruin. At the same time, the affliction which had begun about the time of the epidemic and riots became more widespread and virulent. The nature of this condition, whose outward symptoms consisted of curious deformities of the skull and an odd scaliness of the skin, was still unknown. Disappearances continued without any attempt to discover their cause. Few questions were asked openly, for those who inquired too deeply into things went to join the many who had vanished over the years.

With the abandonment of the railroad to Rowley, the town became more isolated and backward. Those outsiders who ventured there were tolerated, provided they asked no questions and did not probe into matters which were none of their concern.

Such were the facts, half-truths, myths, and superstitions which faced me after reading through those damnable papers and notebooks. As I have said, they instilled in me a desire to visit both Innsmouth and Arkham to examine for myself what truth lay behind such hidden and bizarre happenings. It was not, however, until that summer of 1927 that this strange hankering for knowledge came to fruition. My mother's death in 1922 meant that I had to spend a lot of time tidying up the estate, but at last, having received a comfortable competence left by her, I was able to undertake a sight-seeing trip around New England and Massachusetts, leaving those two ancient towns as the last on my agenda.

New England was a region about which I knew little and initially I was much taken by the unspoilt beauty which contrasted sharply with that of the more populous communities with which I was familiar. Here there were steep hills of grey granite and patches of dense forest within which numerous narrow streams ran swiftly through unlit glens. Only an isolated homestead was now and again visible, glimpsed through the window of the motor coach. The steep, narrow roads in this region forced the coach to travel slowly, affording me an excellent opportunity to view the surrounding landscape.

It was towards the end of the first week that my journeying took me towards the Atlantic coast. Here the countryside changed dramatically with the hills becoming fewer, lower, and curiously rounded. I was on the bus for Innsmouth, intending to remain there for two or three days before continuing on to Arkham and thence to Boston. I suppose the lure of Arkham stemmed from the fact that, so I believed at the time, my maternal family had originated there, and I experienced an odd wish to see that ancient town of still-remembered witchcraft.

I had arrived in Newburyport, further along the coast, the previous day and it was there, on inquiring about the train service from that town to Arkham, that I heard a little more of Innsmouth. Considering the rail fare to be extortionate, I had been informed by the ticket agent that a twice-daily bus service left for Innsmouth at ten in the morning and seven in the evening, Innsmouth being approximately an hour's journey away.

Much of what the ticket agent told me corresponded with what I had read some seven years before. Innsmouth was virtually cut off from its neighbours along the coast, and there was something abnormally queer about its inhabitants. Clearly there was still something about the old sea-port which inspired both fear and dislike among the townsfolk of Newburyport. So much so, that my informant warned me implicitly against visiting the town and especially against remaining there overnight.

Despite what I had read, I was still prepared to dismiss much of his talk as idle gossip. There was, however, one particular statement he made concerning the odd physiognomy of the Innsmouth folk which I had been able to verify for myself.

The driver of the bus, a taciturn man in his mid-thirties, who I was told was Joe Sargent, was one of the most repulsive creatures I had ever seen. There was something ichthyic—or batrachian—about his appearance which sent a shudder of nameless horror through me on first seeing him. The wide, protruding eyes were of a pale blue, so large that it seemed impossible he could close them, and his mouth was far wider than normal, with lips of an inordinate thickness, The coarse, bluish skin was mottled and scaly, particularly along the scrawny neck and around the almost non-existent ears. I took a seat near the rear of the bus, as far from him as possible, and shuddered to think what the rest of his body looked like. Certainly his clothing did not appear to fit the contours of his limbs.

At the time, my feeling was that he suffered from this strange, extraneous malady associated with Innsmouth almost a century earlier, somewhat similar to that which had attacked my mother, although far more pronounced.

There were no other passengers and, to take my mind off him, I concentrated all of my attention on the countryside through which we were travelling. Having left the environs of Newburyport, we were now travelling across a wide and desolate stretch of empty sand with very little in the way of vegetation. A few stunted bushes, leaning in the direction of the prevailing wind, dotted the area and there was no sign of any human habitation. Since the land was evidently so poor, I doubted if many folk had attempted to cultivate it. Once or twice I spotted what looked like crumbling ruins and guessed that, long ago, someone had tried to eke a living from the earth but had long since left.

All in all, there was nothing here to support the information I had gleaned—albeit reluctantly—in Newburyport, and from those old writings, that this had once been a region of great prosperity and commerce. If such stories held a germ of truth, then some terrible catastrophe must have overtaken this region and certainly not less than a century earlier. There was nothing here to suggest more recent occupancy.

About half an hour after leaving Newburyport, the main highway veered sharply to the right and, from the maps I had consulted, I guessed it ran across country towards Rowley and Ipswich. For a moment, I thought the driver intended to follow it, but we then swung precipitously to the left and onto a much narrower, rutted track which presently cut along the side of the beach, and now I could make out the blue expanse of the Atlantic.

Even had we been in total darkness, I would have instantly known that we were travelling close to the sea. The nauseous fishy smell pervaded the bus, catching at the back of my throat and stinging my eyes. Rattling and wheezing ominously, the ancient vehicle somehow climbed a steep rise ahead of us and, as we reached the top, I sat forward in my seat, staring down at the vast panorama which lay spread out before us in the valley. It is impossible to say what I had expected to see. Certainly nothing like the town which straddled the Manuxet River where it flowed into the Atlantic. All I knew of Innsmouth had come by vague rumour from people who had almost certainly never visited the place—and from the writings of a century before.

It was far larger in extent than I had visualized, with the spires of a number of churches rising above the densely clustered houses. These, I soon discerned, were all in a state of advanced decrepitude, with slates missing from the steeples and gaping holes showing in the sides. Huge warehouses stood along the waterfront and I noticed other large buildings near the center of town, most situated along the banks of the Manuxet. One of these I took to be that belonging to the Marsh Refinery Company. In the rooms of the Newburyport Historical Society I had been shown several items of gold jewellery which were reputed to have been made in the refinery from the gold obtained by Captain Obed Marsh, almost certainly brought from some pirate hoard in the vicinity.

One thing which worried me as the bus began its rattling descent was the curious dearth of life. I could see no smoke rising from any of the numerous chimneys. The entire scene was one of utter desertion and decay, suggesting a mass exodus of the population at some time in the past. Despite the shuddersome aspect of Innsmouth, I experienced a resurgence of that strange sense of excitement I had felt on first reading about this place. Those bygone days of colonial affluence and elegance might have passed, but there was some deep, dark mystery here which gave play to my imagination.

The veiled insinuations I had picked up in Newburyport concerning strange disappearances among outsiders visiting the town were forgotten as we drew closer to the outskirts. Here, I felt certain, were hidden secrets of a foregone age awaiting discovery. That it might be difficult, and possibly dangerous, to get any of the people to talk of such things, I recognized at once. But at that moment I was determined to find out for myself what had reduced this town to its present pitiful state of desertion and decrepitude.

I noticed that some of the grander buildings, mostly those set well away from the waterfront area, still appeared to be lived in, retaining a little of their bygone grandeur. Many needed a fresh coat of paint and some had upper windows which were tightly boarded up, adding further to the general air of abandonment. Sitting well forward in my seat, I strove to take in as many details as possible in order to obtain an accurate layout of the town. A railroad had once connected Innsmouth with Rowley, but it was obvious, even from that distance, that it was no longer in use. Whether the tracks were still in place it was difficult to say, but its route was clearly delineated by the telegraph poles which ran alongside it, although many of these were either fallen or missing.

The air of rottenness and decay grew even more pronounced as we drove slowly through the outer environs along a narrow street, cobbled in places, a hint of a sidewalk along one side, but composed mainly of hard-packed earth over which the ancient bus bumped and rattled alarmingly. I took particular note of the houses on either side, searching them for any signs of human habitation. For the most part, however, they were clearly empty. Broken windows stared like vacant eyes in the crumbling brickwork. Numerous gaps existed where buildings had fallen into utter ruin and never been rebuilt, giving the impression that their owners had simply upped and left. Everywhere, the stench of rotting fish permeated the bus through the half-open windows, mingled with that of the rubbish lying in mounds in the street.

Other, narrower streets opened out from the one along which we were travelling. All of them seemed deserted. Where in God's name were all the people? From what I had seen on the way down the hill, the Marsh Refinery Company still seemed to be in operation, and there had been several small fishing boasts drawn up alongside the jetty with lobster pots visible and nets drying in the sun. But not a single being in sight. Not even a cat or mangy dog roaming the empty streets. On the surface, Innsmouth was a ghost town, a place which had been abandoned and left to rot and decay years before.

Since entering the town I had been aware of a sound, faint at first but now growing louder, which I had been unable to identify. As we rumbled over a rusted iron bridge spanning a wide gorge, I realized what it was. Here, the Manuxet flowed through the town on its way down to the sea, and inland were a number of falls which I presumed formed the power source for the refinery and other industries there might be along the river's edge.

Finally, almost an hour after leaving Newburyport, we entered a wide cobbled square where the bus stopped before a large building which seemed to be still in a reasonable state of repair. This, I saw, was the Gilman House.

Grateful for the opportunity to stretch my legs, I alighted from the bus and stood for several moments, staring about me. Now, for the first time, I noticed a few of the inhabitants, but my relief at finding some signs of life was short-lived as I studied them more closely. All bore indications of the same repellent features as the bus driver with long, sloping foreheads, thick lips, wide mouths, and protruding eyes. More and more, I was becoming convinced that some strange genetic ailment had been the cause of that contagion of a century before and that its effects still lingered on in the descendants. If this were indeed the case, I could understand their dislike of outsiders and their desire for isolation. But whether the latter was self-imposed or had been forced upon them by some outside agency, afraid of such a condition spreading beyond the confines of town, was a matter of conjecture.

It was as I stepped into the shadowy lobby of the Gilman House that I noticed something which made me pause. Joe Sargent had followed me out of the bus and was now engaged in deep conversation with three younger men standing on the nearby corner close to a small restaurant whose dust-smeared windows did not look as if they had been cleaned for decades. From the furtive glances thrown in my direction, I guessed that I was the subject of their conversation. I hesitated long enough to see two of the men move off quickly into a shadowed alley, leaving Sargent and his companion in the street as if to keep watch on my movements.

In an attempt to alleviate my growing apprehension, I told myself that any stranger in Innsmouth would certainly come under some form of scrutiny and that news of my presence would soon get around. Approaching the dingy, shadowed desk, I checked in my bag. In answer to the middle-aged man's inquiry as to whether I intended to stay the night, I told him I was merely visiting places such as Innsmouth for historical purposes and much would depend upon my impression of the town and whether there was anything worth viewing.

I had already formed the impression that, in spite of his surly demeanour, the man was not a true native of the town. His features were regular, yet there was something in his manner which made me decide not to question him about Innsmouth. I recalled something the ticket agent had told me concerning the Gilman House; something he had picked up from someone who had stayed there some years before, of conversations overheard in other rooms during the night and voices speaking in some foreign tongue.

Most of the spectral tales I had heard concerning this town had been so wild as to be beyond belief and rational explanation. Yet now I was there, the air of mystery was so intense that I had already decided that, if I was to learn anything definite about the history of Innsmouth, I would have to exercise caution and not appear too inquisitive. These folk had something to hide, something they had concealed from the outside world for decades, and it was likely they would stoop to anything to prevent it from coming out into the open.

Before I left, however, the elderly man leaned forward across the desk and gripped my arm tightly. Thrusting his face close to mine, he whispered hoarsely, "Look around by all means, young fella. But take my advice. Be on that Arkham bus at eight o'clock tonight. There are things that happened long ago that are best forgotten; an' things that *still* happen that are best left alone." I refrained from asking him what he meant by that remark, for there had been a veiled threat behind his warning.

Returning to the square, I examined the scenery in more detail. The contrast with the bustling activity of Newburyport and other small New England towns I had visited was so marked that, in spite of the pleasant warmth of the sun, I felt a shiver go through me. I had taken note of most of the prominent buildings from the vantage point of the bus, but it was immediately obvious I would require a more detailed idea of the general topography of the town if I was to discover anything of importance during my brief stay.

I intended to present myself as someone interested in the architectural aspects of Innsmouth with the historical background assuming secondary importance. Although vague, and at times evasive, my inquiries in Newburyport the previous day had elicited some information, the most accurate undoubtedly being that provided by Miss Anna Tilton, the curator of that town's Historical Society, together with a little more I had been able to find among the Essex County histories on the shelves of the Public Library. In the main, this confirmed what I had uncovered seven years before in Father Conlan's documents. The most important point which had emerged was that the queer tales of neighbouring Arkham had not touched Innsmouth. Whatever had happened here had originated in Innsmouth itself.

I had not been able to find any references to the source of the gold which had appeared in such abundance at the time of old Captain Obed, and most of the accounts detailing the epidemic and riots against Obed and his cronies were of such a garbled and contradictory nature as to indicate that something was seriously amiss with the town. Certainly various trinkets fashioned of gold still appeared in both Arkham and Newburyport, with one or two occasionally turning up in Rowley and Ipswich and even as far afield as Boston.

These, then, were the curious facts I had to go on as I stood in the late morning sunlight outside the Gilman House. That some terrible shadow still lay upon this town I could not doubt. But its nature seemed elusive and vague, as if something so unutterably terrible had occurred that efforts had been made to have it deliberately erased.

Perhaps it would have been far better for me if I had simply strolled around that ancient town and then taken the bus out to Arkham in the evening, without asking any questions, leaving Innsmouth to sink even further into its general decay and obscurity. But my curiousity had been whetted by what little I had heard and read, and some imp of perversity prompted me to delve into its hidden mysteries and concealed background of horror.

I had seen enough of Joe Sargent and those men to whom he had spoken so furtively to know it would be both futile and unwise to question any of the inhabitants who bore that stamp of ichthyic regression which was so noticeable. From my perusal of the shops around the periphery of the square, I noticed a number which seemed ordinary enough to suggest that their owners might be outsiders and, as such, more willing to answer my questions. It was also possible that some of the townsfolk had remained untouched by this odd affliction and, if I could engage one of them in conversation, out of sight of the others, I might learn something more specific than the shreds of information I had already gathered.

Accordingly, I set out across the square, trying to make myself look as inconspicuous as possible. A few rusty automobiles and trucks were parked against the broken sidewalks and most of the small shops appeared to be open for business. I had decided to visit the grocery store first, but as I was on the point of entering, I caught sight of a dark figure emerging from the street on my right, which the half-obliterated sign told me was Eliot Street. For a moment, the incongruousness of the sight held me rigid. The old man was dressed in clerical garb which proclaimed him to be a Catholic priest.

Approaching him after glancing swiftly around to make sure I was not being observed, I introduced myself as a sight-seer anxious to explore the ancient town. At first, he was reluctant to talk, throwing an apprehensive glance over his shoulder back along Eliot Street. Then he clutched my arm in a surprisingly strong grip and urged me off the square and into a narrow, rubbish-filled alley between the drug store and a fish-dealer's office.

Innsmouth, he said in a low voice which was of marked Eastern-European accent, was no place for strangers. As I had already guessed, he informed me that he was Father Iwanicki, originally from Poland, having come to Innsmouth more than forty years before to act as parish priest to the small Polish community on the southern fringe of town. These folk had long since been dispersed until now none of them remained.

When I informed him that I had spoken with Father Conlan in Cleveland and had read through the dossier of papers he had smuggled out of Innsmouth, Father Iwanicki became more agitated but also more talkative.

As he had no longer any flock to minister to, I inquired why he still remained in Innsmouth and had not left it with the other immigrants, to which he replied that a great evil existed there, one which he was pledged to fight in any way he could. When I questioned him about the exact nature of this evil, he became more hesitant and illogical, declaring that demons had taken possession of Innsmouth and its people at some time in the past and were still present, working their blasphemy through the Marsh family and the Esoteric Order of Dagon, which was now the only religion established in the town.

So far, they had left him to his own devices, evidently convinced that he was no danger to them. But since he knew too much, there was no way he would be allowed to leave Innsmouth to tell of what he knew. He had received no replies to his letters written to outside acquaintances, and now he accepted that none of them had left town.

While I might be in little danger provided I remained in the area close to the square and left the town by evening, he warned me vehemently against entering the region to the north of the Manuxet or becoming too conspicuous along the waterfront where the crumbling wharves and warehouses stood in empty desolation. It was also unwise to ask questions of any who possessed what he described as the 'Innsmouth look'. To do so would be to invite the unwelcome attention of the Marshes or the Waites, and people had vanished for such indiscretions in the past.

On the subject of the Marsh family he waxed more eloquent and it was evident that he had delved into their history in some detail, although some of what he told me seemed extravagant in the extreme. Everything had begun with Obed Marsh and his conversion from privateering to trading with pagan folk in the South Pacific. I tried to question him about this pagan religion which now held sway in Innsmouth, but it was clear he knew little, if anything, concerning it. His opinion was that it was some form of devil worship which Marsh had come into contact with during his voyage to distant parts. There had, of course, been rumors of human sacrifices over a century ago, but this was probably nothing more than idle supposition, possibly aimed at deterring strangers from visiting the town. Certainly, people had unaccountably disappeared in and around Innsmouth, but, however much he detested this cult as a Christian, he had found nothing definite to connect it with these incidents. Unexplained deaths and disappearances occurred all over the country in these troubled times.

Before taking my leave of him, I inquired whether it was possible to purchase any of Innsmouth's trademark gold items myself. After some hesitation, he replied that the Marsh retail office, situated at the eastern end of the square close to the river, not more than fifty yards from where we stood, was sometimes open, and that such items were occasionally sold. Whether they would part with any to a stranger was uncertain, but I could always try.

Resolving to do this before I left, I waited in the shadows as he shuffled slowly along the alley, away from the square. Much of what he had told me was vaguely disquieting and had it come from anyone else I might have found it all very difficult to believe. Certainly there may have been some exaggeration in what he had told me, for it was now clear that none of the normal religious sects had been allowed to continue to exist in Innsmouth, and having to stand by and watch the spread of paganism must have made him a very embittered man.

I now had the strongest of forebodings that to continue my investigations in Innsmouth was to court some subtle and insidious peril; yet I nevertheless continued to be motivated by that curious thirst for knowledge which had first come over me on reading those ancient notebooks. Although I had breakfasted in Newburyport, I had no wish to obtain food in the Gilman House and instead decided to purchase some from the small grocery store where I might also be able to obtain further information, depending upon whoever was in charge.

It had already occurred to me that, since this was a branch of a national chain, it might be managed by someone who came from outside the area. This I found to be the case. There were two people in the store, a man in his late twenties and a much older woman who was busily engaged in arranging items on the long shelves. Neither possessed any of the odd distinguishing lineaments I now associated with the indigenous Innsmouth stock. The look of stunned surprise on both their faces on seeing me was instantly apparent, but the man's hesitancy in serving me I put down to the fact that few visitors ever came into the store.

As I paid for the packet of crackers and cheese, I pursued my inquiry, watching his reactions as I questioned him. Where were all of the people? I wanted to know. Why was the town so run-down and deserted? Was the Marsh Refinery still operating? And were any of the Marsh family still alive?

His agitation was instantaneous and I noticed that the woman, who had evidently overheard our conversation, almost dropped the cans she was holding.

Glancing fearfully in the direction of the open door, the manager thrust my change at me over the counter. "Don't go askin' questions like that araound here, mister," he said harshly. "Not if yuh want to git oauta here alive."

I managed to look suitably surprised, although it was the kind of answer I had expected. "Why? What is there to be afraid of?" I asked.

"There be sartin things abaout Innsmouth it's better not to know," he replied enigmatically. "We hev to work heah, and we've learnt it ain't healthy t' staht probin' araound inter things which ain't our consuhn."

"Yew ain't talk with any o' *them*, hev ye?" The woman spoke up in a quavering voice tinged with hysteria.

I was on the point of saying I had already spoken with Father Iwanicki but thought better of it. I had no wish to put the old priest into any kind of danger, and if anyone should discover that my visit was a direct outcome of having read what he had smuggled out of the town years before, it was highly likely some form of retribution would befall him.

Instead I replied, "I've just arrived from Newburyport on the bus, and you're the first ones I've spoken to."

Both looked a little relieved at my answer. Nodding, the man said hoarsely, "Then take my advice. Speak to no one else and leave as soon as ye can. And anything ye see, keep to yourself."

"Ye won't git anybody to tell ye anythin'," put in the woman hastily, "unless it be that crazy old fool, Zadok Allen, an' nobody listens to his rambling—" Here she broke off abruptly at a curious look from the manager.

Thanking them for the purchases, I left the shop. It was abundantly clear I would get nothing more out of them; that they knew a lot more but were mortally afraid to speak openly. But I had obtained one vital piece of information which I had not expected. Old Zadok Allen was still alive and, if I could succeed in locating him, it might be possible to get him to talk.

It was now almost noon and I decided to widen my investigation of the town. The square seemed to be the civic center of Innsmouth, but from the ordinary aspect of the shops it was clear I would learn little here. Whatever was hidden in Innsmouth would lurk in the outlying districts. I had already ascertained that the street I had come in on was Federal Street, which ran almost due north and south through the middle of the town. Not wishing to lose my way among the maze of streets, I left the square on the north side, recrossing the large iron bridge. From here, I had an excellent view along the river. The thunder of the falls, situated on both sides of the bridge, was a loud roar that hammered incessantly at my ears. Eastward, towards the sea, I could make out three other bridges spanning the Manuxet where it narrowed appreciably. The second one from where I stood appeared to have collapsed and never been rebuilt; only rusted remnants of the original structure remaining standing, thrusting out futilely from either bank.

In the other direction, standing on a little bluff close to the falls, was the large building which housed the Marsh Refinery. Although partially obscured behind a curtain of spray, enough was visible to tell me that some kind of activity was going on there. Indistinct figures could be seen now and again, but it was impossible to determine whether they were normal folk or not. My own impression at that time was that the Marshes would have no wish to employ anyone from outside Innsmouth in the refinery.

On the northern side of the bridge I entered a region of utter squalor and decay enshrouded in an atmosphere of oppressive silence. On my way into town I had caught a fragmentary glimpse of a large and imposing building which had somehow intruded upon my consciousness in spite of the briefness of my glance. Now I was determined to get a better look at it. On my left as I proceeded along Federal Street I noticed what appeared to be the ruined remains of large factory buildings. All looked to be more than a century old with the remains of wooden waterwheels visible on the riverward side. Broken windows gaped in the sagging walls and it seemed incredible that such rotten structures were still standing.

A shudder passed through me as I thought of things which might lurk within those rubbish-filled areas, the rat-infested rooms and bat-ridden ceilings where unknown horrors might lie unseen during the daylight hours, emerging only at night. A fresh wave of revulsion seized me as I thought I glimpsed an oddly humped shape through one of the lower windows. Hastily, I turned away from my contemplation of the scene and continued down Federal Street, coming at length to a large circular area covered with thick grass and rank weeds. Around its periphery the sidewalks were of brick, and standing nearby was the building I had noticed from the bus and which had made such a lasting impression on me. The building had, according to the familiar symbol above the four-pillared facade, once been the Masonic Temple. In spite of the obvious external decay, it still seemed to be in use and, from the sign above the pediment, I knew that its present purpose was a very sinister one. This was clearly the meeting place of the Esoteric Order of Dagon mentioned in Jedediah's and Zadok's notebooks.

Fortunately, there was no one in sight as I surveyed it from a respectable distance, yet I still had the *feel* of eyes watching me closely. It was as I stood there that I thought I detected an odd sound, a weird ululation. I could make out no individual words, *and it seemed unmistakably to well up from somewhere within the solid ground on which the temple stood!*

Was it possible there were hidden regions below that forbidding structure? Passages left over from the old smuggling days when much contraband was landed on the beach and hidden from the King's men? I recalled a particular passage from Jedediah Allen's book wherein he had described what he had seen one night from the shore and how a straggling file of men had entered that concealed cove, passing out of sight from where he lay concealed. If there were subterrene tunnels leading down to that deserted stretch of coastline, what better place for them to begin than here?

Since Obed Marsh had bought this place and only his trusted followers were allowed inside for their unholy rites, it would be the ideal place to bring slaves from distant parts without the general population being any the wiser. What terrible fate had befallen those poor wretches, it was impossible to guess.

From the grim warnings I had been given, I knew it would be unwise to be seen taking any particular interest in this shrine of pagan worship and I hurriedly made my exit from the green and headed along Dock Street, in the direction of the waterfront. This was an area of such utter slovenry and decadence that I shuddered at the mere sight of the empty hovels with their sagging gambrel roofs standing out spectrally against the clear blue sky. The stench of fishiness was far stronger here. Here and there, entire buildings had collapsed and were now no more than weed-overgrown mounds of tumbled masonry, clustered with prickly briars and obnoxious growths with a pale, unwholesome look about them, as if there were something in the meagre soil which provided them with an unnatural nourishment.

Although I could see no one, the place was far from silent. Odd noises reached my ears from both sides of the street, and I felt the hairs on my neck begin to prickle uncomfortably as I realized that the majority of these sounds emanated from those buildings which were apparently empty and boarded up, rather than from those which might have been expected to contain some form of life.

It was abundantly clear that the town was beginning to get on my nerves, making me edgy and jumpy. I tried to tell myself that this merely stemmed from those fantastic events I had read in the crumbling notebooks and what little had been hinted at since my arrival in Innsmouth. It was perhaps only natural that there were folk here who were jealous of anyone possessing wealth in the midst of all this squalor and, even a century earlier, those who had lost everything and seen their wealth and authority decline to the vanishing point might harbour a grudge against anyone who was doing well. Those tales which had been spread around concerning the Marshes, Waites, Gilmans, and Eliots were probably nothing more than malicious slander.

All of this which I was now seeing: the empty, deserted houses, the queer looks of the townsfolk, their dislike of strangers and desire to be left alone to continue their own way of life, could be put down to inbreeding and the indisputable fact that Innsmouth *was* isolated from the outside world by the salt marshes on the landward side and the sea on the other.

This line of reasoning was certainly plausible and logical and undoubtedly could explain much. Yet there still remained a nagging undercurrent of fearful horror in my mind as I proceeded cautiously along the ancient street until I came within sight of the sea. One other detail which was beginning to annoy me, and which I found impossible to explain, was a strange sense of *déjâ-vu* which I experienced at intervals. I would come across a small intersection, or distinguish the spire of a small church rising starkly above the background of tumbledown houses, and have the transient certainty that I had seen those places before. Yet I had never been in Innsmouth, nor was it possible to explain such sensations from what I had read.

This odd affection became more frequent and stronger the nearer I got to the waterfront and reached its pitch the moment I stared out across the water where the tide was beginning to come in and discerned the jagged silhouette of the black reef a mile and a half offshore. I had come across several references to Devil Reef and the spectral stories surrounding that ominous black rock beyond which the Atlantic was said to drop precipitously for several thousand feet. Both Jedediah and his son had written of Obed Marsh's nocturnal excursions to that forbidding reef on moonless nights and of strange blue lights seen at times around the dark of the moon.

Doubtless there were many in those days of superstition and myth who put such sightings down to pagan rites being carried on out there, and it had seemed strange to me that neither writer had considered a more commonplace reason; that such lights, which were said to be answered by others from some high structure in the town, were designed purely to lure unsuspecting craft onto those rocks, guiding these luckless vessels to their doom so that their cargoes might be seized to swell Obed's already bulging coffers.

Crossing Water Street, which, to my left, extended in a wide curve around the bay to end on a spit of land across the harbour, I entered what had once been a prosperous part of Innsmouth. The brick breakwater just across the harbour, although crumbling in places, still provided a defense against the worst of the Atlantic, but it was immediately obvious why the port had fallen into decline. Sand and silt almost blocked the entrance and I guessed that only small, shallow vessels would now be able to use the harbour where once the large, fine schooners and brigantines had docked with their cargoes.

I looked in vain for anyone matching my mental description of Zadok Allen. By now, I reckoned he would be a man well into his nineties. There were a number of repellent-looking fisherman in sight, although I forebore to question them, since all bore the now-familiar Innsmouth look about them. Several eyed me suspiciously and then one rose to his feet and approached me with a curiously shuffling gait which I found disturbing. Knowing that it would be foolish to turn and run, I stood my ground and waited until he came up to me. The staring, lidless eyes bored grotesquely into mine as he muttered in an odd voice, "What be ye doin' in Innsmouth, stranger?"

I told him that my only interest in the town was to view the quaint old buildings I had been told existed there.

He seemed to consider this for a little while, then grunted hoarsely, "There be no place like that at the waterfront. You better make your way back into town afore somethin' happens to yuh. We don't like strangers pokin' around here. An' those as does find themselves in a whole heap o' trouble."

Sickened somewhat by the slobbering speech, I inquired which was the quickest and easiest route back to the main square, aware all the time of sullen stares from the other men seated on the tumbledown jetty. I could sense the air of hostility in their expressions and although I knew how to take care of myself and doubted if any open action would be taken against me in broad daylight, it was difficult to suppress the fear in my mind.

Pointing a curiously mottled hand along Water Street, he indicated I should follow it across the bridge and then proceed along State Street, which would bring me out into the square. The fact that he had not directed me back along the route I had come suggested that, for some obscure reason, he did not want me to pass that main temple dedicated to the weird, outlandish cult.

Thanking him as courteously as possible, I walked as quickly as I could over the uneven hard-packed dirt of the street. Now the rushing roar of the river sounded more loudly from directly ahead and for the first time in my wanderings, I came upon a scene of activity. From the stench of fish, I guessed that the tall buildings on my right were what was left of the fishing industry in Innsmouth. Several trucks stood outside the buildings which were still in a reasonable state of repair, and a number of men were visible loading wooden crates into the vehicles. This was clearly still a major business in Innsmouth and, apart from the various items of gold sold by the Marsh Refinery Company, the only one which had any contact with the outside world.

Crossing the shaky wooden bridge where the Manuxet emptied itself into the Atlantic, I located the street on my right which I took to be State Street although there was no sign to mark it, finally arriving back in the square from whence I had started.

By now, it was well into the afternoon and I was glad to be out of those empty, narrow streets and in a place where a few wholesome people still remained. The door of the Marsh retail office on the edge of the square stood open. I had already decided to visit the office in the hope of seeing some of the items reputedly manufactured in the town and which I had been told were totally unlike anything produced elsewhere. I approached the door with an air of self-confidence I was far from feeling inside. There were too many disturbing circumstances associated with this town to make me feel easy in my mind.

To appear simply as an inquisitive stranger was out of the question. I therefore intended to pass myself off as a buyer of such articles for a store in Cleveland interested in purchasing anything out of the ordinary.

Going inside, I found the interior shabby and dim, illuminated by a few lights, and these were all dim bulbs set close to the painted ceiling. A youngish man stepped forward from the shadows as I entered and, as I studied him closely, a fresh wave of disturbance passed over me, for, although not unhandsome, I detected a hint of something bizarre about his features which was reminiscent of the other inhabitants and there was something aberrant about his vocal timbre which I could not place.

However, he appeared ready to accept my credentials and, adopting a professional attitude, I inquired if I might view some of the items he had for sale. Very soon, however, I found it difficult to keep my sense of mental equilibrium. The clerk switched on several more lights and it was with a feeling of growing unreality that I examined the articles in the long rows of cases, for here was something I had never expected.

Certainly the objects were beautiful in their design and intricate workmanship, yet the beauty was marred by the unearthliness of the designs and it was impossible for me to believe they had all been fashioned in that factory which lay but a stone's throw from where I was standing. Here were tiaras, bracelets, necklets, and rings all made of gold, but of a hue and quality I had never seen before. Almost all of the designs had an aquatic motif, giving disquieting suggestions of batrachian and ichthyic symbolism from extremely remote times and places.

My inquiries as to the origin of these pieces brought only oddly evasive answers, although the clerk did intimate that certain of them were extremely old and had been brought back by Captain Marsh during his voyaging to the East Indies and Polynesia, and the majority of these were for display only and not for sale. Others were made in the factory at the refinery and had obviously been based upon the earlier designs, yet with the same intricate and delicate workmanship which I found truly astonishing.

There was also that odd lustre of the metal which denoted that it was an alloy with some unknown metal, and I did not believe that among this decadent community anyone could have produced that amalgam or manufactured any of these items. There was such an air of mystery and alienness about them that I found it difficult to accept that any culture, primitive or modern, had formed them.

A small number, I noted, were devoid of the usual marine design, being purely mathematical in outline. Yet even here, certain disturbing elements were present which increased my uneasiness, for the lines and angles bore a curious relationship to one another. Staring at them in the overhead light, I found myself struggling to follow the amazing contours of interweaving curves and patterns and lines, as if my stunned gaze were being drawn into depths and abysses within them.

By dint of discreet questioning, I did succeed in eliciting some information from the clerk, although he appeared oddly uneasy about imparting it. That he accepted my interest was professional I did not doubt, but he was far from open regarding my inquiries. Yes, he replied, a number of these articles had been sold outside Innsmouth; he reluctantly stated that many larger, and even more intricate, pieces were in the hands of the still wealthy Innsmouth families and were occasionally seen worn in public by the Marsh and Waite women, but it was not wise to ask about these.

I left the office in a state of utter bewilderment. Even accepting the common belief that most of them had formed part of a pirate hoard discovered by Obed Marsh and possibly some of the other sea captains of a century earlier, such jewellery was certainly not of Spanish origin. I had seen photographs of pirate loot which had been uncovered in the West Indies and brought up from various wrecks on the seabed, but none of these bore any resemblance to what I had just seen. Although I knew little of such ornaments, my immediate reaction had been that these objects were far more than a few centuries old. Yet even a comparison with those found in the tombs of ancient Egypt seemed totally inadequate. Furthermore, I could not rid myself of the vague sensation of evil which I had felt on viewing them, and my mind persisted in linking them with the pagan idolatry which Obed Marsh had introduced into Innsmouth and which still persisted from what I had seen of the so-called churches dotted around the ancient squares to the north.

By now, it seemed that my inquiries had reached a dead end and no other source of information lay open to me. It was then that I recalled what I had heard of Zadok Allen. My interest had been so taken up by what I had seen during my wanderings in the neighbourhood of the waterfront that I had forgotten about him. How much I would be able to extract from the nonagenarian even if I could locate him, and how much would be anywhere near the truth, I could not tell. Acting on a sudden impulse, I found a small store in Eliot Street just off the square where I purchased a quart bottle of whiskey, hoping to loosen his tongue with it if I found him.

I knew that my chances of locating Zadok were remote, for he could be anywhere and I had no desire to venture too far from the square after my encounter with those fisherfolk near the jetty. There were, I feared, too many eyes watching my movements and it did not seem unreasonable that my presence in Innsmouth had, by now, become well known and might already have attracted less welcome attention than I wished. After all, there were few people who knew I had come here, and if I should fail to return to Cleveland it was doubtful if any inquiries would lead investigators to Innsmouth.

There were still several hours to go before that ramshackle bus left for Arkham and I guessed the owner of the Gilman House would ask no questions if I failed to turn up to claim my bag.

It was then, however, that fortune seemed to smile on me, for, as I was standing on the corner of Paine Street, undecided what to do next, I spied a curious figure perhaps a hundred yards away; a white-bearded individual of great age who had just broken off a conversation with two men and was shambling slowly in my direction. Despite his advanced years, there was a spark of intelligence in his watery blue eyes, and his lined features were regular with no hint of the reptilian look which I had come to associate with the majority of the town's inhabitants.

Although acutely aware of the fact that, even with no one else in sight in the square, I might still be under observation, I knew I had to seize this opportunity if I was to talk with him and learn something more of the dark and sinister shadow which lay over Innsmouth. Accordingly, as he came up to the corner, I caught his arm and half withdrew the whiskey bottle from my pocket.

The pale blue eyes fixed themselves upon it instantly and he mumbled something under his breath which I did not catch. Retaining my grip on his arm I ushered him quickly along the side of the square, past the Gilman House and a couple of shops, until we reached the intersection with Eliot Street, where I led him into a narrow, rubbish-filled alley and thence into South Street, edging towards the distant waterfront.

At first, he seemed reluctant to accompany me, hanging back as if afraid to be seen with me. Eventually, his desire for the liquor overcame his qualms and he trotted quickly beside me, moving with an agility which totally belied his great age.

I finally halted at an overgrown spot where we were out of sight of any watchers. I had occasionally thrown a hasty look over my shoulder to ensure we were not being followed but had seen no one. All around us lay rotting wharves and the ruinous remains of century-old buildings.

For some reason or other, the oldster appeared unduly disturbed by my choice of venue and repeatedly threw apprehensive glances towards the incoming tide and, in particular, towards the ominous black reef which stood on the horizon. Surveying the stretch of water, I could see nothing amiss to account for his jumpiness apart from a few dark shapes swimming far out which I took to be seals. Yet he was clearly nervous and getting more fidgety by the minute.

I had tried to question him a little on our way along South Street, but apart from a few mumbled monosyllables, I got nothing out of him. Evidently he was afraid of something and, since we had seen no one on the way, I guessed it was something more than being observed talking with a stranger. Taking out the bottle, I handed it to him and waited impatiently while he took several hefty swallows. When he made to put the bottle to his lips again, I caught hold of his wrist and took it from him. I had no wish for him to drink himself into a stupor before he answered my questions.

Before I could begin my interrogation, however, he peered closely into my face, then said in a thin, wheezing voice, "Ye ain't from Innsmouth, mister, and yet—" He broke off sharply, and a curious expression which I couldn't analyze flashed across his wizened features. Then he drew back a little, reaching out a skinny claw for the bottle.

Shaking my head emphatically, I said harshly, "First tell me about this town. About old Captain Obed Marsh and what happened nearly a century ago."

Tugging at his beard as a sudden twitch crossed his face, he leaned forward, lips moving spasmodically. For a few moments, nothing came out apart from a string of curses. Then his voice became stronger, and more articulate words came out.

"Reckon ye must know somethin' o' this accursed town or ye wudna have come here. Don't git many folk visitin' Innsmouth because o' the curse. It be still here as you've no doubt seen for yourself. But those ye've seen on the streets ain't half as bad as the *others* they keep locked away in boarded and shuttered rooms. Them is only seen at night."

Shuddering, I allowed him another couple of sips of the whiskey, for he was now showing signs of definite fright, as if merely taking about these others made him fearful.

After a long pause, he went on, "Reckon it all started with Obed and those voyages he used tuh make to heathen places in the South Seas, places nobody else had visited. He had three ships plyin' the trade at that time—the brig *Hetty*, a barque *Sumatry Queen,* an' the brigantine *Columby.* They all used tuh make regular runs to some island Obed had come across east o' Othaheite. Mind yuh, talk o' what he found there didna come from Obed; tight-lipped devil that he was, he'd say little. But Matt Eliot, him as was first mate, would talk, though it seemed he was agin with much o' what Obed was doin'. Matt didna hold with heathen things like Obed who'd huv sold his soul to the Devil—*and most likely did!*

"Wasn't long afore Obed started tradin' with the natives for bangles an' other baubles they had, all made arter some kinda gold, but it wern't like any kinda gold we'd seen. Matt—he were agin this from the very beginnin', said it weren't Christian to git such trinkets that were all queer with funny picters o' sea monsters all over 'em. Reckon he was allus a God-fearin' man. But the same couldna be said for Obed. He allus said he feared neither God nor Devil and there weren't no difference gittin' this gold this way an' diggin' up pirate loot which some o' the folks around here did, now and agin.

"But then, it seems, Obed ran into a mess o' trouble wi' them natives. He'd tried often enough to git 'em to tell him whar the gold come from, but that was somethin' they'd never tell him. So he takes one o' the natives on board the *Sumatry Queen* one night, brings him into his cabin an' locks the door. Reckon he must've tortured that poor devil into talkin' because Matt claims he heard screams durin' the night an' nobody dares go see what's goin' on. They never did see that native agin.

"The next night, Obed orders three o' the crew to take him in one o' the longboats to a little volcanic island nearby, but they don't find any gold there. Only the ruins o' a temple an' some carvin's so old they was nearly all worn away. Reckon those images must've been pretty awful because none of the men say anythin' when they got back and all o' them was mighty quiet.

"But old Obed wasn't goin' to be put off gittin' what he wanted, an' he started questionin' the old Chief, mebbe threatenin' him a bit. The upshot was that Obed finally made a blood pact wi' them heathens in return for all the gold he wanted. Seems there was one other thing he had to do, and I guess Obed baulked a little at this. The old Chief told him he was to take one o' the natives as a wife so that their religion could be perpetrated forever."

So far, much of what Zadok had told me corroborated what he had written in his notebook decades earlier, confirming that his memory was still not impaired by age.

After a few more swallows of the liquor he continued, his voice getting stronger than before. "Seems there was somethin' strange about that wife o' his. When he brung her back to Innsmouth, they anchored inshore off Devil Reef yonder instead o' tyin' up at the dock like they allus did. Came ashore in one o' the longboats an' landed on the beach north o' town at dead o' night. Reckon ye don't know about the tunnels under the hill and into town from the cove. 'Tweren't only that heathen wife he brung either. Hordes o' them natives was shipped into Innsmouth during the 1830's an' '40's, all having a queer look about 'em, more fishlike than human. That were about the time Obed closed all o' the Christian churches, chased their pastors outa town, or else they jest disappeared and were never seen agin. He bought the old Masonic Hall an' turned it into that temple to Dagon like them natives said he should.

"Them was real bad times fer Innsmouth. Most o' the other businesses had gone and, o' course, a lot o' the younger men had been kilt either privateerin' around 1812, or lost at sea. Funny thing was, plenty o' good ships went down out yonder beyond the reef durin' them bad storms that blew up without warnin', yet none o' Obed's vessels was touched. They'd make harbour wi' full riggin' as if they'd sailed through fair winds an' calm seas and not a man lost, while others runnin' with 'em went down with all hands.

"It were things like that that set folk talkin'. Rumours was rife that Obed, an' one or two others, had sold their souls to that devil god an' there was a curse on Innsmouth which he'd brought from them far-off places, an' it'll remain until the last o' the Marshes, Waites, an' Gilmans is gone, dead an' buried. But they's still here, so I reckon that curse, or whatever it is, will be here long arta I'm gone."

Here he lapsed into a reflective silence, staring ruminatively out across the bay, his lips trembling as if muttering to himself. I waited impatiently while he gathered his thoughts, knowing that as long as there was some of the whiskey left he would remain. That he was still agitated by what he saw, or thought he saw, out where that gaunt black rock rose ominously above the sullen swell, was patently obvious. If half of what he had told me was true, I wondered how he could have remained sane and able to discourse so succinctly and logically on this subject. Any lesser mind would surely have cracked under the strain of knowing this for all these years, speaking of it only to the occasional stranger who would not believe a word of such crazy mutterings.

After a while I let him have the bottle again, watching him closely as he half drained the remainder before I took it from his trembling hand. Wiping his mouth with the back of his sleeve, he continued his discourse, nodding his head slowly.

"Ye don't believe what I'm sayin', young fella," he murmured in a hoarse whisper. "Can't say I blame ye. Well, there was a few Federal men came into town when some o' the young ones started growin' up and showin' certain changes. But they figured it were some kinda unknown disease those seamen brung back wi' them from the Indies, an' there was some talk o' quarantinin' the town until it burnt itself out, but that came tuh nothin' an' after a time, those men left, those still *able* to leave because a lot of 'em just disappeared.

"Things reached a head around 1846 wi' more folk showin' these signs, and that wus when some o' the townsfolk started gettin' mighty suspicious about Obed's activities an' decided to keep a watch on him themselves. Some kept watch on the Marsh Mansion on Washington Street with others watchin' the rear on Lafayette Street. More of 'em took to keepin' the docks under surveillance, an' it soon transpired there was a constant traffic between the two—but not through the town, mind ye. Folks as knew nuthin' about it afore, soon got wind o' them tunnels an' when that heathen chantin' started from someplace under the Marsh Mansion an' the Temple o' Dagon, they reckoned they had tuh take things into their own hands.

"Hundreds o' folk had died in the big epidemic an' mebbe that wus partly to blame fer the riots. A whole band o' folk stormed the Marsh Mansion one night, took him and some o' the others to the gaol. Some were all for lynchin' 'em because o' what they found inside the house, partikularly down in the cellars an' up in the attick. Don't ask me what it was they found theer. None o' that mob would talk about it afterwards, but I figure it must've been somethin' real awful for 'em to act as they did.

"It were the next day that somethin' terrible happened. Without warnin', the town was swarmin' wi' critters. My old daddy used ter say most of 'em came up from the sea from Devil Reef, but my guess is they came from someplace where Obed had hidden 'em. While half of 'em came from north o' the river, the others took to them tunnels, comin' out at the cove an' then into town from that direction. Gawd, the slaughter there was that day! I was only fifteen at the time but it's somethin' I'll never fergit. They smashed in the door o' the *Innsmouth Courier* on Dock Street, kilt John Lawrence, the editor who'd spoken out often agin Obed, smashed all o' the equipment, presses an' the like, and then set the place afire.

"They let Obed outa the gaol, an' from then on he give the orders in town. Them as didn't go along with him just dropped outa sight an' was never heard of again. Some were allowed to leave, Poles an' Lithuanians. Guess he figured nobody ud believe 'em if they repeated anythin' outside. Besides, some o' the old prosperity was comin' back into Innsmouth, better'n before in the old days an' then the refinery set up, turnin' out gold ingots an' more o' that fancy jewellery you'll sometimes see around town or in the retail office. Reckon there must've been plenty o' trade with the outside because it was around that time that Obed got the railroad to put through the branch line from Rowley."

While he had been speaking, Zadok had been eyeing me closely with a shrewd expression on his grizzled face. Now he seemed to have lost some of his fear of Devil Reef and had transferred his apprehension to me, although I could see no reason for it. Perhaps he thought my intention was to repeat any information he gave me to the authorities in Innsmouth and provide them with enough evidence to keep him quiet permanently.

Abruptly, he switched the subject. "You ain't been in this town afore, have ye, mister?"

I assured him I came from Cleveland and that I had no intention of staying here, meaning to take the eight o'clock bus out to Arkham that very night.

He considered that for a moment, then drew in a deep, shuddering breath. After eyeing the last of the liquor with a meaningful glance he finished it off to the last drop before tossing the empty bottle away into the nearby weeds.

"Reckon there ain't much more to tell, mister. Ye'll hev seen for yourself what most o' these folk look like. An' like I said, they ain't the worst. They keep the *others* outa sight, locked away in the atticks and cellars. Had a county doctor here once who took a good look at some of 'em. Jest confirmed what the other physicians said—a disease from somewhere in the South Pacific, but he couldn't say what it was, nor how to treat it. Talked a lot about minglin' with them natives a century ago. Said it'd mebbe get worse down the generations. Didn't reckon it were contagious so there wern't no quarantine order slapped on the town.

"Some of 'em as ain't too bad visit other towns around here, mostly to sell the fish an' a few o' them gold things. But they ain't liked in places like Rowley an' Ipswich an' even the Arkham folk, who know more about these things than most, shun 'em like the plague."

I asked him whether he believed in this disease theory, and he seemed to consider that for a little while before speaking again. Then he shook his head vehemently, and I could see he was becoming agitated again, his eyes flicking in all directions.

"Ye want to know what old Zadok thinks, mister? Even if I were to tell ye, ye'd never believe it. Crazy Old Zadok they say around town, an' mebbe that's why I've lived so long while others have died. To *them* I'm jest an old fool who's teched in the head. But God, if yuh knew what I've seen senct those times, ye'd know what the truth is."

I could see he was wandering from the point and feared he might lapse into stark raving before I got everything out of him. I was also afraid that, now that the tide was coming in, we might be interrupted by some of those fishermen I had seen earlier. Stopping his hoarse flow of words, I repeated my earlier question.

"All right, young fella." he wheezed finally. "I'll tell ye what I think an', believe me, I've lived long enough seein' what's really happenin' around Innsmouth to know it's the truth. It weren't jest the gold that made the folk take so readily to this new religion Obed brung back, nor jest the fear o' him. There was somethin' else, somethin' Obed told everyone who joined that band o' heathens. They wanted me ter join, but that was somethin' I wouldna do, no matter what. But I were promised by Obed that, in spite o' the curse o' the Innsmouth look, I'd never die. All of 'em were told the same thing *and by God, I know fer a fact that it's true!*"

I stared at him in utter disbelief. Certainly, from what I'd read of the Arkham witchcraft trials, this was a common belief among those who worshipped Satan, but it was nothing more than a myth, an inducement to involve people in their unholy rites. Yet there was no doubting the sincerity in the nonagenarian's voice.

"Ye think I'm mad, don't ye? But I wus there when some o' them old coffins in the churchyard in Church Street were dug up more'n forty years ago. More'n haff of 'em contained nothin' but stones an' logs. There weren't any bodies. So where'd they go? Answer me that, stranger. I'll tell ye where.

There never was any. Them folk never died, they jest hid away when they figured their time was come. They're *still* here, hidin' away in them big houses on Lafayette an' Adams an' Washington. Old Captain Obed died, fer sure. *But he vowed he'd come back an' there ain't nothing so sure as that!*"

Zadok had once more gripped my arm, fingers biting deeply into my flesh as he muttered his crazy words. "It was he as made that first pact with 'em off Othanheite an' that was one o' the promises they made. *You mark my words. Old Obed will return—and soon!*"

Releasing his grip, he fumbled in the tattered pocket of his ragged coat, muttering all the while under his breath. Finally, he found what he wanted and brought out something which glittered between his fingers in the waning sunlight. "I've taken a likin' to you, young fella." He chuckled hoarsely, thrusting the object into my hands. "Ye're the fust who ain't laughed at old Zadok an' called him a crazy, drunken old fool. Besides—" here he thrust his face close to mine and I almost recoiled at the smell of liquor on his breath, "—there's somethin' about yuh I can't quite understand. Ye look a lot like—" He broke off sharply as if suddenly aware he was on the point of saying something he shouldn't and pressed his shaking lips tightly together.

Glancing down at the thing in my hand I saw that it was a ring bearing the same strange workmanship as those other items I had seen earlier in the Marsh retail office. It was far larger and thicker than any other ring I had ever seen and was made from that same curious amalgam. Too large for any normal finger, it slid loosely even when I placed it on my thumb.

"Don't ask how I got this," he wheezed breathlessly. "Belonged to Old Obed himself. Was to have bin given to one o' his daughters that he married off to some Arkham man. Keep it safe and let no one see it if you value your life."

I saw him start abruptly at some sudden sound, but it was only an abnormally large wave smashing against the crumbling breakwater. Yet it was enough to set him off into a veritable paroxysm of fear. Lurching to his feet, his voice now rising in pitch, he almost shouted, "Now git outa town. *They'll* know ye've talked to me an' if they reckon ye've found out too much, they'll see yuh never git out alive. Don't wait for the bus. Even if ye git on it, they'll make sure ye never reach Arkham."

Before I could stop him he had turned and, with no show of the drunkenness I had expected, raced for the road, disappearing into South Street as if all the devils in hell were on his heels.

For several minutes I remained where I was, struggling to assimilate all I had been told. By now it was almost five-thirty. I had not realized the time had passed so quickly. Zadok's rambling tale had heightened the feeling of malignancy and evil I felt about Innsmouth. There had been such terror in his tone and such utter conviction that I found it difficult to dismiss it out of hand as the ravings of a madman or the result of some impairment in his memory. Exaggerations there might have been, but if they were based upon some germ of truth, it was quite clear that something awful had visited this town almost a century before and, to some unknown degree, was still present.

Evidence of this curse, or rare malforming disease, was everywhere. In spite of my initial scepticism, I found myself coming round to the inescapable conclusion that the insidious shadow which lay over Innsmouth had a supernatural, rather than a natural, origin.

By the time I reached South Street I could see no sign of Zadok. Slipping the ring into my pocket, I walked slowly back towards the square, knowing I still had more than two hours to wait for the bus to arrive. It was still my intention to be on it in spite of Zadok's warning.

There now seemed to be more people abroad and I was acutely aware of the stares I received as I passed the shambling figures. Now that I had learned as much as I was likely to, I was anxious to leave this legend-haunted town. The oppressive air of watchfulness and malevolence was beginning to have its effect upon my nerves. More than once, in spite of his apparent frankness, I had gained the impression that old Zadok had seen something about me which he did not like, yet I could think of no logical reason for it. Perhaps it was his natural aversion to strangers, whom he only tolerated as long as they supplied him with his favourite tipple and were content to sit and listen to his tales.

Going into the Gilman House to reclaim my bag I was accosted by a second man, whom I took to be the manager, who drew me to one side and informed me that word had been received that the bus from Newburyport would not be able to make the journey that night owing to some kind of mechanical trouble which had arisen unexpectedly. It was patently obvious that, for some reason, the man was lying. On my way in that morning, I had noticed that, in many places, the telegraph lines between Innsmouth and Newburyport were down and unless the news had been brought by some transport making a business run between the two towns (which I thought was extremely unlikely), there was no manner by which such a message could have been received. When I pointed this out to him he merely shrugged and moved away, saying that he had given me the message and there was nothing more he could do.

By eight-fifteen, when the bus had still not arrived, I realized I had no other option but to try to get a room in the hotel for the night and seek transport out in the morning. In this I experienced no difficulty, for the clerk informed me that several of the rooms were vacant and I could have one at the top to the rear for a dollar.

Following him up the dingy, ill-lit stairs I was shown into a large room equipped with an ancient iron bed and a splintered wardrobe. There was a single chair next to one of the two dirty windows and a solitary bulb without a shade suspended from the fly-specked ceiling.

After sullenly informing me that there was a bathroom at the end of the corridor, the clerk left, closing the door softly behind him. It was as I stood there listening to his footsteps on the creaking stairs that I noticed there was no key in the rusty lock, nor were there any bolts on the door. My first thought was that, perhaps, this was an oversight on the part of the management. Not only would they have few visitors, but none of these guests were likely to have anything valuable worth stealing, and this did not warrant the expense of fitting new locks once the keys were lost or the bolts had rusted away. But my apprehension increased when a moment's examination revealed that there had been a bolt in place until recently, for the wood at that point was quite clean and the holes where the screws had been were clearly visible. Someone had deliberately removed it and not long before.

By now, I was becoming alarmed, convinced that this was all part of some conspiracy to keep me in Innsmouth overnight. Old Zadok's warning came back to me as I stood beside the window, staring out into the deepening twilight. It was still light enough to make out details beyond the multitude of sagging roofs and chimneys towards the river and the abandoned railway station where the rusted rails ran out of town through the marshes and then on to Rowley.

Perhaps it is a good description of my mood at that moment that I was already considering that route as a possible way of escape from Innsmouth if things got too bad. I had no intention of sleeping that night, for some inner sense warned me I would have to remain awake and alert if I were to get out of this crisis. I couldn't figure out why these folk should decide I was such a threat to them that I had to be eliminated. After all, what had I seen and heard? Abandoned, broken-down houses, derelict warehouses, ruined churches, that enigmatic temple with its suggestion of pagan rituals, the curious inherent strain of disfiguring degeneracy which had befallen the inhabitants, and a crazy, rambling tale from the oldest inhabitant.

And, of course, the ring.

Taking it from my pocket, I examined it minutely now that I could not be observed. Despite its obvious value and the marvellously intricate figuring, it was not what one would call beautiful. The weird arabesques which adorned its outer circumference were horrible in the extreme, depicting some form of sea creatures which I could not believe were meant to portray any species known at the present day, but were surely the product of the maker's wildest and unfettered imagination. Only in mad nightmare could such creatures have possibly existed. Yet every tiny detail was shaped with immaculate minuteness and perfection. Why anyone should wish to wear such a grotesque adornment was beyond my understanding. There were also a number of symbols clearly representing some form of writing, but the language was totally unknown to me and it would have required a powerful magnifying glass to make them out properly. Oddly, I had the impression that these had been etched into the metal at a fairly recent date.

It was clearly very old, its age akin to some of the objects I had seen in the retail office, and I felt certain it had not originated in the refinery on the banks of the river. Holding it between my fingers, I experienced a queer sense of unease as if the mere touch of it evoked strange memories in my mind. Whatever it was, I intended to show it to someone with a knowledge of these relics for a professional opinion. But that would depend on me getting out of this place of nighted shadows and subtle hints of satanism.

Before settling myself for the night, I decided to get something to eat and, not wishing to use the dirty room in the hotel, I went back into the square, locating a small restaurant which was still open. Here I was served by a sullen-featured woman of middle age who took my order and brought the food without uttering a single word.

In spite of the rundown appearance of the place and the attitude of the waitress and proprietor, the food was hot and wholesome and I ate ravenously. The only disquieting fact which disturbed my meal was the feeling of being closely under surveillance, not only by the two people in the restaurant, but by occasional outsiders who eyed me through the dusty window with more than usual interest. I knew without doubt that my movements were being closely monitored and, if I was to hope to flee Innsmouth, it would have to be under cover of darkness. Until such an opportunity presented itself I had to be careful not to show I was aware of this deliberate scrutiny.

Back in my dismal room at the Gilman House I forebore to put on the electric light, sitting near the window, every sense alert for the first sign of trouble. Something was brewing and the thought of that unlocked door made me fearful, so much so that I could finally contain my emotions no longer. Going across to the heavy wardrobe, I threw my shoulder against it, sliding it across the floor until it stood immediately behind the door. Only then did I feel a little easier in my mind and return to my vigil by the window. I had already ascertained that the connecting doors with the rooms on either side of mine were locked. Since there were no keys in them, however, it was clear they could be opened from the other side.

Darkness was now falling swiftly, but I knew there would be a moon, a little past full, which would hamper my chances of making it through the town unobserved. Deserted as Innsmouth was during the day, I feared its streets and narrow alleys would be far more populous after dark. From somewhere in the distance came the cracked tones of a clock chiming the hour of ten. From the direction of the sound I guessed it came from the small church almost directly opposite the Hall of Dagon, and even that everyday sound increased my tension, jarring on my ears.

I had brought a pair of powerful binoculars with me on my trip and now I took them out of my bag. Even with their enhanced vision, I could discern little evidence of activity in the town. The huddled, decaying houses blocked off much of my view of the streets, although I could make out a few dim lights in the windows of the refinery building, and where Bank Street intersected with Washington Street I thought I detected pale yellow gleams behind boarded windows.

At the moment, the town seemed abnormally quiet, with only the ceaseless rush of the falls marring the silence. After scanning the more distant regions, I lowered the binoculars and turned my attention to things closer at hand. If I was to get out of this decrepit building in a hurry I must choose some avenue of escape other than down the stairs and through the lobby. Undoubtedly the clerk and manager would be in league with anyone attempting to block my escape.

The wall immediately beneath the window was sheer with neither handhold nor foothold in sight, but a few feet away to my right a metal drainpipe clung precariously to the crumbling bricks, and a brief look suggested it might be possible to descend to the weed-choked and rubbish-filled courtyard below.

That it would be a descent fraught with danger was clear from the rusty bolts which held the pipe fixed to the wall. These looked ready to tear away at the slightest tug. But unless I was to risk moving through the corridors outside, there was no other choice open to me. Moving to the other window, I struggled with the catch, finding that it was rusted firmly in place. It resisted all my efforts to open it until I took out my penknife and chipped away at the flaky coating till it finally gave. Very slowly, taking care to make no unnecessary sound, I managed to ease the window up, letting in a rush of the foetid air.

Having decided on what action to take if any danger should present itself, I settled down at the window to wait. It was possible that all of these precautions and plans might be for nothing. Certainly Innsmouth was a town where there had been unexplained disappearances in the past. But all of that was many years ago and I was probably allowing my overwrought imagination to dominate my common sense. That the townsfolk had a natural aversion to strangers had become abundantly clear, but surely that was no reason for them to kill anyone who stayed there overnight. Furthermore, from what I had seen of that ramshackle old bus which was the only mode of transport, it was perfectly possible that mechanical failure had resulted in it being unable to make the journey from Newburyport—and as for that wild tale old Zadok Allen had spun after drinking a whole quart of hard liquor, how much credence could I put in that?

I realized I was trying to calm my nerves by explaining logically all I had seen and heard and to find a partial relief from the mounting tension which was building up inside me. But the oppressiveness of the atmosphere, both inside the dingy room and outside, produced the opposite effect. I could hear no sound or movement inside the hotel. Checking the luminous hands of my watch, I saw that it was approaching eleven. Outside full darkness had fallen, with the moon out of sight around the side of the building but throwing a pallid radiance over the clustered roofs.

When the sense of imminent danger came it was not from any source within the hotel, nor was it any actual sound. Rather it was the disturbing impression of *movement* in the nearby streets. I could see nothing to substantiate this, but the feeling increased swiftly, for there was now a very definite suggestion that something was afoot in the town, and it was nothing to do with the normal nocturnal activities of these folk. I could not analyze the reasons for my certitude that this unseen animation was directed wholly towards me, yet by now I was thoroughly convinced that I was the target and there was not a moment to be lost if I were to extricate myself from this horrible predicament.

Thankful that I had refrained from putting on the light, I hooked the strap of my binoculars around my neck, allowing them to dangle loosely against my chest. Edging towards the half-open window, I peered cautiously out, and in that same instant there came an unmistakable hint of movement on the stairs, a creaking accompanied by a low muttering. A fresh spasm of horror went through me at the sound of those low voices for, faint as they were, it was clear they were speaking in some foreign tongue which I did not recognize; guttural monosyllables and croaks that became louder as the speakers approached the door of my room.

I knew the drainpipe to be only six inches or so to the left of the window and was on the point of easing myself out when a sudden movement below caused me to draw back hastily into the room, pressing myself tightly against the peeling wallpaper. Two dim figures emerged from the shadows at one side of the courtyard. One of them lifted an arm and gestured upward and, with a shock which confirmed my earlier fears, I recognized the coarse, malformed features beneath the wide-peaked cap. That it was none other than Joe Sargent I was certain—and that could only imply that the bus had actually arrived in Innsmouth and had probably been parked somewhere out of sight before reaching the square!

I believe it was only the fact that this entire side of the building was in deep shadow which prevented them from observing the open window. For a moment, they conversed together in low tones, then, after scanning the courtyard, they separated, Sargent returning by the way they had come, and his companion clambering over the tumbledown wall at the rear. I knew I could not afford to waste any more time. Already those muttering voices were outside the door and within seconds the handle would be tried and it would be discovered that I had barricaded that means of entry.

Sucking in a deep breath to steady myself, I gritted my teeth and swung my legs over the ledge, grasping the pipe with my left hand. I felt it give a little and knew that the chances of it bearing my weight during the descent were very slender, and my chance of reaching the ground safely would be nil if either of those two men were still in the vicinity. Swinging myself sideways from the window, I clutched desperately at the drainpipe with both hands, thrusting myself as close to the wall as possible to minimize the pull on the rusty fittings. I would have to lower myself down as speedily as possible before the entire structure gave way, but luck was with me. Somehow, the dubious brackets held until I reached the bottom.

Bent double, I scuttled towards the rear wall and threw myself over it, crouching behind it and listening intently. A sudden hoarse cry followed by the unmistakable sound of splintering wood came from within the hotel, and I knew that a heavy weight had been hurled against that flimsy door and my escape would soon be discovered. Keeping in the moon-thrown shadows as much as possible, I made my way in the direction of the abandoned railway which might afford me the only possible escape route from Innsmouth. I had originally intended striking south along Federal Street towards Arkham but, from what I had been told, this was where the old families of Innsmouth lived and my chances of being seen in that direction were impossibly high.

Eliot Street appeared deserted with only a handful of widely scattered, dim incandescent lamps throwing small pools of yellow light along it, but a few seconds later a group of running shapes emerged from Broad Street, paused for a moment at the intersection, and then divided into two, moving out of sight in both directions into Bates Street where it cut across the junction. The sight had sent a fresh shiver of fear through me, but it also brought a faint sense of hope, suggesting that the townsfolk had already decided I would try to make my escape southward, and the purpose of that group was to block all roads out in that direction.

I was still far from safe, however. To reach my goal I would have to cross several more streets before I reached the western end of Bank Street where the railway lines began. Even then, the rusted rails followed a westward route very closely parallelling Rowley Road for several hundred yards, and if lookouts had been posted there I might find my escape impossible. But that was a risk I had to take.

Very soon, the entire population would be alerted and on the lookout for me. How well the pursuit would be organized I had no way of telling, but if the old tales were anything to go by, these people had done this before on numerous occasions and would be well versed in the art of hunting down fugitives. The thought prompted me into a wild burst of activity. Slipping through the maze of ruined buildings to the west of Eliot Street, every sense strained to the limit, I plunged recklessly on from one shadowed doorway to the next, now acutely aware of the sounds of pursuit from almost every quarter. Again luck was on my side, for I encountered no one as I fled across Lafayette Street and then Adams Street. Most of the shouts and hoarse yells still came from those areas to the south and east, and I began to entertain the hope that I had eluded my pursuers.

Then, at the intersection of Bank and Hancock Streets, I ran into trouble. Advancing along Hancock Street, evidently coming from the south, was a large horde of dark figures, some carrying flaring torches, the latter fortunately picking them out and giving me time to step back into the dubious shelter of a splintered wooden doorway, for they made no sound and without thus being forewarned of their presence I would undoubtedly have been seen. I judged there must have been more than a score of them, moving soundlessly and hideously over the uneven road surface.

The moon had temporarily disappeared behind a bank of dark clouds, and my only real view of them came from the flickering torches. But this was enough to pick out the features of those who carried the brands, and I almost fainted at the repellent contours of their faces as they drifted past my hiding place. The features of those abhorrent creatures I had encountered abroad in daylight had been bad enough, but these were a hundred times worse. Whatever the nature of the curse which Obed had brought down upon this town, it had transformed these men into virtual monsters. Slithering and shambling in a manner which I could scarcely describe, they padded silently in the direction of Bank Street, and it took every effort of will I possessed to prevent myself from fainting on the spot.

Scarcely daring to breathe, I crouched there in the debris-cluttered doorway and watched in absolute terror, praying they would not turn left along Bank Street and thereby inevitably dash any hopes I might have of reaching the railroad. I saw them halt at the corner in a loose bunch, and much guttural croaking ensued, with several gesticulating urgently towards the distant station. Then, to my utter relief, the entire group moved out of sight towards the distant waterfront, leaving the road clear. I knew I had to make a decision, either to remain where I was until that band had proceeded some distance towards the town center, or make a sudden dash for the station lest some of the stragglers turn back and discover me. In the end, I chose the latter course, running as fast as I dared past the looming shadows of the empty warehouses and then across a vacant area towards the station ruins.

The station, with its cracked and chipped stone columns, stood out gaunt and empty in the spectral moonlight which now flooded the scene, giving me ample light by which to see. A single, weed-overgrown track ran alongside the platform with its square clock tower throwing a grotesque black shadow across piles of rotting ties in what had once been the station yard. A couple of hundred yards away was the bridge across the Manuxet, boxed in like a tunnel.

The bridge, I knew, was the first real obstacle I had had to tackle, for it was evident it had received no repairs for many years, and I had no idea how secure the ties might be across the gorge. But there was no turning back now. I had come this far without being detected and, once over the bridge, I had only to follow the railroad across the salt marshes to reach safety. True, I would be in plain view of anyone along the Rowley Road and where the tracks crossed River Street, but by now I felt sure the bulk of my pursuers were to the east of me towards the town center and along the waterfront.

Comforting myself with that thought, I followed the decaying track into the tunnel. Here the moonlight only penetrated for a few feet, but I managed to navigate my way through the bridge successfully, although in one or two places the ties sagged precariously under my weight and the thought of falling into that chasm beneath me almost unhinged my reason. Now I entered more open country, having left the last of the buildings behind. As far as I could determine, Rowley Road was empty in both directions, but a fresh burst of sound at my back told me my pursuers had not given up the chase and, from both the volume of sound and its direction, I guessed they were now widening their area of search and some, at least, were heading in my direction. Having failed to find me, it was now possible they had deduced I might make for this route out of town. Even as the thought crossed my mind, I spotted a dark milling mass pouring in a tide of blackness along Bank Street, while others were searching the empty warehouses which bordered the northern side of that thoroughfare. In almost the same instant, I caught a horrified glimpse of a second group spilling across the bridge on Place of Hawks Street, rushing to link up with the others.

My position was becoming more precarious by the second, and without giving any thought to the possibility of being seen, I plunged into the cutting ahead of me. Thick, intertwining brambles and coarse grass clawed at my legs as I ran. God alone knows how many there were on my trail—there must have been hundreds of them, with possibly twice that number scouring the center of Innsmouth and teeming along the waterfront. Far more than could possibly be accounted for considering the number of empty houses I had seen and the dearth of living creatures on the ancient, crumbling streets.

That such a once-normal, prosperous town could have fallen into such a condition of degeneracy and physical abasement as this seemed impossible. *Dear Lord, the witch cult of nearby Arkham was nothing compared with this!*

Small wonder that outsiders neither cared to visit this place, nor were made welcome there. These were the thoughts which ran riotously through my mind as I fled along the rusted tracks, stumbling and clawing my way through patches of dense, abnormal vegetation with fear and horror riding the night wind and stench-laden air at my back. I knew I had only scratched the surface of the true shadow which lay over that evil-riddled town, and that I somehow had to reach the safety and sanity of Rowley and tell what little I knew to someone in authority.

How I eventually succeeded without being overtaken by that shrieking mob, which must have teemed in hundreds from hidden warrens and burrows deep beneath the town, I shall never know. But reach Rowley I did, after hours of running and walking through the night, with the leering moon lighting my way. It was grey dawn when I finally reached my destination. In Rowley I said little, explaining my dishevelled and exhausted state by saying I had somehow lost my way in the salt marshes. Rowley, for all it was a peaceful, natural town, lay too close to Innsmouth for me to be able to tell all that had happened.

Later that morning, I took the train to Arkham, where I sought out Professor Derby of Miskatonic University, whom I knew to be a recognized authority on the various religious cults of the world. A small, nondescript man in his early sixties with a kindly, lined face, he took me into his office and led me to a chair, offering me a brandy, for there must have been something in my face and demeanour which told him I was no ordinary visitor.

Briefly, I related to him all that had occurred during my brief and frightening stay in Innsmouth, and I noticed his expression growing more grave and troubled as my tale unfolded. It was clear that he already knew a little of that terrible place, but to hear it at first hand in the prosaic surroundings of that venerable seat of learning had a profound effect on him. He waited patiently until I had finished, only interspersing my story with a few pertinent questions, then sat back in his chair, studying me gravely.

After a brief pause, he said soberly, "You were, indeed, extremely fortunate to escape from that place, Mister Olmstead. I myself have known cases where people have visited Innsmouth and never returned, though whether by accident or malign design, it's never been possible to prove. Several of the old legends shrouding Captain Marsh are, of course, well known to anyone like myself who has made a lifetime study of these pagan cults. However, I had never realized things had reached such a terrible state. From what you've told me, these people still worship a god which Obed stumbled on somewhere in Polynesia a century ago. I had thought it had mainly died out and things had returned to something like normal. Apparently, this is not so."

So saying, he rose to his feet and crossed to a small cabinet in the corner. Coming back, he placed before me a large object which was evidently a tiara, hideously reminiscent of those pieces of jewellery I had examined in the Marsh retail office among those which the clerk had informed me were not for sale. The overall design was, as with the others, of a marine motif, beautifully worked but extremely hideous.

This, Derby informed me, had been brought to the university museum some thirty years before by a drunken individual who claimed he had been offered it by a fisherman from Innsmouth in return for the sum of fifty dollars. The museum had purchased it for its collection for the ridiculously low sum of a hundred dollars and, in spite of numerous inquiries from other institutions and much heated debate among various learned professors, it had still proved impossible either to date it or determine its exact place of origin.

There were, he told me, several other similar items manufactured from the strange gold alloy which could be seen in other institutes, most having been obtained in the decade immediately following Obed Marsh's death in 1878. As for the tiara, rumor had it that these were worn by the priests of this debased cult, which was reputedly based upon a strange mixture of pagan rituals and magic.

On my questioning him concerning the nature of the magic practised in Innsmouth, whether it was similar to that reputedly perpetrated in Arkham, which had clearly been based upon that of Medieval Europe, he replied that such spectral tales were associated with a close ally of Obed Marsh, the wizard Ephraim Waite, said to have been buried next to him in the Christchurch Burying Ground. While Waite's sorcery had been occasionally overshadowed by Marsh's nefarious activities, what had been told about him made interesting reading, and it was apparently he who had prophesied that Obed would one day return to Innsmouth to resume his former position as leader of the sect.

I now took out the ring I had been given by Zadok Allen. Derby examined it closely, taking it to the window to scrutinize it more readily, returning to his desk and taking out a large magnifying glass.

"Where did you get this?" he asked finally, looking up at me with an odd expression on his lined features.

I had already related the conversation I had had with the drunken nonagenarian, but had not mentioned the ring.

Once I had told him, he shook his head in a puzzled fashion before handing the ring back. "Either he found it or stole it," he said tautly. "I'm certain that ring belonged to Obed Marsh and equally sure he would not have parted with it, certainly not to anyone not a member of his congregation." So saying, he handed me the magnifying glass. "You will have noticed the ring is far too large to fit a normal hand. There are also curious symbols etched on the inside which, I must add, are unlike any I've come across before, but just here—" he indicated a spot with the tip of his pencil, "—you can just make out the letters—"

"O.M.," I said, focussing the glass on the inscription. "Obed Marsh."

"Exactly." He nodded.

It was at that precise moment that a very odd and totally inexplicable thing happened. I was still gripping the ring in my fingers and was on the point of replacing the magnifying glass on the desk when I experienced an odd tugging sensation inside my skull, and the next second I seemed to be no longer in the conventional office with the sunlight streaming through the window, but in some other place, somewhere infinitely horrible and dark, and there seemed to be a voice speaking in my mind, muttering harsh, archaic syllables of a weird and sinister nature.

The experience lasted for only a few seconds before normalcy returned, but I was aware that Derby was eyeing me curiously from across the desk. If he had noticed anything untoward in my behaviour, he made no mention of it, merely saying that the university museum would be prepared to offer me a substantial sum for the ring should I decide to sell it.

When I declined his offer, he appeared more concerned than disappointed and his next remarks seemed extremely strange. There was, he averred, something about the ring which he did not like; something which had struck him as being malignant and highly dangerous. It was, he hastened to assure me, nothing to do with the fact that it had come from Innsmouth, nor my rejection of his offer. Rather he had the impression that some form of harm might befall me if I kept it.

I pressed him to be more specific, but he evaded my direct questions, merely repeating his belief that my possession of it could lead to disastrous consequences for myself.

It would be impossible to analyze my thoughts and emotions as I left the university. I knew that somehow, following my visit to Innsmouth, I had become embroiled in something which went far beyond my comprehension. Had my presence there, short as it had been, somehow been sufficient to taint me with whatever evil existed in that town? There had been a wholesale horror associated with Innsmouth for which my conscious mind could not account, and no matter how much I tried to put that terrifying ordeal from my thoughts—or at least thrust it down into my subconscious—it continued to haunt me as I followed the directions I had been given to the local Federal office.

Here two stern-faced officials listened to my story in stony silence. I did not expect them to believe me. I was acutely aware that much of what I said was perhaps beyond the belief of such men who understood only stark facts and had no time for myth and local superstition, for little of my tale was based upon anything definite and had, in the main, been derived from hearsay. While one man made notes, the other continued to question me as to what I had actually seen. When I had finished, they told me politely that they had noted everything I had said and that appropriate action would be taken once they had consulted with their superiors and all of the facts had been taken into consideration. As I left, I glimpsed one of the men shaking his head and guessed they considered me to be simply someone who was a little mad and seeking some notoriety. I remained in Arkham for only three days and then returned to Cleveland, determined to put the entire episode behind me. I had done all I could to alert the authorities to what conditions were like in Innsmouth and if they chose not to believe me, there was nothing further I could do. But two events transpired to ensure that my memories of Innsmouth would not go away.

The first occurred less than a week following my return to Cleveland and the old family home. It came to my notice in the form of a newspaper article, tucked away on one of the inside pages. Evidently, in spite of my doubts, the Federal authorities had taken some note of my statement. A raid had been carried out on the town by Federal agents and revenue officers under the guise of arresting certain members of the community on tax evasion charges. Much of what they had discovered on entering the town was never openly revealed and I, perhaps alone among the general public, am able to read between the lines of what was reported and recognize that the real horror lay not in what was written, but in what was never disclosed. Fierce resistance met the invading force, and large numbers of people were killed in the battle. Fires were started among the dry-timber houses and hovels along the waterfront which soon raged out of control. By the time the raid was over, much of Innsmouth was little more than a smouldering heap of rubble. Some arrests were made but, oddly, no reports of any charges came to light, although I searched assiduously through the ensuing papers and periodicals.

Several groups associated with civil rights and liberties attempted to obtain details of what had occurred. Initially some of these well intentioned people proved vociferous in their condemnation of certain acts, yet these outcries ceased abruptly for reasons never yet explained. The curious report that a naval submarine had been dispatched to the area following certain findings, the vessel diving deeply into the Atlantic east of Devil Reef and discharging a number of high-explosive torpedoes straight down towards the ocean bottom, appeared in only one newspaper and, since this particular publication had long been noted for its sensationalistic and spurious articles, it tended to be disregarded.

This news might have been expected to bring me relief after what I had undergone yet, as I have intimated, there was a second event, or rather a sequence of events, of ever-increasing terror, which left me without any hope of shaking off that blasphemous horror which now assails me daily. There can be no more peaceful nights for me on this Earth since old Zadok Allen gave me that strange ring with its even stranger history.

The nightmarish incidents began shortly after my return, always occurring in that odd interval between full awareness and sleep. Immediately following an odd transient time when it seemed that someone—or something—was trying to get into my thoughts, I would find myself back in Innsmouth. It was a singular feeling which I had experienced on only one previous occasion—in Professor Derby's office when I had examined that ring with the magnifying glass. That these frightening experiences were not dreams, but rather vivid visions, I was forced to accept, for, apart from their bizarre nature, there was a logic about them which was unassailable.

Yet from the first, I recognized there was an unusual quality about them which set them apart from my waking survey of Innsmouth. The buildings and streets were all in a far better condition than I had seen them, and I saw none of those curiously disfigured residents. When, for the first time, I saw the waterfront and the wide harbour, I knew that the scene I was witnessing was not that of the Innsmouth of 1927 but as it had been much earlier. There were tall, square-rigged sailing ships moored at the quayside, and the wharves and warehouses bustled with activity. The breakwater was unmarred by any of the ugly crumbling blemishes I had seen during my visit.

At first, apart from their singular nature, these waking visions were not in the least frightening. Naturally, I assumed they were the product of what I had read coupled with my actual visit to that town, but gradually an element of horror crept into them. I would find myself wandering along the streets which had now become weirdly familiar to me, yet those people I passed on the sidewalks took no notice of my presence, as if I were totally invisible to them. It was during later visions that I became aware of two figures, seen with increasing frequency, who appeared to be taking an abnormal interest in me, following me closely as I moved, otherwise unheeded, between long rows of fine Georgian houses and across well kept squares and greens. One was a tall, bearded man, sometimes dressed in the finery of that bygone age and at others in the unmistakable garb of a seafaring man. His companion, by contrast, was thin to the point of gauntness, wearing a long black cloak with the high collar pulled up around his neck. But it was this man's face which shocked me almost to the point of screaming. Never had I believed such evil could have been stamped upon a human being's features.

Perhaps it was this characteristic which finally enabled me to recognize these two as Captain Obed Marsh and the old wizard Ephraim Waite. As the months passed, these two menacing figures gained more prominence. No matter where I would find myself in old Innsmouth, they would be there, lurking in shadowed doorways or along the harbour wall where three fine ships sometimes lay at anchor with men loading or unloading cargoes.

Gradually, however, a fresh taint of horror entered these scenes. Whenever I encountered this monstrous duo, Captain Obed would lift his right hand in an imperious beckoning motion, bidding me to follow. The first time this occurred, the shock was so great that it jerked me fully awake, lying in my bed, drenched in perspiration. It was not so much the threatening gestures which brought me fully out of that shadowy chimera, but the sight of Obed's hand. Abnormally large with fingers far thicker than normal, *they gave the impression of being webbed, and on the third finger something glittered in the pale sunlight.* I recognized it instantly as the curious ring which Zadok Allen had pressed into my hand.

And on the finger of that monstrously scabrous appendage, it fitted perfectly!

So vivid and lifelike were these impressions that I finally decided to consult my physician, Doctor Alexander Morton, for although my waking hours appeared rational enough and my work had not suffered unduly, I was well aware there was the taint of insanity in my family. My cousin Lawrence had been incarcerated in a sanitarium where it seemed inevitable he would spend the rest of his days in complete seclusion.

After examining me thoroughly, Doctor Morton assured me I was in perfect physical health. As to these weird occurrences, it was his belief they all stemmed from my horrifying experience in Innsmouth, stating that the atmosphere of that ancient place, combined with the ordeal of my precipitous flight from its inhabitants, had left this lasting mental impression on me. He averred that he had come across several similar cases with soldiers returning from the Great War whose service under the terrible conditions and privations of trench warfare had scarred them mentally in a similar fashion. Such an experience as mine, he believed, would undoubtedly produce these symptoms, but they were nothing more than very powerful impressions caused by my visit to Innsmouth.

I was not, as I feared, going insane, but if I wished to avoid a possible nervous breakdown I must try to forget all that had happened and put it out of my thoughts completely. He prescribed a mild sedative and told me to make a further appointment in a month if the symptoms persisted.

Rather than alleviating my condition, the sedative appeared to have the opposite effect, for no sooner did I begin taking the drug than the frightening episodes, which had previously been little more than brief flashes of a few minutes' duration, began to invade my dreaming state. There was still that odd sense of tugging which was the major premonitory symptom and then, within seconds, so swiftly that I was scarcely aware of the transition, I would find myself back in old Innsmouth.

I have said that, in the beginning, I wandered those hideously familiar streets unseen by any of the passers-by, as if I were a ghost from the future moving through scenes of a past age. Then, as this odd affliction progressed, I became aware of an alarming phenomenon which, although I could not comprehend the meaning behind it, nevertheless frightened me even more than anything before. It was a simple, but inexplicable, observation.

In my dreamlike state, it seemed that more and more of the people I encountered were becoming aware of my existence in the town, whereas the figure of Obed Marsh was becoming gradually more evanescent compared with the gaunt shape of the accompanying Ephraim Waite. Still, Obed continued to beckon me to follow him, this unspoken command becoming more and more insistent until I knew there would come a time when I would be totally unable to resist.

That dreaded moment came sooner than I had expected. On the evening in question I had taken the ring from the locked drawer where I had kept it since my return from Arkham, with the purpose of examining it closely, and I compared it with that which I had seen on Obed's finger in my strange dreams.

That they were identical, I could not doubt. Handling it almost instantly produced that subtle sensation inside my head, stronger than before, and a moment later, sill clutching the ring in my right hand, I lapsed into that queer, dreamlike state which had haunted me for so many months. Again I found myself in Innsmouth, but on this occasion, unlike all of the others I had experienced, it was night. I was somewhere along Federal Street, facing the old Masonic Hall which now bore the legend "Esoteric Order of Dagon" above its portals. There were only a few dim lights along the street, but the brilliant yellow moonlight was sufficient to pick out everything in amazing detail.

The actual sight of that terrible place of pagan worship was bad enough, but the sight of those two figures standing one on either side of the doorway, through which a throng of people were entering, hinted of blasphemy and madness. What terrible rites had been, and still were, enacted within those unhallowed walls, I could not begin to guess. That some form of sorcery was practised here by Obed and that evil-visaged wizard was abundantly clear, and this time, when Obed raised his right hand in that familiar, imperious gesture, I could no longer resist but went forward without any vestige of physical control, passing into the dim-lit space within.

Grotesque figurines, etched with black shadow, adorned those walls with sputtering brands thrust into metal brackets between them. Down along a subterrene passage I was led into the massive crypt beneath the temple. In my waking visit to Innsmouth, I had been told that when this foreign cult had been initiated into the town, Obed Marsh had assumed its leadership as high priest, and as I was unwillingly led towards the front of that vast congregation, I assumed that he would fulfill this office now. Instead, it was Ephraim Waite who made his way onto the dais at the front of the crypt while Obed remained close to where I stood, as if to prevent any attempt at escape on my part.

Of what followed I retained only vague and hazy memories when I woke the next morning, still seated in my chair by the fire. There had been a terrible dialogue between Waite and the congregation, but as to the nature or meaning of the archaic phrases, I could deduce nothing. Utterly alien to me, the sounds were yet strangely familiar, evoking some odd pseudomemory within my mind. I recall seeing Obed leave my side and approach the dais where a monstrously thick tome lay open on the altar, and the last thing I remember with any clarity was Obed taking the gold ring from his finger and laying it on the open page of the book while Ephraim Waite made a strange sign over it with his left hand.

By now, it had become clear to me that the key to these strange visions lay in that ring which Zadok Allen had given me. How he had procured it I had no means of knowing, but that it had originally belonged to Obed Marsh was now beyond all reasonable doubt. But why had that drunken old reprobate given it to me, a complete stranger in the town? As a resident of Innsmouth, he must certainly have known how valuable it was, yet he had made no effort to sell it to obtain money to fund his obvious liking for strong liquor.

Plainly there was something concerning Innsmouth and old Captain Marsh which I had not so far uncovered—and in some obscure way, it concerned me and my family. The very nature of the visions and dreams now gave an added impetus to search. Fortunately I was on excellent terms with the town librarian and the pastor of the church where my family had worshipped since moving from Arkham. From the former I obtained little of value in my inquiries, although it came to light from my reading of the old records that my maternal grandmother was an Innsmouth woman who had left there to marry my grandfather, an Arkham man.

It was while I was searching through the musty church archives, however, that the real horror was revealed, for there it was written quite legibly, although in ink which had faded appreciably over the decades, that my maternal grandmother's maiden name was Marsh! Perhaps, after all that had happened, this should not have come as a shock to me, for, looking back in retrospect, there had been so many odd incidents pointing in this direction. The way Zadok Allen had peered so intently at me when he had handed me the ring as if he had seen something in my face which told him of my ancestry.

Yet the knowledge was utterly and inconceivably abhorrent, for it meant that my great-great-grandfather was none other than Obed Marsh, and as to the identity of my great-great-grandmother, I did not dare to think. Conceivably she had been one of those natives he had brought back from that dreadful island in the South Pacific, and not only had she brought that wealth in gold as her dowry, but also the curse which had fallen upon Innsmouth and which still lay, like a vast and malignant shadow, over the fire-ravaged town.

It was in a state of terrified bewilderment that I returned to the house and struggled to absorb these horrific revelations. I had solved the mystery, for this discovery undoubtedly explained both that sense of *déjâ-vu* which had assailed me at certain times during my wanderings around Innsmouth and the dominance of Obed Marsh in these curious visions which afflicted me nightly.

Yet, in spite of the plausibility of this explanation, I still felt there was some more sinister aspect of my ancestry which I had, as yet, failed to uncover. What was the hidden meaning in my dream of Obed's placing that ring on the monstrous tome and those weird cabalistic signs which Ephraim Waite had made over it? Was I, in some visionary manner, being warned against keeping it?

I knew it was possible that my subconscious mind had absorbed so much of the weird atmosphere of Innsmouth and those horrific events which had led up to my precipitous flight from that shadowed town that it was inevitable some of it should seep through my consciousness at times, as if the brain were attempting to unburden itself of this episode in my life. After all, most dreams are made up of strangely disordered and disjointed events in one's past life, often strung together in a manner which, in the dream, appear to be perfectly logical, even in recurrent dreams such as those I was experiencing.

So far, all of this had occurred either while I slept or during that twilight period between wakefulness and slumber. Only later did I suffer fleeting visual impressions while wide awake. These visual displacements were, at first, of only a few seconds' duration, but they seemed to possess some profound and portentous meanings connected with myself, which I struggled to decipher.

I would be walking along a familiar street in Cleveland, taking in the sights in the warm autumnal sunlight when, on emerging into a small tree-bordered square, I would find myself abruptly facing a totally different scene. Gone were the red-brick buildings with the shoppers and sight-seers on the sidewalks, and in their place was something equally familiar—but horrible—the Esoteric Order of Dagon hall. It was the advent of these hellish hallucinations which finally brought home to me the insane and soul-shattering reality of what was happening, the ultimate cataclysmic horror of wizard-haunted Innsmouth and that grotesque pagan cult which, combined with the sorcery of Ephraim Waite, had enmeshed me irretrievably in the terminal horror which will soon befall me.

For now I know the hideous fate which is my lot as a descendent of Obed Marsh, his hellish pact with those islanders of the South Pacific and, above all, his terrible bargain with that old wizard. In my mirror, I can see the physical change which is coming over me, the resemblance growing more and more distinct with each passing day, and that terrible tugging at my mind as he becomes more dominant until finally he will take me over completely.

Obed Marsh did not obtain immortality, since that was given only to those members of the cult who were the offspring of that terrible mating with those creatures from that distant island. But, as revealed to me in Zadok's half-crazed testimony, *he would return.*

Very soon, I shall no longer be Robert Olmstead but Obed Marsh, and then I must return to Innsmouth and there carry on those blasphemous rites to resurrect Ephraim Waite. *Together we will restore the worship of the old gods and rebuild that which has been destroyed and desecrated by the outsiders!*

About "Understudy"

Have you ever noticed a certain strange resemblance between a finny creation of Lovecraft's and a much more famous fishy monster of the Big Screen? Gary Myers did, and here's the result, an etiological myth of sorts, intended to explain a piece of sinister synchronicity that must be more than coincidence. Or my name's not Ahab Marsh.

Myers explains, "This one is based on a bit of real cinematic trivia. It seems there were *two* creatures used in the making of the original film: a larger, darker-colored one for the land, and a smaller, lighter-colored one for the water . . . ."

"Understudy" marks, hard as it may be to believe, Gary Myers' first foray into Lovecraftian tales set in the modern era. Up till now his fame has rested on his carrying forward the banner of Lovecraft's Dunsanian dream fantasies. This time, he has taken off the kid gloves. You will be seeing more in this vein. It is not too much to say that, with "Understudy", we are witnessing the debut of a major new Cthulhu Mythos writer, even though Gary was already in the first rank of the New Lovecraft Circle. It's as if there were *two* Gary Myers . . . .

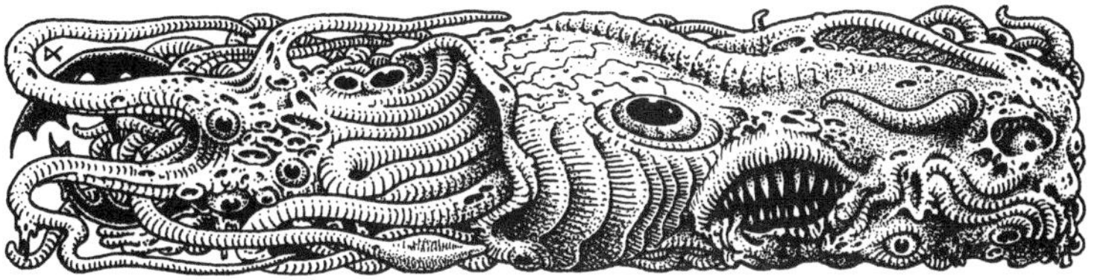

Understudy

by Gary Myers

It started with the monster. Before it ended, an actress was frightened into hysterics on a working set in broad daylight, and two men disappeared from a seaside bungalow in the middle of the night. The police who investigated it were too inclined to dismiss it. They thought the studio had rigged it as a publicity stunt for the new picture. But I know better. I was there. I watched it happen from the first.

I had had considerable experience with monsters in those days, working in the Galactic Pictures make-up department at the height of the fifties science fiction boom. But the Fish Man was going to be something special. I don't mean the creature itself. That was just another bug-eyed-horror, just another missing link between sea life and land life, such as must have been featured in maybe a dozen pictures before and since. No, what would make the Fish Man special was the make-up. For one thing, it had to be a full-figure suit, and that had never been done before. For another, it had to be suitable for swimming in.

But these problems were relatively easy to solve, given time and money and a staff of talented people. The real trick was to make the monster conform to the ideas of the producers. They knew what they wanted, I guess, but they couldn't communicate their desires in any meaningful way. They could only tell us when we had failed to meet them. It wouldn't have been so bad if they had always recognized our failures in the design stages. But sometimes it took a finished suit to show them exactly where we had gone wrong. Then there was nothing to do but stand looking on while several weeks' work got carted away with the rest of the garbage.

I was complaining about this to Ted Marsh that Saturday afternoon on the porch of his Venice bungalow. Ted was my best friend in the department, and he used to have me over to drink beer and watch the pelicans fish in the surf. But today I wasn't much interested in pelicans. Today I only wanted to let off steam over this latest in a long series of workplace disasters. And Ted, always the perfect host, sat quietly by and let me do it. He sat quietly by, that is, until somewhere around the middle of my fourth beer.

"Maybe it wasn't *all* the producers' fault," he said then. "That last design wasn't exactly wonderful."

"Wasn't exactly wonderful! You've got *that* right. With those lobster claws and that lizard tale, it looked more like a bad case of the DT's than a product of earthly evolution. Lobster claws! My five-year-old nephew could do better than that. We could do better ourselves, if we were a little more sober."

This sort of thing was not unusual. Ted was an odd fish at the best of times. Oh, he was nice enough when you got to know him, but more than a little eccentric. But maybe his odd behavior went with his odd appearance. Ted was nobody's idea of handsome. With his pop eyes and flat nose, his wide mouth and receding chin, he looked more like a frog than a man.

As I said, this sort of thing was not unusual. I guessed that he was tired of the subject, so I turned the talk to other things. But on Monday he came to work a good fifteen minutes late, with a great big artist's portfolio under his arm.

"What have you got there?" I asked him.

"I'll tell you that later."

Then, as the old man passed through the shop on his way to his office at the back, Ted gathered up his portfolio.

"Wish me luck," he said.

"What for?"

"I'll tell you that later, too."

Before I could answer, he turned away and started toward the old man's door. He knocked and went inside and didn't come out again for a long time. When the door did open maybe half an hour later, it was the old man himself who came out to call the rest of us in to a departmental meeting. I went in with everyone else, and saw Ted standing at the back of the room looking nervous and excited. But I forgot all about him when I saw his big portfolio lying open on the table.

Nowadays the Fish Man has become so familiar that it's hard to appreciate the striking originality of the design. Well, it was the original design I was seeing now. It was all there. The body armored in overlapping plates of horny reptilian hide. The oversized hands and feet, with webbing between the whole lengths of the fingers and toes, and wicked-looking claws at the tips. The weird head, noseless and chinless, with bulging eyes, a thick-lipped gash of a mouth, and, instead of ears, a fringe of gills growing down around the curves of the jaws. It was a monster, all right, and ugly enough to satisfy even the most demanding producer. But it made me smile all the same. For clearly Ted had put a lot of himself into it. Except for the webs and gills and things, it looked like an extreme caricature of his own peculiar physiognomy.

After the meeting I cornered him at his work bench. "So that was your big secret, you mysterious bastard," I said jokingly. "I didn't know you had it in you. Where did you get the imagination to dream up something like that?"

"What imagination?" he answered, his face a perfect deadpan. "I drew it from life."

After that we had our work cut out for us. For the next several weeks we labored to translate Ted's design into three dimensions. We sculpted and cast, painted and tested, then sculpted all over again. In many ways this was a reprise of the work we had been doing for the last three months or more. But there was one thing that made it different, and that was our belief in the new design. There wasn't one of us who didn't think that we were working on something big this time. There wasn't one of us who didn't think that this new creature, from the warts of its domed head to the claws of its great webbed feet, had the potential to take on a life of its own. And the first time the old man led Frank Sellers out on the floor in full Fish Man regalia and announced, "Well, boys and girls, it looks like we've got our monster," there wasn't one of us who was inclined to disagree.

Frank was the man in the monster suit. He had been involved in the project from the very beginning, since the suit was built over casts of his body to ensure that it would fit him like a second skin. This made it a large skin to fill. Frank was an athlete, a professional dancer and a strong swimmer, important assets to a role in which movement on land and in water were the only means of expression. But what must have set him apart from other contenders was his height. At six feet, five inches, he was tall enough to make any monster look threatening. Frank took his punishment pretty well. But I've often wondered whether some of the Fish Man's on-screen savagery didn't grow out of Frank's resentment of those grueling make-up sessions.

Ted and I had plenty of opportunity to observe this savagery close up, since our work didn't end when the suit was finished. We were assigned to ride herd on it throughout the production, to help Frank into and out of it, to make sure he didn't try to sit down in it, and to repair any minor damage it might sustain in the course of filming. This meant that we had to be on the set with him while his scenes were being shot. This was less interesting than it sounds. The scenes were seldom shot in chronological order, so they made little dramatic sense to begin with. After the actors ran through them two or three times, they were drained of even that. But for sheer mind-numbing dullness they couldn't begin to compare with the periods between, while the crew set up for the next shot.

Still, the experience was not without its bright spots, and the brightest of these was Eve Capulet. Eve was our leading lady and the Fish Man's love interest. She was also about the prettiest little thing that ever put on a bathing suit, which our script gave her ample opportunity to do. All leading ladies are pretty. But Eve was also very sweet and friendly to everyone, and not all leading ladies are that. Not many of them would deign to notice the poor make-up men, but Eve came to see us on the very first day. It was Frank who brought her to us. He came up to us with Eve on one arm and his second head under the other.

"Eve is really impressed with the suit," he told us after making introductions. "She's been asking all kinds of questions about it. I know when I'm in over *my* head, so I brought her along to see the boys who built it."

"You brought her to the right place," I said, stepping forward. "Miss Capulet, I'm at your service. Just tell me what you want to know."

But all I got for my offer was a polite smile. She turned from me to Ted.

"Frank tells me *you* invented it," she said. "Where do you come up with ideas like that?"

For a moment I almost hated him. I *would* have hated him if he hadn't looked so trapped and unhappy, like a deer caught in headlights. Poor Ted! The attentions of a pretty girl were something new in his life, and he didn't know which way to turn. This should have come as no surprise. In the two years we had worked together I had never heard him talk about women, and I had always figured it was because he couldn't have much to tell. As I said before, he was nobody's idea of handsome. But I had never realized until that moment just how bad off the poor guy was. It was all he could do not to bolt.

Eve caught on pretty quickly to what the trouble was, and she did what she could to help him through it. She kept him focused on the subject under discussion as if it were the most interesting thing in the world. And I have to say, her approach worked. In no time at all she had old Ted eating out of her hand, explaining the mysteries of hooks and zippers, rubber and paint as well as I've ever heard it done. They went on like that for a quarter of an hour, while Frank and I just stood there looking foolish. They went on right up to the moment Eve was called to take her place before the camera.

"I want to thank you, Ted, for giving me so much of your time. It's been very interesting. Thanks."

She smiled and held out her hand to him. He took it without hesitation.

"Thank *you*, Eve," he said. "The pleasure was all mine."

She smiled again and ran off, leaving Ted looking dumbly after her. Clearly, she had made an impression on him. But that was to be expected. Half the crew was in love with her. I was a little in love with her myself. But none of us would have thought that this meant anything. We would have understood that what had passed between Ted and Eve was nothing more than the momentary camaraderie of two people thrown briefly together by their common livelihood. I would have thought that Ted understood this too. But Ted saw things differently from the rest of us. I wouldn't know how differently until a few days later.

We were on the lake that doubled for the Amazonian lagoon, shooting a long sequence in which Eve's character goes for a swim. She stood a moment on the deck of the boat, looking stunning in her white bathing suit. She dived over the side and struck out through the water with strong and graceful strokes. She went through a number of aquatic gyrations. She swam back to the boat again. Not very exciting stuff, at least not when viewed from shore twenty yards away. But Ted saw a lot more in it than I did.

"It's beautiful, Dave," he said in an awed whisper. "We can't see him, but the Fish Man is down there too, swimming a few feet beneath her. He's too shy to touch her, too drawn by her to pull away. So he swims beneath her on his back, mirroring her every move in a beautiful courtship dance."

I was too surprised to answer him. And yet, I thought, why should I be surprised? Half the crew was in love with Eve, so why not Ted? But wasn't it ironic that this ugly man, whom no self-respecting woman would ever look at twice, should nevertheless have an advantage over the rest of us? That he alone could carry on a vicarious romance with the girl of his dreams, through the person of the monster of his imagination.

Ted didn't notice my silence. He was too caught up in thoughts of his own. When he spoke again, it was in a voice almost too soft for me to hear.

"If the picture has a heart, this is it."

I had reason to remember this a few days later. Word got out that the producers were unhappy with the underwater sequences as they appeared in the dailies. Frank Sellers might be a strong swimmer, but he was evidently not strong enough to make a good showing while encumbered with a thick layer of foam rubber. He did well enough swimming right-side up, but when, as in Ted's beloved water ballet, he had to swim upside down, the effect was downright ludicrous. "Somebody call a life guard!" was one screener's brutal summation. The bottom line was that the scene must be redone or dropped altogether.

Ted was so upset by this rumor that he stopped the old man on his way to his office. "Is it true what they're saying, sir? That the water ballet is being cut?"

The old man frowned and shook his head. "It looks that way, Ted. Unless we can find a way to fix it, and I don't see how we can do that. Even if we had the resources to build a new suit, we don't have a swimmer to build it for. And there would be no assurance that the new man could maneuver in it any better than the old one."

"Let *me* fix it, sir."

The old man was genuinely surprised by this. "Ted, I know how much this project means to you—"

"I can *do* it. I can have our new Fish Man here ready to shoot on Friday morning. But you've got to give me the chance."

The old man looked thoughtfully at the younger one. "OK, Ted. You get your chance. Have your Fish Man on the lagoon set on Friday morning."

After the old man passed on I confronted Ted myself. "Are you nuts?" I asked him.

He considered this for a moment. "No, Dave, I don't think so."

"Well, think again. You heard what the old man said. Where are you going to find a swimmer who can *wear* the suit, let alone *swim* in it? You sure as hell can't build another one between now and Friday. The thing's impossible!"

I must say, he took it very calmly. "You may be right. All the same, be on the lagoon set on Friday morning."

Ted didn't report to work the next day or the next, which left me with my hands full. These were Frank's last days on the shoot, and they included two of his most important scenes: the girl's rescue from the Fish Man's grotto, and the monster's subsequent death in the hail of her rescuers' bullets. These were also the last two days of primary filming, which meant that on Friday Ted would have the production unit pretty much to himself. It also meant that I would be free to go down to the lagoon set and get a look at what he had come up with.

He must have come up with something, because I arrived to find Eve already in the water, running through the gyrations of her lonely swim routine. No cameras were in evidence, since the scene was being played for the benefit of the underwater cameras only. I saw Ted standing beside his old van on the far side of the lake, watching like the rest of us. I couldn't get closer to him while the shoot was going on. However, I saw Frank Sellers standing in civilian clothes a few feet away from me. So I approached him and asked how things were going.

"Pretty well," he told me. "Old Ted got his Fish Man, all right. He drove up with him in the back of his van about two hours ago. The new guy—Ted introduced him as his uncle Asa—is smaller than me, and his coloring is a little lighter, but in everything else he's identical. He's not very friendly, though."

"No?"

"No. I went up to him before the shooting began, to introduce myself and compliment him on his costume. The son of a bitch ignored me!"

Before he could tell me anything more, our attention was drawn back to action on the set. The filming had stopped. The director was walking down to the edge of the lagoon where the divers were standing chest-high in the water, giving him thumbs up. They had got what they needed, they seemed to be saying, and it looked good. Eve was being helped out of the water and into a robe and slippers. But where was the Fish Man?

"There he is," said Frank beside me. "He's coming ashore now."

And so he was. Nobody helped him out of the water, but he didn't seem to need it. A moment later he stood on the shore, dripping and gasping. Now that I was getting a good look at him, I realized that Frank had been a little harsh in his assessment. Asa and Frank were certainly *not* identical. The new Fish Man was superior to the old one in every way that counted. But Frank had been right about one thing. Asa didn't share his easy professionalism. Frank might be the Fish Man while the camera was rolling, but afterward he would take off the head and make jokes about it with the crew. Asa took it more seriously. I don't think I ever saw him out of character, and I know I never saw him out of the head.

Frank wasn't the only one that this attitude rubbed the wrong way. Eve had always gotten along well with Frank, in and out of costume. But Asa seemed to make her anxious and unhappy. As soon as she noticed him standing by her, she turned without a word and hurried to her trailer. As for Asa, he just stood there looking dumbly after her, much as Ted had done under similar circumstances a week before. He stood like that until Ted himself came up and led him back to the van.

The director had been crouching on the shore, conferring with the divers in the water. He must have been satisfied with what they told him, because now he came up and called everyone to their places for the next shot. This was the big abduction scene, where the monster leaps off the boat with the girl in its arms and carries her down to its underwater lair. Asa and Eve reappeared from their van and trailer and took their places on the deck. Asa looked the same as ever, but Eve had changed from her white bathing suit into white shorts and a dark print blouse. Her dark hair was still a little damp from her swim, but this didn't matter since the only cameras were in the water. She seemed less nervous than at the end of the last shot. But I noticed that she still kept her distance from Asa.

Then the call for action came, and Asa threw his finny arms around Eve's waist and threw them both over the side and into the water where the cameramen were waiting. Nobody but the cameramen saw what happened then, but less than a minute later Eve broke the surface alone and let out a terrified scream. I had heard actresses scream before when their roles called for it, but never like that. Everyone who heard it was as alarmed by it as I was. At least three crew members jumped into the water fully clothed to get her out of there. She didn't scream again, but she was sobbing hysterically as they helped her ashore.

"Keep it away from me!" she said over and over. "Just keep it away from me!"

Asa came ashore behind them and stood there looking after them, his masked face frozen in an alien bug-eyed frown. The crew members looked at him in anger and disgust. "Somebody ought to teach that guy some manners," I heard Frank say in a low voice beside me. I guess that summed up how we all felt. But I noticed that all of us kept our distance.

Ted was in the first wave of those who had rallied to Eve's side. I saw him break away from the crowd just as Frank and I were coming up to join it. He didn't speak to us, or we to him. He didn't look like he wanted to be spoken to. He went straight to where Asa was standing and ordered him into the van. Then the two of them drove away.

I could understand how Ted must be feeling. I mean, to put so much of himself into a project he felt so strongly about, and then have it blow up in his face, that had to hurt. And to have his beloved Eve get caught in the explosion, that had to hurt like hell. I thought more than once in the course of the day that I should give him a call and find out how he was doing. But I always decided against it. He was big enough to handle his own problems, and I would hear all about it on Monday morning. But late that night the phone rang, and I answered it to find Ted himself on the line.

"Hello, Dave. I'm sorry to break into your evening like this, but I couldn't think of anyone else to call. I want to ask you about Eve. Is she all right?"

"Yeah, she's all right. She had a bit of a scare, as you know. But by the time you left she was recovering from it nicely. You mustn't blame yourself, Ted. It isn't your fault that your uncle got a little too deep into his character. Is he there now?"

"He's in the bathtub. He can't hear me out here. But, Dave, it *is* my fault. Though God knows I never meant for anything bad to happen, to Eve or anyone. I only wanted to save the picture. It was so important to me, saving the picture, and I could see no other way to do it. But they're not like us, Dave. They're wild and dangerous. And they don't mix well with humans."

"What are you talking about, Ted? *Who* doesn't mix well with humans?"

"Listen, Dave. You know the premise of the Fish Man story, the idea that our world was once inhabited by a race of beings half man, half fish? Well, what if I told you that it's true? What if I told you that there really *was* such a race, not limited to the backwaters of the Amazon, but spread over the oceans of the prehistoric world? And what if I told you that they're still there today?"

"Ted, I—"

"Just hear me out, Dave. This is no fantasy. It isn't even much of a secret. Plenty of people have known about them for years. There are any number of fine old New England families that have made their fortunes trading with them. And some of those families have engaged in more than trade. Families like mine. Like mine and Uncle Asa's.

"You see, Dave, I wasn't kidding when I told you that I drew my Fish Man from life. Asa really is my uncle. But he's also a creature like the one in my drawing. His home is in the sea, but he can still venture out on the dry land when the need arises. It was lucky that my design was accepted, because nothing else could have enabled me to produce a double on such short notice. But it was *un*-lucky too, for the same reason.

"Because there's been a complication. It seems Uncle Asa is quite taken with Eve. Well, I can hardly blame him for that. But he wants to do more than just admire her. He wants to take her back home with him. I've been trying to tell him how impossible it is, but he won't listen to me. That doesn't leave me with a lot of choices. I'm going to kill him, Dave, if I can. And I want you to know, if anything happens—"

That was as much as I could take. "Now *you* listen to *me*, Ted" I said. "This is crazy talk. You've been working too hard, or drinking too hard, or both. You don't want to kill your uncle. You want to go to bed and try to get some sleep. I'll come down first thing tomorrow and we'll talk about it over breakfast—"

But he had hung up.

I decided I had better not wait for morning. I headed out for his place at once. But when I pulled up in front of his bungalow about an hour later, I thought I had made the trip for nothing. The house was as dark as if he had taken my advice and gone to bed. But then I saw that the front door was open, literally hanging half off its hinges.

The state of the front door hardly prepared me for what I saw when I managed to turned on a light. The place was a wreck. It looked like the set of a western saloon after the big fight. Lamps were broken, chairs overturned, upholstery slashed. The carpet was soaked with water, and something else that wasn't water. And where were Ted and his uncle?

Ted had sounded pretty crazy on the phone, but had he been crazy enough to attack his uncle under the delusion that he was a monster threatening the woman he loved? Had he been crazy enough to kill him, to drag his body out on the beach, to cast it adrift in the water? I didn't know, and it wasn't my job to find out. I dug Ted's phone out from under the wreckage and put in a call to the police. Then I went out on the porch to wait for them.

And it was there that I saw something to make me think that maybe poor old Ted hadn't been so crazy after all. Someone had gone out this way before me, tracking water from that soggy carpet across the wooden deck. But that someone wasn't Ted. I knew the feet that had made the tracks, because I had spent many hours trying to duplicate their features in rubber and paint.

They were the webbed and taloned feet of the thing Ted had brought up from the sea to save his picture, the terrible thing he had called his Uncle Asa.

About "The Doom That Came to Innsmouth"

Well, what did you expect? You mean to tell me you didn't think there was *some* kind of link between the amphibian populace of Ib in "The Doom That Came to Sarnath" ("they had bulging eyes, pouting, flabby lips, and curious ears") and certain others with the "Ibsmouth look" elsewhere in Lovecraft's fiction?

Brian McNaughton has not written a huge amount in the Lovecraft Mythos, true, but what he has penned is memorable, including his recent "The Dunwich Lodger" (*Deathrealm* #23) and "Beyond the Wall of Time" *(Lore* #6, Autumn 1996, the concluding installment of a round robin tale, "The Challenge from Below" appearing in #s 3-6, by Robert M. Price, Peter H. Cannon, and Donald R. Burleson). But Lovecraftian interests made themselves evident considerably before that. McNaughton's trilogy *Satan's Lovechild (*1977), *Satan's Mistress* (1978), and *Satan's Seductress* (1980) featured the bold innovation of a copy of the *Necronomicon* masquerading between the covers of a Manhattan phone book propping up the short leg of a guy's office desk!

"The Doom That Came to Innsmouth" delivers a bracing corrective of sorts. After Lovecraft's original "The Shadow over Innsmouth" has persuaded some readers to share narrator Olmstead's "born again" perspective on the Deep Ones as a sublime and superior culture, we find ourselves brought up short here, reminded the hard way that the Deep Ones were in fact pretty monstrous. You find yourself sharing the narrator's pro-aquatic sympathies, precisely because he is the narrator, and then suddenly you find yourself thinking, "Hey! Wait a minute! What have I got myself into here?"

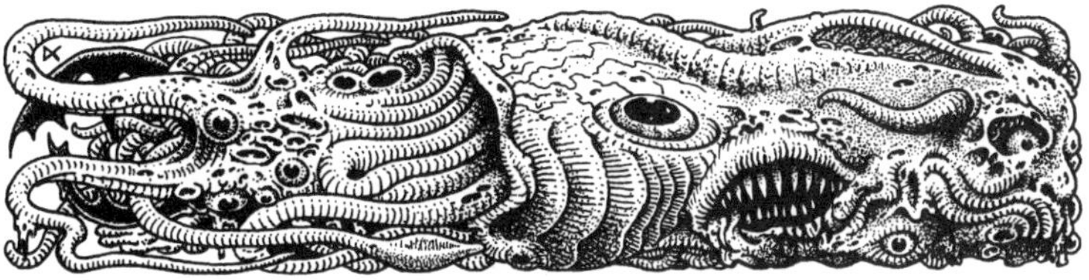

The Doom That Came to Innsmouth

by Brian McNaughton

We need not dust off the history of our nation's dealing with the Indians to find examples of genocide, nor even go so far from our doorsteps as Montgomery, Alabama, to see instances of racism. Right here in our own state of Massachusetts, in February of 1928, agents of the U.S. Treasury and Justice departments perpetrated crimes worthy of Nazi Germany against a powerless minority of our citizens. . . . When the dust of this jack-booted invasion had settled, no citizens [of Innsmouth, Massachusetts] were found guilty of any crime but the desire to live their peaceful lives in privacy and raise their children in the faith of their fathers. The mass internments and confiscations have never been plausibly explained or legally justified, nor has compensation ever been so much as attempted to the innocent victims of this official hooliganism.

—Sen. John F. Kennedy, Commencement Address to the Class of 1959 at Miskatonic University, Arkham, Mass.

* * *

Grandma had been a bootlegger, according to a family joke that we didn't share with her when we visited the nursing-home. I did . . . once. "Is it true that you got busted by Eliot Ness, Grandma?" I asked, wise-ass kid that I was. She started carrying on about "Loch Ness", and getting very worked up, because that place was important to her religion.

"You got a golden crown waiting for you there, Joe, a crown that outshines the sun," she croaked in her liquid way, a way that nobody but me understood half the time. Even when I got the words, I wasn't always sure what they meant.

My name isn't "Joe", by the way, it's Bob, Bob Smith, but she always got me confused with her brother that she adored, Joe Sargent, long ago passed over. Ignored or even mocked by the bitchy attendants who kept her strapped in her bed, she clung to a pathetic scrap of pride that her brother—

or I—used to drive a dinky bus in Massachusetts that connected the Back of Beyond with the Middle of Nowhere.

She thought it was a big deal that he had been allowed to hobnob with "outside folk." Her religion had been dead set against contact with non-believers, and only a few special people were allowed to "swim beyond the school", as she called any travel outside of Innsmouth. She bitterly regretted that she had been forced to swim way beyond the school and, what with one thing and another, never swam back.

Her life was pretty dismal. She was brought up in the strict cult that owned her hometown, not much of a town at its best, but she'd loved it. She never recovered from the shock when the Feds invaded and trashed her birthplace. Mom theorized that it was a Prohibition raid that got out of hand when some deputies recruited from nearby towns grabbed the chance to express their prejudice against Innsmouth people. They roughed them up a lot, I guess, but to hear Grandma tell it, they herded people into cellars and set fire to the houses, then opened up with tommy-guns on anyone who tried to escape. But this was the United States of America, after all, and I was sure she had confused real events with movies about Nazis.

They sent her to a camp in Oklahoma, where she said a lot of people died of "separation from the Great Mother", which meant they missed the ocean. Swimming was a sacrament to these people.

Franklin D. Roosevelt inherited the mess when he came into office in 1932 and was reportedly horrified, although he had bigger problems on his mind at the time. Even though a U.S. Senator from Massacusetts, Marcus Allen Coolidge, tried to prevent or delay their release, the president just closed the camp with as little fuss as possible, leaving the inmates to find their own way home. I guess having a few hundred more bums on the road during the Great Depression seemed preferable to letting J. Edgar Hoover run a concentration camp.

Funny thing about that: Grandma insisted that Hoover had Innsmouth blood, that he had "the look", and that he persecuted his own people because they reminded him of a heritage he rejected. But she was always claiming famous people as "really one of us", Gloria Swanson and Edward G. Robinson, for instance. The only famous person she claimed to be certain about was Albert Fish, a cannibal and serial child-killer who went to the electric chair in 1936.

She tried to make her way back east by hopping freight trains, a pretty rough way for a woman to get around, though not all that uncommon in those days. It was not the most direct way to get anywhere, and with stops at jails and hobo jungles, with detours that took her from Louisiana to Minnesota, she finally gave up when she got to Seattle. It was the wrong side of the continent, she said, but it was near an ocean.

There she met a fisherman named Newman, a bastard who married Grandma for no other reason than the universal superstition that her people had a way with fish. You can say "Innsmouth" to a trawlerman from Norway or Japan and, if he's old enough, you'll get a startled look of recognition, even though he usually doesn't want to talk about it. Newman used to take her along on his boat as a good-luck charm. When he didn't catch anything, he would beat her.

Grandma started to go round the bend after Mom was born, but it was fifteen years before Newman put her away. Mom left home not long after, and I was twelve years old before she made an effort to locate her mother and visit her.

I nagged her into doing it, because I have always been intensely curious about my roots. As far back as I can remember, I felt different from other people. I used to daydream about the magnificent welcome I would get when my *real* parents—the King and Queen of Mars, maybe—tracked me down. I had night-time dreams of flying, or maybe swimming, through the stupendous galleries of a twilight city like nothing I had even heard about on earth. I believe I had those dreams even before I was exposed to some of Grandma's wilder ravings.

For Mom, the reunion was shattering. "God, she's ugly! And she's crazy as a bedbug." Mom shivered with loathing. "And she smells." She cried all the way home on the bus. Later I would sometimes catch her looking at me in a strange way, as if trying to decide whether I was starting to take after Grandma.

She wanted nothing more to do with her mother, and she would have forbidden me to visit her if I asked, so I never asked. Knowing I was different, I learned early to protect my secrets and wriggle around the rules made for other people. In case you think I'm bragging, nobody even suspected me when I finally helped her escape, to say nothing of other things I've managed to get away with. But in those days I got to see Grandma once or twice a month by making up stories or skipping school to walk and hitchhike my way to the nursing home, which was way out near Issaquah.

I didn't think she was ugly, I thought she was beautiful, so sleek and graceful in her old-fashioned way. Her huge eyes would transfigure her face when she talked about her home and her beliefs and seemed actually to be gazing on the vasty deep. I didn't think she was completely crazy, either, not when her stories raised echoes from my own dreams. As for smelling bad, that was the fault of the attendants, but I would raise hell whenever I went there until they cleaned her up and tended the sores from her restraints. Even when I was a kid, people knew I meant business when I looked at them in a certain way.

Since I was so different from other people, it stood to reason that my religion should be different from theirs, so I embraced Grandma's. I only wish I'd listened harder and understood more, and that Grandma's ordeal hadn't left her so confused. The story about the beautiful princess sleeping under the sea, waiting for me to wake her with the stones and the baptism, fueled my teen-age masturbation fantasies. I hated to consider the possibility that this was all wrong, that Grandma had mixed up her religion with the story of Sleeping Beauty.

Even though I searched every library and old bookshop in Washington and Oregon, even though I wrote dozens of letters to professors and churchmen, I never found any solid information about the beliefs and practices of the Esoteric Order of Dagon. Maybe there just weren't any more Dagonites.

Maybe I was the last one.

* * *

"My Grandma's brother used to drive this bus."

The driver glanced at me with annoyance.

"Not *this* bus, I mean, one that traveled the same route between Newburyport and Innsmouth back in the old days, before—"

"See that sign? Don't talk to the driver," he said in the flat, Yankee way that reminds me of ducks quacking.

"You still don't much take kindly to Innsmouth folks around here, do you?"

"Sure, we do." At last I got a sort of smile out of him in the rear view mirror as he added, "Because there ain't any."

I believed him. It was hard to imagine a romantically ruined town and its otherworldly cultists in this wasteland of strip malls and Dairy Queens, where summer shacks had been converted into year-round homes for people who couldn't afford trailers. In this clutter that had been dumped willy-nilly onto a strangled marshland, you knew you were nearing the sea only when the junked automobiles in the yards gave way to junked boats, when the cardboard signs in the windows said "LIVE BAIT" instead of "BEAUTY SALON."

The last of the other passengers had got off at a mall with a K-Mart a few miles back. I had studied them all guardedly for any resemblance to Grandma, or maybe to myself, but they were nothing but long-chinned, quacking Yankees in John Deere hats or pastel hair-rollers. Nobody but me was going all the way to Innsmouth. I would have liked to ask the bus driver if he thought I had "the look", but maybe his attitude said it all.

My own look is pretty damned odd, ever since alopecia hit me like a truck last year. Some people with the disease can brazen it out: Yeah, I got no hair, no eyebrows, no eyelashes, this is how I look, so fuck you, Jack. I admire such people, I even like their clean, smooth appearance, but I have spent my lifetime trying to blend in, so that's not my way. Besides, I couldn't have done that even if I'd wanted to, not after the onset of psoriasis a few months later. A perfectly bald head might go unremarked, but a perfectly bald, *peeling* head draws jeers in the street from children.

One alternative is to use false hair, and that might pass muster if you are rich enough to afford a very good rug and have the skill and patience of a make-up artist. I wasn't rich. Pop had called himself an entrepreneur, which meant he would start doomed businesses and run them, or get me to run them—like the famous Ice Kween Ice Kreem Co.—until he got bored or they failed. After he died and I sorted out his disastrous affairs, I was left with a second-hand record shop in one of Seattle's more blighted areas, which I hung onto because I thought it would be a good way to find girls. I hadn't realized that it's mostly guys who buy old records. Correction: mostly guys who *shoplift* them.

A second alternative is to look for miracle cures. The first doctor I consulted had told me the brutal truth, that my hairlessness was hereditary and incurable, tough luck. He was more hopeful but no more helpful about the rash, which he said I would have until it went away. That didn't stop me from going around in my cheap wig, often-crooked eyebrows, and ruddled face to every charlatan in the phone book.

None of them helped, but one doctor, Dr. Errol, who went to the trouble of asking for my medical and personal history, had heard about Innsmouth. He was up on all the angles of squeezing money out of patients, insurance companies, and the government, and he urged me to apply for assistance under the Kennedy-Keaton Act. I didn't imagine it would be as simple as filling out a form and cashing a check, but I was floored by what I did get by registered mail within two days:

> Pursuant to provisions of the Federal Reparations Act of 1962, as amended in 1994, which offers compensation to residents of Innsmouth, MA, or their legal heirs or assigns for actions by agents of the U.S. Government on or about February 14, 1928, *et seq.*, you are required to present yourself to the Field Office of the U.S. Public Health Service, 291 N. Eliot St., Innsmouth, MA 01939-1750, in order to duly process your claim. Failure to appear is punishable by a fine of not more than ten thousand dollars ($10,000) and/or imprisonment for up to five (5) years.
>
> Food, lodging, and appropriate clothing will be provided for approximately ten (10) days while you undergo such

tests and interviews as are required by law. Additionally, you are permitted to bring any personal effects which may be carried in a case no larger than 40x30x7.62 cm and weighing no more than 2.3 kg. The importation of photographic equipment, audio or video recording devices, firearms or other weapons, alcohol, tobacco, combustible materials, or controlled substances into the Facility is prohibited by law and punishable by a fine of not more than ten thousand dollars ($10,000.00) and/or imprisonment for up to five (5) years.

At the time of your induction into the Facility, you will be required to present your birth certificate, Social Security card and photographic ID (passport, state driver's license, or other deemed acceptable by the Examiner), current bank and credit-card statements, along with any documentation in the form of personal letters, diaries, family photographs, etc., that may relate to your claim. Additionally, it is required that you complete the enclosed Questionnaire, Medical Release Forms, and Waiver of Liability and return them, duly signed and notarized, to the above address, postmarked not later than five (5) business days from receipt of this communication.

Failure to comply with this notice or any of its provisions, or with any rules, regulations, or provisions not explicitized herein, is punishable by a fine of not more than ten thousand dollars ($10,000.00) and/or imprisonment for a period of up to five (5) years.

(signed) I. M. Saltonstall, M.D.
Field Director
Innsmouth Facility
U.S. Public Health Service

Because I am the way I am, my first thought was to change my name and make a run for the Fiji Islands. Not only did I vividly recall Grandma's stories about tommy-guns and concentration camps, I had my own reasons for avoiding government scrutiny. No amount of money was worth this kind of grief.

But . . . I had always wanted to visit Innsmouth. I had been held back by the fear of barging in where outsiders were mistrusted. This summons gave me a legitimate reason to visit my ancestral home and question people who might have answers. My clerk could run the record-shop at least as well as I could in my absence, and the government promised in fine print to pay my travel expenses.

I had misgivings about the tone of the summons, but I told myself that was how bureaucrats did things, and I still believed that I wasn't living in the People's Republic of China. I filled out all the forms as honestly as I dared and sent them off. I actually began looking forward to my trip. I would go by bus and see the country. It would be the first real vacation I had ever had, and it would be free.

Was it too much to hope that I might at last meet the torpid beauty beneath the sea, Mother Hydra, the Ice Queen who would be woken by my kisses and the special stones?

* * *

The jolting of the bus roused me from a half-doze. The road had become narrow and potholed, and on either side the marshland reasserted itself. Black little creeks ran through it, with here and there a boat forlornly anchored. I wondered how the owners could get to and from them in the trackless swamp without using other boats, and I laughed silently at the picture of confusion this evoked.

I was shocked to discover the bus driver studying me sourly in the mirror. I wiped the smile from my face and tried to check my wig and eyebrows without seeming to.

My embarrassment vanished when I realized that the ocean shimmered before me through the windshield. The sight has always stirred profound emotions within me, the nameless but powerful feelings evoked in others by great music or poetry, and this, the Atlantic, the very ocean of my dreams, stirred me as I never had been before. I sat up straighter and wriggled for a better look, wishing the driver were the sort of person who would have let me run forward to gaze out beside him.

Then, in the foreground, I saw the town.

I had assumed it would be not much different from other depressed towns I had glimpsed on the way. Despite hard times and a genuine disaster in the past, the indomitable Yankees would have put a bold face on things and got on with their God-given mission to make money. Seaside real estate was worth something, wherever it might be, and I had half-expected to be affronted by a welter of marinas and condos, with maybe a theme park, a water slide, and a gauntlet of shack-up motels. In my worst imaginings, the weird charm of the town would have been buried under a Sea-Tac Strip East that stretched all the way to Boston, complete with hookers who quacked like ducks.

I was wrong. The Feds had killed it seventy years ago, and it was still dead. Toward the beach, where you might have expected some rebuilding, the devastation was complete. The burnt-out shells of industrial buildings remained, but the sites of former houses were marked only by free-standing chimneys and clogged cellar-holes.

Just before we reached the bottom of a hill and the oceanfront dropped out of view, I noticed a metallic glimmer stitching the rubble. It looked like a fence topped with razor-wire, separating the seaward ruins from the rest of Innsmouth. Oddly, it looked shiny and new.

* * *

After contemptuously scrawling the receipt I required and ignoring my sarcastically cheerful promise to see him in a week or so, the driver dropped me at the Gilman House in Town Square, a once-gracious building in the Georgian mode whose upper windows, like most of the shops in the square, had been boarded up.

The clerk looked like a forlorn refugee from Woodstock who took his style from David Crosby, his tie knotted loosely as if worn under protest. As a further comment on his job and perhaps the town itself, his tie bore a reproduction of Edvard Munch's *The Scream*. He asked suspiciously, "Will you be checking in, Sir?"

"No, I have to stay at the Facility on Eliot Street, but can I check this bag here?"

"That Public Health thing?" His desire to peer closely at me struggled painfully with one to retreat beyond the range of contagion.

"You see many people going that way?"

"None at all until lately. Then a couple weeks ago, four or five turned up. And there was a girl last week, Ms. Gilman, just like the hotel, she asked for directions." He added, as if to distinguish her from me and the others, "She was nice."

He put a receipt on the counter beside my ten-dollar bill, which he hadn't picked up.

"Hey, if you see Mr. Marsh out there, ask him what he wants done with his suitcase. We can't hang onto it forever, and I ain't heard a word form him since he left it."

Marsh, Gilman: These were both names from the old days. I was unprepared for a stirring of what you might call nostalgia-by-proxy. I looked away for a moment, and the seedy lobby was dimmed by tears. At last, I would actually get to meet some of *my* people!

"What's chances of getting in a swim before I go?"

"We got no pool. You'd have to go to the Ramada out on 1-A—"

"No, no, I meant in the ocean. Is there any place by the beach to change?"

"You don't want to swim in the ocean here. Well, maybe you do, but you can't. Everything east of the Old Square has been off limits since I been here, and that's twenty years come September."

"Off limits?" I'd seen the fence, but still the authoritarian phrase surprised me.

"Didn't you see that burnt-out area? An Air Force plane crashed. Back in the nineteen-fifties, I think it was, a terrible tragedy, wrecked half the town, and it was carrying a bomb they never found. I ain't caught myself glowing in the dark yet, so I guess it's safe enough here, but you don't want to go swimming in nookie-leer waste. That's why you're here for the Public Health thing, ain't you? Children of people who got zapped?"

"I guess," I said, hiding my amusement. "Are any people still living here from the old days? People named Marsh, or Gilman, or Sargent?"

"Some, I think, but you really want to ask Old Lady Waite, she's our local expert. Most of the people in town now are Portuguese; they came here to fish, only they have to go to Marblehead to do it on account of the pollution. But they live here because houses are really cheap."

"Where would I find her?"

"You want to go down Bank Street, that's the second left as you leave the hotel, and you can't miss her house, it's the only one on the river side of the street. Past her house, you hang a left on Adams, and that'll take you into Eliot. But the Facility is a long walk, it's halfway back to Ipswich, and Larry, that's our only cab driver, he took a fare to Boston this morning and ain't come back yet."

"I don't mind the walk. I'd like to do some sight-seeing."

He withheld comment, even though I knew he wanted to make one.

Leaving the hotel, I happened to glance back through the streaked glass of the door. The clerk hadn't touched my money or my bag before I left, and I now observed him taking the bag from the counter. He had first wrapped his hand in a red bandana to protect it from germs. Or radiation.

* * *

A Portuguese bar at the corner of Bank Street, outside of which a few swarthy loafers muttered about me to one another, marked the apex of Innsmouth's social scene. Beyond that point, the houses on the left side guarded their inhabitants behind drawn shades, lulling them with a varied chorus of air conditioners. Here and there shadows would stir at windows as I walked up the steep street, but the residents were good at concealing themselves. I saw no one, not even a hand at a drape as it shifted.

Above a picture-postcard falls, the Manuxet grew far more energetic and noisy than any human as it raced between bulkheaded banks, and even frightening. The river had penetrated the ancient pilings to undermine the footway on the right. Gaps yawned in the sidewalk. I'm sure the road was next on its list, then the buttoned-up houses, until it swept all of Innsmouth and then New England out to sea. Its continuous roar, made up of a million gurgles and mutters, was alarmingly loud as it echoed off the blank house-fronts, and I seemed to eavesdrop on a wealth of incomprehensible conversations in a din that threatened at any moment to become clear.

I stayed to the left-hand side, but no one came out, as I half-expected, to glare at me and demand I account for myself. In the far distance a lonely dog barked an interminable litany of grievances that probably had nothing to do with my return to the seat of my ancestors.

The river roared more loudly, constricted by a granite outcropping of the bank where some scruffy woods and a small cottage, the only house on the river side, clung perilously in a fine, perpetual mist. The house was very old, to judge by the small, lead-filled windows of imperfect glass, and I fancied that its unpainted cedar shakes might have been made with an ax. It was oddly out of proportion, as many old New England houses seem to me, with the single story dwarfed by a bloated chimney and roof.

I knocked, then repeated it before the door opened. I took a step back from a disturbing figure, a tall, slim and impenetrably veiled woman.

"Excuse me, my name is—"

"No, don't tell me. It's *Sargent*, isn't it? You could be Joe, just a couple years before he passed over."

And hers could have been my Grandma's voice, either because of a local accent or locally hereditary quirk. Before I even suspected that I might, I burst into tears.

"Alma Sargent was my Grandma, yes, Joe's sister, but my name is Bob Smith," I said when I could speak.

"Bob is a good name, a real Innsmouth name. Come in, Bob."

I was about to sit in a straight chair opposite her rocker when she demanded, "What's that you got in your pocket?"

"Nothing," I mumbled, feeling like a trapped kid.

"Show me! In the name of Mother Hydra!"

She was definitely not a lady I could refuse. I pulled out the three pyramidal chunks of granite that had caught my eye on the way to her house. She studied them closely, then spat on them and held them tight in her gloved hand for a moment as if willing them to reveal their secrets.

"These are okay," she said at last, handing them back. "These'll do." She added playfully, "Figure on finding somebody to baptize while you're in town, Bob?"

"Well." I coughed, looked away, wondered if my rash was bad enough today to hide my blushing.

"I see you follow the old ways, that's good. I expect Alma taught you? It's a cryin' shame you can't do the baptizing out on Devil Reef, like Our Lord intended, but the Navy blasted the bejesus out of it in twenty-eight. But if you do it with the right spirit, you can perform a baptism even out in the middle of Kansas."

I had spent sleepless nights struggling with that point of theology, and her words took an enormous weight off my soul.

Before I could thank her, she said, "Love that name! Bob. I do believe I can prophesy a truly glorious future for you. So tell me all about yourself, Bob."

I did. My God! I never thought I could have revealed such secrets to a stranger unless I had gone stark, raving mad, but they just tumbled out. And she accepted them. Instead of ordering me out or screaming for help, Old Lady Waite nodded and murmured . . . approval. Often I knew that she was smiling gently behind her veil, amused by my account of my clumsy efforts to be true to my heritage, but her amusement was in no way contemptuous.

Even as I spoke so unguardedly, I wondered about the spell she had cast over me. The unfamiliar emotion I felt was as strong as love is reputed to be, but it would be crazy to suppose that I had fallen in love with a woman almost three times my age whose face was veiled. She was in fact concealed completely in dark, old-fashioned clothing, and might have been a mannikin if she hadn't murmured from time to time, if her rocker hadn't moved rhythmically.

I was forced to the conclusion that I felt *at home*, and that I had never felt that way anywhere, not even in my boyhood home with my own parents. The feeling seemed to be generated by a combination of subtle influences that I didn't perceive until I tried hard to sort them out. Nothing around me, not the spare furniture of colonial design, the home-hooked rugs on the mirror-polished floor with its wide and irregular boards, the huge, unlit fireplace that doubled as an oven with its iron doors, was inconsistent with the eighteenth century, a time that has always seemed more congenial to me. I saw no television set, no tawdry magazines, no brightly packaged products of mass consumption. I believed that the unlit lamps were fueled by kerosene, for I saw no electrical outlets or wires. Despite the absence of air conditioning, the house was comfortably cool and dank behind its small windows, beaded by the river's mist, and under its huge roof: This atmosphere, together with an indefinable odor that came from the woman herself and all she had touched, must have been responsible for my profound sense of comfort.

But none of these factors really explained my feelings as well as my first impression, that I had fallen under a magical spell.

"Alma must have passed over," she said. "I'm surprised she hasn't come by. We were best friends, and I thought she'd just love to tease me about the long time I'm taking."

"It was fourteen years ago when I helped her with the last rites, but it was a long ways off. Puget Sound."

"Oh! Then I expect she'll be by one of these days."

"Actually it was a river that runs into the Sound," I admitted a bit guiltily. I have a deep aversion against speaking the name of one place, but I forced myself: "The Green River."

The name provoked no special reaction. She just said, "Fresh water is okay."

"But pretty swift."

Her laughter was surprisingly youthful. "This river out here is pretty swift, but it doesn't stop old friends from coming to call on me when they're of a mind."

"Do you suppose I could . . . ?"

"Meet them? Sure, why not? How long you plan to be in town? You can stay right here with me, so's not to miss anyone."

"I wish I could, but I came here to take advantage of the federal reparations. I have to stay at—"

"Not the Facility! Oh, my," she groaned. She stopped rocking for the first time since she'd sat down.

"What? What's wrong? The program was sponsored by President Kennedy, and he seemed—"

"Son, what he mostly seems now is *dead*, and laws have a way of getting amended. This one got amended with bells on, to say nothing of books and candles. The Facility caught some local folks when they first set up shop, but I saw right through them, and I wanted no part of it. I told that wicked Dr. Saltonstall to take his stethoscope and stick it up his sphygmomanometer. Fortunately Ramon Medeiros, he's the mayor now, is a good friend to all of us, and he's moving heaven and earth to get that place shut down." She chuckled. "He leaves the sea to me. I'd give Ramon a call right now if I had one of those goddamn telephone machines—"

Someone knocked on the door. It was a loud, peremptory, no-nonsense knock.

"I bet that's not Ed McMahon and Dick Clark, come to make me rich," she said.

"What should I do? Is the back—"

"You don't really suppose they're not out there, too, do you? If you were foolish enough to sign anything you better go, because Uncle Sam is an alligator: dumb as hell and easy to avoid, but once he gets his jaws set, he won't let go. Your best bet is to go along with them now so you don't get hurt, and let me do what I can on the outside."

The sight waiting for me at the door was unnerving, for the heavy-set older man and his grinning, dapper companion bore a skewed likeness to the pitchmen she had named.

"Mr. Smith?" the dapper one said. "We heard you might need a lift to the Facility."

"Want to go for a nice ride, too, Mrs. Waite?" the other one said to the woman standing just behind me. "That would save everybody a lot of hassle."

"You don't know what hassle is, sonny-boy. You'll find out if you do Mr. Smith, here, any harm."

"Harm? We're here to *help* you people, don't you understand? How long do you think you can fuck with the U.S. Government?"

"How deep is the ocean?" she laughed.

"Ed" hummed the tune she had quoted all during the ride. It was proof that spells of a sort really can be cast on others, and I tried to take that as a good omen.

* * *

I was unprepared for the Facility, a Victorian fantasy of sooty bricks that managed to look both brutal and whimsical, a bad combination. The high fence around the grounds, capped with broken glass, was part of the original design, but the electronic gate looked brand new. The guard who controlled it was armed. As I was hurried up the front steps, I saw that the new sign over the door only partly concealed the original name in bas-relief: MANUXET ASYLUM FOR THE INSANE.

The interior corridors were huge and ill-lit, wainscotted in dark wood. Most alarming was the emptiness. Except for my escort and a few attendants who were trying to avoid notice or look busy, I suspected that I might be the only one here.

This suspicion was born out in the days that followed, but I didn't regret my isolation. The first thing they did was take away my false hair and give me a chemical shower that aggravated my rash. Bald and scabrous, clad in an orange jumpsuit, I might have been an imperfectly fashioned android under study by the normal-dressed people and white-uniformed keepers who hustled me here and there to determine where my creation had gone wrong. Under these circumstances, I wanted to meet no one whose opinion might have mattered to me.

* * *

Forced to choose the one thing about the Facility I liked least, I would pick Dr. Isaac Mordecai Saltonstall, the director. A long-faced, long-fingered scarecrow in tweeds, he treated me like a child, or worse. Sometimes when he stared at me blankly over his tented fingers I imagined he was trying to decide whether to have me gassed now or later. At least he didn't quack, but he swallowed his vowels, except for an occasional "a" as broad as a barn door. His diplomas said he had gone to Harvard and identified him, curiously enough, as a psychiatrist.

"The Seattle police questioned you in July of eighty-three and again in September of that year," he asked as he studied my distressingly thick dossier.

This was the first time that subject had come up. I was sorely tempted to babble, but I followed the rule I had observed since arriving: Say nothing unless asked a direct question. That had always worked with the police.

"Why do you suppose that was?" he said at last.

"I guess they were being thorough."

"But why you?"

"I was there."

"At the murders?"

That was a low blow, but I took it without flinching. "No, not at the murders!" It seemed reasonable to inject a little anger into my voice. "I drove by the Strip, where many of the girls were abducted, in my ice-cream truck every day. The hookers were my customers, I recognized some of the victims. Maybe the Green River Killer was a customer, too. But it turned out I couldn't help. I was never a *suspect*!"

"No need to get excited," Dr. Saltonstall said. "We have to be thorough, too. Now your grandmother went missing from the nursing home not long before the first murder, didn't she?"

"She wandered off, yes."

"You didn't help her *pass over*, did you?"

I tried to conceal my shock at his use of these words with more anger: "What, killed my Grandma? I loved her!"

"That's not what I said."

"Yes, you did. People use euphemisms for dying, like *pass over*. Do you think I helped her commit suicide or something?"

"*People* do?"

"*Other* people. I always try to say what I mean. So, do I get my money? When do I get out of here?"

"Do you still have your rocks?"

The previous interviews had covered only medical details. I guess he had been trying to lull my suspicions. Today he was coming at me from all sides, jabbing me where I least expected it.

"Rocks?"

"You had some rocks in your pocket when you came here."

"Oh. Those." I made a show of searching the deep pocket of the jumpsuit. "Yeah."

"Why do you carry rocks in your pocket?"

Better than in my head, you know-it-all son of a bitch! "I picked them up in town." I smiled. "Genuine Innsmouth rocks. Souvenirs. *I* don't know why I do it. If I see an odd-shaped rock or a bird feather, or, I don't know, an unusual bottle cap, I pick it up. For luck, I guess."

He wrote something in my dossier. If he had believed me, it was "obsessive-compulsive."

"Where is everybody?" I asked, deciding to go on the offensive. "Do you have a Mr. Marsh here?"

"He left. How do you know him?"

"The clerk at the hotel told me he never returned for his bag. If he left here, why didn't he go back for it?"

He wrote something else: *Have clerk killed?* No, the hotel clerk was one of their spies. He must have told them I was at Old Lady Waite's house.

"Mr. Marsh left the day you arrived. He probably picked up his bag after you spoke to the clerk."

It pleased me that his lie should be so transparent, but maybe it shouldn't have. Maybe he didn't care if he was believed by a man who would soon follow Mr. Marsh into limbo.

"What about a girl named Gilman?"

"Ondine Gilman? She's here. Haven't you met her?"

"No," I said evenly, "I haven't."

"It's a big place. You're sure to run into her."

* * *

It was no surprise at all when I went to enter the cafeteria that evening and saw, for the first time, another person seated at one of the plastic tables. She wore a jumpsuit like mine, but she exhibited no pathological symptoms.

I was reluctant to enter, not just because of my appearance but because I knew that she or I, or both, was being manipulated by Dr. Saltonstall. I forced myself.

"Ondine Gilman," she responded when I brought a tray to her table and introduced myself.

"Really?"

"What do you mean?"

"Nothing. I heard the name, and I thought . . . well, I thought Dr. Saltonstall might have planted an impostor."

She laughed. "He makes me paranoid, too."

She tried to avoid looking at me directly, but I stared hard at her. Her blue eyes were large and rather protuberant, but not as much as Grandma's or mine. I saw no hint of extra skin between her fingers, no rash, and certainly no alopecia: Her auburn hair was real.

"You don't look like an Innsmouth person," I said.

She grimaced. "I'm not. And since they *know* I'm not, I wonder why the hell I'm still here!"

She had raised her voice for the benefit of the bored server at the counter, but he continued to look bored.

"It's none of my business—"

"Sure it is, we're in this together. You'd think if they won't let me go home, they'd at least let me have a goddamn cigarette, it's not as if this place is bursting at the seams with people whose lungs I can pollute. Why can't I go home?"

The last remark, in her flattest, hardest quack, was also addressed to the server, who retreated to the kitchen without comment.

"I'm sorry," she said.

"If you're not an Innsmouth person—"

"Then why am I here? It's embarrassing. No, it isn't, it's funny, actually. My father looked sort of like you before he—"

"Passed over?"

She seemed startled. "That was what he said he was going to do, that's the phrase he used. Only he didn't die, he ran away. I never knew why, but maybe I do now."

"Why?"

"He wasn't my father, that's why. They found that out as soon as they took my first blood test, and then they confirmed it with DNA. My father, Wade Gilman, had Innsmouth parents, but my biological father must've been the mailman or somebody. I never even suspected that until they took the blood test, but maybe my father suspected it long before, and that's why he left."

She strove for a light tone, but her voice shook. I said, "I'm sorry."

"It's a bitch. I just came here to get some money for art school in Providence, so they lock me up without cigarettes and tell me my mother was screwing around. Have they put you in the tank yet?"

"What's that?"

"They truss you up and dump you in a tank full of water to see how long you can hold your breath. They make damn sure you're not faking, too, they keep you under till you pass out. And they do it again and again. They put me in the tank even after they *knew* I wasn't a Kermie!"

"A what?"

"I'm sorry, that's not nice, I guess. That's what they call Smouthies—Innsmouth people, I mean—in Rowley, where I come from. For Kermit the Frog?"

"Why won't they let you leave?"

"That's *my* question, Dr. Einstein!" Annoyed by the close scrutiny I had given her, she stared back at me and added coldly: "You've got enough problems of your own, I guess."

"There were some other people—applicants—when you came here, weren't there?"

"Oh, yeah, this place was really hopping . . . ." She looked as if she wanted to bite her tongue.

"They looked like me, you mean?"

"No, I meant . . . okay, If that's what you want, they looked like you." She didn't like being put on the defensive, and she stopped trying to hide her contempt for me. "It should have been obvious that *I* didn't belong."

"What happened to them?"

She shrugged. "One day they were gone. We didn't become best friends. Nobody said good-bye. I guess they just took their money and hopped away."

"Did you see them leave?"

"No." She glanced uneasily toward the counter, but we were still alone. "What's your point?"

"Maybe they didn't leave."

"Huh? Oh, come *on*! You mean they killed them?" Her surprise was overdone. I think she had considered that possibility on her own and was trying to reject it. "But they wouldn't kill me. I'm not like *them*."

"I guess it was all a terrible mistake," I said mildly. "They'll ask you to promise not to tell anybody that they tortured you, or that all the *Kermies* disappeared, and let you go. Tomorrow, probably."

"You son of a bitch. Being sarcastic doesn't help."

"Do you want to go? Without waiting for them to tidy up all the paperwork, or whatever it is they say they're doing?"

"Damn. Are you serious? You don't look exactly like a—"

"A knight in shining armor?"

"A man of action, I was going to say."

"My looks are deceptive." This misplaced nitwit had irritated me. Born in an earlier time, she would have egged on the thugs who massacred the detested "Smoothies." My tone was bitter as I added, "Just think of me as the Frog Prince."

"Jesus, don't look at me like that!" She failed to repress a shudder. "I think I believe you."

* * *

The second floor of the wing where my room lay had originally been composed of four cavernous wards, but the one on the end had been divided with drywall into thirty cubicles under a false ceiling, each barely large enough to contain a single bed, plastic chair, and fiberboard writing desk, all of them bolted in place to discourage their use as weapons. A reproduction of a bland Matisse seascape was similarly bolted to the brick exterior wall. Mine could be considered a first-class accommodation, I suppose, since it shared one of the old madhouse windows, heavily barred and screened, with an adjoining cubicle. Standing on the chair, I had a view of the gatehouse in the distance and, under the window, most of the parking lot.

The door was the most interesting feature of my cell, for it wouldn't have met the security standards of a dollhouse. I believed the lock could be spread with one of the long but sloppily installed bolts I had extracted from Matisse. I hadn't experimented, though, for fear of marking the door or even splintering it.

Swathed as he was in medical degrees and patrician breeding, I don't think Dr. Saltonstall ever considered that anyone would mistrust him or try to escape his prison. And if they did, his omnipotent drugs would stop them. Every night I had been given a big red capsule that I dutifully swallowed, and every night it knocked me out within ten minutes. Tonight I concealed it under my tongue until I could spit it out.

I lay quietly in my bed for an hour or so until I heard cars starting up, four in succession. I climbed onto the chair and watched as they drove to the gate and were let through. While I watched, the doctor himself strode across the parking lot to his car and left. Two others followed him within the next ten minutes, leaving only one car. When a fat man in uniform trudged from the gatehouse to the main building carrying a brown bag, I was sure the Facility had now shut down for the night.

The gap between the door and the jamb wasn't as wide as I'd thought. I couldn't push the bolt in even when I leaned on it with all my weight. I hesitated to hammer it with the heel of my shoe, but I had no choice. If the guard heard me, I told myself, he would assume I was signaling for help and take his time about responding. I had another bad moment when the cheap bolt I was using as a lever seemed on the verge of bending. Again, I had no choice. I pushed harder. The bolt held and the door sprang open.

I had the freedom of the new, plasterboard corridor, but an insuperable hurdle might remain: the heavy, iron door of the former ward. If they had locked that door—but they hadn't. This was more of the doctor's smug faith in drugs, I supposed.

I prowled along the outer corridor, where the only light glowed in an "EXIT" sign. I heard tinny voices and laughter as I approached the main stairway, where a broad landing overlooked the lobby. The guard I had seen sat at a desk by the front door, watching television and eating a sandwich. It seemed rather melodramatic not to just stroll naturally across the landing, but I tiptoed.

At the end of the next wing I found another ward converted to cubicles, and it seemed likely that this would be the women's quarters. The first ten doors were unlocked, the rooms empty. When I found the eleventh locked, it seemed likely I would find Ondine Gilman behind it.

This door was just as flimsy as the one on my own cell, and since it opened inward, I believed I could simply kick it open. This worked, but the thunderous crash of the door against the wall made me cringe. I ran to the outer corridor to listen. Minutes passed. I heard nothing except the canned laughter of the television until a human guffaw joined in, testimony that the guard's attention was fully occupied.

I felt confident enough to snap on the light after I had closed the woman's door behind me. She didn't stir.

"Ondine?" I said, and, more loudly, "Miss Gilman?"

Curled on her side, she breathed deeply and evenly. Her breathing didn't change even when I shook her by the shoulder. I stood considering my options for a moment, then lifted her covers and pushed her green hospital gown above her waist. She continued to sleep soundly even when I peeled her underpants down and extricated her feet.

I wasn't displeased by what I saw and touched, but I wished I still had my ice-cream truck. An hour in the locker would have done wonders for her superior attitude. I restored everything as it had been except for the panties, indecent, red ones of the sort favored by roadside whores. After using them to wipe the evidence of my visit from her buttocks, I wadded them into my pocket and turned off the light. She continued to breathe evenly.

I was tempted to try the stones for size, but decided she would keep while I explored the Facility.

* * *

The stairs marked as an exit led me down to an unguarded rear door. I stepped outside and savored a warm night that was loud with crickets, frogs and . . . sirens? I strained my ears, but I couldn't identify the sounds in the distance. They might have been sirens, or even thin screams.

The stairs continued down to the basement, where I knew the medical department was housed. I had been given tests here, but I hadn't suspected its extent. There was a fully equipped operating theater and other rooms that held machines liberally plastered with radiation warnings.

The last room, and the largest, was obviously a morgue. Nevertheless, it was a shock to pull out a drawer and find a naked body. And a second. And a third. And . . . they were Innsmouth people, every one of them, and they were dead. I couldn't say what had killed them, but they had all been stitched up crudely after autopsies.

My knees wobbled, the room swam, and without further warning I found myself throwing up until my stomach clenched down on itself like a hard, painful, empty fist.

My shock and sickness gave way to fury. I raged down the line, pulling out drawer after drawer. Fifteen of them. Twenty! Someone would pay, someone would pay dearly. These were my people, my own unique, precious people, standing even further above Saltonstall and his henchmen than those butchers fancied they stood above worms. Left to evolve in peace, they would have shed their simian traits and passed over into magnificent beings who would have lived for all time in the glorious kingdom of the Lord. And now they were just so many dead chimps.

"Father Dagon!" I screamed. "Mother Hydra! Where were you?"

I came at last upon a drawer whose contents shocked me into stillness. Those evil savages had succeeded in meddling with something they couldn't even begin to comprehend. It was the ultimate obscenity, a blasphemy for which no human words exist, and I forced my imperfect tongue to struggle with curses that were more appropriate, but still woefully inadequate to the horror. With drugs, perhaps with surgery or radiation, they had forced a Deep One to pass over on dry land.

It was huge, and even in its desiccated state it was beautiful, god-like. My hands fumbled reverently over the dry scales, the pathetically limp crest of spikes that should have stood proud. Sobbing bitterly, I promised a hundred sacrifices, a thousand, a holocaust that would rouse Father Dagon and make the sea rise up to the sky and draw down the moon in its awful wrath.

Stroking the massive chest, I realized that I felt no stitches. I looked closely. I saw no obvious wounds at all. I felt no heartbeat or respiration either, but it was possible, just barely, that he had shut down all his systems hard when faced with the horror of a landlocked metamorphosis. As Grandma was so fond of quoting, "That is not dead which can eternal lie . . . ."

I dashed back to the next room, where I had seen a sink. I looked about for a bucket of some kind, but—better! I smashed the glass case holding a firehose, oblivious to the shrieking alarm this set off, and wrenched the wheel over until the hose came to life like a wrathful dragon, spewing a destructive jet that smashed cases of fiendish instruments and foul drugs open and hurled their contents clattering and crashing through the torture-chambers.

I manhandled it back to the morgue and directed the stream on the ceiling above the Deep One, bouncing down a flood of life-giving water on the poor victim.

I didn't notice when the alarm was silenced. I couldn't understand why the hose suddenly went limp and dry. Then I became aware of the man quacking furiously at the door to the next room.

"Put that down, you goddamn loony! Drop it, asshole, or you are dead meat!"

I had found what I wanted, a human being to absorb the full force of my rage, and I threw the hose aside and stalked toward him.

"Don't you realize what you're doing here?" I screamed. "Don't you know—"

"I know what I'm doing is catching a goddamn loony who's fucking up the hospital. Stop! Stop right now! This here is a .357 Magnum, shithead, and it's about to tear out your spine and pin it to the far wall. I am not joking with you."

I stopped. What could I have been thinking of? All hope of escape was lost. Dr. Saltonstall would lock me up tight. More probably he would take no more chances with me, and I would be filling one of these morgue drawers before lunchtime tomorrow.

"That's better. Assume the position."

I knew what he meant. I turned to the wall, leaning forward to support my weight with my hands on a closed drawer. He strutted up behind me and took great delight in kicking my ankles wider apart.

"Scabby son of an Innsmouth bitch," he snarled, "I'm really hurting to blow your baldy-ass head all over the wall just for laughs, so don't try nothing, you hear? I just want an excuse to blow one of you scum-suckers away. What the hell you got here?"

He had found the rocks I had been saving, which he hurled on the floor. He thrust his hand into my other pocket and extracted Ondine's panties. After a moment of baffled silence, he made a gagging noise of utter loathing.

"You goddamn *pervert*!" he screamed.

The wall hit me in the face, cracking teeth. I only then became aware of a worse pain where he had hit the back of my head with his gun. I wondered how I had wound up on my knees. They hurt, too.

"Bastard bastard bastard!" he screamed, kicking me in the back as if trying to squash a bug to paste. "You got me to touch your goddamn frogspawn jackoff rag—"

He stopped kicking me. I tried to stop my sobbing and groaning so I could hear what he was saying, though his words were strangely muffled. It sounded as if he were choking. Was it too much to hope that he was dying of apoplexy?

I managed to twist my head around. I couldn't imagine what was happening to him. Most of his face was covered by a wet, black cloth, and he was apparently standing a foot off the floor, his heavy-duty oxfords and white tube socks jerking spasmodically.

But it was no cloth that covered his face. It was the huge, webbed hand of the dark figure that loomed behind him, the Deep One I had revived.

"Praise Mother Hydra!" I sobbed.

"Praise her name!" a rich, deep, croaking voice responded.

* * *

"'S' okay, sweetie," I slurred, dumping Ondine Gilman into a lobby chair of the hotel that, most inaccurately, bore her name. "Jus' get us a room, okay?"

"Wha . . . ? Where?" I leaned forward and, under the pretext of giving her a kiss, pressed her carotid arteries until she lost consciousness again. After changing my *modus operandi* in the Northwest, I had learned that this was every bit as effective as an ice-cream locker for draining the will of baptismal candidates.

"Excuse me, Sir! Just what—oh. It's Mr. Smith, isn't it?"

"Bob. It's good ol' Bob," I said, steering a wayward course for the desk and the clerk I had seen before, the one who had used a bandana to pick up my bag. He was still wearing his Munch necktie. The image was a deliberate slur against my people.

"What's going on?"

"Celebrash. Celebration. We're outta that damn crazy-house."

"I can see that. What's going on outside, I meant."

I pretended to hear the sirens for the first time. And there were indeed screams, too.

"They're celebratin', I guess." I heard a burst of automatic gunfire.

"God!" he cried, starting from behind the desk.

"Hey, wait. Need a room for me and my sweetie."

"I can't rent you a room, you're drunk. And I'm closing."

"Then gimme my bag," I said. "Left my bag, remember?"

"Oh. Sure. Then will you go?"

"Drunk, huh?"

"Where am I?" Ondine cried.

"'S'okay, honey." He dumped my bag on the counter, forgetting to protect his precious hand from my contagion in his confused haste. He fretted and fussed as I opened it, and he grew even more flustered at another burst of automatic fire in the distance.

"I'm not really drunk," I said clearly as I pulled the nine-millimeter Browning out of the bag and jacked a Black Talon round into the chamber.

"What?"

"I'm just very different from you, that's all."

I put the bullet right through the Screamer's bald, distorted head and through the clerk's breastbone.

"I'm coming, dear," I told Ondine, and hurried over to deprive her simian brain of yet some more oxygen.

* * *

I was afraid she might not be able to understand what I was doing after I had stripped her and tied her to the bed in the room I had assigned us, but she came around as good as new. Nobody would have paid attention to her screams and curses over the similar noises in Town Square.

I took all the time I wanted to amuse myself, but it surprised me when dawn broke while I was still thrusting into her. I turned and saw that it was floodlights, powerful floodlights from the section of town sealed off by razor-wire. The gunfire had become constant, but it seemed as if fewer guns were in use.

"You fucking bastard!" Ondine sobbed.

"You got part of that right," I grunted, "but I'm the one who's legitimate, remember?"

"Freak!"

I'd had enough of her and her filthy mouth. I pulled out and rummaged among my clothing for the stones. Her screams found surprising new energy as I inserted them in the secret places, but I managed to ignore her as I recited the words. I'm not sure if the words and the procedure are exactly right, since Grandma explained them fully only at the very last, when she had passed over and was in a fearful hurry to rejoin her people, but I have always used them.

I suspect that any human being who reads this account may think that my baptism of forty-eight women between 1982, the year Grandma passed over, and 1984 was somehow *excessive*. On the contrary, it was based on an *exact* calculation of the yearly baptisms Grandma was prevented from performing while she was interned in Oklahoma (four), and while she was confined in the nursing home (fourty-four). Despite all the hard work and laborious planning involved, to say nothing of the danger, I wanted to complete Grandma's hecatomb and ensure that she was granted full honor among the Deep Ones as quickly as possible. Don't you think she had suffered long enough and waited long enough already? If you still believe someone should be censured for upsetting the public with such a concentrated flurry of "criminal" activity, you might look to President Hoover, whose agents disrupted her life and prevented the free exercise of her religion, or to Sidney Newman, my grandfather, who did the same.

It was my turn to scream as the door opened. I recoiled from the figure in black that stood there, but then I saw that it was Old Lady Waite.

"I don't know what you did, Bob," she said admiringly, "but you sure stirred up the Host of the Sea. However," she added as she set a crocheted bag on the bedside table and withdrew a large black book and a butcher-knife, "that's not really the way to go about *this* business." To Ondine she said, "Hush, now, child, this won't take much longer at all. To baptize your soul we have to separate it from your body. Take heart from the fact that your suffering won't be wasted. Even now your pain and shame are floating out like incense to feed those whose glory you can't even begin to comprehend."

While I watched and listened, she showed me exactly how it should be done.

* * *

The flapping roar of helicopters deafened us as we ran through the marsh. They raced right toward us, flying barely higher than the reeds. I thought this was the end, but they passed right over us to the town, where they blasted the beach with rockets and cannon-fire.

"They're killing them!" I cried.

"I doubt it," Old Lady Waite said. "The Deep Ones are not stupid, you know. They wanted to destroy the Facility and give the boys in the back room something to chew on, and they've done it. They're long gone by now, taking their dead with them. You'll read in the papers tomorrow how some foreign fishermen got out of line when they thought they saw a sea monster, or maybe a mermaid, and how the dumb state troopers called in an air strike. There's no fun on earth like reading the papers, if you know what to look for."

Whatever the papers might say, our position was untenable. Dr. Saltonstall knew what I'd done in the Northwest, he hadn't just been on a fishing expedition, and he couldn't be the only one who knew. I had made no attempt to hide the remains of Ondine and the hotel clerk. As for Old Lady Waite, she was sure that they would come hunting for any lingering Dagonites in Innsmouth, with her at the head of their list.

She had kept a small sloop ready for just such an emergency, and now it ghosted through the black creek under a small jib while she steered it expertly.

"Where are we going?"

"You mentioned Fiji. It's nice there. There's an island where the Deep Ones mix freely with the people, just like they used to do in Innsmouth. Just like they'll do again here when this blows over and Ramon does what I told him."

"We're going to . . . to the South Pacific in *this*?"

"Not *we*. I'll be passing over before very long at all." She laughed at the horror on my face. "What's the matter, can't you swim?"

"Yes, of course, but—"

"Don't worry. I'll make sure you know how to sail it before I pass over. Then I'll stick by you, or maybe our friends will."

Old Lady Waite—but that was merely the name of her larval shell, soon to be discarded as she assumed the glorious form that I came to know and love, in every sense of those words, as Pth'th-l'yl'-l'yth.

It was the magnificent soul of that companion and lover-to-be who had guided me, and who now gestured at the black water. I saw nothing at first, then a glow in the depths, a trail of phosphorescence to one side of the boat. A second followed on the other side. Large, submarine creatures escorted us.

It comforted me to think that one of them might be Grandma.

About "Return to Y'ha-nthlei"

Every writer is drawing on a smaller or larger repertoire of basic premises, ideas, character types, actantial roles, and types of turns of events, as well as vocabulary and style. If this were not so, we would never be able to point to a story or a passage and say, "There! That's typical Lovecraft!" Or Poe. Or Hemingway. The best writers are not necessarily those who do not repeat themselves, but rather those who do it without you catching on. Again, the most skilled writers may be either those who recycle the same elements less often because their subconscious fund of ideas is so broad, so rich and diverse. Or those who manage to ring so many different changes on a smaller collection of motifs that we do not notice. Lester Dent ("Kenneth Robeson") was such a one.

It is important to keep all this in mind when one sets out to play the challenging game of pastiche, a sport in which John Glasby is an Olympic champion. In pastiching Lovecraft, he understands as few others do how one must master the primary writer's repertoire (like Absalom usurping his father David's throne and then proceeding to appropriate his royal harem, too) and then simulate his method of ringing certain *kinds* of changes on them, variations within a prescribed range, that HPL set for himself, most definitely *not* striking out in some new direction. "New Wave" Mythos fiction may be right and proper, but Lovecraft wrote none of it, and thus no successful Lovecraft pastiche can do so either.

Glasby has become a regular visitor to Innsmouth. He has an address there now. In stories like "Return to Y'ha-nthlei" he gives us a guided tour. As for the Lovecraftian modules he has utilized, certainly we may discern here the basic *fabula* of the journey of serendipitous self-discovery through antiquarian research. This *fabula* is the cell-nucleus of both *The Case of Charles Dexter Ward* and "The Shadow over Innsmouth." Glasby has chosen this syntagm, common to both Lovecraft tales: It provides his story's skeleton. But there is still the matter of the meat on the bones. Here Glasby has mixed paradigm options from the catalogs of both stories. The result is something like *Charles Dexter Ward* but with Innsmouth's Robert Olmstead as the protagonist. It is almost as if *The Case of Charles Dexter Ward* has undergone "the change" to become "The Shadow over Innsmouth." But, as in the latter tale, the strange mutation is only possible in the first place because the potential is already there in the narrative DNA, the common *fabula*.

"Return to Y'ha-nthlei" first appeared in *Lore* #7, Summer 1997.

Return to Y'ha-nthlei

By John S. Glasby

That Dr. Eldon H. Torrance died by extreme violence at the hand of an unidentified assailant is an undisputed fact and was recorded as such at the inquest in the County Courthouse in Arkham on July 28, 1934. Strangely, many aspects of this horrific murder were hushed up by the authorities, and a small number of witnesses who claimed to have vital information relevant to the crime were never called to give evidence.

Only one newspaper—the *Arkham Gazette*—whose editor was well known for publishing wild and often uncorroborated reports concerning Innsmouth, mentioned that the primary suspect, a strange young man by the name of Arthur Minchell, and undoubtedly the last man to see Torrance alive, had never been arrested, or even questioned, by the police, nor was any attempt made to find him after the events of that fateful afternoon.

That Minchell attended Torrance on a regular basis over a period of four months at his Innsmouth surgery was firmly established, and the doctor's receptionist, Miss Eliza Cousins, confirmed that Minchell had arrived for his appointment on the day in question promptly at two o' clock and had been shown into the doctor's consulting room at precisely five minutes after the hour.

In her evidence, Miss Cousins was adamant that no one else had entered the room, and it was not until almost an hour later, when the insistent buzzing of her desk intercom, immediately followed by the most awful sounds, had indicated that something terrible was happening inside the room, that she had run to the door, only to find it locked from the inside.

She had immediately gone for help, and, with the aid of the janitor, they had succeeded in breaking open the door only to find the dreadfully mangled remains of her employer, his body ripped and twisted almost beyond recognition. There had been no sign of Minchell, and although the window was open, the day being excessively hot, there was a sheer drop of more than fifty feet outside with no possible means of egress in that direction.

On further questioning, Miss Cousins testified that she had noticed one peculiar fact on entering the room—a faint but definite odor which she described as like that of decaying fish, although the source of this odor was not apparent. By the time the police arrived the fetor was no longer evident, nor did the janitor notice it.

Whether the mystery surrounding Torrance's murder will ever be solved is a matter of conjecture, as is the equally inexplicable disappearance of Arthur Minchell, for no trace of the man has ever been unearthed.

Rational investigators remain content to allow the entire case to be buried and forgotten, maintaining that if the testimony given by the principal witness, the receptionist, is true, if Minchell could not possibly have made his escape while she had been absent seeking assistance and then somehow locked the door again from the inside, while leaving the key in the inner lock, then there can be no logical explanation for Torrance's death.

There are others, however, who have collected and correlated everything pertaining to Arthur Minchell and are also inclined to accept the unheard testimony of other witnesses who were never called to present their evidence. These scholars adhere to more singular and unorthodox theories, pointing out several odd incidents which occurred during Minchell's early life and the verified fact that he attended Dr. Torrance, not for medical treatment, but for sessions in hypnosis.

While it is not possible to judge conclusively between these two opposing views, one may draw certain conclusions which allow the open-minded reader to gain some insight into the probable events which led up to that fateful day. What subsequently occurred behind that locked door can only be guessed at, but if we accept what certain people believe they saw that afternoon and examine objectively what lies behind the entries Dr. Torrance made regarding Minchell's curious case, then what happened was a hideous outrage of nature which has no place in a sane and orderly universe.

Arthur Minchell was abandoned by his natural mother when less than a year old, and no entry of his birth exists in any official register. He was apparently found on the steps of St. Patrick's Catholic Church in Boston early on the morning of June 6, 1902 by Father O'Leary when on his way for early morning service. The child was warmly wrapped in a blanket and shawl and placed in a basket. The name, which he was to bear all of his relatively short life on Earth—for most of the more heterodox investigators firmly believe he is no longer alive as we know life—was given to him by middle-aged clothing manufacturer James Minchell and his wife Margaret, who officially adopted him when he was two years old.

From about the age of five, Arthur exhibited signs of abnormal behavior, much of which appears to have stemmed from frequent nightmares from which he would waken screaming strange words which frightened Margaret

Minchell, since the words were in no language she knew. When questioned about these hysterical dreams he would say little, merely intimating that they always consisted of floating within great pillared cities and along vast colonnades of graven obelisks peopled by hideous creatures.

By now, he had learned to read and write with an astonishing rapidity and astounded his adoptive parents with his prolific knowledge of far distant places, knowledge which they were certain he could not have obtained from any books available to him. He would speak fluently of distant islands in the faraway South Seas, sometimes giving vivid descriptions which were later found to be correct in every detail.

His culinary habits were also strange in the extreme, as he preferred to eat his food raw rather than cooked, his particular delicacy being raw fish, for the consuming of which he was often reprimanded and sometimes beaten.

He did not mix well with the other children of the neighbourhood, having a moody, solitary temperament which set him apart from most of his companions. His only friend, Peter Thorpe, was a year younger than Arthur, and on numerous occasions the two of them would be found sitting by the edge of the lake in the park where Minchell would stare for hours into the water with a curious expression on his thin, angular features. This odd affinity for water, noted from his earliest years, was to be a dominant characteristic throughout the rest of his life.

Then, on February 15, 1913, there occurred an incident so astounding that it merited a paragraph on the front page of the *Boston Globe*. That winter had been particularly severe, with snow and ice covering the streets and houses for a full three months. All of the lakes and ponds were frozen over, and on this particular afternoon Arthur and James Minchell had gone for a walk through the park taking young Peter with them. It was a dark, overcast afternoon with more snow threatening from the northeast.

It was as they were approaching the lake with its thick covering of ice that Peter Thorpe ran forward to join several other children sliding on the frozen surface. There had been no hint of danger until there came a sudden, sharp cry of alarm as the ice in the middle broke, pitching Peter into the icy water. The cries of the other children brought an instant reaction from young Minchell. Without any show of hesitation he raced across the ice toward the widening hole into which his friend had fallen. Before anyone could stop him, he had plunged in, grabbing the boy around the waist and somehow thrusting him to safety on the lip of the ice. The next second, Minchell had disappeared beneath the surface.

While the rescued boy was rushed home with all speed, where he was placed before a roaring fire and his frozen clothing removed, James Minchell and several others searched in vain along the ice for any sign of Arthur, then waited in vain near the hole which was rapidly icing up once more. As night fell, all hope of finding the boy alive was abandoned. Twelve-year-old Arthur had evidently given his life to save his friend and his frozen body was now trapped somewhere beneath the four-inch layer of ice.

It was a little after midnight that Arthur Minchell was spotted by a patrolling policeman wandering slowly through the park. On examination he was found to be totally uninjured and none the worse for having been submerged beneath the ice for almost seven hours. Even the biting chill appeared to have no effect upon him. James Minchell, subsequently recalling the details of that night, gave an interesting account anent certain statements the boy made on being questioned.

Arthur claimed that he liked the water, that he did not feel the arctic chill beneath the ice, and that it never occurred to him that unless he escaped quickly he would die. He appeared quite unperturbed by what had happened, unable to comprehend the reason for the anxiety he had caused and the utter disbelief on everyone's part that he was still alive.

While there are those who insist that he must have drifted into an air pocket trapped under the ice, others point out that even if this had been the case, it was virtually impossible for such a small air supply to have kept him alive for so long and it was an absolute certainty that the sub-zero temperature would have killed any normal being in the space of a few minutes.

Over the next two years, Minchell continued to read avidly, although confining his attentions to matters relating to the sea and, in particular, to those pertaining to its deepest regions.

The nightmares which had plagued his infancy had largely left him and for almost three years his sleep had been virtually untroubled by dreams of any kind. His grades at school were good, although his teachers went to great lengths to point out that they could have been excellent were it not for his weird obsession with the ocean. During his vacations he would spend much of his time in the library in Copley Square searching out rare and quaint volumes, several of which were pronounced as unsuitable for a youth of his age, dealing in the main with records of ancient myths and pagan worship.

The Polynesian culture was uppermost in his researches, but later he added to his reading by consulting volumes on such varied subjects as the laying of communication cables across the floor of the Atlantic and Pacific Oceans; whether any untoward and unexplained accidents or difficulties had been experienced when these crossed the deep trenches known to exist under the sea; unexplained disappearances of sailing ships and modern vessels; and old nautical legends of monstrous sea creatures, the latter going back for several centuries.

These strange studies did not pass unnoticed by Mr. and Mrs. Minchell, and their feeling that there was something peculiar about their adopted son was heightened when it became known that he had also taken to conversing with strange sailors down at the dockside, inquiring about far-off ports of call in the East Indies and the possibility of obtaining passage on one of the ships which plied between Boston and those distant places on the other side of the world.

That he fervently wished to make such a voyage in the near future became increasingly evident from remarks he made, but in this respect neither of his adoptive parents intended to indulge him, declaring that such an unaccompanied voyage was out of the question for one so young.

It was not until shortly after his nineteenth birthday, following the death of James Minchell in a car accident, and having been left a tidy sum of money, that Arthur succeeded in persuading Margaret Minchell to allow him to go. After doing all she could to dissuade him from such a foolhardy, and possibly dangerous, venture, she finally acquiesced with great reluctance. She did, however, extract a promise from him that he would write on a regular basis to keep her informed of his whereabouts and when he intended returning home.

Accordingly, on August 11, 1921, Arthur Minchell departed the shores of America from the pier in Charlestown aboard the SS *Eastern Star* bound for Port Moresby in Papua, steaming the short route via the Panama Canal, which had been officially opened a year earlier.

A letter confirming his safe arrival was received by Mrs. Minchell, also giving details of his initial failure to obtain a passage to certain islands lying much further south which he needed to visit in order to gain some vital information. Apparently, this unlooked-for delay was not being wasted, since he had been able to talk with a number of the natives in the area about matters concerning their tribal deities and, on one occasion, he had succeeded in witnessing one of their secret ceremonies deep in the jungle, secreting himself in the dense undergrowth where, fortunately for him, he had remained undetected.

Yet, in spite of these discoveries, he remained convinced that he would not learn what he wanted until he could visit the more southerly islands which lay well off any normal trade route.

His second letter, received two months after the first, spoke mainly of trips along the coast to tiny, out-of-the-way places unvisited by tourists, all the while seeking the origins of the numerous myths and legends of the natives. Occasionally he told of visiting ruined temples deep within the encroaching jungle, of struggling ineffectually to interpret weird glyphs chiseled on time-eroded stone columns covered with vines and creepers which had almost totally obliterated them.

Then, finally, his long-delayed journey to the southern island materialized when he took passage on an ancient tramp steamer whose captain was suspected of illegal trading and was willing to take any passenger provided the price was right. Thereafter, there followed a long hiatus during which no word was received from the traveler and Mrs. Minchell was on the point of believing the worst, that something drastic had happened to him, when a letter arrived at the home in Boston: a curiously rambling and disjointed epistle which was utterly unlike his usual precise form of writing.

In spite of the fact that the letter assured her that Arthur was in good health and spirits, the contents were oddly disturbing, more in what it did not say than what was written. It had clearly been penned by someone in the throes of great excitement, speaking of his landing on an unnamed island in the South Carolinas where he intended to remain for some considerable time since he was now convinced that it was here he would discover the answers to the many questions which had been troubling him over the years.

Worried by certain references contained in the letter, Mrs. Minchell showed it to Dr. Winston Armitage, a family friend, whose field of study at Harvard was in Ancient History. From his perusal of the letter Dr. Armitage concluded that young Minchell was searching avidly for evidence of age-old pagan rites among the natives of these farflung islands, in particular those relating to some sea deity whose name was not given in the letter, and the existence of a vast palaeologic city of gray stone reputed to lie on the ocean floor off Ponape Island.

Such ventures, he declared, while almost certainly doomed to disappointment, were not the sort of thing which should be actively pursued by an impressionable young man and might lead him into danger. There were grave hazards associated with delving into forbidden matters, and, while the old pagan gods might not exist, their cults were still present and active on Earth, and they guarded their aeon-old lore jealously.

Before leaving, the worthy doctor inquired about the strange nightmares of Arthur's young days which appeared to have been the initial cause of his curious obsession. He urged Mrs. Minchell to try to recall as exactly as possible those words Arthur had uttered on waking.

While she could now remember very little of Arthur's frenzied shrieks, she recalled that her husband had, on three occasions, written down the archaic, gutteral syllables, forming articulate words as nearly as possible from the boy's unintelligible jumble of sounds. Even at the time, it had been apparent that the same phrase was being uttered again and again.

After a great deal of searching, Mrs. Minchell succeeded in finding the paper in her husband's desk, handing it to Dr. Armitage, who stared down at the scrawled letters, an expression of growing horror on his face. The words, as written several years earlier from the utterances of a bewildered and frightened six-year-old, read: *Shtunggli grah'nn fhhui Y'ha-nthlei vra Dagon chtenff.*

While Dr. Armitage, for all his learning, could give no rational interpretation of the phrase, the name Dagon was familiar to him. He recalled that while it was usually associated with the god of the Philistines, there was a much older reference which reputedly went back far beyond prehistoric times to a monstrous sea deity which had been worshiped at a hugely remote period in Earth's history.

Dr. Armitage said nothing of this to Mrs. Minchell, but did ask to be shown any further letters which Arthur might send, merely intimating that it was just possible that the youth might discover something of importance in the field of anthropology. After extracting a promise that he would be kept informed of Arthur's whereabouts and when he might be expected to return, Dr. Armitage took his leave and returned immediately to the university, where he spent the remainder of the afternoon poring over several old volumes, his trepidation increasing by the hour as he probed more deeply into a labyrinth of ancient cults and myths. Some of these which he found in the oldest tomes purported to date from such distant eras that he found it difficult to place any credence on them.

It was within the yellowed pages of the infamous *Xhanggh Fragments* that he found much of the information he was seeking, although even here there were numerous gaps where the letters had faded over the centuries. For almost two hours, Armitage sat immersed in a web of mounting horror and disbelief as he read the rambling account of untold ages before the coming of mankind, of gods and their minions who had come to Earth countless millions of years before Man had appeared, seeping down from the black spaces between the stars.

When he came across the reference to Dagon and the Deep Ones, his fear for Arthur Minchell's safety and sanity knew no bounds, for it was here that he stumbled upon the name which had puzzled him on reading that piece of paper with Arthur's waking utterance on it. Y'ha-nthlei—the vast stone city of the Deep Ones which was said to lie in the deeps off Devil Reef near Innsmouth.

Yet how in God's name was it possible for a six-year-old boy to wake from sleep screaming that name?

Clearly there was something disturbing associated with Arthur Minchell which went beyond all reason and common sense. Whether there was some ancient race memory, inherited from his unknown parents, which was responsible for these odd manifestations, it was impossible to tell, and Dr. Armitage knew he would gain no further information regarding Arthur Minchell's mental aberrations and overriding obsession until he had a chance to question the youth on his return.

This did not take place until September 23, 1924, when Arthur Minchell arrived back in Boston, accompanied by three large and heavy wood crates which were delivered the following day and taken up to his room under his direct supervision. To his adoptive mother he explained that they contained a number of rare and extremely valuable artifacts which he had picked up during his stay on the island from where he had last written.

For some reason he refused to explain, he would not allow her to witness what these crates contained, locking his door and insisting on unpacking them himself in private. Several times that night, Mrs. Minchell was woken by the sounds of heavy objects being moved across the floor, and when Arthur came down to breakfast the following morning it was evident he had slept little, if at all, during the night.

To her urgent questions he would say little, merely saying that he had made several discoveries beyond all his expectations and that once he had thoroughly studied the objects and catalogued them, he intended to visit the university and ask a number of the professors if they would care to examine them and give their authoritative opinions regarding their authenticity, age, and meaning.

It was later that same day that Dr. Armitage, being informed of Arthur's return, decided to visit the youth, a proposal to which Mrs. Minchell acquiesced readily since it had immediately become apparent to her that Arthur had changed in some queer way during the three years he had been away. It was not simply that the stay in tropical climes had altered him, for this was something she would have expected and accepted. Having known him and watched him all of his life, she sensed that this peculiarity went far deeper than certain subtle changes she noted in his outward appearance.

There was, for example, an odd far-away expression in his eyes, as if his thoughts were completely divorced from his present surroundings, and his normally pinched features had taken on a strangely repellent cast, almost as if some foreign ailment had afflicted him, one which had altered the underlying bone structure, flattening out the forehead.

On arrival at the house, Dr. Armitage went immediately to Arthur's room, where, after a long period had elapsed since his knocking and announcing himself through the door, he was finally admitted. For over a minute, Dr. Armitage was unable to take in everything he saw. Where young Minchell had discovered the fiendish articles in that room, or what means he had used to obtain them and smuggle them from their original site, Armitage could not even guess. Grotesque beyond all of his imagining, they occupied almost every piece of available space.

Against one bare wall stood two tall stone columns almost six feet in height, the greenish stone exuding an air of antiquity and alienness which sent a shudder of nameless dread through him. But it was the deeply incised carvings on their surfaces which filled him with the most dread for, in the main, they represented creatures which could never have walked upon the

Earth, certainly not in any times known to Man. All were evidently meant to depict some form of aquatic life, fishlike or octopoid in their general delineations, yet with a vaguely horrific hint of something human about them.

On the small table were stone statuettes of all sizes, each carved into the monstrous shape of an idol closely resembling those shown on the graven columns. Squidlike abnormalities stood side by side with reptilian aberrations in a zoological assembly of such extraordinary diversity that Armitage felt his head reel at the mere sight of the collection. Only by a tremendous effort of will did he succeed in pulling himself together sufficiently to question the youth concerning his reasons for traveling across the world in order to get his hands on such monstrosities.

Although clearly reluctant to speak of the reasons behind his obsession, either because of uncertainty or a desire for secrecy, Arthur did appear amenable to answering several of the doctor's questions. He could not explain this ungovernable bewitchery with the ocean and those islands he had visited, a mental possession which had bedeviled his thoughts for as long as he could remember. He did know that it was associated with those dreams of childhood and that he would never be free of it until he had discovered certain vital knowledge which could not be obtained by normal means.

The old, forbidden tomes in the university library and that in Copley Square had provided him with tantalizing hints of what he sought, but that had not been enough. It had been of vital importance that he should visit for himself those places mentioned in the books in order to determine the source of this weird compulsion which seemed to have set him apart from other men. What he had found certainly went a long way toward providing him with some explanation but, as yet, he could not be sure whether even these aeon-old artifacts which he had obtained surreptitiously and at great personal danger would be sufficient.

He fully intended, at some time in the near future, to allow them to be examined by the professors at the university, although he was extremely doubtful if they would be able to shed any light on them, since such men were prone to understand only what they could see or measure with their scientific instruments and lacked the ability to comprehend that there were far greater things which belonged outside the realm of science.

When quizzed by the doctor about the contents of his childhood nightmares he was quite open, and it was obvious that the memory of them had not dimmed in the slightest over the intervening years. In every instance he had found himself as an unwilling spectator in some vast subterranean world of massive colonnades and towers whose overall proportions bore no relation to any human design. The outlandish phrase he was said to have uttered on waking he had seen engraven above an immense portal and, although engraved in symbols which had no earthly counterpart known to him in waking life, he had known its pronunciation in his dream. As to its meaning, he had no idea, although he felt sure the key to its decipherment lay within his grasp.

In spite of Dr. Armitage's insistence that such delvings into ancient myths could be dangerous in the extreme, Minchell laughed at his fears, maintaining that many of the old myth cycles from all over the world were now being actively studied and no harm had come to these investigators.

Dr. Armitage left feeling even more disturbed than when he had arrived. Despite Minchell's apparent openness, he was certain the youth was hiding something, that he knew far more than he was willing to tell. Arthur's mind held some dark secret which he did not intend to share with anyone. In addition to the youth's curious mental state, Armitage had also noted his physical appearance. He had anticipated some change, for, after all, Arthur had spent three years in an alien environment and possibly under conditions of extreme privation.

Yet not only did he seem to have aged considerably during his absence, there were also those queer changes to his physiognomy, the wide, staring eyes, the curious flattening of the forepart of the skull, and a perceptible stoop which was so unlike his former erect posture. What fiendish sights he had witnessed all those thousands of miles away, Armitage could not imagine, yet they seemed to have had a pronounced, and adverse, effect upon him.

During the weeks that followed, the doctor paid several calls on Arthur, who received him courteously but declined to answer any further questions, giving the impression that he was engaged upon important research which took up all of his available time. While he was aware that his adoptive mother was extremely worried by his general behavior, especially the secretive way in which he conducted his affairs, he assured the doctor that he was perfectly well, in mind and body, and there was no danger associated with his investigations.

He was, he hinted, attempting to decipher certain very old inscriptions which he had photographed during his stay on the island, but so far with little success. Once this had been accomplished, however, he would then invite the university professors to examine his trophies and, if they wished, certain of them could be put on public display, since they clearly represented an art form which was unknown at the present time.

With this Armitage had to be content, and, when the invitations to Professors Waldron, Curtis, and Hewitt were duly received, Armitage accompanied them. Having seen most of the specimens on previous occasions, he had already decided that the monstrous effigies bore not even the remotest resemblance to the normal Polynesian type of sculpture, nor were they anything like that of the vast Australasian continent or New Zealand.

This view was readily accepted by his companions as the statuettes were passed around amid a growing perplexity. Apart from the nightmarish contours which, in the majority of cases, appeared to be hybrids of various marine creatures, the anatomical quintessence of the idols, the grotesque tentacular nature of their limbs and misformed torsos, were suggestive of long, prehuman eras. The nature of the material from which they had been fashioned also evoked much heated discussion. A pale, nauseous green in color, flecked with minute black striations, it was extremely hard and heavy and as to its composition, no one could hazard a guess.

Only Professor Curtis could recall ever having seen anything like it before and Armitage noted how Arthur listened with undisguised attentiveness as Curtis related how, fifteen years earlier, he had stumbled upon an ancient medallion, while holidaying in Corfu, which had been made of a stone very similar to this. From the inscriptions and design, Curtis had concluded that it was Phoenician, possibly three thousand years old. In spite of the ridiculously large sum he had offered for it, the old shopkeeper had refused to part with it, although he had been willing to divulge what he knew of its history.

There was, the old man had told Curtis, a legend relating to that particular object, although whether it was to be believed was a matter of opinion. Briefly, the piece of stone had been brought up from the sea in a fisherman's net more than four thousand years ago when men had marveled at its curious color and consistency, claiming that it must be a gift of the sea god. The image depicted on the front was understood to be that of some ocean deity and according to the legend it had then fallen into the hands of a sea captain who carried it with him whenever he set out to sea. It was, perhaps, noteworthy that even in the most violent storms, his ship was undamaged even when many others were lost.

There had been vague, queer rumors associated with it over the millennia since then, but of these the old shopkeeper knew little except that it was said that whoever possessed it *would neither drown nor die if lost at sea*. Somehow, it had come into the possession of his great-grandfather who, on his deathbed, had adjured his son never to part with it and to ensure that this same oath be taken by all succeeding generations of the family.

After plying Professor Curtis with several more questions, young Minchell then suggested that his visitors should choose from among the artifacts those which they might like to place in the university museum, indicating that there were, however, certain pieces which he intended to keep for himself, particularly the two graven stone columns which stood against the wall.

Once this had been done and the relevant items carefully packed in strong cardboard boxes, the professors left, leaving Armitage alone with the youth. Although not wishing to agitate Arthur further, for he could see that the youth was in an unusually excited frame of mind, Armitage realized there were certain questions he had to ask, not only for his own peace of mind but also for that of Mrs. Minchell, who had remained downstairs during the professors' visit.

During the conversation which followed, which lasted for a good three quarters of an hour, one particular incident was to occur which, although he made every effort not to show it, frightened the worthy gentleman more than he cared to admit. At first Arthur reiterated his now-familiar view that there was far more truth in the ancient legends and myth cycles than present-day scientists were willing to admit or accept; that there had existed on Earth several long-lived species prior to the advent of mankind; and that if one only knew where to look, the positive evidence for this could be found.

In response to Armitage's assertion that no archaeological proof existed for the great stone cities which young Minchell claimed had been erected millions of years before, Minchell dismissed this argument by saying that such ruins had been buried deep beneath the pre-Cambrian rocks aeons before by the great crustal movements on the planet's surface. Others, he argued, still moldered virtually untouched and undecayed on the ocean floor after the land on which they had been built had sunk during that cataclysmic event when the Moon had been torn from what was now the Pacific Ocean to take up its present orbit. Who was to say what hellish remains existed, unseen and unsuspected by mankind, on the far side of the Moon?

In reply to Armitage's scathing denials, Minchell pointed to the hideously carved columns, insisting that the indescribable glyphs could not have been chiseled less than fifty, possibly a hundred, million years earlier. Once he succeeded in translating them he could present such conclusive evidence to the scientific world at large. Naturally, such a task would not be easy, since there did not exist any Rosetta Stone to provide the key for such decipherment. But there was other evidence which he possessed which he had not yet shown to anyone else.

Crossing to a small desk in the corner, Arthur unlocked one of the drawers and took out a small bundle tied with a piece of red ribbon. Armitage saw that it was a collection of photographs. These he did not give to the doctor at once but proceeded to extract them carefully one by one, after first perusing them, handing them in turn to Armitage. The first five were innocuous shots of an island, clearly taken from the deck of an approaching vessel.

The next depicted a large clearing in dense jungle showing tall columns similar to the two which rested against the nearby wall but more than thirty feet in height, several canted at crazy angles where the ground beneath them had evidently subsided. The structure had obviously been a temple at some time in the remote past, yet there was an odd *alienness* about the disposition of the stones, so much so that Armitage found it impossible even to visualize what it must have looked like when it had first been erected. Certainly it resembled no type of native architecture with which he was familiar.

There followed a number of close-up shots of several of the rearing columns which revealed, in surprisingly sharp detail, the outlandish hieroglyphics inscribed thereon. These photographs, Minchell maintained, would form the basis of his work in decoding this horribly ancient script.

It was at that moment that the incident occurred which so unsettled the old professor. Reaching out to take back the photographs from Armitage's outstretched hand, Arthur dropped the others upon the floor. Before the youth could move, Armitage automatically stooped to pick them up from where they had fallen in a heap. Almost immediately, Arthur uttered a sharp cry and attempted to scoop them up, virtually snatching from Armitage's fingers two of the photographs he had retrieved.

The doctor caught only a fragmentary glimpse of them before the youth grabbed them and hurriedly returned them to the desk; but what he saw, leering blasphemously from the glossy surface of the prints, shocked Armitage to the core and it was only by a supreme effort that he stopped himself from crying out aloud.

Both had clearly been taken at night, but by the light of a full moon so that, even in spite of the poor lighting conditions, each detail was as sharp and clear as in the other photographs he had seen. One showed a rocky promontory from which a group of figures were diving into the pounding surf while the other exhibited what were, in all likelihood, the same figures swimming away from the island. Dr. Armitage's head reeled as he recognized the figures for what they were, for there could be no doubt whatever: They were identical with those depicted in the hideous statuettes, a number of which still reposed on the polished top of the table in front of him!

Dear God in Heaven! What monstrous survival from Earth's distant past had young Minchell stumbled upon? No wonder he wanted to keep such foul things secret from everyone.

In spite of his scientific training, Armitage undertook a hurried departure from that room of cosmic horror and unholy secrets, nor could he ever bring himself to visit the house again. He could tell no one of what he had seen, for who would believe him? Confronted with such a possibility, Minchell would undoubtedly either conceal or even destroy those damnable pictures and deny that they ever existed.

Over the next nine years, Arthur Minchell remained a solitary figure in Boston. From certain inquiries he made among the police and doctors, it appeared he was anxious to trace his natural parents, something he had shown no inclination for until two years after his return from the South Seas. Mrs. Minchell died in 1931 and he continued to live in the house on Providence Street, having little intercourse with his neighbors, whom he had known all his life. His visits to the various libraries continued, and he took to haunting old bookshops in the narrow streets, evidently searching for information he could not obtain elsewhere.

His stoop became more pronounced and it was often remarked by those who knew him how much he appeared to have aged since his sojourn in the tropics. His skin, too, had assumed a curiously wrinkled appearance, and the wide, vacant eyes made him an object of derision among the children of the neighbourhood.

Then, in December 1933, it appears that he made a discovery of extreme importance, for the librarian at the library in Copley Square clearly recalls the incident. Minchell had been sitting in his usual seat near the window poring over a stack of ancient books when he suddenly uttered a loud, triumphant cry which disturbed the other readers. Making a hasty entry in the notebook he carried with him, he rose so abruptly from the table that his chair fell back with a crash, and, without bothering to replace it, he dashed from the library in a state of tremendous excitement.

Neighbors noticed signs of frenzied activity in the house that night, with the light in the upper room burning continuously until dawn. Eight weeks later, he moved out of the house where he had dwelt for almost thirty-two years, took all of his belongings, and moved away from Boston for good, having purchased a decrepit, ancient building close to the wharves in Innsmouth.

Whether it was something he had come across in that particular volume or the dreams which prompted this precipitous move, there is no way of telling. Yet from Dr. Torrance's notes it is clear that the horrifying nightmares which had plagued his early years had now returned to haunt his sleep. There is no doubt whatever that it was the dreams which led him to consult the doctor and that he had chosen Torrance for a very particular reason since the latter was one of the first practitioners to practice the virtually unknown procedure of hypnotic regression. Although a new technique, it is clear from Dr. Torrance's notes, which he transcribed in meticulous detail after each session, that he achieved some remarkable results.

From the very first, Minchell proved to be an ideal subject for hypnosis, although Torrance chose this course with some reluctance and only after hearing a full account of the terrible nightmares which were now a nightly occurrence. Whether Torrance had any inkling of the strange malady which had afflicted Minchell for so many years, it is only possible to conjecture, but from the notes which the doctor scribbled down verbatim from Minchell's sometimes erratic and hesitant speech, it appears that he regressed the patient more than three thousand years on that first occasion. The notes themselves, though inevitably disjointed, have an obvious bearing on this strange case:

". . . Standing on the deck of a ship, my ship. . . . tremendous storm which has driven us far to the west beyond the Pillars of Hercules. May the gods protect us! Difficult to see anything in the darkness and the water lashing over the sides. . . . our two accompanying vessels faring worse than us. Perhaps the amulet of green stone I wear around my neck will save us.

"Something in the ocean around us, just visible whenever the lightning strikes. Demon shapes . . . tentacled but beings with curiously human faces . . . swimming all around the ship. Now hundreds swarming onto the other two vessels, dragging their crews into the sea, bearing them down out of sight. Why do they not attack us? Can it be they fear the amulet I carry?

"The storm abating although the lightning still flashes. They are all around the ship now. . . . I see their eyes staring at me . . . strangely luminescent . . . their voices are in my ears, sounding loud even above the roaring of the thunder. Strange words yet they have a meaning for me. . . . I see images . . . vast cities more splendid than those of my native Phoenicia . . . a pillared temple within which something unimaginable lurks, sculpted in the side of a titan undersea cliff . . . Y'ha-nthlei . . . Y'ha-nthlei . . . Aaaaah!"

There are other notes indicating that Dr. Torrance took down everything Minchell said during his trancelike states, all being in a similar vein, and all apparently relating to times in the distant past with but one notable exception. Two weeks before the murder, Torrance put Minchell into an hypnotic trance and, from the scrawled jottings the physician made, he apparently regressed his patient only a century into his past lives.

Here, unless we accept that these notes represent nothing more than latent memories based upon evidence which Minchell had collected during his perusal of ancient books, many of the incidents related may be accurately correlated with known historical facts.

"Another long voyage and the Sumatra Queen again anchored off the island east of Othaheite . . . Hallowe'en and all the crew jumpy. . . . special night for the Kanakas who row out to the small volcanic island a couple of miles offshore. Talked with Matt Eliot, first mate . . . he reckons many of the Kanakas are left there for human sacrifice to some fish god in return for gold trinkets. Eliot has pleaded with Captain Marsh to stop this trade but he won't listen.

"Reckoned to be weird ruins on yon isle unlike those here, maybe millions of years old. . . . supposed to have lain at the bottom of the sea for thousands of years. Captain Marsh has ordered Colter and me to row him out in the dory to the island tonight. . . . utter madness . . . sheer suicide!

"Have approached the island from northeast. . . . full moonlight but no sign of Kanakas . . . on other side of island. Can easily make out ruins . . . must cover most of the island . . . all crazy angles and odd features, eroded almost beyond recognition.

Chanting has begun beyond the strangely shaped peak. . . . things coming up out of the sea . . . frog-fish that walk like men . . . glowing green in the moonlight.

"Sounds coming in answer to the chanting of the natives. . . . croakings and piping whistles that somehow make sense for me, some memory I have of hearing those sounds before, some horrible remembrance deep in my brain. Dear God in Heaven, those images flashing through my mind . . . Y'ha-nthlei . . . great grey R'lyeh dreaming eternal on the ocean floor . . . Father Dagon . . . Mother Hydra . . . Great Cthulhu!"

The testimony of these notes, taken over a period of four months, accurately recording Minchell's utterances while regressed hypnotically, has been seized upon by those who prefer the more unorthodox theories to that put forward in the Arkham County Courthouse to satisfy the hard-headed authorities, maintaining that some latent ancient race memory, first manifesting itself in his childhood dreams and now dramatically confirmed by Dr. Torrance's pioneering work with hypnosis, had been growing stronger year by year until it seemed inevitable it would soon take over complete control of him.

Naturally, there is nothing which can be conclusively proven from Dr. Torrance's writings, which are all that remain to tell us what may have happened on that fateful afternoon. The possible explanations of how Minchell came to utter such words are many, and no one can say with certainty that the technique Torrance used is absolute proof of past lives, certainly not going as far back in time as he reputedly took Arthur Minchell during those hypnosis sessions.

Dreams are, after all, illusions and not substance, and those hypnosis-induced ramblings may easily be put down to subconscious nightmares, to what he remembered from that voyage to those fantastic islands of the South Sea, and, above all, to his reading of forbidden tomes kept under lock and key in the university libraries.

Common sense and logic dictate that one should accept the more prosaic alternative, that at the very end Arthur Minchell was insane and attacked the physician with such ferocity that Torrance's body was literally mauled out of all recognition and that somehow Minchell succeeded in making his escape while Miss Cousins was absent seeking help, that he is now somewhere at large, either well concealed among those squalid, archaic waterfront lanes of ancient Innsmouth, or elsewhere in the country.

To believe otherwise would be to concede that there are hideous survivals from remote aeons still present in this world, hidden in the ocean deeps and other inaccessible places.

Only two things, neither of which was brought up at the inquest, speak against such a conservative theory. There is the evidence of three people of the utmost reliability, testimony which was curiously denied a public hearing.

While what all three saw was so outlandish and bizarre that it took them several days to recover from it, there is no reason to believe it was a trick of the light or something conjured up by their imaginations.

Patrick O'Docherty, a level-headed Irish lawyer visiting Innsmouth to interview a client, had just passed the building housing Dr. Torrance's surgery when he heard what he described as a nauseous sucking noise coming from some distance above the street and, on turning, witnessed an anamorphous, tentacled shape descending the sheer outer wall with astonishing rapidity which, on reaching the street less than fifty yards from where he stood, rooted to the spot in horror and disbelief, scuttled away in the direction of Water Street, where it disappeared around the corner.

Less than five minutes later, the greenish monstrosity was also sighted by John Kentman and James Durran, both well educated and sober citizens, who witnessed it moving swiftly along the waterfront where it dived into the sea, swimming out in the direction of the deep water beyond Devil Reef, where the sea bottom drops precipitously for more than two thousand feet.

Second, there is the pad on which Dr. Torrance recorded his notes at that last meeting. These were found on the floor close to his mangled body. For the most part they were nothing more than a meaningless jumble of virtually unpronounceable syllables with only one name standing out: a name with which the doctor was doubtless familiar by then—*Y'ha-nthlei!*

At the top of the sheet, however, he had written in perfect English and a precise, legible hand: *As a final experiment I intend to regress the patient at least five million years!*

About "The Old Ones' Signs"

Despite the claims of today's fundamentalist demagogues, the United States was not a "Christian country" at its founding. The minority of colonists were church-goers, and a good number of the Founding Fathers were anything but Orthodox Protestants. Many were adherents of Deism, Universalism, Natural Religion, etc. Jefferson, for instance, was an avowed Unitarian, and he compiled his own version of The New Testament gospels, omitting all the miracles. Thomas Paine wrote a withering broadside against biblical religion (*The Age of Reason*), as did Ethan Allen (*Reason: The One Oracle of Man*). It is in this context that Obed Marsh's "village atheist" tirades against Christianity must be understood. Marsh appealed to common sense, to empirical results, even as did the Deists and skeptics of early America. He might even be viewed as something of a precursor to the notorious agnostic lecturer Colonel Robert Ingersoll. Ironically, like Colonel Ingersoll, Captain Marsh preached a creed of scientific rationalism and even of implicit evolutionism! It's just that Ingersoll couldn't have known of the remarkable ethnological/zoological discoveries to which Marsh was privy. Pierre Comtois' "The Old Ones' Signs" focuses on the religious tension of the Innsmouth community.

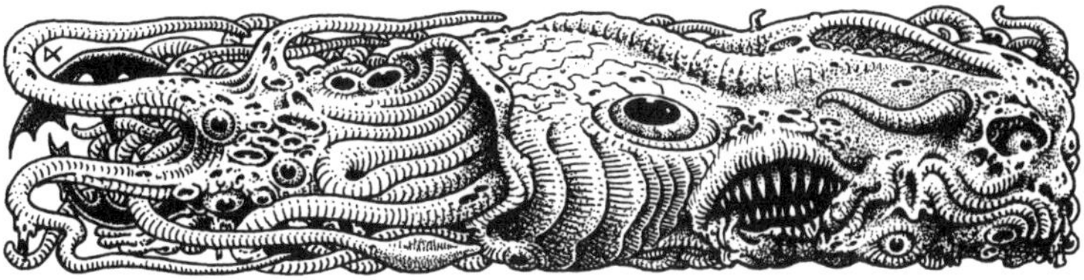

The Old Ones' Signs

by Pierre Comtois

From: United States Department of Justice Federal Bureau of Investigation
To: Mr. Pierre Comtois
Reference: Freedom of Information Act Request #900048
Subject: Government Document #0534225 Hosiah Peters, testimony of

My name is Hosiah Peters. It was early Spring as I recall it, in 18—, and I had just come off four months of wintering on the old homestead outside Pepperell in Massachusetts. My parents and two brothers still lived there, cajoling a living from the rocky New England soil, but spent the winter cutting wood and bottling preserves in the root cellar. I don't usually mind such work when the sea grows frigid and gray and the ice cakes on a ship's hull, but when the sun begins to stay up in the heavens and temperatures to rise, I get the old urge to feel the swell of water beneath me and to smell the brine of the ocean. Such was the case that season when I hefted my sea bag, kissed my mother on the cheek, shook the men-folks' hands and took the road toward Boston. Little did I know of the strange and heathenish ways I would meet with and the even stranger temptations. Mind you, I was not ignorant of the peculiar delights of the world's more exotic ports of call, but as I am a God-fearing man and a proper Yankee, I like to consider myself made of sterner stuff, my will reinforced by staunch faith. The sea itself and the honest wages due me at the end of a voyage were my delights, and the attractions of the French ports, the crowded cities of Araby, the gentle women folk of China, or the savage wantonness of the South Sea isles held no interest for me. But none of those experiences would prepare me for what proved to be the final time I would cross a body of open water.

There was an early thaw that season and when I arrived in Boston I found that every ship had already hired its complement of seamen. Disappointed, I made my way to Salem and Marblehead, where the same situation prevailed. It was in Salem, however, that I was advised to try Innsmouth further north, where ships were said to still need men. It was growing late in the trading season when I arrived in Innsmouth, a bustling seaport whose warehouses and factories along the main wharves would soon be packed with goods. The sun shone full but gentle, and the gulls called enticingly from the housetops as I climbed the stone steps into the custom house. There I inquired about employment and the old pensioner behind the counter looked up surprised. "Kinda late, aintcha, boy?" I mumbled an excuse and waited as he slowly rose from his swivel chair and made his way to a bulletin board crowded with postings. He tore one off and returned to his chair. "Here y'are, boy," he said, handing the paper to me. "The *Sumatry Queen* sets sail with the tide, skippered by her owner no less, Cap'n Obed Marsh. Find his Fust Mate, Matt Eliot. He'll square ya away if'n he hasn't already hired the full crew." I thanked him and left the building.

Outside, I approached the sea at last as I followed the whole length of Stone's Wharf, the stink of low tide tickling my nostrils like perfume. At last, I found the *Sumatra Queen*, a sleek, three-masted barque that at the moment sat motionless, its sails furled. A gang plank extended down to the wharf where men worked feverishly loading her with Nantucket candles, New England butter, mountain ginseng, salted fish, and a dozen other local products for the European market. The dock master indicated a rough-looking character standing on the ship's deck as the first mate, and I heaved myself up the gang plank. I introduced myself and told him of my desire for work. He looked me over well before saying, "We do need a few more men, and I can tell by the way you hold yourself, you're a tried seaman. So I'll take you on here and now. Wages are fifty cents a week and a standard share of the profits. The Cap'n sails a tight ship and brooks no sloth. He is hard but fair. You will bunk in number 12 with Worthy for'ard." He shook my hand and went back to his business.

I was in the stern when our Captain ordered the lines to be cast off and watched as men heaved at the oars of two boats, tugging the *Queen* into open water. With the tide in, the ship was taken by a hidden current and slowly drifted away from the yards. The roofs and gables of Innsmouth gleamed in the sun as they began to shrink on the horizon, and I could see a dozen handkerchiefs fluttering their farewells. Finally, it was time for the Captain to order the sails up and for a time I was too busy to appreciate the fine weather as I helped with the hoisting of the spanker. Then, under full sail, the huge sheets filled with wind and billowed outward, and I felt the ship beneath me jerk forward as it eagerly sought the deeper water. My heart leaped with the knowledge of being at sea again.

I had a chance to size up our Captain later that afternoon when he assembled the crew amidships for the customary welcome. He stood above us on the poop, not a large figure, but impressive in his self-possession. He told us a bit about himself but nothing I did not already gather from the chatter of my fellow crewmen. He said he ran a tight ship and if we all pulled together and obeyed him and his mates, then all would go well and we would return in two years with handsome wages to show for it. It was then he said something which made me uneasy. After mentioning our due wages, he added that we would get much more from hard, honest labor than the same time spent in prayers that never were answered. Now I am the first to say that not all prayers are answered, but there are times in men's lives when it is all they have. If nothing else, they bring comfort and are aimed not simply to ask favors, but as a way of communing with the Almighty. This attitude on the Captain's part set a false note with me that was to last throughout our voyage. And it was this seeming interest in the things of earth over those of heaven that was to drive the Captain and the crew of the *Queen* into the abominable situation that is the ultimate reason for this narrative.

It was with some self-consciousness that I would pull the well-worn Bible from my sea bag at the end of my watch and read its familiar passages. There was no jeering or mocking from the other men, of course, it being one of the unwritten laws of the sea that, against the vast oppression of the open ocean and its sometimes unpredictable and terrifying nature, a man had a right to his own form of spiritual comfort. It was true that many men found theirs at the bottom of a bottle, but many more shared my sentiments.

Thus did I pass the time aboard ship as the *Queen* made its expert way across the chilly Atlantic waters to arrive at last in the port of Liverpool in England. There we off-loaded our American goods and took on a cargo of fine linens and colored cloths. The men were given little time to spend ashore and, in any case, had even less money to spend on the sort of women to be found there. Consequently, a number of us sober crewmen had to be sent around to drag our mates from the dockside grog shops preparatory to our departure.

With the *Queen* once more riding low in the water, we drifted down the Mersey into the Irish Sea and began one of the longest legs of our route. We sailed southward, across the old Spanish Main and the Canarys, then swung outward along the Guinea Current avoiding Cape Bojador on the West African shore. We continued southward after that, at last rounding the Cape of Good Hope and entering the Indian Ocean. The strange, jungle-laden coastline of Madagascar with its dusky denizens giving obeisance to the god of Islam slid past our port side too slowly for my satisfaction. Who knew what unholy activities that green hell hid? When the northern tip of the island at last sank from view, I breathed a sigh of relief.

The next several weeks were an unending series of battles with fast-moving squalls and deadening calms under a burning sun, and it was a great relief for all when the enchanted coast of India loomed on the horizon. The Captain ordered the sails trimmed as the *Queen* approached the great city of

Bombay. The men crowded the starboard rail shouting and pointing as the shore grew nearer and they could see the throngs of people jamming the seashore doing their laundry, bathing, or performing nameless esoteric rites in the shallows. As we passed beneath the brooding bulk of the Towers of Silence up on the Malabar Hill and entered Mahim Bay where the shipyards lay, the sea turned a muddy brown in color as the accumulated filth of a million people emptied into it from inland rivers and streams. Once even a shrouded body bobbed past the ship. Shuddering, I ruminated on the heathen practices of the people here and mumbled a prayer in thanks that my ancestors had the benefit of the Lord's enlightenment. In Bombay, we traded our linens and cloth for a load of opium which would be under guard for the length of our next leg to Macao in China.

By that time, I had earned a reputation for honesty and fastidiousness aboard ship, by no means qualities disparaged by the crew. In fact they were appreciated, and their utility was not lost on the first mate, who recommended me as one of the guards below decks for the opium. Thus it was that I saw little of our voyage along the coasts of India or Annam. Finally, we reached our destination after passing between the city of Macao and Hong Kong, beneath the resentful eyes of a British man-of-war, and into The Bogue. Immediately, we were hemmed in by a ragtag fleet of junks, including a grand affair bearing the local customs officer. The expected bribe was paid and we berthed comfortably at Whampoa. While the Captain and his first mate bartered away our cargo, the men at last had the time to spend ashore that allowed them full vent for their lusts. The women of China are as wondrous and beautiful as you may have heard and altogether too easy to bundle with. Amid the crowds, one could easily see the luckless fruit of the thousands of illicit unions the natives had been made to endure since the arrival of white men in their country.

Once more, when it was time to depart, I was called upon to help round up the men. It was more difficult this time, and we ended up losing two to the myriad drug dens that riddled the city. To replace them, Captain Marsh took on a couple of the huskier natives who could speak a kind of pidgin English. With the hold loaded with fine porcelain and furniture and tons of rice, we slipped port and made our way back out to open sea. It was not official knowledge, but the scuttlebutt had it that the Captain was of a mind to steer a course southward to the spice islands to trade our load of rice for some spices and peppers that would bring a great price among the dealers in Boston. He had hopes of finding an island not recently visited by traders and so ill-versed in the worth of rice for spices.

Well, I am sure that the search went on a good deal longer than even the Captain had expected. The *Queen* at first made good time south of China as it crossed the Philippine Sea, passed the Carolines, and threaded its way beyond the Gilberts and the Tuamotu Archipelago. After that, landfall became a rarer thing, and when we transited the Tropic of Capricorn, we at last entered the great, empty reaches of the South Pacific. At first the Captain made for islands marked on his charts, but soon after, he began following leads to others that were not charted, names given to him by the ignorant riffraff we had met at previous ports. Most of the stories we heard proved false; some led to actual islands. Eventually, these specks of land seemed to run out and we drifted out onto the wide empty ocean far below New Zealand. Weeks passed with nary a hint of dry land, and the men began to grumble, expecting momentarily to spot stray icebergs from the not too distant polar regions to the south.

It was on one of those later evenings as I held the stern watch by the spanker that my doubts about the Captain's intentions and his irreverent attitude toward the Christian religion began to add up to something. The surface of the sea was as still as a soft shroud, while the silvery light of a full moon silhouetted the length of the ship toward the bow. Unfamiliar constellations twinkled between the ropes and spars of our empty masts as the *Queen* lay in wait for a strong wind. The hour was late, and so we had only a minimum crew on deck, allowing my thoughts to wander. I lit my pipe and leaned against the rail, feeling the cool night breeze against my face.

"Reckon we must be nearin' the Pole as some o' the crew been sayin', Hosiah?" came a voice from behind me. I looked over my shoulder without altering my position at the rail.

"It's true that this wind is colder than normal, Worthy," I replied, "but the Pole's still a long way off. More 'n likely it's just the season." My bunk mate took a place beside me at the rail and lit his own pipe.

"Couldn't sleep," he said, looking out at the moon. "Ain't familiar with these parts," he continued. "The strangeness of it all: the stars, the currents, the not knowin', it all spooks me." I told him I agreed with him and wondered aloud if the Captain knew what he was doing.

"Cap'n Marsh is a crafty old seaman," said Worthy, "but he's got one weakness: profit. It ain't enough for him to return to Innsmouth a rich man, he always needs to have more."

"No good can come of a man who worships only at the altar of Mammon," I observed. "The Captain's god is gold and silver."

Worthy did not dispute this observation but merely changed the subject: "What do ya hear about our provisions?"

"They are still good. We have plenty of fresh water, but we lack fruit to prevent scurvy."

"Aye, we haven't been able to stock up on fruit for over three weeks." Suddenly, the moon slipped behind an approaching cloud bank and plunged the surrounding sea into what seemed pitch dearkness. As the minutes passed, we could actually see the shadow of the clouds as it creeped over the water and swallowed the *Queen*. I immediately looked to the spanker as a few more hands came up from belowdecks. The second mate was shouting orders to trim sails when a terrified scream pierced the night air.

"We're bein' boarded!" someone yelled, and immediately the ship was plunged into a chaos of shouting men and screaming savages as what seemed a hoard of dusky-skinned, painted, and file-toothed natives swarmed amidships, flailing spears and truncheons at the night watch.

I saw Jim Caneford have his skull crushed beneath the weight of a war club and Isaac Kearns gutted with a spear. Their killing slowed the savages down a bit as they jumped and hooted in glee at their swift victories. Then the bulk of the crew emerged from belowdecks armed with pistols, cutlasses, and belaying pins. Captain Marsh was at the forefront, shouting encouragement at the men and curses at the natives as the two sides met and mingled amidships. Almost immediately, the decks were awash with blood as limbs were hacked off and heads rolled. It was all I had time to see as I was suddenly grasped from behind in a rough embrace and felt the prick of a stone knife against the flesh of my back.

A foul reek of sweat and fish guts assailed my nostrils as my captor's breath whistled in my ear. I twisted suddenly and reached behind me, my hand seeking to stay the plunge of the knife. I found the savage's wrist and we stood there a moment or two, he with his arm about my throat and I with my hand at his wrist. The sounds of the melee below died away until we struggled in silence, the perspiration beading my face and streaming along my body with the strain. Finally, I felt my assailant shift his weight and in that instant, I acted. I pushed the knife hand against his belly and threw myself backward. In doing so, the arm around my neck pulled away enough for me to use my free hand to seize and twist it away. In the meantime, the force of my rearward lunge prolonged the savage's imbalance and he toppled back. I threw my full weight against him, and in another moment his back was arched against the horizontal beam of the spanker. I spun and flung my right hand to his throat; with the other, I struck the knife from his hand. Our relative positions were in my favor as I continued to force him back. Now both his hands were desperately grasping at mine as I concentrated on crushing his larynx. Already, the breath was wheezing from his open mouth, where I could see that two of his sharpened teeth had been broken long ago. At last, his struggles grew weak, his arms fell to his sides, and he began to slump. Cautiously, I removed my hands from about his throat and had the peculiar satisfaction of seeing him crumple to the floor.

Fleetingly, I felt the guilt a proper Christian must feel when he kills a fellow man, but it was only fleeting because just then I heard, as if from very far away, the voice of Worthy Hunnicut calling my name. He was asking if

I was all right, and I replied that I was. I could see through the tatter of his blouse that his shoulder was smeared in blood. Behind him lay the corpse of a native, the broken haft of a spear protruding from its side. I looked at my own hands and saw that they were smeared in the earthy paints that had decorated the native I had slain.

Then the silence retreated and the clamor of battle reemerged into my consciousness. The level of noise had lessened somewhat, and as Worthy and I rested warily against the rail overlooking the main deck, we could see the last act of the epic battle. A score of bodies lay strewn across the blood-drenched deck, and we could see with some relief that only one more of our crew had gone on to join poor Jim and Isaac. The rest were savages in various modes of dismemberment. Captain Marsh was still standing, still shouting and cursing and spattered in blood. He looked more than a match for the nickname the men had taken to calling him: Old Limb of Satan. The enemy were in full retreat as the last of them fell and leapt over the side. Some regained their war canoes, others simply began swimming toward the horizon, while still others merely sank beneath the surface of the sea. By then it was near dawn and just as the men began to catch their breath, another shout arose, this time with an even more fearful warning: "Fire in the hole!" it yelled.

There was a momentary scramble as the crew looked anxiously about until someone spied the smoke rising from the bow trap. "Form a bucket line!" ordered the Captain as tired men gained sudden new strength and began hoisting buckets of water up from the sea with ropes, then handing them on down a line of their mates. As the smoke dissipated, and the seaman's worst nightmare began to recede, the first mate was lowered into the hold to view the damage. When he reemerged, it was to report that the trade goods were undamaged but that our victuals had all been spoiled. There was silence then as everyone looked to the Captain, who moved swiftly to nip any discontent in the bud.

"These savages," he said, pointing to what remained of the dead natives, "boarded our ship in war canoes, which means that they didn't come from very far away. We'll find their island and restore our supplies there." This seemed to reassure the crew, even though the natives who had survived the battle were already out of sight and no one aboard had marked which direction they had fled.

As I ruminated upon this new problem, the sound of a groan at my back arrested my attention. When I turned, I saw that the savage whom I had thought I had slain was yet alive. I immediately informed the Captain of this stroke of good fortune and watched as he and Matt Eliot climbed the stairs to where the savage lay on the deck. "Matt, you speak the lingos of these parts," said the Captain, "see if the brute can understand any of 'em."

The first mate grunted some words which the native at once understood. I was not too surprised at this, as past experience had taught me many of the native populations of the Pacific Islands were related in some way and shared much the same language.

The native grunted something back which Eliot translated as the whereabouts of his own island. The Captain smiled, then stopped. He had noticed something around the native's neck and, stooping, ripped it from about his throat. The savage made as if to stop him, but thought better of it. The Captain looked closely at the object, which seemed to be a necklace made of finely worked gold. Grinning, the Captain handed it around the knot of crewmen that had surrounded the native, who still reclined on the deck.

After passing from hand to hand, the necklace finally came into my possession. It was very fine indeed, not heavy. And the man who had shaped the figures on it could have made his way in any civilized city in the world. Upon closer examination, I could see that the figures etched in the gold were strangely amphibian men who seemed to be in the form of frogs or fish, as well as fish with legs and arms, emerging from the waves. There were other, less recognizable shapes, but by then the short hairs on the back of my neck had begun to rise and I sensed that there was something not right with the native imagery: something beyond simple pagan iconography, for I had seen much of that in my travels and none had ever affected me in the manner that the necklace had. I handed it absent-mindedly to Worthy, and when I brought my attention back to the small drama before me I could see that the Captain's ploy of handing the necklace to the men had worked as he had planned. The lust of riches was plain in their eyes, and none seemed to be as disturbed as I was about it.

"Ask him where he got that there necklace," ordered the Captain. When Eliot reported that the native refused to tell, the Captain became exceeding wroth and told Eliot to threaten the native with bodily harm if the information was not forthcoming. Again the native refused to comply, and the Captain ordered Barnston, the second mate, to take him below with two other men and use what physical persuasion they wished to convince him to cooperate. The broad smiles that creased those crewmen's faces needed no explanation. They were the sort who took pleasure in the sound of other men's bones breaking. I did not hesitate to protest the action and was surprised to find that I had an ally in Matt Eliot, but our suasions were wasted on the Limb of Satan, who confidently asked the rest of the men if they felt the way I did. They bellowed their negative reply and the issue was settled.

A short time later, the second mate returned and he and Eliot were beckoned by the Captain to follow him to his cabin. There they remained for some time until emerging around noon. The first and second mates split up, bellowing orders to the crew to trim the sails and bring the *Queen* about.

With our experienced hands, it did not take much time to put words into action, and presently we found ourselves bearing a course to the south-southeast. Every eye aboard strained ahead to be the first to spy our destination, even though every one knew the honor would fall to the man in the crow's nest. The sea was still as glass and smooth as it had been during the night, and a preternatural calm had suddenly settled in the air itself so that our sails soon went limp. Anxious to arrive at the island the native had spoken about, the Captain ordered a boat lowered with sixteen men to man its oars. A line was made fast in the bow, and the men soon were bending their backs and singing a seaman's dirge to the calls of the second mate. Slowly, they pulled the *Queen* along toward the horizon, and presently, as the afternoon waned, a great tower of birds could be seen wheeling in the sky like a living tornado. It was a strange sight even if we had not been away from land for so long, and it elicited much excited discussion until the lookout in the crow's nest called out "Land ho!" Instantly every member of the crew followed the direction of the man's pointing arm, and, dimly, a dark smudge began to resolve itself on the horizon. The men in the boat began to pull with renewed vigor, but it was clear that it would be after nightfall before we arrived within the vicinity of the island. When the time came, the Captain ordered a halt and the boat brought back. The anchor was thrown overboard and the ship made fast for the night. It would remain for the dawn to see us make our final approach to the island.

That night, most of the crew slept abovedecks with their weapons close at hand. I found it difficult to sleep at my position aft with the regular scuff of Captain Marsh as he paced the deck throughout the night. He seemed more anxious then he usually was when near to closing a deal. Sometime in the dark nearest dawn, I gave up attempting to sleep and approached the port rail. The faintest tinge of the approaching sun glowed dimly near the horizon, silhouetting the shape of the island. We were within a mile of it and already I could tell it rose steeply out of the water at that point. As the light increased, its bulk began to take on more detail. At first, I guessed the irregularity of its summit was due to a thick overhang of jungle growth, and, indeed, my surmise soon proved accurate and more. Great tendrils of leafy vines festooned the face of the grayish cliffs much as we are told of the hanging gardens of cursed Babylon. Then, as the sun rose fully into view, and as more of the crew joined me at the rail, the full wonderment of those cliffs was revealed to us. Far from being a single sheet of rock, the cliffs were actually a grouping of colossal stones, tumbled as if from a great height untold ages before. It betokened some sort of volcanic activity on the island some time in the past. But as the sun slowly moved its rays over the surface of those stones, their true disposition became startlingly apparent. Many of them sported the likenesses of men. They proved to be great stone effigies whose visages stared unseeing and eternally out to sea, as if waiting for something. I had seen such handiwork before in the Ponapes, but never dreamed the practice could have reached to other islands. Also, these stone faces were of more intricate work, as if they were the originals of which those on other, better known isles were but crude copies.

Others of the crew were also marveling at the discovery even as the Captain ordered another sixteen men to take their places in the row boat. "Ole Limb o' Satan ain't wastin' any time is he, Hosiah?" said Worthy at my elbow.

"He has the scent of gold in his nostrils," I replied, without taking my gaze from the stone effigies.

Worthy saw my stare. "Seen things like those once in Easter Island, somewheres east of these parts," he said.

"There as well?" I observed and told him about my own experiences.

"Reckon there's some connection?" asked Worthy. I shrugged.

"I would not be surprised. How else could such widely separated peoples participate in identical endeavors to rival the labors of Hercules?"

"Aye, it would seem ta be a colossal waste o' time for folks otherwise dirt poor."

The *Queen* moved forward inch by inch as Eliot called out the soundings. The water there reached only fifteen or twenty feet before a hidden reef reached up dangerously for the vulnerable hull of the ship. The Captain continued to push it farther to the east, circling the island, and when the soundings finally reached a safe depth, an inviting, sandy stretch of beach was clearly visible on the island. By this time, the strange carvings had sunk from view and the island's elevation had flattened until the surf could wash far up onto the beach. An impenetrable jungle edged the sand, hazy in the morning's growing heat, and a mist still clung to the land farther back where it sloped up to the hidden heights. With those heights cleared, the birds that we had spied the day before were again in view, but apparently were not centered upon the island before us, but at some point beyond it. Still towed by the boat, the *Queen* was maneuvered through an opening in the coral reef that ringed the island. Members of the crew manned long poles to either side, probing the depths for unexpected coral projections that could rip open the ship's hull in seconds. Eliot gave the word that we had cleared the reef, and the rowers were ordered back to the ship. The *Queen* drifted with the tide a bit before the Captain signaled for the anchor to let fly. It was done and the ship made secure.

The Captain wasted no time in having the captive brought from below decks. The poor wretch had to be supported between two crewmen. His face was bruised, and I could see two fingers had obviously been broken. At the Captain's order, Eliot put some questions to him to which he nodded and grumbled a reply. Presently, a boat was lowered, and the Captain, together with Eliot and the captive islander, ordered a handful of other men including myself to clamber aboard. We headed for the distant beach.

Although the journey to the beach was short, it seemed longer as we pulled our oars, our backs to the land and only the comfortable familiarity of the *Queen* to be seen on the bosom of the sea. The captive managed to keep up a stream of commentary at the instigation of Eliot, who translated for him. It seemed that the people native to this island were resented in no small way by the inhabitants of the surrounding waters. There also seemed to be some undercurrent of revulsion in the words Eliot translated; whether it was the inadequacy of the translation, or something actually intended by our savage companion, I could not tell, but in any case, there appeared to be a subtle element of disgust in the words, but at what, I could not have said at the time.

Then, just as I noticed the swirl of sand in the water about my oar ends, the boat scudded into the soft beach. We all debarked and hauled it the rest of the way out of the surf until it was securely above the water line. I turned then and received my first close-up look at the island. It resembled any number of other such islands I had visited in the past with its fringe of jungle growth and gently curving beach. Suddenly, there was movement in that jungle, and there appeared a small group of dusky savages arrayed in primitive implements of war and no less bizarrely painted than those who had attacked the *Queen* the night before. They were in all respects like those others except in one: They were decorated in various and sundry articles of gold. Necklaces, armlets and ankle rings. Ear rings and finger rings and head bands. The crewmen around me began to mumble in eager delight until the Captain ordered them to keep silent and display as little interest in the gold as possible. Shrewd as ever, even in this first, uncertain contact, the Captain then ordered the trade goods we had brought from the *Queen* taken out of the boat and laid on the beach. Soon, the newcomers approached warily and after glancing interestedly at the various colored cloths and beads on display, their leader, who we later learned was named Walakea, pointed at our captive and said something.

"He wants to know what this man is doing in our company, sir," said Eliot.

"Tell them the whole story, Matt," instructed the Captain, "but leave out our interest in the gold." Eliot turned and did as he was told.

Walakea said something again, and Eliot said, "He says this man's people are their traditional enemies and demands to take possession of him."

The Captain hesitated not at all. "Then give him to him." Eliot said something to Walakea and signaled the men holding our captive to give him over. He was taken roughly in hand and marched off into the jungle by two of the natives. Then followed the introduction and the discovery that rudimentary communications could be had with sign language. The natives, whom we later determined to be a tribe of the Kanaka, were enthralled by the goods we brought, being completely ignorant of the products of civilization. What was more, they had no compunction about trading their golden baubles for it. But the art of the trade does not involve coming directly to the point. A roundabout method is often called for in order to arrive at the desired end. Consequently, the Captain began trading for other, less desirable items among which were small, carven stone effigies, miniature versions of those giant heads on the cliff sides. An invitation to their village soon followed and when we returned to the *Queen* the Captain informed the crew of the celebration Walakea planned for our reception the next day. Knowledge of the easy trading on the beach fired the men's excitement and their greed and, I must admit, my own for the anticipated meeting.

The night passed uneventfully. The next day, leaving a minimal crew aboard ship, the Captain led the remainder of us to shore, where we were met by one of Walakea's warriors. We were led inland a few hundred feet to where the village stood beside a small, deep stream of fresh water. At least two dozen canoes lay pulled up to the narrow beach there while the village proper extended through the nearby jungle and straggled almost down to where the boats lay. The village was a collection of grass huts, each perched on sturdy palm logs, typical for the South Seas. Pools of sunlight shone here and there where the natives had cleared parts of the forest. But the people themselves, of whom there appeared to be many hundreds, were decidedly queer looking. Admittedly, there were some, including Walakea and his wives, that were quite handsome as natives in those parts are judged, but the greater majority seemed wan and pallid with an odd, scaly texture to their skin. In addition, all alike suffered from bad posture, seeming to find it more comfortable to stoop than stand erect. Several more of the golden ornaments were in evidence but not so many as we had expected judging by the group we had met on the beach the day before.

In the center of the village, a great feast had been laid out for us with every sort of native fruit and vegetable and a wide variety of sea food. Indeed, there was so much that even the tight-lipped Captain Marsh was moved to comment on it to Walakea, who shrugged and indicated it was thanks to the beneficence of their gods. As we took our places at the table, the exotic strains of native music welcomed us. The women passed among us with wooden plates stacked high with steaming native viands and succulent fruits. From where I sat, I could see that the Captain lost no time in getting Eliot to sit with him beside Walakea to begin the bartering. I could tell by his demeanor that the chief was not disposed to discuss the matter, but that did not dissuade the Captain from continuing his efforts periodically thoughout the meal. By the end of the fifth course, most of those present were becoming rapidly satiated and a sort of torpor began to set in. Native and white man alike lay back, some to sleep and some even to seek out the pleasures of the native women. I continued to study the Captain as he plied Walakea for information, and I could tell that Marsh was already stitching together a rudimentary understanding of the native tongue, needing Eliot less and less.

I also noticed the singular lack of any elderly members of the tribe; in fact there were none. There also seemed to be fewer young people than would be expected in a village of that size.

It was about then that Worthy came back from somewhere I knew not, slightly drunk on the native beer, and threw himself down next to me. "Look what I have," he said, holding out a gold head-band to me. "Traded it for my brass shoe buckles," he said. I looked at it at first with envy but then, as I observed its markings more closely, with vague repulsion. Whereas the previous pieces I had seen were decorated with froglike men, the object I held in my hand had the figures of less distinct aquatic-looking creatures in obvious postures of sexual coupling with humans.

Disgusted, I threw it back at Worthy, swearing, "I will have nothing to do with such unnatural idolatry! The rest of the crew can keep what gold it acquires here, but for my part, I will remain satisfied with my honest wages." Here, Worthy looked at the etchings and shrugged, his greed apparently getting the better of his Christian upbringing. From that moment on I grew increasingly wary of the island people and their degraded interests. As the evening progressed, I began to notice their strange little idols everywhere, and when I next looked to find the Captain, he was gone together with Eliot and Walakea. The unaccustomed surfeit of food proved too much for me, and I rose drowsily from the table and made my way to one of the huts assigned us. The rude pallets, though no doubt no worse than our hosts slept on, were scarcely more comfortable than our bunks aboard ship. But, as they say, weariness is the best pillow.

It was only the next day when I saw Marsh and Eliot again; or rather, I saw Eliot. He was sitting alone beneath a palm tree near the beach when I came upon him. Naturally I was curious as to how he and the Captain had fared with Walakea, so I made bold to walk up to him to ask. Ordinarily there would be no reason for a first mate to confide in a mere member of the crew, but I have since felt that he may have remembered my stand against the Captain's torturing of the native prisoner and there seen a kindred spirit. In any case, he had a story he needed to share with someone and perhaps I was the most convenient. It was a story so outlandish, so bizarre, and yet so hideously obvious, that it would shake my perception of the world to the very core and test the mettle of my Christian faith.

I approached Eliot that fateful day and casually asked him if he and the Captain had made any progress in their talks with the chief. Eliot grunted and remained silent for a moment, then said, "Hosiah, I have observed you for a good portion of this voyage, and I think I might have your measure. We think alike in many ways, and I can see you have much book learning about you. You think straight, not like the other members of the crew. Hosiah, what if I told you that the real order of things is not quite what we suppose it is?" I must have made the expected facial expression, because he continued.

"Have you noticed the queer looks of the natives on this here island? The way their big eyes seldom blink? Or the slippery feel of their skin? Hosiah, the carvings on those golden ornaments and statuettes are not the figurings of ignorant savages, but the literal truth their own eyes have seen and, God help me, *my own as well!* When I left yesterday with the Captain, Walakea had already hinted to us about how his people acquired their gold. At first, I thought it was just more heathen superstition trying to explain things they could not understand, but then Walakea showed us the island. No, not this one, but another on the lee side of this one. We boarded one of his war canoes and, accompanied by a handful of his most trusted warriors, were taken downstream to the sea. From there, we skirted the shore until we came into sight of another, smaller island. Only a few hundred yards of water separated it from this one and, at that proximity, I could see that it seemed less an island than a jumble of oddly carved stones. Overhead whirled that mighty column of birds we had seen from far off. The stones were odd, I say, not because of the well-worn carvings of various sea creatures that dominated them, but because, for some reason, they were hard to see. Not with distance, but because of their shapes. It was as if a man could get an idea of their shape out of the corner of his eyes but when he tried to look at them straight, they blurred somehow. In any case, right then, I started feeling that we may have stumbled into something we had not bargained for.

"As we drew nearer, I could see that much of the rubble was buried in black silt, suggesting that the island had once been beneath the sea and perhaps had been hurled up sometime in the past. When I questioned Walakea on this he confirmed my opinion, saying it had appeared from the sea one morning when his grandfather had been chief. At that time, he said, his people had been extremely poor and they had made an excursion to the island hoping to find something of value to trade with their neighbors. What they found were strange, fishlike creatures, like those depicted in the carvings. Of course I dismissed the chief's remarks as ignorant exaggeration, but, to my surprise, Captain Marsh nodded and took the whole matter seriously. He began to question Walakea in word and in sign and grew increasingly excited as the chief continued to speak. According to Walakea, his forebears had learned to communicate with the island creatures and soon arrived at a mutually beneficial agreement. In return for their worship and the sacrifice of a certain number of the tribe's young men and women, the sea things ensured the Kanakas plentiful supplies of fish and a steady stream of golden artifacts.

"Well, we reached the island at last, and on closer examination, I could see that many of the carvings, besides the half-fish, half-manlike things, consisted of other less familiar creatures: all tentacles and ropy filaments. I thank God that those carvings were as old as they were, because if they had been any more distinct, I think I may have lost my mind. As it was I reeled as Walakea steered us toward a single gargantuan block while his men pulled thick strands of old and rotted seaweed from about its face. When they had finished, they all fell to their knees, and the chief led them in some kind of prayer. I noticed then how the image on that great stone resembled those of the small idols the natives possessed back in the village. This was the image of their god, a god who answered their prayers in a most concrete way, a way easily understood and appreciated by a poor and backward people. I actually found myself feeling jealous of them! I must admit that the thought did not immediately strike me as absurd; it was all a part of the hideous nature of the situation. After a few minutes my senses returned and I was able to rethink my feelings. Of course it was all absurd! Their god could not be a real god. I thought I had the problem settled in my mind until Walakea revealed the ultimate secret about the Kanakas' relationship with the sea-things.

"We re-entered the canoe and paddled back to the main island, but instead of taking us back to his village, Walakea took us to the opposite side of the neighboring stream where a second village site stood. It seemed deserted, but as we soon learned, all those who lived there lurked indoors. We approached a lone hut and Walakea led us inside. I followed the Captain, stooping to pass under the door frame; when I straightened up again, my eyes fell on a sight I hope I never see again. Even with the interior of the hut in shadow, I could make out the features of the figure before me. Have you ever caught sight of some awful freak in a madhouse or that a family locked away in the attic room? Something that should have been killed at birth? Remember how you felt? Didn't you ask yourself how the human frame could have gone so wrong? That will begin to show you some idea of what I felt when I saw what was in that hut! It had to be human, I couldn't deny that, even though I wished I could! But, by far, it was more fish than man! It had all the same queer deformations as most of the villagers, but they were all horribly exaggerated; the eyes were great, unblinking orbs without pupils, the hands and feet were webbed, and the skin, where the light fell on it, glistened in thousands of iridescent scales. What must have been rudimentary gills opened and closed at the side of its misshapen head as if the creature had difficulty breathing. Entirely hairless, it crouched on the dirt floor staring at us with the emotionlessness of a fish.

"I was repulsed and even the Captain took a step backward. Then Walakea told us the final horror. After his people had been sacrificing their youths to them for some time, the sea-creatures began to tire of them and made a further suggestion: they wished the opportunity to mate with members of the tribe. At first, the idea was resisted, but soon they were persuaded to comply. Over the years, almost the entire tribe had been tainted with the fish blood, thus the queer looks we noticed among the villagers. But the looks did not come all at once; they came over time. When a villager advanced in years, the changes began to come over him faster and faster until, at great old age, he looked like the creature I saw in the hut. Soon after that, the urge to go to the sea would become too strong; he would be unable to resist it and would join the sea-creatures beneath the waves, probably never seen on the shore again."

I began to protest his story, to suggest alternative explanations for what he had seen, though they sounded pathetic even in my own ears. Eliot shook his head.

"It's all too frighteningly true, Hosiah," he said. "But the sight of that fish-thing was not the worst of it. Do you know what the natives received in return for their bestial mixing? Immortality! You don't understand, do you? They have gods who not only answer their prayers, I mean, truly answer them, but who even grant them eternal life! Without having to die forever! What argument is there against it and in favor of our own Christian religion? We are only promised our eternal reward and we go to the death bed in secret fear and trembling. And mostly our prayers go unanswered, though we never admit it. Honestly, Hosiah, can you deny it? That is the most insidious fact about the whole thing; do you think that men, ruled mostly by greed and lust, could long resist the lure of such a practical faith? Yes, yes, I know it's all preposterous. They are not true gods, just mortal creatures like us, but with preternaturally long lives. But I say to you, they could easily prey on the ignorance and selfishness of many men. They must remain here, unknown."

I suggested an immediate return to the *Queen*, but he shook his head.

"The Captain, unbeliever as he is, is the first of those fools to embrace these devils. Even now, he speaks seriously with Walakea on the whys and wherefores of their worship. Oh, he does not believe in the creatures' godhood any more than I do, but his greed yet leads him into a venture that will damn not only his own questionable soul but those of anyone else he introduces to the secret.

"The Captain will surely work on the men's greed to win them over to his way of thinking. He will swear them to silence and you will see, a regular run to the Kanakas for trade gold will become an accepted fact back in New England."

I protested that I would take no such blasphemous oath.

"I believe you, Hosiah, but are you prepared for the consequences? I have sailed for Captain Marsh for many years; I feel I know him as well as any man. You saw the lengths he was willing to go to force the native warrior to talk? Believe me, he will display little more compunction to *keep* you from talking. Would you like to remain behind on this island? Perhaps to end up as another sacrifice to those creatures?"

I shuddered and shook my head.

"Then we both will take whatever oath is demanded of us and keep our mouths shut. There's no shame in it as it will be a vow made under duress. Our real problem will be in trying to find a way to thwart the Captain should he decide to work directly with those sea-creatures himself. Aye, he would do that if it meant cutting out the middle man and increasing his profits. Already, when I left him, he was working on the chief to show him how to call up the monsters."

I asked him how we could do such a thing; who would believe such a wild tale back in Innsmouth?

"I have an idea about that too," he said. "Most folks here are tainted by the fish-blood except for Walakea's immediate family. He had to stay clean of it; otherwise there would be no opportunity of intermarrying with the daughters of neighboring chiefs. And there's one other person that is untainted. . . . "

"The witch doctor!" I said.

"Aye, there must be a reason why he has managed to hold on to his humanity while everyone else has succumbed. We'll go and see him." At that, he rose and began making his way back to the first village. I followed him, not knowing what else to do. In truth, I did not even know if I believed all that he had recounted to me. It was all so utterly fantastic, completely incredible! And yet, I had seen the queer look of the villagers, wondered at the meaning of the disgusting carvings on the golden ornaments and the inspiration of the tiny idols. In my mind they added up to irrefutable evidence of Eliot's story. In addition, a strange disquiet had been building in me ever since our arrival in these distant waters, and I was loath to remain oblivious of any threat to myself or the *Queen*.

It did not take long to locate the witchdoctor's hut. It stood alone a good ways off in the surrounding forest, and one smelled it long before seeing it. The remains of dismembered animals lay all about the site, and drying and rotting fish hung from the structure's outer walls. We called out and received a reply from within. Eliot led the way inside, and I followed, vainly holding my breath against the overpowering stench. The witchdoctor himself was one of the ugliest humans I had ever seen, but even then he seemed more pleasant-looking than the tainted creatures his brethren had become. His hair was a tangled, dirty mass, and his skin was smeared in fish oil. He was naked but for a loin clout about his hips. As he squatted to the side of the hut, I noticed one thing immediately; there was no sign of the island's gold nor any aquatic idols. Eliot spoke to him and must have received a positive reply because he bade me sit. I sat cross-legged as far away from the old man as I could as Eliot sat alongside me but a little ahead. He leaned forward and asked the conjure man a question. The following is the translation he gave me of his conversation with the witch man, who barked a sort of laugh before he spoke.

"He says he knew we would come around to see him sooner or later. That any normal men, even sickly looking white men, would be repulsed by what had happened to his people and be compelled to seek out their own kind. He is laughing at his own joke, and I cannot say as I blame him. We white men always think ourselves the superior of other races, and now we can see just how closely related we really are to them. Our differences amount to nothing compared to the gulf between us and those 'Deep Ones', as he calls them. Aye, he has a name for those creatures whose likenesses I saw carved on that island. He says everything Walakea told me is true, and I gather he and the chief are not on friendly terms. It seems when the Deep Ones began mating with the Kanakas, his forebears held out and kept their line pure. Seems the medicine man, here, is jealous of the Deep Ones. Ever since making their unholy bargain with the creatures, the villagers have had little need for his services. They get all they want from the Deep Ones. These days, he ekes out a living by working a few cures for bellyache and infection. I asked him if there is anything the Deep Ones fear and he said how do I figure he and his father and his grandfather were able to remain pure-blooded all these years? The Deep Ones fear only two things he says: someone or something called Clooloo, I think, and a certain kind of symbol of things called the Old Ones."

By this time, I was a bit confused, no doubt the result of a mixture of Eliot's inadequate translation and the old wizard's ignorance. Who were these Deep Ones and Clooloo? They seemed nothing less than the embodiment of the Philistine fish god, Dagon, abominated in scripture. There was a pause in the conversation as the old man reached into a pouch and pulled out a small roughly star-shaped stone. He showed it to us by the fading light of afternoon, and I could see the simple marking of what looked like a crooked cross on its face. I had seen something like it on articles imported from India. Quickly, he returned it to its place and resumed speaking.

"He says he can tell that we are still having a difficult time believing his story, but that perhaps he can offer us more proof." The wizard stood and preceded us out of the hut. The sun was well down on the horizon when we started up a path different than the one we had followed earlier. As we walked, it grew darker, and soon I could hear the sound of the surf in the darkness. We came upon a rock-strewn beach. The old fellow bade us be silent on pain of our lives and indicated a spot laden with concealing underbrush. A hundred yards or so in front of us, the beach was well-lit with many torches, and Walakea stood there with a great number of his people. The light of the torches flickered over the incoming waves. In the distance, I could make out the dim outline of the island of the Deep Ones. Suddenly Eliot took my arm in a painful grasp and hissed a warning. He inclined his chin toward the crowd on the beach, and for a moment I did not see what he was attempting to point out to me. Then it was my turn to stiffen as I saw Captain Marsh step out from behind one of the warriors and take his place beside Walakea. The witch doctor nudged us and pointed out to sea.

At first I thought he meant for us to observe the island in the distance, but as my eyes adjusted to the weak torch light, I saw that there was something else out in the water between us and the island. It was a jagged log, or something, that thrusted itself a good six feet from the surface of the water. There was an irregularity upon it that I suddenly saw move.

"It is that native prisoner the Captain gave to Walakea yesterday," whispered Eliot in my ear. "They've got him tied to that log. They intend the poor creature to drown in the incoming tide."

Unfamiliar stars began to twinkle overhead, and a dull glow was all that remained of the setting sun in the west. All was silent except for the lapping waves when Walakea began intoning a guttural prayer. Soon his followers began to join in. There was a disturbance on the surface of the water a little distance from the bound native. I tried to focus my eyes upon it, but failed to see what was happening in detail. I thank God to this day that I could *not* see it! Slowly, the disturbance grew in violence until the captive ceased his struggles in momentary confusion. Then the motion halted and all was calm once more. I had turned a moment to ask Eliot about the phenomenon when a blood-curdling scream pierced the gathering gloom. My head shot around in a flash, and I could see the captive struggling mightily against his bonds to no effect. All the time his screams continued, melding with the droning chant of the group on shore. Then, if possible, the man's screams became even more shrill as his body seemed to stiffen. I saw something break the surface of the water around the native's legs. It slid slowly upward, its hide glistening wetly in the torchlight. I watched transfixed as the thing inched its way ever higher, now to the man's thighs, now his waist. It seemed against the descending darkness that it was a giant slug, as its movement suggested an arching and contracting to help pull its bulk along.

The screams continued until they seemed to become a part of the universe, a natural noise like that of the wind or the surf. Then the gelatinous mass seemed to begin to tug, to drag its massive weight downward. The native's bonds snapped with a sound clearly heard even over his screams as his body began to slide downward into the water. By then, his mind must have been completely emptied by the horror that had hold of him. I gulped heavily and breathed, I think, for the first time since the screams had begun. Another snap and the native, one arm flailing, slid beneath the waves as his screams bubbled into silence. The only remaining sign of the horrid scene was a shiny slick left upon the upright log. Dimly I heard the chanting die out and saw the crowd turn back toward the village. I do not know how long it was before I was shaken by Eliot and pulled back along that path to the witch doctor's hut, but I remember watching Eliot working frantically through the rest of the night with the old man's inadequate tools to reproduce the Old One's signs on a few smooth stones. The conjure man's ironic chuckling, tinged not at all with madness, will remain with me the rest of my days.

As expected, Captain Marsh demanded an oath of silence from the crew. His explanation, appealing to their greed, was smooth to be sure, and Eliot and I forced back our reluctance and swore with the rest. Eliot was unable to completely control his voice as it shook slightly, and his hands would never lose the ague-like trembling they acquired that night when we witnessed the thing rise from the sea. For myself, I think that I betrayed no outward signs of the terror I felt. Perhaps I was paralyzed with fear.

Thus the long voyage progressed until, early one morning, just after two bells, the cry most dreaded by seamen echoed below: "All hands on deck!" Immediately, Eliot and I joined the rush to the top, spilling outdoors into harsh moonlight and a placid sea. We were far southward by then, in the currents that skirt the Pole. The Captain was on deck, smothered in his cold weather gear and pointing out to port.

I moved to the rail with the rest of the men and looked in the direction the Captain was pointing. At first I saw nothing in the gloom, then a sound of disturbed water broke the silence and one of the men shouted and pointed, too. Instantly, every head turned. There was activity in the water about half a league out, a small whirlpool of swirling water that indicated something of immense bulk had recently submerged. We all leaned just a little bit more forward then as whatever the thing was breached the surface once more. It slid wetly toward the southward and I could see immense ridges or rings that segmented its length as though it were a gigantic serpent or worm. I stiffened and recoiled at the sight, my hand immediately seeking the comforting shape of the stone in my pocket as I recognized the contours of the monstrous thing worshiped by the damned Kanakas. In the meantime, immediately upon catching sight of the creature, the entire crew reeled back as one, some crying out to the Lord, others cursing, but all deeply frightened.

"It's just like in the Book o' Jonah!" someone cried out, echoing my own racing thoughts. I looked about for the kindred soul and imagine my surprise to find that it was none other than Captain Marsh himself! Amazed, I listened as he harangued the crew, controlling their panic, with biblical allusions and assurances of the Lord's mercy until his true intentions revealed themselves. "The thing's only lookin' fer sustenance," the Captain said. "There cain't be much food for a creature so big hereabouts. But still, something had to bring it up from the deep. Someone among you must have aroused its wrath through sin and unbelief." With that, his eyes fell squarely upon mine, and in a flash I saw the Captain's evil plan. He himself had called up the thing using the idolatrous methods of the Kanaka islanders and then had made the suggestion of offering the creature a sacrifice when he knew the crew were already resentful of Eliot and me. Perhaps the Lord was yet with me that night, however; how else to explain the timeliness of my next words in that situation?

"But Cap'n Marsh," I said, not unmindful of the irony of trading scriptural quips with Old Limb of Satan himself, "don't forget that Scripture says each seafarer called upon his God, and I will call on Jehovah, even as Jonah did! And thus let it be known who is God!"

Then something even more amazing and terrifying than the nearby sea beast followed: Lightning crackled amid a cloudless sky and the stone in my pocket became almost too hot to hold. I bit my lip and continued to grasp it firmly as the sea off the port side was churned into a gleaming froth in the throes of the maddened beast. At last, the monster seemed to disappear, and the sea returned to normal, and the crew, their resentment for Eliot and me temporarily forgotten in the relief of the moment, dispersed amid fearful mutterings. Eliot and I remained behind, the comforting feel of the Old Ones' sign still warm in my hand. The look he gave me indicated he, too, had resorted to the protection of the stone, and I was on the verge of voicing my guilt at our reliance on such idolatrous and pagan objects over that of the true God when I noticed the form of the Captain where he still stood at the rail. His eyes burned hatefully into mine and I knew for certain my life was not worth a penny aboard the *Queen*. Muttering, Captain Marsh turned and retired to his cabin, leaving Eliot and me to ruminate upon the strange protection obviously afforded us by the star-shaped stones in our possession.

How we endured the interminable agony of the long voyage around Cape Horn is more than I can explain here. Where once the sea had beckoned me with its gentle swell and even violent temper, now it struck me with ineluctable fear and loathing. Its boundless reaches and mysterious depth filled me with terror and, although there were no further attempts by the Captain to rid himself of Eliot and me, we took to spending as much time as we could belowdecks. At last, though, the shores of home hove into view, and the *Sumatra Queen* arrived at Innsmouth again.

But even back among the civilized haunts of men, I could not find peace. Almost as soon as we arrived, Captain Marsh began his damnable crusade to convert the citizenry of Innsmouth to the ways of the Kanaka religion. Even I had to admire the old seaman's canny arguments; such casuistry would have impressed even the most wily Jesuit. For some, he promised riches from gods who rewarded their worshipers with items they could use such as gold and silver, and for others he used the insidious and tempting arguments first promulgated by Thomas Paine and Ethan Allen. Each man had his weakness and Marsh had no compunction in exploiting it. He debated the local clergy, sometimes pointing out their hypocrisy and other times demanding of the congregation why they allowed themselves to be led by these men, why could they not think for themselves? Compelled to witness against such unscrupulous tactics, Eliot and I spoke out at every opportunity. In the public rooms, in the churches, and on the street corners we spoke to whomever would listen, but it was difficult to combat a man who could pass out bits of gold. In increasing numbers and regularity, men began to meet in cellars and basements and then in homes and halls to participate in the new rites of worship. Whom Marsh could not convert, he bought with gold. Thus he was able to drive first the clergy and then those citizens who refused to follow the new belief from the town with the help of its own elected officials. At last, there was no more Eliot and I could do, and it was decided that I would journey to Boston and seek help from Commonwealth or Federal officials who might at least act upon Innsmouth's official corruption.

It was with great trepidation that I deserted my companion, but it was felt to be necessary by the both of us that I did. In Boston, I met with resistance to my imprecations. It was out of their jurisdiction, it was none of their affair, and there was no evidence, they said. I spent days wandering the cobbled streets searching for anyone who might listen to my tale, but no one did. Suspecting that Marsh's gold had arrived there before me, I considered moving on to Washington, but by then I was growing fretful of Eliot's lack of communication. Finally, some weeks after my arrival in the capital, I gave up and began my return journey to Innsmouth.

It was on my final night on the road, after I had arranged for a room in Arkham, that I had the dream. In it, I found myself on a vast field of ice and snow. Before me, in the misty distance, rose a range of snow-covered mountains, and at my back was a great empty ship held fast in the ice.

Snowflakes fluttered in the cold air and, suddenly, there was the strangest shape I had ever seen erect before me. It was cone-shaped and somewhat taller than a man, and its plastic make-up seemed undisturbed by the weather. But the strangeness of the event was not borne out of my encountering it in those frigid climes but rather, the shape of what I presumed to be its head. For that member was shaped much like the Old Ones' sign I still clung to in my pocket. Could this creature actually be an Old One? Then I saw it twist about at its mid-section as if it intended to indicate some point to the side. I looked and beheld the figure of my friend, Eliot, as he lay in the snow, his cold body partially buried in the drifting stuff. Now, at last, a shiver passed along my body as the meaning of the scene bore itself upon me.

Upon awakening, I tried to convince myself of the essential meaninglessness of dreams, but however I tried, I could not shake off the feeling that it had been a kind of premonition or warning. It was not an hour later, as I had breakfast in the tavern below my room, that I learned the sad fate of my friend.

A local resident, enjoying a pint of rum at the inn, overheard me say that I was bound for Innsmouth and asked me what I might know about a lynching that had occurred there not two days before. It was from him that I learned Matt Eliot was dead. It seemed that the affair had begun with a simple theft when Marsh had goaded the town prankster, a boy named Zadok Allen, to steal a strange stone Eliot always kept on his person. I did not say so to my informant, but the theft of the Old Ones' sign would have left Eliot unprotected, as Marsh surely knew. It was after that, said the man, that Marsh accused Eliot of all kinds of foul deeds, whipping the town's residents into a self-righteous frenzy that resulted in his being lynched.

With this crushing news, all the hope and enthusiasm I may have had for combating Marsh and his followers evaporated. I paid for the man's drink and left the inn. There was no coach scheduled to go southward until the next morning, but I could not bring myself to remain in such close proximity to the scene of such a depressing turn of events. It was a long and lonely walk back to Pepperell.

Although I have not had the opportunity since then to keep abreast of events in the larger world, or even of those closer to home, I have still heard news from time to time from the vicinity of Innsmouth, including its rise in prosperity even as it shuns outsiders. I have heard it said that Captain Marsh made many subsequent voyages to the Kanakas, always returning laden with strange worked gold and sometimes even in the company of certain of its natives.

For myself, I have resided here on my family's farm in Pepperell since the day I returned after hearing of the fate of poor Eliot. In that time, my loathing of open water has only increased, further circumscribing my movements. From time to time, I seek to test those fears, but whenever I approach a body of water I balk and begin to tremble violently; I begin to perspire and an urge to turn and run overcomes me. The nearby Nashua River is a terror to me and the smallest brook takes all my fortitude to cross. Consequently, I mostly stay on the farm. I am safe here, and land-bound. Here, far from the sea, I am well out of reach, the long reach of Dagon or the Deep Ones or Clooloo or whatever it was I saw emerge from the waters that damned night in the Kanakas. I also have my charms, the Old Ones' signs; my Bible I read less frequently now. Why should I? The Old Ones have proven their power. The sign will ward off Dagon. I have them close at hand, here in my room. But Dagon's reach is not so long as that, is it? I cannot say, for the one thing I do know for certain is that the thing I saw that night drag the screaming native into the water, and again in the colder southern climes, was not a giant slug or enormous jellyfish nor even a serpent, *but merely the tip of an appendage belonging to an infinitely larger creature* that had been trapped beneath the sea for uncounted ages and now is not only free, but aware of our larger, more populated world here in America . . . .

About "Fleas of the Dragon"

All critical analyses of Lovecraft's work and the pessimism motivating it sooner or later run aground on two characters, Dr. Armitage in "The Dunwich Horror" and Dr. Willett in *The Case of Charles Dexter Ward.* Why? Because in both cases, the puny, negligible human race manages to stem the invading tide of the Outside. Come to think of it that's pretty much what always happens in *all* heroic adventure fiction: Evil is never more than set back temporarily even in a Superman comic book. So it will not do to say that Armitage's and Willett's victories are merely temporary, that the ax will fall anyway sooner later. Yeah, and maybe Lex Luthor will win sooner or later, too.

C. J. Henderson's occult detective, Teddy London, carries on that heroic tradition battling the Old Ones and their minions. In doing so he also dispels the old saw that a good vs. evil tale cannot be truly horrific.

"Fleas of the Dragon" happens between the fifth and sixth Teddy London novels, *The Only Thing to Fear* and *Some Things Come Back*. (These books appeared under the pseudonym "Robert Morgan" from Berkley Books. Planned Chaosium editions will restore the author's intended titles: *Steer'd by Fate* and *That Gives Us Absolution*.)

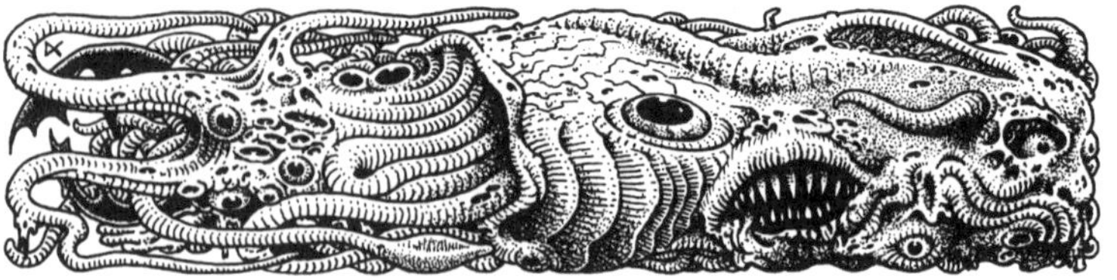

Fleas of the Dragon

by C. J. Henderson

"Study the past if you would divine the future."—Confucius

"So," started the man behind the desk, "tell us about your problem, Mr. Lin." Lin, a middle-aged Chinese-American with dark but thinning hair did not seem at ease with telling anyone about his problem, especially the man behind the desk. To the casual critic, his hesitation might have seemed bound up in some cultural bias—a delay born of the thought that an Anglo outsider might not understand what he had to relate.

Such was not the case. Mr. Lin had come to the London Agency with a number of assurances from within his own community that they would be quite open-minded to his problem. The trouble he was having was that, in truth, he did not actually know *what* his problem was.

"Mr. London," Lin finally began after too many nervous seconds had collected in the room, "I, I wish I knew what to say. I wish there were some easy path to it. But. . . ."

Lin held his hands up helplessly. Behind the desk, Theodore London suppressed the urge to push him for more. He had already caught the glint in his prospective client's eyes—the flashing shade of panicked fear that said the man had seen, or at least *felt,* things he could not describe—not without most people thinking him mad, anyway. London understood.

He had seen the look before.

The detective had seen the same terrified and confused tint in the eyes of a corpse torn apart by flying monsters . . . in those of a woman whose community had been attacked by vampires . . . as well as those of a man who had sold his soul to the devil . . . but most often he had seen it in the eyes that stared back at him every morning from his mirror.

In its time, the London Agency had run up against all manner of horrifics. Over the years its various members had battled winged lizard-men, cast the abomination known as Lilith back into the pit, destroyed a werewolf that had lived since the beginning of time, faced down the power of the fallen angel, and even thwarted the rapacious desires of more than one inter-dimension traveler.

They had, however, not done such without cost, which is what was putting London ill at ease with his prospective client.

In the years since the detective had first crossed over the line of conventional reality into the dark beyond, he had seen his oldest friend taken by a horror that eventually killed nearly two million people. He had witnessed the slaughter of more than a score of his friends, coworkers, and clients—including his blood brother—dead at the hands of an unstoppable beast which ripped the man's heart from his body just before it went on to butcher a score of his associates.

The London Agency had not once stood forth against the world's dark forces that it had not seen blood pouring—freely and deep. Years before, the detective had discovered that Fate had chosen him to be the world's protector. It was not a mantle he desired to wear on any kind of regular basis. Looking over his desk at Lin, feeling the depth of the fear bleeding off the man into the surrounding air, the detective knew his desires had once again come to naught.

He was not surprised. Despite all he and the others had done to keep the facts of their more unusual investigations private . . . word had a way of getting out. They did not like it, but there was not much they could do about it. Resigned, London waited quietly, knowing that sooner or later the man across his desk would find his nerve.

Then it would start again.

Across the desk, Kong Lin fought against the paralysis numbing him. Hammering at the fear freezing his brain, he retraced the steps that had led him to where he was. It had only been a few days earlier when he had let slip to a friend over drinks some of the "unusual" kinds of problems he had been having outside the city.

He had been spewing through a haze of drunken belligerence—had not remembered half of what he had said next day. But his friend had remembered it all. The tale Lin had told that night was whispered from one end of Manhattan's Chinatown to the other. In a matter of hours, the story had traveled the length of the ancient neighborhood from this person to that one, reaching friends of friends, *et cetera*, until finally it came to the ears of Mrs. Si Wan Lu.

The venerable old Mrs. Lu performed many duties for the Chinatown community at large—from reading the *Kow Cheem* to studying the *feng shui* of new property, advising prospective buyers and builders how to go about their business so as not to affect the sleep of the dragon westerners called the Earth. She was related to Mr. Lin in a distant, third-cousin manner. But it was enough. Mrs. Lu had seen disaster coming in her daily readings. Finding Lin's name attached to the coming darkness, she had sent word out from her advisory shop on Pell Street for him to be brought to her.

Once he had been found, he had been advised most strenuously to go to Mrs. Lu at once. Many people added their urgings, including several of his partners. Desperate, Lin had gone to Lu's shop. She had listened to his story, then told him she would look at his property. In the meantime, she told him, "You go London Agency. They take care you. I go see land. You go see them."

With that, his audience had been ended. One of her assistants had given the badly shaken man an address and suddenly Mr. Lin had found himself directed to midtown Manhattan—to the thirteenth floor of the Greeley Arcade. Fifteen short steps from the elevator had put him into the agency waiting room. Another ten had taken him into London's office.

And that was where he had hit a wall, one whose bricks were leavened with as much terror as clay, as much confusion as straw. London did not pretend to know what Lin's problem was, but he understood the man's difficulty in coming to the point. He knew all about "the things that are not there", and people's general embarrassment in confronting them.

Professor Zachary Goward, one of London's original comrades—now fallen—had coined the phrase initially, describing its subject as "those things we see out of the corners of our eyes, only to turn and find nothing. These shadows that travel in the far angles of our fields of vision—oh, they are unnerving beasties. They can freeze a man in his tracks, slow his blood, and numb his brain. And the reason is no more mystical than the getting of fire from the striking of a match."

A lover of the dramatic, Goward had then struck one of the large blue tips he kept near his ashtray, setting its flame to the bowl of the pipe. Then, after sucking in a great draught of blended smoke, he had let it roll back out over his lips and through his beard and moustache as he explained.

"The human brain is often compared to a computer. If we had computers advanced enough to store information in the form of electrical impulses held between water molecules, the analogy would be more complete—but still, the comparison is sound enough. You see—whenever we come across something we don't recognize, our brain sifts through everything we have on file—at the speed of light, of course—until it finds a match-up. How quickly we recognize something foreign depends both on how vast our experience is and in what order of importance we've arranged the files in our head."

Goward had been talking then about why people froze when they saw things beyond their comprehension. London knew the conversation applied to the man across his desk. Lin was certainly embarrassed by his fear, but that was not his problem. His lack of articulation sprang from the fact that he simply did not have the words to describe to the detective what he had come to him for. London let the man sit in discomfort, as the detective fought voices within his own head.

You could cut through this for him, you know, said one, to which another side of London's brain snapped back instantly, *Why? Why bother? Let someone else take the heat. Let someone else pile up their dead friends. I'm tired of it.*

I'm sick to death of it.

Oh, all right, came the first voice again. *Sure—ignore the problem. Good idea. That'll make whatever it is go away.*

Stop it, he told himself, knowing he had already lost.

Of course, of course. After all, Fate didn't bring this boob to us. N*oooooo, destiny didn't deliver him to our doorstep. There's got to be, what? A thousand other guys that could handle his problem.*

Right?

Leave me alone, Goddamnit, London snarled within his mind. Feeling another second of Lin's helplessness pass, he thought, *Why should I have to do this? Why do I have to drink from every cup that gets set on the bar? Why me?*

Because, answered another voice, one he heard so infrequently he had almost forgotten it, *there* is *no one else. If you do not take up this challenge now, you will only be forced to do so later.*

The detective froze, his life spinning before his eyes. There had been such a comfortable span since death had come to London last—snaking toward him and his from out of the shadows. He slammed away the twisting desires within him—to cry, to scream, to simply break down into the warm bosom of comforting hysterics. Knowing, though, that such could not bring him even temporary relief, he snarled to himself, *All right—fine. You win. We'll do it your way.*

The detective stared across his desk, his eyes drilling into Lin. It had only been a few seconds since the man had become lost within his own panic, but each had been a hateful eternity for the detective. Tired of waiting, London could feel the atmosphere in the room changing, could smell the air burning around him. Extending his hand in Lin's direction, the detective snapped his fingers.

Startled, his client blurted, "Evil—evil. That's all I can tell you. Evil—all right? *All right?* There. I've said it. I'll say it again. Evil. That's all I know—*evil!*"

"Yeah, right," answered London, sighing to himself. "Isn't it always?"

Then the detective's nerves began to open certain little-used sensors, even while other vast parts of the same system began to cloak themselves in protective layers. He felt the familiar shift coming again, rumbling unbidden through his body—recognized it from so many times in the past. He could feel his muscles tightening, his lungs stretching, his daily radar expanding its usual field outward ten-, twenty-, fifty-fold. Shoving aside conscious awareness of his internal realignments, he said, "Now, why don't you tell me just what *kind* of evil you're talking about."

"You, you . . . huh, ha huh, you certainly make it sound simple," the frightened man snapped back. "Like there's some kind of menu I could just point to."

"There is, Mr. Lin," London assured him wearily. "And it covers breakfast, lunch, and dinner—soup to nuts. Now, why don't you get started before the waiter shows up with a check neither one of us can cover?"

Lin looked into the other man's eyes, startled by his answer. Then, suddenly more frightened by London than by what had sent him to the detective in the first place, he slowly made his way around the gagging knot of terror that had been strangling his ability to respond.

Finally, Lin talked. The detective listened. Outside the window, darkness fell at its appointed time.

* * *

"Now, lemme get dis straight, boss." The speaker was Paul Morcey, London's partner and right-hand man. It had been seven years since the balding man had given up his job as the head of the Greeley Arcade's maintenance corps to join the London Agency—more than one since the darkness had encroached on any of their lives. "It's startin' again?"

"That's what I've been told, Paul," answered London, staring out the window.

"Perhaps," interjected the woman in black to Morcey's right, "you will tell us everything that you have been told, so that we might apply our own judgment. As well as why we had to pack bags and meet you at the train—?"

"Sure," answered London with a trace of bitterness. "Why not?"

Turning back from the window and the scenery moving beyond it, the detective caught hold of the building terror within him. Running the fingers of his mind over his comforting fear, he shoved it aside once more. Then, feeling more in control, he told the others, "I had you two meet me at the station to save time. We were offered twenty-five thousand for a weekend's work—this weekend. When the offer comes in at 10:00 on a Friday morning. . . ."

London let his voice trail off. Morcey and the woman both nodded, seeing his point. After a couple of quips about the rising costs of overtime pay in a free market society, the detective got down to filling the others in on the nature of the urgency that had put them on the 11:05 for Massachusetts.

"Our Mr. Lin is a developer. He and his partners purchased a piece of prime coastal property in Massachusetts up toward the Vermont border for a song. Their idea is to build a retirement community. It would come complete with a mall that would service the surrounding towns while giving business opportunities and employment to the retirees. They get to live in a walled-in security village, run their businesses in the mall down the road, and then go back to their beautiful oceanview homes at night."

"Sounds choice," said Morcey drily. Brushing his graying, near-half-foot-long ponytail back off his ears, he asked, "Do they need a detective agency branch office?"

"They need something," answered London. "The investors are all set to go. They have support from the surrounding towns—Newburyport, Ipswich, Rowley—already had the area surveyed, equipment and building supplies moved in, even got work started. That's when their troubles began."

"You are not referring to zoning difficulties," asked the woman in black. "Are you?"

"No," agreed the detective. "But I think I wish I was."

The woman's eyes moved sharply as London said these last words, framing him and the area around him. Her name was Lai Wan. A psychometrist, she had been with the agency since its first brush with the beyond. She could feel through the air—through her feet touching the same floor as his—that the detective had gotten to the important part of his tale. Saying nothing, she opened herself to the waves of energy coming off him, focusing not so much on his words but on his mind. Digging through his mood, she burrowed away from the surface of present time back to his meeting with Lin.

London noted Lai Wan's eyes closing, knew she was searching for clues as to what their client's problems might actually be by tapping the detective's recent past for the kind of fact only her talents could pick up. *Good,* he thought, and opened himself fully to the probing as it continued.

"I wish I could say that Lin had a lot to tell us—but he didn't. This isn't some B-movie nonsense with a lot of unexplained accidents or equipment malfunctions. It's more that the atmosphere there is . . . *terrorizing* everyone."

As Morcey simply stared, Lai Wan added, "I think 'terror' too polite a word for what is being felt by our client." All eyes turned toward the psychometrist. Neither of the men questioned her as she continued, "There is something horrible brewing ahead of us. Something is hanging in the air around our destination. It is a thick curtain of darkness—ugly and revolting—hung in a manner the eye cannot avoid. But, as horrific as it might be, what it drapes from view is infinitely worse."

"But, darlin'," asked Morcey, "what's it up to? Why's *this* batch of hell-crap—whatever it is—wanta keep a mall from gettin' built?"

"You misunderstand me, husband," answered the woman in black. "I said nothing about the force desiring a halt to Mr. Lin's construction."

All eyes remained focused on the psychometrist, waiting for her to continue. She obliged them, saying, "If anything, it is trying its *best* to stay out of the way."

Lai Wan paused at that point, taking a breath. Outside, the train's wheels screeched as friction and pressure struck out at each other. The engine had just reached the sharp bend before the Norganza tunnel and, as always, the entire train was feeling the effects of the turn.

Having caught her breath, the psychometrist pulled at the ebony lace shawl around her shoulders and said, "Whatever its hidden reasons, that which we are seeking can barely contain its excitement over Mr. Lin and the thought of his plans reaching fruition."

Then sudden darkness enveloped the three.

* * *

The trio spread out from their rental car, looking over the construction site as they did so. As they approached the vast cyclone fence running the length of Lin's property line, an unshaven black man on the other side of it took note of them. With almost an exaggerated slowness, he moved away from the bulldozer he had been leaning against. His dark blue down jacket did sport a Truman Security patch, but the rest of his outfit—faded jeans, sweat shirt, white socks, scruffy old sneakers—did not look much like anyone's usual idea of an official uniform.

London and the others stopped where they were, waiting for the man to reach them. The detective unconsciously scanned the man as he drew closer, noting the tight set of his shoulders, his large hands, quick eyes. He was a hard man—his deliberate walk, closed expression, everything about the approaching figure warned caution to London. Despite his extremely weathered appearance, the detective knew the man was not quite as old as his thinning crown of close-cropped graying hair made him appear. Lai Wan whispered to the others, "This man is armed."

The psychometrist could sense the aura of threat the man unconsciously projected, could smell steel and lead and powder in the air around him. London and Morcey were already aware of the fact, however, having noted the slight bulges at both the man's right armpit and left ankle. London had just begun to wonder if the approaching figure's peculiar gait was due to the presence of a possible third weapon on the back of his belt when the man asked, "You the detectives?"

After Morcey assured him they were, the man began unlocking the gate, saying as he did so, "Thought so. No one else be crazy enough come out here except us what gets paid to. The old lady already been and gone, but she said she'd be back."

When the trio inquired as to whom the guard was talking about, he answered, "The old Chinese lady. Lin called, said let her go wherever she wanted. She got here early this morning. Walked all over. Left about an hour ago, said she'd come back later. Didn't say nuthin' else, sos I'ze can't tell yous no more then dat."

London, going on the information Lin had given him, decided that the old woman must be Si Wan Lu, checking on how the dragon ran through Lin's property. Shoving the information aside, he framed the older man on the other side of the gate with his gaze and said, "You must be Mr. Mitchell."

"Dat's right. Corporation tried hire a watch force—couldn't gets no one ta stay. Finally these folks," the man pointed to the patch on his jacket, "got tired of lookin' for a shift—started askin' round for someone who'd just live out here."

"And that'd be you—right?" asked Morcey, taking a liking to the older man.

"Yeah," answered the security man, his face not betraying any emotion. "That'd be me."

"Mr. Mitchell has declined to add that he took this job because there is a great need in his life for cash at the moment."

All eyes turned toward Lai Wan's except London's. He watched the security man's face as the woman said, "Covering three eight-hour shifts a day, seven days a week, throws him into a quite healthy overtime bracket. The management corporation is paying Mr. Mitchell quite well. It is worth it to them, of course, because of the great reduction having armed security brings in their insurance rate. But . . . Mr. Mitchell has begun to think that it may not be enough."

Noting the tightness building in the guard's eyes, London turned the man's attention toward him by asking, "Something bothering you about this job, Mr. Mitchell?"

"Dat woman got no right ta say I'ze scared."

The detective disagreed, telling him, "Actually, she has every right in the world. First off, she's never wrong in any of the things she says. Get used to it. Secondly, it was you yourself that said no one would be crazy enough to come out here if they weren't being paid. So tell us, why is that?"

Mitchell took a backward step, as if simply moving away from the strangers that had invaded his private world might detach the connections they had somehow made to him. His eyes narrowing, he answered, "I'ze supposed ta open the gates for yous and let yous in and out as you please. Nobody told me I hadda do no more."

The guard turned to walk away. Then suddenly he turned back toward them. Anger raging in his old eyes, he snapped defiantly, "My daughter be goin' on ta graduate school. I never made it ta the eight grade, but now, my baby girl gonna be a professor. *If* I can gets the money. Yous wanted ta know what's enough ta make the crazy nigger stay here in this damn sick place—fine. Now you knows."

"Hey, no sweat," answered Morcey for the group. Not able to sense the man's fears or needs the way his partner or his wife could, but understanding them better, he added, "There ain't any of us here that's not being paid great for doin' it."

London, readily seeing what his partner was up to, motioned to Lai Wan with his eyes for her to walk off to the side with him. As they wandered away, Mitchell said, "Money ain't no good if yous ain't alive to spend it."

"Yeah, don't I know it," answered Morcey. His mind flashed the faces of scores of his former coworkers and acquaintances who had died during the agency's past investigations. Shutting the memories off with a shudder, he said, "But, that's why ya just gotta stay alive."

Mitchell snorted. It was a short noise, but enough of a break in the wall he had built around himself to allow him to relax. Given that one tiny opening, the tension that had been building within him for weeks poured forth through it, almost leaving the man too weak to stand as it escaped. Looking at Morcey differently, the guard said, "Yous not like them other two."

"I guess we're all three from different backgrounds—that's true. We do the same work now, but I spent mosta my years before I became a detective in the wonderful world of custodial maintenance."

"Yous was a janitor?" asked Mitchell with disbelief. To the guard, the cut of Morcey's suit suggested he was kidding. When the balding man insisted he had spent the first near-thirty years of his adult life in the janitorial services industry, the guard asked, "Okay—what would yous use ta pick oil or grease up off'a the floor?"

"Paint thinner. Then I'd cover it with cat litter, sand, dry cement—somthin' like that. Let it sit overnight, sweep it up in the morning. If there was still a stain after that I'd probably bleach it."

"Yeah?" answered Mitchell, impressed but not convinced. "How can you tell which side'a the window the streaks is on?"

"Depends. Easiest way is to wash the outsides north-south, and the insides east-west. Then, whichever way the streak is runnin', dat's where it is."

The security man smiled. Convinced, but happy for the diversion after living for so many weeks by himself at the construction site, he asked, "Okay. Okay. But tell me, if you had'a keep track of what color da room's been painted—how'd yous do it?"

"Mark down da brand and shade and everythin' on da back of da light switch cover. It's about da only thing ya can count on always stayin' in a office."

"Lord love a monkey—yous the real goods, alls right," admitted Mitchell. Putting out his hand, he said, "I'ze a garbage jockey, too. Took a leave of absence ta hold down dis gig. Make the money for my Sarah Jane."

"Always pleased to meet another brother of the broom," said Morcey, shaking the man's hand.

After a moment, the two released their grips and then, tired of standing still, began to move off toward the construction equipment in the distance. They talked as they walked, mainly covering simple incidentals, feeling each other out. Finally, however, as they neared the two-room trailer Truman Security had moved onto the site for Mitchell, the man changed the subject radically, asking, "Yous and them two others—yous been at this a while. Yous seen some real shit—ain't ya?"

"Shit that would turn you white, chief."

And then Mitchell stopped outside his trailer, threw back his head and laughed. It was a deep and cleansing sound, one that welled up from his core, tearing at the roots of the fear that had been forcing its way through his resistance since he had first come to the construction site. Tears broke from his eyes as his laughter finally calmed, allowing him to say, "Okay, okay, yous win." Slapping Morcey on the back, he added, "But—oh, Lordy—how I needed that."

"Yeah," agreed the balding man, "I've noticed keepin' yer sense of humor can help."

"Yous live out here a few weeks and can keeps yous sense of humor—yous the funniest fuckin' man in the world."

Putting his hand on Mitchell's arm, Morcey asked him gently, "Why don't ya tell me about it?"

The security man thought for a moment. Then, unable to look into his new-found friend's eyes and still know the fear that had been gnawing at him, he asked, "Yous really wanta hear it?"

"Hey, dat's what I'm here for."

"How to explain?" asked Mitchell. He held his breath for a moment, then said, "I'ze been over this ground a thousand times—okay? Walked miles on end. Ain't nuthin' live 'round here. Ain't never seen no animals, never found no tracks—none that made no sense, anyway—no turds, nuthin'. And I means snakes, bugs . . . I ain't never even seen no bird what will fly over this land. For miles. *Miles*. An' yet, night, day, don't matter—yous sits around here for a while—yous starts feelin' it."

Mitchell's voice went low, his eyes locking on Morcey's as he said, "Eyes. Watchin'—all the time. Even when I'ze inside the trailer—I'ze can feel 'em, studyin' me . . . crawlin' over me. After a while, yous can smell things goin' by, feel their stink stickin' ta yous skin." The guard rubbed at his hands unconsciously as he continued. "There's somethin', everywhere arounds here, but yous can't find it. Yous can hear it, but yous can't see it. It just hangs in the air—waitin'. Shit's been makin' me crazy."

"Yeah," the balding man responded, his eyes looking over the barren site. "I understand."

Mitchell cocked his head to one side, his eyes not breaking their link with Morcey's. He stared for a long minute, wondering just what kind of man his fellow janitor was. Finally deciding he was the kind that could be trusted, he started them walking again, saying, "Yous know, part'a my brain be scramin' at me to warn yous as to what yous'all's gettin' into. Another, though, it stopped me. Now, yous wants to know how? By askin' me just exactly whats I'ze thought I'ze could tells ya. And, sweet Lordy, I'ze wish I knew."

"Look, man," offered Morcey, "You ain't gotta explain nuthin' to me. I've been through this kinda shit too many times—I know what it's like. Besides, Lin—the guy who hired us—he could barely tell us anything, either. All he said was that he couldn't get anybody to work the land. He and his people've got millions tied up in this deal, and it's all goin' south on them. His basic pitch was that everythin' was cool at first, they inspected the land, got it surveyed, no problem. But, after that, once they had machinery and crews out here, after a while everyone started walkin' off the job. Pretty soon word had spread that the job was hoodooed and they couldn't get anyone to stay—not even security people. No one except you."

"That's because dey didn't done woke it up at first. One, two guys in for a few hours here and there, it didn't catch up ta 'em right away. But, after dey started bustin' through roads, rippin' down the old trees, bringin' in supplies . . . workers here every day . . . lotsa noise . . . lotsa activity—dat's how dey woke it up."

"No offense, Mr. Mitchel—."

"Call me 'Dixie.'"

"Paul," responded Morcey, adding, "But, anyway—you're sayin' this feelin' is what chased everyone off—right?"

"Yeah—why? Yous wonderin' if'n it could run off a couple hundred construction workers, how come it can't run off the crazy nigger?"

"Well," admitted the balding man with a smile. "Sumthin' like that."

"Dat's okay. Makes sense. And I'ze can tell ya, too. When there was lotsa folks 'round . . . first woke it up . . . it came up too fast . . . droolin'. Couldin' hold itself back. Runned everybody off."

Mitchell paused for a breath. Then, his voice dropping low again, he added, "It can't help but make itself felt. But, now it's woke up, it's tryin' to keep quiet. It leaves me 'lone 'cause it's tryin' to trick folks inta comin' back."

Morcey felt a cold twitch crawling through his spine. A trickle of sweat broke from his hairline and rolled down under his collar. Making its way down the center of his back, it focused his uncomfortable mood all too clearly. Knowing the answer to his question, but needing to hear Mitchell give it, he asked, "Why?"

"I'ze think it knew what the crews was here for. I'ze think it could tell what was comin'—stores and homes an' all. Dat's why it didn't bother no one. It's waitin' for dem ta build dis place, sell all the homes, move in the folks—and put dat big wall up all around everythin'. Den, when it's locked up inside with everyone—den it'll do what it's been waitin' ta do."

"And what'ya think that is?"

The two men stopped walking. Turning to Morcey, Mitchell said, "All I'ze can tell ya is whats I'ze been feelin, that whatever this thing is everyone been feelin' . . . it's old. Old and been sleepin' for a long time."

The line of sweat dripping down Morcey's back reached his belt, began working its way underneath. Squirming uncomfortably, the ex-maintenance man said, "And now it's awake, an' lookin' for breakfast."

"Yous got it."

Great, thought Morcey. Already he was beginning to hear the same whispers, smell the same dark reeking, feel the same clammy dread that had been stalking Mitchell for weeks.

Just fuckin' great.

* * *

It had taken London and Lai Wan even less time to sense the otherworldly presence in the area than it had Morcey. As the pair moved over several acres of the densely overgrown land, the psychometrist said, "There is something hidden from us here, and something hiding within that which is hidden."

The detective stared at her, his head cocked to one side, his expression slightly puzzled. When he asked her if she could make herself any clearer, she answered, "Yes," she answered simply. The woman paused—uncomfortable—her voice thinning tensely. Pulling herself together, she said, "This forest . . . it is hiding something from us. And something else is hiding in that which is being hidden."

"You know," said London, "we've been at this too long. I actually understood that."

Pointing to some of the trees around him, he continued, saying, "I've been noticing something peculiar. I don't know if it ties in with what you were saying or not, but these trees all around us, all of them—the oldest is only fifty, sixty years old." Turning from side to side, indicating the way they had come and the way before them, he said, "There isn't one of them that's any older."

Unlike Lai Wan or her husband, London had been raised in the country. The psychometrist was well aware that his rustic skills far outstripped those of anyone she knew. Pulling in on herself, she allowed him to fall into his own space. Seconds later, she knew he was talking more to himself than to her, trying to make the connections between whatever nagging clues the back of his mind had spotted but could not pull together on its own.

"No stumps or trunks that are older, either," he mused, wondering himself where he was going with his observation. "There's plenty of younger stuff around . . . clumps of it everywhere . . . sure, but what—"

The detective stopped, information piling up so quickly in his head he could barely process it.

"Maples. They're all maples." Spinning in a fast pair of circles, then a series of far slower ones, London's tone went curious as he whispered, "They are. There's no pines, birches, oaks . . . nothing. Just maples."

Then an odd thought hit him. Stepping up to one of the oldest of the nearby trees, he closed one eye, squinting off in the direction of the next closest one. Bit by bit, he screened the newer foliage out of his sight, ignoring the younger trees until he could look from side to side once more—this time his sight only taking note of the oldest trees in the forest. As he began to get lost in thought, Lai Wan sensed it was the moment for her to return him to their conversation.

"Theodore," she asked softly. "What is it you have found?"

"The oldest trees," he told her, having no explanation for what he had discovered, "they're all growing in straight lines."

* * *

"The government done it," said Mitchell, reaching back to his childhood memories. "I'ze can still remembers it." The older man told the tale quickly, of how the entire area had been flat when he was a child, totally barren. Then, when he had been roughly five or six years old, the federal government had started a work program in the area, building walls and bridges, clearing roadways, planting trees.

"Theys put in the trees. Kept 'em real nice for long time, too. Then, theys stopped keepin' the area up. Right away, it started gettin' overgrowed, alla that."

"So, our question is," said Morcey, "why'd the government plant trees, and then why'd they stop taking care of them?"

"That's part of it, anyway," agreed London. Turning to Mitchell, the detective asked, "Can you tell us what was here *before* the government came in? You said the land was flat when you were a kid . . . that there was nothing growing here?"

"Dat's right."

"Do you know *why*?"

Mitchell scratched his head at London's question, answering with an apologetic tone, "No, sir, I'ze sorry, but I surely don't. It'd just been . . . flatlike . . . you know? Long back as I'ze can remember. Sorry."

"That's all right," the detective assured him. "You've been doing your job. Finding out the answers here is ours." Before London could say anything further, Lai Wan felt a sudden compulsion that took the shape of a single word.

"Marsh." When everyone turned to stare at her, she asked, "Does the name mean anything to anyone?"

"Are you certain it's a name?" asked London.

"Yes. It came to me just now—a feeling out of the air or the ground—it was just a whisper I picked up. All I can tell you about it, however, is that it was a name."

"Well, then," said the detective. "Perhaps we should find out just *whose* name it was."

* * *

Later that day, Morcey and Lai Wan found themselves nearly a hundred miles away at the county seat's Hall of Records. Although they had been there almost an hour, they had so far not been able to find anyone willing to help them. Now that it was almost closing, they were both getting a bit impatient.

"This, my dear," said Morcey under his breath, "is gettin' a little too obvious."

"I agree, my husband," answered the psychometrist. "What would you suggest?"

"I suggest we nab someone and make with a little friendly persuasion." With a slight note of concern in her voice, Lai Wan said, "Do not be reckless, Paul."

"Who? Me?" Morcey smiled at his wife, blinking as he added, "Perish da thought."

The balding man went back to the front counter. Once more he approached the older woman posted there. She had already given him the run-around twice. The look on her face, the set of her shoulders, everything about her screamed that she was ready to give him the same run around for the rest of the year.

Glancing at her name tag, the pony-tailed man took a deep breath, then said, "You know, Mrs. Bennett, I hate to say it, but I don't think you're really tryin' to help me."

The woman rolled her eyes in a bored, contemptuous gesture. Before she could say anything, though, Morcey added, "But, that's all right. I figure you really want to help me, you just have to be coaxed into it."

"I told you before, there are no records for that area of the coast."

"Sure. Right—now I'm gonna tell you somethin'. You see that woman over there?" The ex-maintenance man pointed toward his wife. "She's a witch if you ever met one. She knows everyone's dark secrets. Includin' yours."

Mrs. Bennett raised one eyebrow. Morcey noted that the woman's eyes shifted—left, then right—gauging the distance between herself and the closest of her coworkers. The ex-maintenance man smiled.

"I can tell by the look on your face that you don't believe me. But it's true. Whatever dirty little bit of your life you've been tryin' to hide—no matter how long you've kept it buried and hidden away from people . . . she knows it."

The clerk turned away, saying, "I don't have time for this."

"Suit yourself," answered the balding man. "We'll just tell whatever it is to some of your coworkers."

"No," Lai Wan interrupted in a cold, emotionless tone. "We will tell her brother, Jordan."

Mrs. Bennett froze. Morcey had done his part by getting her to think about her darkest secret. Lai Wan, of course, could have forced her way into the clerk's mind and rooted about if she had to. But that would have been hard on both of them. With her most guilty moment labeled and brought to the surface of her mind, however, it was no trouble for Lai Wan to read it out of the air. Standing, the psychometrist moved toward the counter.

"If you do not help us at once, we will call Jordan and tell him about what happened after your mother's funeral. We will tell him that you did indeed take the silver cup from her dressing table, as well as the Irish lace from the dining room."

The woman's face went pale. The blood was draining from her head so rapidly that she almost fainted. Morcey chuckled, saying, "Looks like you struck a nerve, sweetheart."

The clerk backed away, her eyes stricken with an uncomprehending terror. Weakly, she intoned her familiar lie, "But, there are no files—"

By this time, however, the woman's mind had become an open book to the psychometrist. Reading the surface of her thoughts as if they were printed on a roadside billboard, Lai Wan answered coldly, "No. There are files. They have merely been sealed." When the clerk gasped, Lai Wan added, "No one has asked to see them in all your tenure here. You were instructed by your predecessor never to show them to anyone."

"But . . . but—"

"Be silent," snapped the psychometrist. "Do what I have told you or Jordan will not be the only person called. Would you like Alice to know where her husband used to go on Thursday nights? Would you care for Mr. Shannessy to know how your seminar days were really spent? Do you desire for your daughter to learn what really happened to the money she was promised for college? Would you—"

"I'll get them!" sobbed the nearly hysterical clerk. The older woman was shaking. Unable to look at Lai Wan's face, seeing the psychometrist as a hateful dark outline, she implored, "I'll get them. I'll get them. *Please* . . ." The last word was a dread-filled plea followed by the begging whisper, "No more."

As the clerk scrambled away, Morcey asked his wife, "You okay? You didn't strain yourself, did ya?"

"No, husband. I am fine. Her mind was no challenge. But I fear we may be in for one."

"Why?" asked the balding man. "What's up?"

"Just a feeling," she answered absently. Mrs. Bennett had never read the old files. They had been officially sealed and that had been good enough for her. Therefore Lai Wan could not pick up anything about their nature from probing the clerk's mind.

But the psychometrist could read more than individuals. The longer she stayed in the Hall of Records, the more vibrations leaked out to her from the walls themselves concerning the mysterious sealed files. Nothing that came to her did anything but heighten her sense of dread.

Nothing.

* * *

"What yous find there?" asked Mitchell.

London was on his knees, tearing at the ground. As he pushed at the soil, he answered, "I don't know. Some kind of hole."

"Best be careful. I ain't seen nuthin' movin' 'round here for a fact, but dey is a lot of critters in dese parts will tear yous up for pokin' in they front doors."

"Thanks for the warning, but it doesn't look like any kind of natural occurrence, including an animal warren." London played his pocket flash inside the hole but the tiny light could not illuminate the interior to the point of satisfying the detective's curiosity. Actually, the hints it gave of a large chamber intrigued London's interest to the point where he could think of nothing else.

For some time he merely sat back on his heels, wondering at what he had found. Finally, however, he turned to Mitchell and asked, "Is there a shovel or a pick around here?"

"One o' each. Which one yous want?"

"I'll take them both," answered the detective. Staring at the slight enlargement he had made, he said, "I think I'll need them."

Twenty minutes' work later, London stood over what his efforts had uncovered. Mitchell stood behind him, staring down into the gaping hole in the ground. So far, the two men had more questions than answers. The detective's efforts to expand the opening had given them some baffling moments. Numerous pick blows and shovel bites brought away bits of stone and wood buried beneath the ground. But that was not what kept London digging.

There was something ominous about the jagged oval in the dirt. Something not natural. The longer the two men studied it, the more queer the entire situation seemed. There was a slight gray pallor to the ground, a lifeless quality to the soil around the opening that disturbed both men. Finally, Mitchell asked, "What the hell yous done found here?"

"I don't know," responded London. "But I'm thinking that whatever it is, it was man-made. That's why I've expanded the opening out to where we can fit inside."

"We?" asked the security man in a voice bordering on honest shock. "Like yous and mes?"

"That was the idea," answered London. Setting the shovel he had been using next to the pick he had finished with earlier, he reached into his jacket to retrieve his pocket flash, adding, "Care to join me in a look?"

"In *there*?" Mitchell could not have sounded more incredulous. "Does the phrase 'not on your life' have any meanin' for yous?"

London raised his eyebrows, smiling as he did so. He understood the older man's reservations. Crawling down into a hole in the middle of any forest was not most people's idea of a good time. Having to crawl down under the ground in the middle of that particular one would have disturbed practically anybody.

"Don't sweat it, Mr. Mitchell," answered the detective. "You've done your duty as far as this place is concerned." London took a first, tentative step into the black oval he had dug. "This is my gig."

Bending over, the detective grabbed onto the surface and then lowered himself into the hollow under the earth. Before he could stretch out completely, his feet touched what felt to be a dirt incline. He tested the stability of the mound with several solid back kicks, then let go his hold. Not moving any further into the chamber, London played his small light about, checking to see exactly what it was he had discovered.

"What'chu see, man? What da hell be down there, anyway?"

"Not sure yet. But it's no cave. Somebody *made* it."

The detective moved his light around slowly. Above him, the hole had a definite ceiling—a stout one made of thick beams he guessed to be oak. The walls to either side and in the distance were of bald stone—slabs of rock roughly hewn and tightly set. The incline he had come down onto seemed to have poured in through what at one time had been the entrance from above.

Above? thought the detective. Questions piled up in his head. *And what was above? Did someone build a cabin out here at one time? A cabin with a basement? A basement this solid?*

Why? asked another part of his mind. *A lone building here? What for? And when? Look carefully at that workmanship—this place was no trapper's cabin. This was something sturdy—made to last.*

And, spoke yet another voice within his head, *it is old . . .* old.

When London had first encountered the supernatural, he had developed the ability to communicate with all the ancestor memories recorded within his racial memory. Everything all the men and women of his past lineage had ever learned was available for him to sift through. Calling upon the voice that had just given its opinion on the age of the room, he asked it, *How old?*

Two hundred and fifty, three hundred years. Look at the fit of the wall stone—perfectly seamed, but the exteriors were left chiseled. That was the practice—built quickly, but made to last.

London turned his attention away from the chamber itself. He knew its age, had assured himself that it was not going to collapse on him. Instead, he moved forward off the incline, heading toward the center of the room and the rectangle of blackness that sat there waiting for him.

"What yous doin?"

"This isn't a cave," shouted London. "It's a basement."

"A basement?"

"Yes. And an old one at that." The detective reached the dark block in the center of the chamber. "My guess is the house or whatever was above was knocked down a long time ago, but the basement wasn't filled in." London thought of the earthen incline he had just left and added, "At least not completely."

"Okay—fine. Yous in a basement. But," said the older man, scratching his head, "I didn't ask yous where yous was . . . I asked yous what yous was doin'."

"Looking at a big slab of stone," answered the detective. Playing his light over its surface, London was slightly taken aback. The block was huge, covered with bas-relief carvings. None of it made much sense to him, though. It was all marine-inspired monster heads and crudely rendered scenes of ritual slaughter. Then London touched the surface.

What? he thought. *Glass?*

He ran his fingers over the cold smoothness. What he had taken for a large piece of black stone he now discovered was in reality obsidian. Suddenly the crude carvings took on the aura of near genius. London stared at the work etched in the dark, conchoidal glass. What he had been ready to dismiss as the efforts of a barely competent hack now staggered him with its depth.

How had it been done, he wondered. *How?*

None of the edges seemed particularly sharp. What tools could have been used to create the carvings before him, especially given the time frame of the work, London could not imagine. There was a delicate grace to the lines the detective could scarcely believe had been made in the volcanic glass. He was actually better prepared to accept that the black rectangle had been spat out from the molten center of the Earth as was—that when it had cooled it had hardened in its present form—and that no human artisan had ever touched it.

Perhaps, one of the ever-present voices in his head intoned, *none ever did.*

Then London suddenly noticed the slight depressions in the top of the slab. A few seconds' examination showed they perfectly fitted the form of the average human back . . . at least, the average human back of roughly two hundred years ago. The detective also noticed something else. The top of the black rectangle was not exactly the same color as the rest.

Something had been poured over the slab—maybe a thousand times . . . maybe ten thousand. Something that filled the nooks and cracks in the various carvings. Something long dried and yet still vaguely sticky.

Something red.

And then Mitchell screamed.

* * *

Morcey tried without complete success to keep the small cellular phone cradled between his shoulder and his ear as he eased the rental car around a bend in the road. Leaving one hand on the wheel to steer, he straightened out the phone, then continued talking.

"Sorry, phone slipped. Anyway, we got some news for you, boss."

"Yes," said London. "I've got some for you. You scared Mr. Mitchell here out of a year's growth."

"Ten years," shouted the older man. "Twenty."

Smiling, London continued, telling Morcey, "It was nothing, really. I was in a hole in the ground and Dix was getting a little concerned as to when I was coming out. My phone was in my jacket back outside. Its ringing gave him a bit of a start."

"Yeah?" answered the ex-maintenance man. "Sorry I missed it. But we do have some news for you. That whole area, it used to be a town called Innsmouth."

"Figures," answered London. He explained about finding the basement.

His partner told him, "The entire place was leveled in 1930. The government came in, took the land away from the state, and then just plowed the whole place under . . . closed it off and knocked everything down. A few years later, during the Depression, they turned it over to the forestry department. They planted the land, but surprise, after a while they gave the land back to the state. Apparently they couldn't find any rangers that would work it."

"But," asked London, wiping at his brow, "what happened to all the people who lived in the town?"

"From what we can tell, the government took them, too." Morcey slowed for a red light. He kept talking as he brought the car to a halt, telling the detective, "What happened exactly, we're not sure yet, but we've got a call in to Roth."

Michael Roth was an FBI man who had been assigned by the government years ago to watch London and his people. He had switched sympathies after coming to the hard realization that the fate of the world was better off in the detective's hands than in those of the politicians Roth worked for.

"Where are you now?" asked London. Morcey gave his partner his approximate location, then asked if he and Lai Wan should head back to join him. The detective told him, "No. We have to stay the night anyway, so just find yourselves a motel in town. I'm going to keep Mr. Mitchell here company . . . find out what this place is like after dark."

"Whatever you say, boss. Better you than me."

The two men made some further small conversation but finally broke their connection. It was growing dark. Morcey and his wife needed to make the rest of the drive back to town and then find lodgings for the night. London needed to mark the area where he had found the entrance to the long-forgotten basement and then set up his own camp. The detective tied his shirt around the tree closest to the hole and started back to the job site entrance with Mitchell. As they walked, London told the older man what Morcey and Lai Wan had discovered.

As they neared the edge of the trees, the security man asked, "So, what yous gonna do now?"

"Now I'm going to get my bag, clear a place to camp, and then settle in to see what this place is like at night."

"Camp?" asked Mitchell, an edge of shock running through his voice. "Yous mean outside?"

"That's where I usually camp."

"Hey—dat's crazy. Dat trailer dey gived me is plenty big for two. You can't be stayin' outside."

"Don't worry," answered London. "I'm not trying to play martyr or hero. And it's not that I don't believe what you were telling us about this place earlier. I do. That's the main reason why I want to be outside."

The older man stared at the detective in disbelief. London reminded him, "My job is to find out what's wrong with this place. I can't do that hiding from whatever's been terrorizing everybody."

"But, but I means . . . I shouldn't be—"

The detective cut Mitchell off. He knew the man was feeling guilty over the thought of staying inside while London slept exposed to whatever it was he had been hearing—and feeling—move about him every night. Stopping the older man before he could articulate his thoughts, the detective said, "No—I need to be alone. And I need you inside, ready to come if I call, but safe in your normal place. To whatever's been slinking around here, I'm new. I'll be a curiosity. With luck, you'll be forgotten by it."

The two men broke free of the trees. Moving out into the clearing created by the developers before work had ground to a halt, they headed across the rough expanse toward Mitchell's trailer. As they did, London said,

"And maybe, not being the center of its attention for once, you might even be able to get a good look at whatever it is."

The older man said nothing. Reading the question he wanted to ask, the detective told him, "Fear's a funny thing. We see or hear something we don't understand, our brain does everything it can to get us away. How many times have people gone running in terror from a shadow? It's all in the angle of our perceptions. Show someone something from one angle, and it appears monstrous. Show it to them from another, and it makes them laugh."

"Yous mean like dat old puzzle—dat drawing dat looks like a cup if yous look at it one way, but then it looks like two people starin' at each other if yous looks at it another."

"Yes," agree London, nodding his head. "Just like that. Understand me, Dix—I know you're not a coward. You've worked this site for quite a while now while everyone else has run for the hills. My guess is that you're more worried about your nerve than I am. Trust me, if I need your help, I'll scream like a stuck pig. I'm no superhero. I'm getting paid to be here just like you are."

The two stopped at the door to Mitchell's trailer. Both men could tell the sun would be below the horizon in less than half an hour. As London grabbed up his travel bag, the older man put his hand on the detective's shoulder, then said, "Okay. Yous clear yo'self a spot and do what yous has to. But, what's yous gonna do for dinner?"

London patted his bag, saying, "I always travel prepared. Protein bars, a couple cans of sardines, dried fruit, crackers. It doesn't take much."

"Dat's true. But if'n yous wanted, I do have a pot on the simmer inside."

Mitchell opened the door to his trailer and reached around the edge to his stove. Pulling up the lid of a crockpot right around the corner from the door, he released a thick aroma that cut through the evening air. London sniffed at it involuntarily. He could make out the distinct fragrances of garlic, mushrooms, spinach, and curry in the first wave. The second told him of basil, chicken, tomatoes, onions, and red potatoes.

Dropping his bag, London gave out a high-pitched squeal, sounding so much like a real pig that the older man almost dropped the glass lid he was holding. Laughing hard, he set it back atop its pot, saying, "I gots a loaf of that real crusty-type Italian bread to dunk ins it, and some smooth, fine red to wash it all down with, too."

The detective moved his eyebrows up and down rapidly several times. Mitchell chuckled, then threw his door open so London could enter the trailer. The detective took another deep breath of the thick aroma filling the interior of the mobile home. The slow-cooking stew beckoned to him, promising to be a meal to remember.

Outside, other things began to beckon as well, making promises all their own. Meanwhile, far beyond them, the sun disappeared beneath the edge of the world, plunging the long-cursed land into darkness.

And, deep within the woods, in the no-longer-hidden chamber under the ground, the scarlet coating on the obsidian altar began to bubble.

* * *

London lay in his sleeping bag, fingers threaded behind his head. He had rolled his jacket up and placed the bundle atop his boots to make a passable pillow. His .38, Betty, he had slid inside one of his boots, along with his stiletto, Veronica. Mitchell was already long turned in for the night, but the detective was still awake—watching, listening.

The sky above the trees was cloudless and blessed that night by a near full moon. For some reason, however, no light seem to filter down through the forest canopy. It did not disturb London. In fact, he had asked Mitchell to lower the site's electric lights as far as he could, killing as many as was legally possible. The detective had then crawled into his bed roll and started waiting.

Waiting, whispered a tiny voice from the back of his mind. *Waiting for what?*

Good question, he told it. *Let's keep listening and find out, shall we?*

The tiny voice went silent, joining the rest in the detective's mind in concentrating on their surroundings. There was no argument—the forest was deathly still. Building on what Mitchell had told Morcey, there were no more animals evident in the area during the night than during the day. No level of concentration brought London the slightest evidence to the contrary.

No insects came to feast on his blood, despite his lack of a camp fire. No sounds came from the thick underbrush—nothing slithered, crawled, or hopped anywhere near the detective's camp. No nocturnal hunters were about. The land was dead—the only sounds were coming from the rhythmic beat of the waves along the shore away on the other side of the forest. The sound of it gave London the impression the tide was coming in. He was not positive—the ocean was some distance off. But, outside of the quiet sound of Mitchell's breathing coming from inside his trailer, it was the only noise of any kind to be heard.

"Going to be a peaceful night, I guess," muttered the detective. Twisting his body, shoving the ground beneath him about with his spine, he maneuvered himself into a more comfortable position, adding, "Too bad."

Then, not seeing the point in prolonging the inevitable, he plunged into the back recesses of his mind and allowed his body to fall asleep. When he was younger, he would have sat watch the entire night—half as a precaution, half because he knew he could do it without paying any great physical penalties. Now, however, having just passed forty, he was not as inclined to heroics or self-matching endurance contests. Settling in for the night, he opened his eyes to glance about—just in case there was something moving about that his other senses could not register. Seeing the same, familiar blackness, he closed his eyes again, and then allowed himself to drift off.

It was not the greatest mistake of his career, but it came close.

* * *

Green waves broke against the ground, receding back up into the sky, then splashing across the earth once more. The aerial tide crashed against the forest, dripping closer with every inward swing. Oozing lime spray splattered against the ground with each receding of the mindless tide, thick putrid drops that burned the ground . . . not with fire, but with decay.

Distant voices gurgled in the cascading water, words barked out from thick phlegm-filled throats. An eerie beat was set by the strangled croakings, one that registered not as any kind of human tonal pattern, but which had its own dragging compulsion nonetheless.

Gray light shattered its way through the trees, falling up from out of the Earth. It had a filthy, decadent odor, a rotting smell that clung to the air like mist. The deformed illumination did wash away with each return of the impossible tide, but only for the moment. As soon as the reeking green curtain was lifted, the blighted light would filter upward through the ground cover once more, seemingly heavier and fouler with every renewal.

Through the ground, a sickening rumble started, one that shook the trees from top to bottom. It set the leaves to rustling at a frantic pace, branches whipping back and forth in violent frenzy. The noise of it joined the harsh whispers and the continual deluging tide waters to create a hissing cacophony that filled the air.

London opened his eyes. The gray light crawling up out of the ground all around him had begun to sting his flesh. Making his way out of his sleeping bag, he pulled on his boots, pocketing Betty and Veronica at the same time. His eyes darted in all directions, taking in the unbelievable insanity infecting the construction site. Closing his eyes again, he focused on the voices in the distance. Then, after he had pinpointed their direction, he started off toward them, thinking, *Maybe now we can get to the bottom of all this.*

He stayed close to the trees, using their foliage to avoid the blistering tide as it drenched downward. His mind darted toward Mitchell for a moment, but he let the idea of waking the other man pass.

This must be what he's been going through every night, thought the detective. No wonder he stays behind a locked door until morning.

You think that's it? asked a separate voice in his head. *You really think that old man's been seeing this?* This?

London wondered where his mind was going. Giving it free rein, he asked himself, *This is supposed to be some special show just for me?*

Maybe it is, maybe it isn't. That's not the point. I don't care how much that old man loves his Sarah Jane—if he'd seen the tide falling out of the sky and then falling back up again—let alone light coming out of the ground, and all the rest of this shit—he'd have been out of here like he was shot out of a cannon.

So what is this?

Maybe we got here at just the right moment. Maybe only someone with our perceptions can actually see what's happening. Maybe it's all an illusion.

Then a cold dread sliced through the detective's nerves. The questioning voice in his head went silent for a long moment, startling London with its abrupt disappearance. He could not concentrate on the fact, however. He had too much else to worry about.

The gagging odors all about him continued their assault on his senses. So strong was the putrid fetor that the steam of it had begun to scald the detective's eyes. The sum of it all, along with the burning tide dripping from the trees above, and the harshly glaring light shining up from below him, was a world of insane abstraction—one so intense London was beginning to find it almost impossible to concentrate on anything.

Then, as he pulled another breath in between his fingers—the only way he could breathe in the gagging atmosphere—the questioning voice returned, asking, *Are your feet wet?*

What? asked London, still working his way toward the foul choir hidden from sight somewhere off in the distance. *What do you mean?*

Your feet, hissed the voice in his head. A thread of panic worked its way into the words as it continued. *Are they wet? Is there* really *any water falling on us?*

As the detective tried to concentrate, the voice swelled to fever pitch, screaming within his skull. *This is wrong! Completely wrong*—don't you see? Don't you understand? *This is a distraction!*

"A distraction from what?" muttered London aloud.

From whatever's really going on, you asshole!!

The detective stopped moving. Knowing that something was wrong, but not knowing what, he told himself, *One step at a time.*

Then, he reached down, feeling his boots.

"No," he said in a low voice. "They're not wet."

Faced with proof that something was more amiss than he had suspected, London awoke. Above him, a harsh voice croaked noises in a tongue he had never heard. He knew, however, that something was giving an alert that he had awakened. Focusing his eyes, he saw what that thing was. Two figures stood to either side of him, one each holding his legs and arms. London gagged at the sight of them. Their skin was various shades of mottled green, except their bellies, which were a flat, dull white. Their skin's individual coloring followed the patterns of any number of earthly reptiles, but not its texture. It was neither snake-smooth nor alligator-rough, but layered and veined in some manner the detective could not quite bring into focus.

As his head turned from left to right, he noted that the hands holding him were webbed and clawed, seemingly too large for the bodies to which they were attached. The things' heads were similarly oversized, each topped by a pair of protruding, bulbous eyes. The mouths clicking above him were lipless, long gashes filled with double rows of broken, razor-pointed teeth.

All of this flooded London's brain in a split second. The horror of it would have paralyzed a normal man, but London had seen too much like it in his time to be affected by anything as ordinary as mere physical repulsiveness.

As the reality of his situation began to flood his senses, the detective suddenly realized he was in the ancient abandoned basement he had discovered earlier that day. More precisely, he had been stretched out on the carved obsidian block in the center of the room.

An altar, he thought. *It's a goddamned altar!*

London tried to kick, but his legs were too tightly held in place. He worked at moving his arms as well, but the horrors grasping him had him too tightly—too securely. Then, a dozen yards off in the far corner of the room, the detective saw another of the monstrosities moving forward. His eyes focused on the slowly loping creature, more exactly on the ornately carved, black glass dagger in its hand.

Something's wrong.

He croaked out some sort of gangrenous oath, but London forced himself to pay it no attention. The terrified voice in his head was right. Something was wrong. As before, something was out of place.

But what? *What?!*

The detective tried to avoid staring at the advancing creature, but he could not help himself. All around him, its fellow horrors had taken up its chant. Sweat poured off London's forehead, stinging his eyes. He knew the thing was coming for him, bringing its ancient blade to do him some kind of damage—assuredly painful, probably permanent. Closer it came, yard after yard, its bulging, unblinking eyes drilling their way into the detective's brain . . . calling to his fear. Forget it snarled another, older voice in his head. Ignore it. Think. *Think! Figure out what's really going on here before it's too late.*

Thhe detective was suddenly startled by a still older, heavily accented, female voice that whispered in his ear.

"Do it, Mr. London. Quickly."

"I can't," he shouted, his nerves fighting the terror eating at him. "That thing's halfway across the room. It's going to kill me! It's almost here!"

Halfway across the room?

He understood.

The subterranean chamber he had been in had been a basement. Twenty by forty feet in dimension—maximum.

"This isn't real!" he shouted.

Then he opened his eyes—again. Once more he was in his sleeping bag, but this time the only other being in sight was an elderly Chinese woman who said, "You almost get the big bite that time."

The detective caught hold of himself, forcing away the panic throttle that had started to shake his body. Sitting up, he wiped at the sweat and mucus that had made a slick mess of his face, then said, "Almost, Mrs. Lu. Almost."

London took stock of the situation. Letting all the levels of his mind loose at one time, he scanned what appeared on the surface to be his current reality. After a few seconds, he relaxed—he was certain he had indeed stripped away the layers of dream that had gotten hold of him in his sleep and finally come fully awake. The arrival of Si Wan Lu had helped. The old *feng shui* woman had found him just in time. Taking that into consideration, he told her, "You couldn't have gotten here at a better time, Mrs. Lu."

"No problem. Me come this morning. Read *feng shui*. Then go back town, call Kong Lin—give report. After that, I walk back like I tell old black man."

"You walked?" answered London with a surprised voice. "Why didn't you just take a cab?"

"Cab cost money," said the old woman indignantly. "Besides, knew you wouldn't need me until now. Knew if I come too soon, fleas catch me in dream web. Wait until now, wake you up. Save life. Earn bonus."

"Haaaaheh-heh," laughed the detective. Dragging on his boots, he indicated Mitchell's trailer with a jerk of his head and told her, "Yeah, sure—all right. I agree. I'd say you earned a bonus. And now, please be so good as to go wake up the security man for me."

"It two o'clock in morning. What for wake up sleeping man?"

London quickly slipped Veronica into her accustomed place inside his boot, then slipped into his shoulder holster. Sliding Betty into place within it, he told Mrs. Lu, "Because we're probably going to need him, considering what's coming for us."

Then the old woman began to notice the pattering, flopping sounds coming toward them from the dark forest beyond. The detective had heard them minutes earlier. Turning toward the trees, her still-sharp eyes picked out the same crouching, shambling figures he had.

She lost no time in moving off toward the trailer. By the time she was banging on the metal door, London was already firing into the trees.

* * *

"It's two o'clock in the mornin', Roth." Morcey whispered, staring at the phone in disbelief. By the time the balding man and his wife had driven back to town and gotten a room for the night it had been almost eleven o'clock. He did not really mind getting the call, however. The members of most other security agencies would have taken the phone off the hook. Then again, the members of most other agencies were not accustomed to being attacked by horrors from beyond time and space.

"I could hang up and tell you all to go fuck yourselves," came the tired voice of the FBI man on the other end. "If you'd like that better."

"No, no—this is an abusive enough reminder of what workin' with the government is like." The ex-maintenance man yawned, then threw his feet over the edge of his motel room bed. Sitting up, he stifled a second yawn as he asked, "So, to what do I owe this honor?"

"You called me—remember? Wanting to know about a place called Innsmouth? Ring any bells?"

"Yeah, yeah," answered the balding man. As the seconds passed he came more awake, realizing more fully with each moment that the FBI man would not have called him in the middle of the night if it were not important. Shaking his head, he continued, "Sorry. I'm with ya. What's goin' on?"

"Heap big piles of trouble, Paul," answered Roth. "You can trust me on that."

"I can trust ya, I just can't quote ya. Right?"

"I'd say there's nothing worse than a funny Jew, but, pots and kettles and all that, I'll just let it pass. Besides," the FBI man's voice went low, "You don't have the time to fool around."

Morcey came fully awake. The sharpness of his attention crackled out from him, waking Lai Wan. The psychometrist felt the shift in her husband's mood even though she was sound asleep. Despite his desire not to disturb her, he could not help it. She sat up without making a sound, listening to the mood of the room while her husband continued his call.

"So spill it, Roth," said the balding man, reaching for a pad and pen. As the balding man flipped open the spiral notebook he had left on the stand near the phone in anticipation of this moment, the FBI man told him, "Innsmouth is the site of the nation's first internment camp."

"Who was it got interned?"

"The whole town. 1927 to '28—it's one of the oldest of the Bureau's black files. You asked about a guy named Marsh? It was a whole family named Marsh that ran the place. The entire town was evacuated and then leveled. All the residents were put into detainment camps for the rest of their lives."

Morcey whistled a low, dark note. Regaining his breath, he asked, "Why? Sweet bride of the night, what'd they do?"

"If you read between the lines, I'd say they pledged allegiance to some dark god and got turned into fish people." The ex-maintenance man said nothing. He had come across such people in his time. "And . . . that includes the guy that blew the whistle on the place. One Robert Olmstead."

"What?" asked Morcey, somewhat confused. Continuing to scribble, he asked, "He was one of them, but he turned everyone in?"

"No. Olmstead called the government in when he thought the flounderettes were going to sacrifice him or eat him or whatever. Later, he discovered that he was related to the Marsh family, and that the entire transformation process was a hereditary thing. He later escaped, broke into a mental health facility where his cousin was being held, and helped him escape."

"Were they ever found?"

"Their clothes were found on a beach along the ocean. Neither was ever seen again." While the ex-maintenance man let everything he had just been told sink in, Roth instructed him to hook his portable fax to the phone saying, "You want the rest of this, you can read it. It's two o'clock in the morning where I am, too. You're not the only Jew in the world who wants to get some sleep tonight."

Morcey did as the FBI man had requested. Then he sat back, listening to the machine's soft hum. As he waited, he could feel his front teeth sliding across each other, tops grinding against the bottoms. Lai Wan had felt a presence when they had first arrived at the job site which she could only identify as "Marsh." Now the presence had been identified. Olmstead, the man who had seen to the destruction of Innsmouth, had turned out to be one of the Marshes himself, a prodigal returning home. But by then it was too late. So he had found the only remaining one of his kind and returned it to the sea, presumably going along with it.

The balding man's mind was racing with a thousand questions. But as long as the phone was being used as a fax line, he could ask nothing. Besides, he was used to Roth—knew how the man operated. He would always cooperate with the London Agency, but only so far. By faxing the pages, he was cutting his involvement. When the machine on the nightstand stopped producing copies, Morcey knew the FBI man would no longer be on the line.

As of that moment, he knew they were on their own. He also knew that his sleep was over for that night. The balding man turned to tell his wife that they would have to leave soon. He was not surprised to find her already dressing. Stretching his arms above his head, he moaned, "Man—I'm gettin' too old for this job."

He thought about what was to come next—driving back to the job site at night on only a few hours sleep—hoping that the only thing that would happen would be his rousing London and Mitchell from a sound sleep to give them the new information. He also thought about the likelihood of that being the only thing that was going to happen tonight.

"Yeah . . . way too old."

And then he turned his head. For a moment, he thought he had heard something, for lack of a better word—strange—coming from outside the motel room.

"Paul . . . ?"

"Yes, dear . . . ?" answered Morcey, not catching the note in Lai Wan's voice at first.

"I believe something has arrived."

The balding man came alert. He had learned never to doubt his wife's premonitions. Thanks to his faith in her, he had just enough time to drag on his pants before the first crushing blows knocked in their motel room's door.

* * *

"Fuck, man—*fuck*!" shouted Mitchell as he flipped on the spotlights attached to the roof of his trailer. "What the fuck be dat shit?"

"Things to kill," shouted London. Taking aim, he squeezed two rounds off. Both bullets hit their target. Instantly the bug-eyed head of one of the loping monstrosities in the distance exploded. Its grotesque body staggered forward a few more steps, then fell over sideways. Others pressed on past the still-flopping corpse.

"Dey's hundreds of them!" screamed Mitchell.

"That's right," answered the detective. Not turning around, he added coolly, "Better bring lots of bullets."

The older man stood in the doorway of his trailer, wide-eyed and staring. He had heard the gurgling whispers in the darkness, smelled the foul sea stench, found the dripping, salty footprints in the morning. But no amount of clues could have prepared him for what he saw now.

Slack-jawed with amazement, he stood frozen in place as the forest beyond erupted, spewing forth an army of insane creatures into the piercing light spewing from the trailor's roof. The fact that London was shooting them down one after another did not seem to register in Mitchell's brain. All he could do was stare unblinking . . . and shake with terror as the freakish army drew closer.

On the ground, London emptied his brass with a flick of his wrist. Grabbing his last two half-moon clips from his belt, he reloaded in seconds, then snapped the cylinder back into the frame, saying, "All right, who wants breakfast?"

Three of the obscene shamblers groped their way to the front of the awkwardly loping crowd. The detective sighted, sending a bullet through each of their brains. Another two stepped forward, pushing their way past their falling comrades, rushing headlong into the same fate.

Behind him, Mrs. Lu grabbed at Mitchell's arm. Shaking him violently, the old woman screamed into the security man's ear, "Wake up, you. Wake up. You want get killed? You want get eaten? Wake up—wake up!"

The old man twitched, trying to swim back to a level of consciousness that would allow him to react. He was trying to make his brain function. Every second London held off the advancing line of horrors helped Mitchell clear some more of the static out of his mind . . . but it was still too much.

He had been waiting for something to arrive for so long, and now that they were in front of him the dread that had been building within him held him in a vice of terror. On one level, he knew that if he did not act the dragging horrors would soon be on him.

But, his mind screamed, *what can we do? There's so many of them. Them . . . them . . . whatever in Hell they are! Good great God almighty—what are they? What are they?!*

All too aware of Mitchell's problem, but not able to divert his attention toward the older man—or to anything else at that moment—the detective took a deep breath, then another. There was nothing he could do for the drooling, crying man behind him that Mrs. Lu could not do. The detective had other problems. Before him, the grotesque line of needle-toothed attackers continued to move forward. London lowered his head for a second, closing his eyes. Sucking in one last, deep breath slowly, he raised his head, again looked over the advancing monsters. Then he raised Betty once more, holding the revolver out before him.

"Well," he said, picking a target at random on which to use his last shell, "how . . . about . . . you?"

He fired. The horror threw up its arms, as if catching its balance would somehow keep it from dying. Its almost comical flailing slowed its fellows for a moment. London took the additional seconds to slide his spent revolver back into its holster. Then he withdrew his blade, thinking, *Well . . . this is it.*

Ahead of him, the nightmare army made its way around the still-flopping comrade. The detective counted his advantages. His enemies were numerous, but slow. Their design showed them to be built more for underwater locomotion.

Don't think they're stupid just because they're slow, a voice in his head told him. *They'll take you down on your first pass through if you make that mistake.*

London nodded grimly. The way the things were spreading out, it was obvious to him that they could think. They were working at encircling him and the others, a tactic the detective was in no position to forestall. Bending down into a crouch, he twisted his neck, preparing for the hand-to-hand work to come, when suddenly the night was split asunder.

"Die, yous motherfuckin' gators—*die!!*"

Mitchell sprang down from his trailer, pumping shotgun blasts into the line ahead. London smiled. The older man swung his weapon from side to side, laughing as he screamed, "I can kill yous! I can kill yous! Yous just a bunch of fuckin' alligators! I'ze be makin' boots out yo' ass come mornin'!"

A loud, crashing noise tore open the night on top of the shotgun explosions. Behind them, a car had just smashed its way through the cyclone gates. The vehicle's lights blinded both sides of the conflict as it bounced along the uneven ground. Then the driver wrenched the wheel violently to the right, sending the car into a reckless spin.

The car whipped around out of control, slamming into the forward members of the attacking things' left-hand flank. Two of the horrors bounced up over the top of the hood; several more were knocked aside or thrown through the air—before the spinning car smashed itself against a tree stump and flipped over.

The car came down on top of three of the hideous sea-spawn, crushing them instantly. As the dust kicked up by the crash billowed out into the morning darkness, London grabbed Mitchell's shoulder, yelling, "Let's go!"

Far beyond the ability to think for himself, the older man followed the detective's lead. The pair charged toward the car. Mitchell pumped out three more blasts, knocking down five more of the creatures. Suddenly, he realized he was out of shells. Wild-eyed, raging, he threw the weapon from him, screaming, "Dat ain't stoppin' me. No way—motherfuckers. No way!"

Pulling a heavy automatic out from under his arm, another from behind his back, he started shooting again, sending round after round at the monsters closing in on the car. Unfortunately, using hand guns instead of a shotgun, he was no longer hitting very many of them, but he kept shooting nonetheless. He emptied the first weapon, then the second. Digging extra clips from his vest pocket, he slid them home and started again.

In the meantime, while Mitchell drew the attacking creatures' attention, London busied himself with getting the driver out of the car. Shattering the left-hand side window with a solid kick, he reached in, helping the somewhat shaken Morcey to crawl to safety. As his partner cleared the window, the detective shouted, "Where's Lai Wan?"

"I dropped her at the local police station," answered the other man groggily. Trying to get to his feet, he shouted to be heard over Mitchell's firing. "She'll be safe there."

London nodded. Getting Morcey's arm over his shoulder, the detective started back toward the trailer, screaming for the security man to follow. As they stumbled along, the ex-maintenance man filled in his partner on the contents of the FBI faxes which Lai Wan had read to him as they drove back to the construction site.

"A wall'a the same creeps showed up at the motel. Lai managed to give me just enough warnin'. I blasted our way to the car. And we think we got an idea of where these damn things came from."

The two men reached the trailer. London settled the slightly limping Morcey on the mobile home's stairs, then turned to make certain Mitchell had not stayed behind. Fighting the dazing effects of his crash, the balding man said, "The FBI closed this whole place down in the twenties. It used to be a town, but the people in it sold their souls to some South Seas devil god or something'. One of 'em, guy named Olmstead, was some kind of renegade, turned informer. Called in the G-men. The government even had the Navy torpedo the reef that used to be here, but I guess it didn't do much good."

As Mitchell came running up to the trailer, London said, "No, I guess not."

The detective grabbed Mitchell as he came in under the lights. He was amazed to see the older man had grabbed his shotgun back up on the way. He was not amazed, however, to see that Mitchell's nerves were going. London could see that the security man's sanity was teetering on the line. A part of the detective wondered what had kept him from falling over already. Not caring, he steadied the older man, telling him, "You're all right. You hear me? You're in one piece, and you're going to stay that way."

"Them things," sputtered Mitchell. "What are them fuckin' things?"

"Don't worry about that," snapped London. "They die. Bullets kill them. All you need to do is keep it up. Keep killing them. Can you do it?"

"But, but, but . . ." the man stammered. The initial burst of adrenaline that had kept him and the detective alive until Morcey's arrival had faded. As his fever passed, his earlier fear began to return. "They keeps comin' and comin' and *comin'!* We gotta run! We gotta run!"

London slapped the man.

"No!" he barked. Turning Mitchell around, London grabbed a box of shotgun shells from the doorway covering their back. Then, shoving the box into the older man's hands, he pointed out at the still-advancing monsters and snapped, "We have to fight!"

Reaching down, London seized the pick he had left against the trailer earlier. Straightening up, he turned to his partner and asked, "You ready?"

Morcey had already pulled his large auto-mag out of its holster. Making a grimace, his head beginning to throb from the crash, he held the heavy automatic up, saying, "Bring 'em on, boss."

London smiled. Giving his partner an encouraging nod, he told him and Mitchell both, "Hold them off best you can. I think I know what to do to end this. Hopefully some of them will follow me."

Hefting the pick, London stared out at the again-advancing line of creatures. Selecting the safest path through their ranks, he took a deep breath, then ran for the forest, shouting, "Just keep them back as long as you can!"

He disappeared into the darkness. As he had predicted, his running off into the trees disrupted the shambling monstrosities' attack. As the creatures slowed, suddenly uncertain as to what to do, Mitchell cried, "Where's he goin'? How can he see anythin' out dere?"

"Hell," asked Morcey. "That all you worried about? Shit—let's give him some more light."

Taking aim, Morcey fired a tracer round into the ruptured gas tank of his ruined rental car. The leaking tank exploded, sending a driving wave of shrapnel through the nearest creatures. An ugly black cloud blasted its way up into the sky as a rain of flame and burning metal showered the area, setting the forest and a number of the deep fathom dwellers afire. Shaking his head to clear some of the pain building in it, Morcey pulled himself to his feet, then told Mitchell, "Okay—dat oughta get things started."

In the space between the trailer and the burning car, a score of the horrific things croaked and bleated as they burned. Around them, however, their fellows turned an indifferent eye to their dying comrades' fate, eyeing the two men responsible.

They had come up from the sea as they always had, to move across the land and claim the lives and souls of the fragile surface dwellers. It was the appointed day. It was the time for the sacrifice. Only once before had they met such difficulty. But that time, they had been unprepared—caught off guard by a force a thousand strong and armed with tanks and submarines.

Thus they had pulled back. They had licked their wounds and bided their time. Bit by bit, their strength returned. First, the traitor had returned repentant. Then he had brought others. Dozens in the beginning—hundreds later. Together they had survived and bred and waited. Waited for the right moment—for the time when the stars would again align and they could make the last sacrifice necessary.

At the darkest moment in time—when night was at its deepest—one more soul needed to be spilled across the ornately carved ebony rectangle Captain Obed Marsh had brought back from the Kanakas. The freakish nightmares realized, at that moment, the one they had been awaiting so long was racing to their dark altar to throw himself across it.

Many of them turned back toward the forest to make sure he did not escape his fate. Many more of them, however, stayed behind. Their attack thus far had been a careful thing. They had not wanted to damage the sacrificial soul before its time. Now, however, the surface pups standing beneath the blinding lights—the insignificant souls that had caused so much damage among their ranks—they could be disposed of without concern.

Turning toward Morcey and Mitchell, the sea-bottom dwellers began moving toward the trailer once more. Their needle teeth clacking, they loped forward with glee. Now they could kill without hesitation.

Soon the doorway would be open, and their long servitude would be rewarded with an entire world as their plaything. Ahead of them, the air shattered with noise. Around them, their fellows began to fall once more. It mattered not.

In a handful of minutes, the Earth would be theirs. Theirs finally.

Forever.

* * *

London dashed through the forest, heading back to the underground chamber.

Moron, he thought to himself. *Idiot. How could you have left that damn thing in one piece? How could you have not smashed it the first second you laid eyes on it?*

He forced his mind to focus, dispelling the chiding voices within it. He was willing to take the blame for not having realized sooner what he should have done, but he had no time for recriminations.

Weaving his way through the dark forest, he ducked for cover as the air behind him heated with the thunder of an unexpected explosion. He did not have to look back to know it was the overturned car that had been obliterated.

Hope it doesn't attract the police, he thought.

Mitchell had been preparing himself to see something horrific for weeks, and he had still almost slipped over the edge into madness. If he had not seen London killing the mind-numbing monsters, there would have been no saving him.

A squad car or two of deputies out on night patrol . . . they would be helpless—worse than helpless. The detective knew that, although Morcey had left Lai Wan at a police station, the psychometrist would not be trying to rally anyone to their aid. The uninitiated would only die there in the forest.

No, he thought as he made his way deeper into the brush, *this one's up to us.*

Then two heavy-breathing forms loomed up in front of London. Their webbed and clawed arms outstretched, both grabbed for the human clumsily. London ducked easily but, thrown off-balance by the heavy pick, he slipped on a clump of heavy vegetation. The detective fell forward and sideways. The sea-spawn croaked wildly, one of them throwing itself atop him.

Its piercing claws sank deep into London's back and side. Refusing to acknowledge the pain, the detective buried his elbow in the creature's snout. At the same time, he snapped his other hand forward, driving his bent fingers into the thing's throat. Not waiting to see if he had done the creature any lasting damage, the detective gathered up his pick and leaped to his feet, swinging the sharp tool as he rose.

The curved axe's tooth broke through the creature's chest, smashing its bones and bursting its heart. Putting a foot to the thing's white belly, London kicked it free from the pick and was immediately on his way once more. He could hear a multitude of the monster's fellows moving in his direction and did not intend to make an easy target of himself.

Sliding silently between the trees, London fought off the panic trying to enslave him. Cutting himself off from his emotions, he pushed himself downward into his cold, logical center. Straining his senses, he sent them searching for any trace of his destination.

His eyes searched for a hint of white hanging from above. His ears filtered out the noise of the things around him, listening instead for any slight trace of his shirt flapping in a bit of breeze filtering in from the sea. Then, suddenly, he had it. A moment only—but he caught a trace of a scent . . . man-made fibers mixed with human sweat. . . .

His head snapped in the direction of the breeze. There was his shirt, still hanging in the branch where he had tied it earlier. The detective's first instinct was to race directly for the marker, but he held back. Employing more caution than ever, he moved forward quietly, determined not to fall prey to his emotions so close to his goal.

He covered the remaining yards slowly, inches at a time. In the distance he could hear the muffled crack of gunfire.

How much longer can they hold out, asked a voice in his head.

Long enough, he told it, not breaking stride.

Then London was at the entrance to the subterranean chamber. A soft, flickering glow now rose from out of the hole he had broken open during the afternoon. Clutching the same pick he had used to perform that operation, he lowered himself cautiously through the opening once more.

Noiselessly he descended onto the dirt incline. This time, however, the long-forgotten basement was not empty. One of the creatures stood within the chamber, hunching over the obsidian altar, its back to the detective. Pausing to catch his breath, London took in the obscene picture before him.

The thing was predominantly grayish green. Most of its body appeared shiny and slippery, but the ridges running the length of its back were scaly. London marveled at the misshapen thing. Its form still vaguely suggested the anthropoid more than the others, but its head was clearly that of an amphibian. The detective noted the palpitating gills on the sides of its neck, laboring hard in the open air. Then creature turned toward him.

It stared unblinking at him with its prodigiously bulging eyes. But it was not the freakish abomination's face that stole London's attention, but that which sat atop it. Resting on the thing's ridged brow was an oddly shining tiara. It was tall in the front and seemed crafted predominantly of gold, though a weird lighter lustrousness hinted at some strange alloy. The crown was covered with a wealth of striking designs—some simply geometrical, some plainly marine—chased or molded in high relief on its surface with a craftsmanship of incredible skill and grace.

The thing took an awkward step toward its intended victim, its lipless mouth curling into a sad grin. Holding a dagger aloft, one fashioned of the same black glass as the altar, it croaked, "Right on time, Mr. London."

Before the detective could move, a half-dozen of the monster's comrades fell on him from above. Instantly they wrenched the pick from his hands. Seconds later they had him completely helpless, each one holding an arm or leg. At the direction of the one in the tiara, the horrors dragged London across the room and pulled him down onto the carved ebony rectangle—holding him there as they had in his earlier dream.

"You have thwarted the designs of Mother Hydra and Father Dagon in the past, Mr. London . . . but no more."

London marveled that the twisted visage before him could speak at all, let alone intelligibly. None of its comrades had emitted more than froggish bleats and croaks. Breaking through his fascination, however, he told himself, *Don't look at it—don't fall under its spell. For God's sake*—for everyone's sake—*hold on to yourself. Hold on.*

"Now," the thing told him, "you have come to the end of your ability to interfere with us. And with your end comes the end of your species' rein on this world."

The thing turned from London, looking away toward the far wall as it intoned, *"Iä! Iä! Cthulhu fhtagn! Ph'nglui mglw'nafh Cthulhu R'lyeh wgah-nagl fhtagn. . . ."*

The other sea-devils in the room turned in the same direction as the thing wearing the crown. As those holding London did so, their grips shifted slightly. Taking a deep breath, the detective let it out slowly, then shouted, "Now!"

Ramming his left hand downward, he broke the hold of the monster that had been restraining his left wrist. Before the others could react, London had shoved his hand down into his boot and come back up with his stiletto. Pulling the wicked blade free, he swung it in a wide arc, slitting the throats of two of his captors with the one motion.

Bedlam broke out as some of the monsters tried to move forward while those mortally wounded floundered about, blocking their way. Taking advantage of the scant seconds he had bought himself, he kicked away the last of the creatures still holding him, then twisted his body and threw himself at the monster in the tiara.

London hit the thing full force. The two toppled over, hitting the ground with a violent thud. Now he could see what the crowned sea beast's body had hidden from him. On the far wall, a portal had begun to open. London dragged himself to his feet, stunned by the unexpected apparition. It was a vague, purplish oval of pulsating energy, filled with a mist that appeared to be hiding a background landscape filled with minarets and pyramids.

Second after precious second he stared transfixed into the beckoning portal, until finally that voice which spoke to him only rarely screamed within his head.

Turn away!

The detective broke off his gaze, whirling away from the luring vision. As he did, the mitred monster sprang to its feet and moved forward on him. Behind it, others of his kind were crowding forward. Still more were pouring in through the entrance from above.

Heedless of the others, London charged the leader even as it staggered forward toward him. The two rammed into each other. The monster's claws tore across London's chest while Veronica sank deep within the thing's heaving, slick white belly. The hopping monster bleated—a high-pitched squeal that echoed off the walls of the subterranean chamber—while a rush of dark black ichor vomited from the gutted horror.

As the foul smell of the creature's fluids filled the room, London tore the tiara from its head. Then, kicking the dying beast out of his way, he sneered, "Nice try, Olmstead," and hurled the heavy crown into the pulsating opening across the room.

* * *

"So, dat's dat, huh?"

London looked at Morcey harshly, casting the set of his eyes to indicate that he was not amused. Straining to keep a straight face, the ex-maintenance man looked back at him innocently through the thinning darkness, saying, "Hey, what'da ya want from me?"

They had all survived. Now that the danger had passed, the balding man was feeling giddy. The detective merely sighed and shook his head, not seeing any point in rising to his partner's bait. The two men, as well as Mitchell, were muddy and smelled of sweat and dried blood. All of them had been injured—gashes and wicked bruises—but nothing serious.

Lai Wan and Mrs. Lu, both in fine shape, sat within the security man's trailer waiting for the water he had put on for them earlier to come to a boil. The old *feng shui* woman had already gone over the job site again, checking it out for her third cousin, as well as for her usual hefty fee. Now she wanted her morning tea. When Mitchell had hesitated, she had scolded him loudly.

"I no like leave home. Too much trouble. World too crazy. But I come here anyway because I am too good. Almost get kill, but come anyway, and save whole world. Save your life, you know . . . now it too much to ask for hot water? No wonder I never want leave home. Nobody worth meeting outside anymore."

Mitchell had gotten the point and had put a pot of water on the fire. Mrs. Lu's rant had broken the heavy mood hanging over everyone in the early morning darkness that still enshrouded the forest. Despite their survival, the five had still needed a couple of hours to regain their composure.

Their troubles had stopped when London had thrown the tiara through the shimmering portal. The dimensional gateway had begun to recede the moment the golden artifact had passed over to the other side. He had kicked the creature that had been wearing it in the same direction, but it did not make it completely through. The portal closed on it abruptly, slicing it cruelly into two uneven sections.

Everything unraveled for the monsters with the loss of the tiara—or perhaps its wearer. Suddenly lacking some unseen guidance, the remaining creatures turned as if of one mind and hurried off for the ocean. Both those in the chamber with London and the others still plaguing Morcey and Mitchell—all of them jerked sharply at the moment the portal vanished, gasping—spewing forth sickening, foaming belches.

Most of them did not make it, but instead fell far short of their mark, dying on the way back to their true home. None of the human survivors felt any great remorse. And, as London had hoped, no one outside of himself and his companions seemed to have noticed the raging confrontation.

All for the best, he had thought, and had made his way wearily back to the surface.

At that same moment, Lai Wan had sensed that the conflict had ended and simply walked out of the police station. The construction site was only an hour's hike. With the monsters vanquished, she was eager to rejoin the others. The psychometrist instinctively knew her husband had survived. But she wanted to see him for herself.

Just because.

Lai Wan watched him clowning with London and smiled. She knew if he was joking that everything was truly all right. Relaxing, she asked Mrs. Lu, "So . . . how does the *feng shui* read now?"

"All fine. All good. Dragon happy. All fleas gone. No more scratching. Good."

"Excuse me, ma'am," asked Mitchell. "But if y'all don't mind . . . what is this 'funk she' stuff?"

Fielding the question, Lai Wan told the security man, "The Earth is a great sleeping dragon. *Feng shui* is the art of reading the lay of the land to determine where the dragon is, and how it is resting. If one wants to do anything with a piece of property—erect a building, plant crops, pick a grave site—it is always best to first consult someone skilled in *feng shui* to make certain that one proceeds in a manner which will not upset the dragon. This avoids disharmony and allows one's venture to prosper."

"Well, while we're at it, I've got a question, too," said London. Stretching out the kinks settling in his back due to the predawn dampness, he said, "Mrs. Lu keeps talking about fleas. My guess is she's talking about those damn things that were trying to kill us—but why's she call them 'fleas?'"

"Because they not right," said the old woman. "They not natural. They crawl about on dragon, but give nothing—only take. Not right. They just fleas."

"Awwwwwwful damn big fleas," laughed Mitchell.

"Yeah," agreed Morcey. "Oh, what big damn teeth you have, grandma."

The lid to Mitchell's pot began vibrating loud enough for everyone to hear it, indicating that the water was indeed boiling. As Lai Wan busied herself with transforming it into tea, Morcey said, "So, I guess we can chalk up another one for capitalism."

"What?" London looked at his partner skeptically. Narrowing his eyes, he asked, "How do you figure that?"

"Look it . . . Lin wants to develop the land. He runs inta things beyond his comprehension. But he's got too much dough tied up to just cut and run, so he hires us. First he hires Mitchell ta watch the place, then us to clear out the trouble, and Mrs. Lu to scratch behind the dragon's ears. Now, we all get our paychecks while he and his partners build their town and get rich. Right?"

London looked at Mrs. Lu. As the old woman accepted a cup of tea from Lai Wan, she said, "Right, right. *Feng shui* very peaceful now. Lin build lovely homes here. Make much money. Everything good."

"Don't you get it, boss?" said Morcey with an exaggerated drawl. "It's no wonder all these monsters that could kick such ass in Babylon and

Mesopotamia and the like always fall down and go boom every time we come up against 'em. They never run inta no capitalists before."

The detective smiled. Taking the tea offered to him, London held the hot cup in his hand, leeching its warmth hungrily. Behind him, the sun was just beginning to break above the ocean. Lifting his cup toward the others, London said, "Well, then, here's to free enterprise."

"Dat's right," added Mitchell. "God fuckin' bless da U. S. of A."

Everyone agreed, sipping at their scalding tea. And in the distance the sun began its work, warming the land, lighting the way, and drying up the putrid remains of the fleas of the dragon.

About "Mail Order Bride"

Ann K. "Ankh" Schwader will be known to many readers as an inspired poetess in that rare tradition of verse that the late Lin Carter dubbed "Innsmouth Jewelry", in the same rare reliquary alongside Lovecraft's *The Fungi from Yuggoth*, Donald Wandrei's *Sonnets for the Midnight Hour*, Doc Lowndes's *Annals of Arkya*, Duane Rimel's *Dreams of Yith*, and the verse of Richard L. Tierney to name a few.

But here she ventures out for a smooth narrative ride into the deep and choppy waters off Devil Reef. In "Mail Order Bride" Schwader revisits the subtext under the waves of "The Shadow over Innsmouth", that of race-mixing, especially with Asians. Remember that Cap'n Obed was first thought to have brought back a froggish-looking Polynesian bride. When she later turns out to be something from a different phylum altogether, we are just witnessing the fictive mythologizing of the basic idea, horrific enough to Lovecraft, that a solid Yankee like Obed should dally with the impure-blooded wenches of the South Seas—and have children by them! Schwader returns to this pregnant motif—with a vengeance!

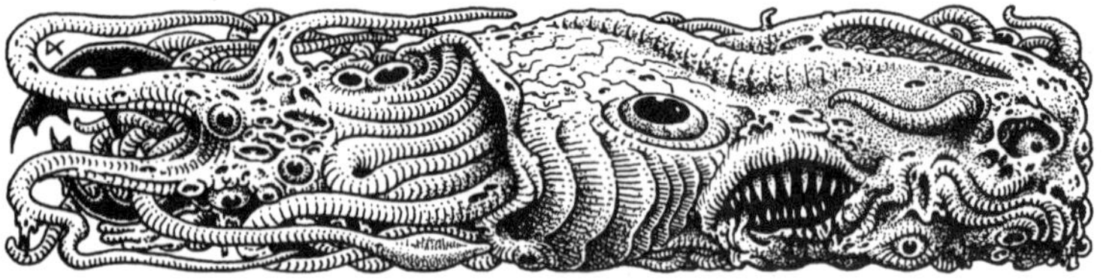

Mail Order Bride

by Ann K. Schwader

She wasn't much to look at, but George had learned not to expect much from life. Lupe in her worn pink suit, still picking carnation petals from her tightly curled hair, was as good a wife as he was probably ever going to get. Pulling his own carnation from his lapel, he let the girl put it in water while he checked over their JOP wedding papers. They looked simple enough, unlike the bull that attorney from the Island Love Introduction Agency had fed him these past two months. If he'd known in advance what it took to bring one Filipina to Ashton, California—

George froze. Lupe was staring at him again, her moss-green eyes just a little too bulging and wide. They were the first thing he'd noticed about her when she had arrived. Her black and white agency photo hadn't looked so bad, but now he wondered what he'd been stuck with. Last thing he needed was a wife going blind on him.

"You got a problem?"

Lupe shook her head without blinking. "No problem. Just wanted to know what you'd like for dinner tonight."

"Depends. What'd you get at the store today?"

When he'd left for a half-day's work at the garage this morning, the fridge in his battered mobile home had held the basics: stale bread, half a pizza, and a six-pack. He'd left Lupe a few bucks, but hadn't checked what she'd bought yet. The girl had served fish four out of the five nights she'd been here.

He was getting sick of fish.

"They had specials on steak and shrimp, so I got both," Lupe said. "With rice and salad."

Getting better. "Steak's OK for tonight. Anything but beer to go with it?"

Brushing her small dark hands on her skirt, Lupe frowned. "I didn't know you wanted something else. Is tequila all right? I could go get some."

"Fine."

Digging into his pocket, George found two fives and the car keys and handed them to his new wife. She was out the door before he could wonder how she'd bought all that food with the money he'd left her.

He didn't wonder past one beer, though. Two of his bowling buddies had already married Island Love girls this spring—and they both said their wives were completely different from American women. Remembering his ex, Maureen, George sure hoped so. He didn't need her kind of mouth again.

He just wanted marriage the way it used to be.

* * *

For the first couple of weeks, things went fine. His clothes got washed, his beer was cold . . . and if the rest of being married wasn't so great, George did his best to ignore it. At least Lupe wasn't fat, the way Maureen had gotten. She just felt a little different. A little cold, no matter how stuffy their bedroom was with the swamp cooler busted again.

Then they had their first fight about that stupid figurine.

It wasn't actually the figurine he'd noticed first, but the flowers Lupe had placed around it. He had found the whole set-up one night after work: a TV tray by his wife's side of the bed, with wildflowers in two juice glasses and a little heap of sea shells in front of . . . whatever it was.

Carved from dull black stone, the figure wasn't more than six inches high. It felt oddly heavy in his hand, greasy-slick, and the design itself was worse. A few details—flared gills, needle teeth, veined webbing fanned between clawed fingers—stood out, but the rest was nothing he wanted to dwell on. Most disturbing of all, the thing had *tits*. Big centerfold ones like a mermaid's.

"George?"

Lupe stood in the bedroom doorway, looking even more popeyed than usual.

"Yeah?" He gripped the figurine more tightly. "What is this, anyway? You into voodoo or something? The agency didn't say nothing about voodoo."

Hurrying toward him, Lupe tried to pull the little statue from his hand. "Please put that down!"

It was the first time she'd crossed him. George held the thing high out of reach, feeling disgusted. Suddenly, he didn't even want to be touching it, any more than he wanted to be fighting with his new wife.

"What is this?" he repeated, more gently. "Something from home?"

Lupe nodded and reached for it again. This time, he released his grasp. The girl polished the statue on one knee of her faded jeans before replacing it between the flowers.

George scowled at the homemade shrine. "Takes up an awful lot of room . . . and it's ugly. Put the damn thing outside."

"Won't work there," said Lupe quietly. "You leave it alone, OK?"

He couldn't, of course; not after that. The first night, he tossed it in the outside garbage. No way in hell the girl could've heard him—she never even turned over in her sleep—but next morning the statue was back. He ate the eggs and bacon she fixed him in silence, satisfying himself with the worry in her weird green eyes.

On his way home after work, he bought a ball peen hammer and hid it in the shed. When he changed out of his coveralls, he noticed Lupe's shrine had fresh flowers, and a higher pile of shells. She must have been goofing off down on the beach again.

"Haven't you got better things to do?" he asked during dinner.

Lupe just stared at him as though she didn't understand English, and refilled his plate with deep-fried shrimp.

He waited until after midnight this time to take the statue outside. It felt *pricklier*, somehow; all edges and spines against his skin. Clambering down the weedy hill behind his trailer, he nearly twisted an ankle getting to the beach and finding a convenient rock.

George smacked the statue a good half-dozen times with his new hammer. When he didn't hear anything cracking, he fumbled for the flashlight on his belt—then wished he hadn't. The sea thing's eyes weren't black stone after all.

More like moss-green, and far too large.

Cursing, he grabbed it and ran for the shoreline, heaving it far out into the waves. A distant splash reassured him, but his first glance across the bed the next morning didn't. The statue's needle grin looked even creepier in broad daylight.

George didn't bother waking Lupe to make him breakfast. Toast and three shots of tequila sounded like a better idea.

* * *

Thursday was bowling night, thank God. Glancing over his beer at Ray and Phil—the first two to marry—George struggled for the right words. He didn't want to sound like a paranoid idiot. He just needed to know whether anybody else's wife had a statue like Lupe's, and what they'd managed to do about it.

"Sure is weird," he said, "the stuff Filipinas keep around. My wife's got this ugly little—"

Phil's hand twitched, nearly spilling his beer.

"*Statue?* About so high, and fishy-looking?"

George glanced at Ray, but he was busy pouring another glass. Tony and Art, the other two guys on their team, were busy looking anywhere else. Phil was a damn good mechanic, but everybody knew he had problems. Having his first wife walk out on him last year hadn't helped.

"Yeah," George finally said. "Something like that."

Phil seemed to relax a little, but Ray didn't. Running a hand through his sparse, graying hair, he reached for his bowling bag.

"Gotta make this an early one," he murmured, to no one in particular. "Just remembered I promised Inez. . . ."

None of them expected him to finish the sentence. George finally got another pitcher from the bar and watched Tony drink most of it. Nobody blamed him, even though Phil wound up having to drive him home.

Tony was getting married tomorrow.

* * *

A few weeks later, Lupe's makeshift shrine disappeared. George first noticed while changing for bowling: He wasn't getting that creepy feeling the statue's popeyed gaze always gave him. Even its TV tray was gone, though he could still see indentations in the worn carpet.

Shrugging into his shirt, he searched the room's crowded closet and sticking drawers, even under the bed where he'd shoved his ten-year collection of *Sports Illustrated*. Nothing. The ugly thing had apparently vanished—accompanied, he hoped, by all his bad dreams.

Unable to believe his good luck, he asked Lupe about her missing figurine at dinner. To his surprise, the girl blushed.

"It's gone because I don't need it any more. It's already done its work."

George frowned.

"What work? You didn't say that . . . whatever it was . . . was supposed to do anything." He forked mashed potatoes into his mouth to keep from admitting that he'd never *asked*, either. "So what does it do, anyway?"

Lupe smiled and laid one hand over her flat stomach.

"No way," he said, over and around the potatoes. "You can't be. I haven't even got health insurance at work, damnit!"

The girl's pug-dog eyes widened. "I thought you'd be happy. I thought all husbands wanted—"

"Well, I don't."

Pushing back from the table, he headed for the fridge and the last two cold beers. Kids weren't something he'd counted on yet. He just didn't have the money—hell, he'd never had it—and pregnant women got demanding. They expected you to hang around all the time, work steady and stay sober.

"Look at this place!" He gestured with his free hand at the cramped kitchen. "Do you see any room for a kid around here?"

Lupe followed his gestures with her usual unblinking stare.

"Plenty of room." She finished her fish and laid its bones aside. "Babies are small, very small. You'll like her."

George downed his first beer in four swallows, though it didn't help much. Late June plus a bum swamp cooler made one hell of a combination—and now this.

"You're wrong about the room," he said, ignoring the rest of her statement. "You're wrong about everything. I didn't want a kid, that's all. Was that too much to ask?"

When he didn't get an answer, George drained his second beer and tossed both cans into a corner. Heading for the door, he yanked it open hard enough to make the whole house rattle. His car didn't want to start—as usual—but he gunned the Ford's balky engine until it got him the hell away from his problems.

This wasn't what he'd expected from marriage at all, even after Maureen. Maureen had at least yelled back at him.

Lupe just sat there watching his life go down the tubes.

He was ten minutes late getting to the lanes, but Tony's black Camaro still wasn't in its usual parking space. Taking the next space over, George grabbed his bowling bag and headed inside quickly. Even summer league people bitched about late starts.

Art, their team captain, already looked steamed. Ray and Phil seemed equally gloomy, but Tony was nowhere to be seen.

"So where's the hot shot tonight?" George forced a smile. Tony'd been their best scorer all season, though they had no chance at a league championship.

Art finished lacing his shoes and stood up, frowning.

"In jail, that's where." His pudgy face creased with disgust. "Got hauled in last night for beating up his wife. God alone knows why that girl's not pressing charges."

George's pale eyes widened. Tony was the youngest member of their team—with the shortest fuse—but he wasn't one to beat his women.

"What the hell happened?"

If anything, Art looked more disgusted. "Didn't want to pay the piper for his honeymoon. When Tia told him about the baby, he just went nuts."

* * *

By August, they'd all paid that piper . . . even Art, to George's secret vindictive joy. Art's Island Love bride turned out to be a cousin of Lupe's, who was somehow related to Tia. Tia was either related to Phil's wife or Ray's wife Inez or both, but by now none of their husbands really cared.

It was weird enough watching them get ready for the babies.

At first, George hadn't minded—much—when Lupe started inviting the others over to make baby clothes. Lupe didn't ask for more than a few dollars, and she never mentioned prenatal care. None of the women were seeing doctors, though Art and Ray tried to insist on it.

George just figured it was one more Filipina custom. If Lupe wanted this baby, taking care of herself beforehand was her business. She never threw up in the mornings, though she did seem to be getting bigger awfully fast.

What *was* starting to irk him was they way their wives just took over a place. Sometimes he'd have no warning, and there they'd be when he got home: five popeyed pregnant women, all sewing and chattering away incomprehensibly. He'd thought it was Spanish at first, but Phil said no. Too many consonants in the wrong places . . . and it sounded like a tonal language, which Spanish wasn't. George didn't know any of this from jack, but he did know Phil had lived down in Mexico for a few years.

He knew Phil was losing it, too. They all did.

Come fall, their bowling nights turned into beer nights; and more of them. They told each other Tony needed company down at the Star Liter—he was tending bar almost every night now, with the baby coming—but George knew better. He knew it in the headache he always arrived with, the heartburn he couldn't get rid of.

Truth was, they were all getting afraid to go home. Even Tony seemed reluctant to call for last rounds some nights, though George couldn't remember him raising any hell since that night he'd hit Tia.

* * *

Phil tried to kill himself in October. He picked Halloween, though George had been half-expecting something long before. Phil was the top mechanic in Ashton's only garage, but he'd been slipping for months—losing tools, screwing up estimates. Nothing George himself hadn't done far more often, but at least George knew why.

Phil didn't even come in with hangovers, for chrissakes.

Tony had invited them to spend Halloween at the Star Liter—dollar draws all night—but Phil never showed. As it got later, George found himself starting to worry. Tony brought more beers, tried to joke about Phil and his wife making their own party, but both beer and joke tasted flat.

They were arguing halfheartedly about the Raiders when the Star Liter's front door banged open. All dozen or so customers stared. Washed in the bar's dim lighting, Phil looked so damn appropriate for a Halloween midnight—

"Somebody call an ambulance," Tony said in the sudden silence. "No cops, OK?"

Art ran for the pay phone. George helped Tony get Phil into the back room, gritting his own teeth the whole time so he wouldn't puke. Phil still clutched the hunting knife he'd used on himself. Maneuvering the bleeding man through the doorway, George tried to forget how many suicides took somebody along.

"C'mon, man," Tony coaxed as the door finally swung shut. "Hand us the knife, will you?"

Phil dropped it and collapsed. Both wrists kept dripping on the stained tile floor: He'd done a panicked, messy job. Grabbing a stack of bar towels, Tony did his best to wrap up the damage.

"Why'd you do it?" Geroge blurted before he could stop himself. "Jesus H., *why?*"

The question seemed to relight something in Phil's blank eyes.

"Down a' the beach tonight . . . saw 'em there, alla them. Alla women. Talking t' sometin' . . ."

"Someone, you mean." Tony didn't sound at all certain.

Phil shook his head frantically.

"*Sonethin'*. Wasn' human. Came outta th' waves . . . part way out . . . an' tol' 'em . . ."

Despite the cold in the back room, sweat beaded on George's forehead. Sure, Phil was crazy—he'd have to be, right?—but the panic in his eyes looked too convincing.

"Told them what?" he asked, ignoring Tony's high-sign for quiet.

Phil's mouth worked silently for a moment. Tears welled in his eyes. "God, our kids . . . their kids . . . what they're all gonna be . . ."

One bloody hand gripped George's wrist. Gritting his teeth again, he fought the urge to shake it off and run. He was no good around blood, and there was too damn much blood here—blood and craziness and whatever Phil had seen.

Or thought he'd seen. He was nuts, right?

Tony was holding Phil's shoulders, trying to prop him up against the wall somehow. Phil didn't look good. His face was dead white now, clammy white, and Tony's wasn't much better.

"Almost sounded like some kinda *warning*," the younger man muttered. "Go find out where the hell that ambulance is, will you?"

George couldn't get out fast enough. Catching a gasping breath in the now-deserted bar, he hit the door just in time to hear sirens. Art and Ray were waiting on the sidewalk. George wondered if he ought to mention Phil's warning—or whatever it was—then decided not to. Ray and Art were both solid guys, not the nervous kind.

Not the kind to understand.

The ambulance crew rushed into the bar a few moments later, then out again with Phil on a stretcher. The sheet wasn't over his face. Tony came out shortly after that and told them all he was closing before the cops arrived. Nobody said anything walking out to the cars, but George noticed they all took off like bats out of hell.

The trailer was dark and quiet when he got home. A lingering smell of fried fish nearly turned his stomach. He moved carefully, flipping on lights as he headed toward the bedroom. Phil's crazy story had left enough shadows in his mind.

Lupe lay curled small on her side of the bed. George resisted the urge to wake her, but she woke anyway, green eyes staring huge and unreadable in the hallway light.

"How was your evening?" she asked. "Have a good time?"

Phil's face in the dim bar lights, his blood spattering the floor as they watched. Phil's hoarse, broken voice muttering about something coming out of the sea . . . .

George shut off the light quickly.

"Not too bad, I guess. Pretty quiet." He hesitated. "How was yours?"

Only quiet, even breathing came from Lupe's side of the bed. George decided it wasn't really worth asking again. Not with morning still hours away, and that faint fishy stink everywhere.

* * *

The babies started arriving in January. None of the Island Love women went to Ashton's hospital, or even called their husbands at work. They just dealt with birth on their own, the way they'd handled their pregnancies.

Lupe's child came first. After a cold, hectic day at the garage (Phil hadn't been much help since October), George arrived home to find the place practically overrun.

Ray's wife Inez met him at the door, but did little more than let him in.

"What's the problem?" George stared at the four women gathered in his kitchen. "Did Lupe get sick today or something?"

Inez shook her head. "Lupe is fine. Your daughter is fine. They are resting now, I think."

Daughter?

George didn't know much about babies, but he knew his wife shouldn't have had one yet. Not for two months. Edging past Inez—who was making no effort to get out of his way—he tossed his jean jacket onto a chair and headed for the bedroom.

Inez and the others stared after him with their bulging eyes.

The room held none of the home birth mess he'd expected: no bloody sheets, no pans of water. Lupe just lay in the center of their bed, propped up with pillows and holding something red and wrinkled against one breast. She was humming tunelessly to the baby.

When she noticed him in the doorway, she pulled the sheet over herself.

Geroge smiled a little at her unexpected modesty. "Why didn't you call me?" he asked, trying to catch a glimpse of his daughter under the sheet. "I know what I said about money, but I sure didn't expect you to have it at home like this."

Lupe stared up at him and shrugged, the fatigue in her narrow face emphasizing her eyes. George wondered how badly the baby's were loused up.

"Inez says it's a girl," he persisted. "Let's see her, OK?"

Lupe hesitated, then lifted their daughter into sight. George reached out to hold her, but his wife's thin fingers wrapped tightly around the wriggling body, keeping it from him.

George frowned. All newborns were ugly, but he'd still expect this one to look more . . . well, human. Wide eyes even greener than Lupe's blinked at him flatly. Her mouth was wide as well, with knife-thin lips; her tiny neck was marred with creases like vertical wrinkles.

George's hands dropped to his sides. He knew he ought to feel *something* for this new life, but it didn't seem to want him to. There was nothing of him here at all.

"What's her name?" he forced himself to ask.

"I thought you might want to name her. We never talked about it, so I didn't. . . ."

Guilt pinched at him. Whatever this baby looked like, it was still his daughter, the only child he'd ever admitted to fathering. "How does Cynthia Elaine sound? Cindy for short?"

Lupe nodded and pulled the child to her. Watching her wriggle under the sheet, George tried to think of this newborn as Cynthia Elaine Myers—and failed. The normal, pretty name seemed to slide off and vanish, leaving a cold little stranger in his bed.

Murmuring apologies, he backed out of the room. His wife didn't seem to notice. She was watching Cindy as though nothing else existed in the world—certainly not him. Closing the door behind them both, George regretted giving this child his mother's name. Safe in her nursing home in Portland, of course, she'd never know.

But it still didn't seem quite right.

* * *

By the end of February, all the Island Love brides had had their babies—and Phil had had another breakdown. He wound up threatening his own newborn daughter with the same knife he'd used last time. Fortunately, his wife was smart enough to call his doctor instead of the cops. He ended up in the state hospital, which might or might not have been better than jail.

Art told them all about it one night at the Star Liter. Almost all of them had had more than enough, and George waited for the older man's usual disgust at the situation.

Instead, Art bought the next pitcher himself and proceeded to drink half of it.

"Hell of a shame," he said, to no one in particular. "Leavin' that girl all alone with a new baby . . . ."

Tony glanced at George, but neither of them said anything. Bar nights weren't much for conversation. They'd tried bringing baby pictures once, but five infant girls all looking alike put a chill down George's spine. He must not have been the only one: After that, there'd been no more pictures on the bar. None in anyone's wallet.

But they stayed around anyhow in the back of his mind.

Looking at his buddies, George started noticing what the past year had done. Ray's scalp showed clearly through his hair now. Art's face flushed with high blood pressure and stress. Phil was . . . getting help, they all hoped. Somehow.

Even Tony was thinking of selling that Camaro of his, getting something safer for Tia and the kid.

Wiping one hand over the lines on his forehead (had *those* been there a year ago?), George wondered why people said motherhood aged women. Their wives still looked like last spring's young brides. It was they who'd aged, trying to provide for women they couldn't understand and kids they hadn't asked for.

Maybe it was time to find out why.

Afterward, George wasn't sure if beer or anger had made him leave early, heading home with confrontation on his mind. As he pulled into the gravel in front of their trailer, he was glad to see only a single light in the living room window. Walking in on one of Lupe's little get-togethers was the last thing he needed.

From the kitchen, he could see her curled in his big recliner, nursing Cindy and humming softly as usual. Light from behind the chair fell over her shoulder. Her thin cotton blouse gaped open, showing brown skin flecked with red on one small breast . . .

George froze. *White*, his mind insisted. *Milk is white.*

When he looked again, the flecks were still scarlet.

Tossing his car keys on the kitchen table, he ran into the living room just in time to see his wife pull Cindy from her breast. The baby's mouth was smeared with red.

Lupe covered herself quickly, but the blood soaked through her blouse. Cindy started howling. Setting his teeth against the noise, George grabbed the front of his wife's shirt and ripped. What looked like a nasty cat bite still oozed above one dark nipple.

With no sign of milk anywhere.

God, our kids . . . their kids . . . what they're all gonna be . . . .

He couldn't make himself look at the baby again. Lupe had squeezed both herself and Cindy into one corner of the recliner, as far from him as possible. She wasn't yelling, or crying, or even trying to cover herself again. She just stared—as though he were the one with a problem.

"What the hell were you doing?" he demanded. "Feeding her *blood*?"

Lupe fixed him with her moss-colored eyes and nodded.

George's stomach lurched. He sure as hell hadn't expected her to admit it! Cindy kept screaming, wriggling against her mother as though trying to get away from him.

"It is . . . a custom of my people," Lupe finally said. "To make the baby strong, you know?"

She tightened one arm around their daughter and began to clean the twisted little face with a tissue. George clenched his fists. "That's plain bull-shit. I read every damn word in that booklet the agency sent, all about the Philippines. Nothing in it about blood, let alone feedin' it to babies!"

Part of him wanted to hit her. Instead, he turned back to the kitchen, to the tequila in the fridge. Still watching Lupe over his shoulder, he took a swallow straight from the bottle.

His wife didn't move. She just kept staring with those bulgy eyes, her flat narrow face uglier than ever.

Hers and Cynthia Elaine's.

"She makes you sick, doesn't she? She's not what you wanted. I'm not, either."

George took another slug of tequila, hoping it might help things start making sense. It didn't.

"I could take her away, George. We could both leave tonight—go back home. Isn't that what you want?"

Somewhere behind the beer and tequila, he knew it was. Nothing would make him happier than to wake up alone—no cold, strange woman beside him and no weird baby staring up from her thrift-shop crib. He'd already checked on the lawyer's name and address on that Island Love con-tract—a Gilbert Orne in Ipswich, Massachusetts. If Mr. Orne got him into this mess, he could sure as hell get him out.

The way Maureen had gotten out four years ago.

The way a couple of girlfriends since then had, making him the butt of his buddies' jokes weeks after.

"No way," he said, wishing for better motives. "After the trouble I went to getting you here? You didn't have squat when I married you, girl. One lousy pink suit." He took another swig from his bottle. "I busted my ass to make you happy, an' now you wanna leave like all those other ingrates?"

He'd never mentioned his past to Lupe, but she didn't question this last statement. She just gave him a chilly little smile—sad and hard and distant all at once.

"I am grateful, George. Really I am. That's why I'm offering to go away, back home where you wouldn't have to—"

"Shut up," he said. "You're not going anywhere."

Lupe stared at him a moment longer, then took Cindy into the bedroom. When she was gone, George found some orange juice in the fridge, then mixed it with more tequila in a juice glass. Straight booze was doing his head no good tonight. What he needed now was his recliner and a soothing drink.

Half-asleep within minutes, he never noticed his wife peering down the hallway. Her smile was sadder now, but just as cold.

* * *

Two weeks later, Art keeled over with a massive heart attack, right in the middle of the hardware store he managed.

The funeral was fast and quiet—his widow wanted it that way—but the reading of his will turned out even shorter. George remembered Art mentioning a couple of sisters, plus a father still living back east somewhere. None of them inherited a cent, though one sister had flown clear out from Montana for the service.

Instead, Art's wife and baby daughter got everything . . . which amounted to considerably more than anybody had suspected.

After the sister and her family left in a huff, George went up and had a look at Art's will himself. Most of it didn't make sense, of course; but a signature at the bottom stood out. The attorney who'd drawn up the document was one Mr. Gilbert Orne.

Of Ipswich, Massachusetts.

* * *

They quit getting together at the bar after that night. Even when Tony had time off, any booth they sat in felt empty. Phil still hadn't come home from the state hospital. Maybe his wife knew when he'd be getting back, but George didn't feel like asking Lupe about it. She was spending most of her time with the other Island Love brides again.

He hoped to God that didn't mean another baby.

When George came home and found the trailer full of women, he generally went to the liquor store to forget about it. Sometimes Tony or Ray happened by, and they wound up forgetting together on the beach or in somebody's car. Sometimes George forgot alone on his own back steps. Either one beat hanging around Lupe and her friends—not to mention the kids. Those five little girls were all growing so fast, and they looked so damn much like their mothers.

At the end of April, Lupe mentioned that it was time to start Cindy on solid food. George looked up from his fish sticks in disbelief. Most kids Cindy's age—normal ones—didn't even have teeth, but who knew in this case? Pushing back from the table, he walked over to the baby's high chair to check.

Protruding from pinkish-black gums was a tiny but full set of teeth. Needle-sharp, glass-white kitten teeth.

He yanked his finger out of Cindy's mouth and backed away. "What d'you need for baby food? Five dollars, maybe?"

Lupe didn't answer. Pulling out his wallet, he sorted through its sparse contents and laid a five on the counter. She watched him the whole time, eyes wide with a strange chilly sadness.

"Gotta get back," he finally said, dumping the rest of his fish sticks in the garbage and heading for the door. "Promised the boss I'd take a look at his Chevy's V-8 tonight."

Overtime had never held much attraction, but that was before he'd married Lupe. By the time he got the classic '57 running properly, it was nearly eleven o'clock. Putting tools away and cleaning up killed another half-hour. After that, there was nothing left to do but go home.

And hope his wife and daughter were already asleep.

When he pulled up in front of their trailer, it looked that way. Unlocking the front door quietly, he reached for the kitchen light—and found himself facing an unexpected sinkful of dirty dishes. For all her weirdness, Lupe kept house well. It was one reason he hadn't written that damn lawyer weeks ago . . . .

The five he'd left her still lay on the counter. George frowned as he shoved it back into his pocket. Lupe never asked for much, but she generally spent it as fast as she could pry it out of him. Maybe she'd gotten sick or something?

Helping himself to a beer, he decided he'd better check on her and the baby. Just by turning on the hall light, he could see that their bed hadn't been slept in—and Cindy's crib in the corner was silent. He reached for the bedroom switch. No baby. No baby blankets, no ratty baby toys.

Nothing on Lupe's side of the closet.

Taking a long swig of beer, George stared at the tangle of hangers wondering what the hell to do next. Maureen had called him at work the day she'd moved out. His girlfriends had at least left notes. Lupe'd just taken the kid and her clothes and disapppeared, without even a car to get anywhere.

Had she gotten help from one of the other women?

Another *man*?

He was drowning that last thought with the rest of his beer when the phone rang in the kitchen. The voice on the other end was Ray's, either half crocked or hysterical.

"George, is my wife over there tonight? I went to the store after dinner—couldn't have taken more'n an hour. Came back an' all her stuff was gone, baby gone, no note, no nothing . . . ."

Short hairs prickled the back of George's neck.

"She's not over here, Ray. Lupe's gone, too . . . with Cindy." He wondered if *he* sounded hysterical. "Didja check at Tony's?"

Ray hesitated, but George could hear him chugging something.

"Tony's the one who called me," he finally said. "Tia must'a left while he was at work. Didn't take the car. Couldn't have, Tony had it." He took another audible swallow. "George . . . d'you suppose the other wives are missing, too?"

George wasn't listening. The window beside the phone was open and uncurtained, giving a good view of the beach below. Somewhere on that beach, a small fire had been kindled, and slim shapes danced in front of the flames. He peered into the darkness, but couldn't identify any of them.

Then the shapes moved faster, and he thought he heard singing: high-pitched female singing, against a rising wind from the ocean.

"George . . . ?"

The receiver dropped from his hand, hitting the floor hard enough to crack. Digging his flashlight from the junk drawer, he dashed through the living room, out the back door. Sea wind hit him in the face. It smelled more strongly than usual tonight, its tang fishier and ranker.

Covering his nose and mouth to keep from gagging, he started picking his way downhill toward the beach.

Lush spring weeds and vines caught at his ankles the whole way down. George swore and kicked himself free, hardly noticing that the growth seemed to worsen as he went on. His flashlight's jittery glow wasn't giving him much help—and neither was the weather. The sky had been clear when he'd left the garage, but now thick clouds congealed rapidly, building to thunderheads as he watched.

The reeking wind tore at his shirt and trousers. Whitecaps frothed and leaped and menaced the shoreline, higher than he'd ever seen them in the spring.

A few yards inland, the flames he'd spotted from the kitchen threw twisted shadows on the sand. George's grip tightened on his flashlight. Five women—short, slight women—circled the fire in a ritual dance, chanting softly. He couldn't make out individual words, but he recognized the language . . . the one Phil knew wasn't Spanish. It had sounded creepy enough in their living room. Out here, set against wind and ocean, each guttural syllable chilled his spine.

Iä-R'lyeh! Cthulhu fhtagn! Iä! Iä! Hydra fhtagn!

Lupe's worn pink suit glowed in the firelight, then passed into darkness as the dance spun faster. Peering between the dancers, George saw an inner circle: five babies squirming in the sand, staring up at the flames. Small piles of belongings lay scattered around.

Iä! Hydra! Hydra-mg'fhalma! Hydra fhtagn!

The fire was licking much too close to the children, nearly touching their waving hands. Whatever Lupe and Tia and the others thought they were doing out here . . . no matter how damn unsettling it looked . . . they had no right dragging kids into it. Conveniently forgetting that he hadn't wanted his kid to start with, George walked straight up to his wife and grabbed her arm.

The dancing and chanting stopped abruptly.

"I don't know what's going on," he yelled over the wind, "but you'd better get yourself home." His grip tightened. "You an' Cindy, right now. Understand?"

Lupe stared at him coldly. Her bulging moss-colored eyes held nothing at all he recognized.

"I can't," she said. "I'm leaving. We're all leaving, very soon."

George looked around. There were no cars on the beach, and none waiting anywhere else he'd seen.

"You're crazy, Lupe; you know that? A genuine psycho—"

Some shift in her expression made him stop short.

"I am not 'Lupe.' I am called Rl'hya-thi, priestess to Hydra Mother. From Below we came to bear these daughters; to Below we are returning." She fixed him with a gaze that twisted his gut. "Now leave us to our journey."

Firelight flickering across her face turned it masklike, horribly other than human. Pale needle teeth like Cindy's flashed in her open mouth. George dropped Lupe's arm and backed off, but all the women and babies kept watching him, like a squashable insect crawling away.

Like a horse's ass, more likely!

Sudden anger stung him. Lupe could call herself all the bizarro names she wanted, but she wasn't any damn priestess. Just the same dirt-poor

Filipina he'd married, treated a lot better than she'd ever deserved. Maybe that was the whole problem—

Dashing forward again, he grabbed Cindy from the circle of babies and held her away from her mother.

"I don't care who you think you are. This is *my* kid, *my* daughter, and I'm taking her home now."

Sudden, astonishing pain shot through his forearm. Looking down, he saw the baby had bitten through cloth into flesh, hanging on with her tiny mouthful of white needles. Cindy didn't look much like a baby now. More like a big rat . . . a rat-frog with those teeth . . .

He raised his flashlight and whacked her with it hard. Lupe screamed somewhere behind him, but Cindy didn't even blink. She just kept on chewing—and *swallowing*, good God!—as blood streamed from his arm and bone started showing through. George shrieked and tried to shake her off, beating on Cindy again and again.

While Lupe . . . and Tia . . . and Inez . . . grabbed his shoulders to pull him down.

Iä! Hydra! Hydra-mg'fhalma!

He squirmed and yelled and tried to scramble up, but babies were crawling all over him now. Girl babies with impossibly sharp teeth. *Oh God*, his sickened mind screamed, *solid food* . . . .

The women weren't even paying attention. They'd turned their back on his struggle to watch the waves leaping, reaching higher and higher with something inside towering above everything, threatening the storm clouds and bright crescent moon.

Iä! Iä! Hydra-mg'fhalma! Hydra Mother!

Late recognition hit him like a new agony but none of the women noticed. They were all running toward the waves now. Toward Lupe's ugly figurine turned huge . . . flared gills and dagger teeth and clawed fingers webbed together, reaching to gather in her daughters and *their* daughters . . . toward slimed, heaving breasts draped with seaweed . . . .

Shrieking, he tore his one remaining eye away from the sight and rolled onto his flayed stomach, away from the thing in the waves. Lights flickered on the hillside above. Twin lights like stars, wishing stars he'd never reach. He gulped air for a last warning scream.

Then his daughter's teeth flashed: the last light in the world.

About "The Idol"

Lovecraft did not mind using the same horror subtexts in story after story, perhaps figuring that even the least sentient among the "yaps and nitwits" of the *Weird Tales* audience would get the point sooner or later. He hated immigrants, non-Aryans, that is, and he found them so monstrous that it was no great stretch to depict them as outright monsters or Nephilim-spawn like the Innsmouth Deep Ones, but he could make the same point with a slightly less heavy hand by sketching the squalid portrait of Southern Europeans and non-Europeans as he saw them, clustering thickly on street corner and dock, no doubt plotting to do white folks mischief. This clandestine cunning he transmogrified into full-scale witch-worship and alien diabolism. This he did to great effect in "The Horror at Red Hook", directly inspired by his period of residence on Clinton Street, Brooklyn. One can only imagine Lovecraft's white-knuckling agitation (probably a lot like Aspinwall's apoplexy in "Through the Gates of the Silver Key") at encountering today's street scene in Brooklyn, boom box radios blasting rap and hip hop, adolescent cocaine tycoons wearing suits (once, then trashing them) that poor HPL could never have afforded with a lifetime's earnings.

This is just the dissonant note that Scott Aniolowski picks up on his antenna tuned to frequencies no earth station ever sent. He discerns the coordinates where the Dionysian orgies of youthful vigor impinge on the nostalgia-cosmos of the Old Gent. Here a teen idol, not a Cthulhu idol this time, hears the call of the wild, and it turns out to be a lot wilder than he thought.

The Idol

by Scott David Aniolowski

Rivulets of sweat ran down Sam Kinney's fat face, glistened like tiny jewels in the hot August sun. He wiped his brow on an already damp sleeve, panting to catch his breath. It came in short wheezes. He staggered to a cluster of trees. Even in the shadier spots of the Boston Common it was uncomfortably warm. And muggy. His heart burned in his chest, he could hear it pound. His puffy hands trembled to light a cigar. "Hey kid, slow down," the fat man spat, wide mouth full of cigar smoke.

"Come on, Sam, let's go," came the distant reply.

Sam's eyes stung with sweat, everything was out of focus. He wasn't sure which jogger was his anymore. Teens on bicycles and roller blades swept by, and somewhere a baby wailed, setting his nerves on end. And everywhere pigeons. Dirty, shitting pigeons pecking and cooing. Everywhere. *It was like being in that Hitchock flick*, Sam thought. *Which one was it? That one with all the birds.* But then Sam hated birds. And babies. And if it wasn't for the fact that he made a goddamn good living off throngs of screaming adolescents, he'd hate them, too. Well, secretly he did.

"Come on, big guy, get a move on," that voice came again, more distant now.

"Yeah, fuck you, too," he mumbled not so much under his breath. He dabbed his greasy face again, tossed the smoking cigar into a trash bin. Then it was off to the beckoning call of his star. Not any star, but The Star. The kid had made a name for himself—and a fortune for Sam—in the span of several busy months. The CD had gone to the top of the charts. He'd made the rounds of all the important late-night talk shows, was soon to embark on a lengthy North American tour.

Sam had found Mikey just when that other pants-dropping shirtless white kid from Boston was fading away. He'd discovered him doing some impromptu rap at Quincy Market one day during lunch. The kid was pretty rough, but he drew a crowd. And Sam Kinney knew a talent when he saw it. Well, most of the time. His last client—a professional wrestler—went nowhere fast, ended up sticking Sam with more bills than profit. But part of being a talent agent was taking risks. You never knew when The Next Big Thing might fall into your lap and bring with it Big Money. And with Mikey Sam had finally found the goose that shit gold.

So he cleaned the kid up, bought him some new clothes, and began an ambitious publicity campaign. Radio play. Television spots. Magazine interviews. Videos. Personal appearances. And the public bought what Sam Kinney was selling. They bought it hook, line, and sinker. Public appearances got to be like frigging Beatles gigs. The clutching hands, the teary eyes. Lusty stargazing adolescent girls screamed and swooned. It wasn't even the kid's singing (who could call *that* singing?)—it was the kid himself. Sam was convinced of it. And that's what he sold. He marketed as much of Mikey as he could. He had the kid peel his shirt off whenever and wherever possible. Sex sells. It's the oldest marketing scheme in the book. And the kid's face and half-naked body were splashed across T-shirts, bookbags, buttons, posters, magazine covers. He was The Next Big Thing.

And somewhere along the way to becoming The Next Big Thing, Mikey signed over the lion's share of his growing income to his agent.

There was a high-pitched shriek. The kind of shriek that shatters glass, sets teeth grinding. It was a sound that Sam had come to be used to. The sound of a teenage girl, her love for Mikey. It was the sound of cash registers.

Mikey's adoring fans had spotted him. Sam stopped his ponderous trotting, stared ahead. A sea of grasping arms and writhing bodies was all that he saw. It was always the same. They came out of nowhere. It was creepy. Like hordes of screaming banshees.

By the time Sam had stumbled to the flailing screamers a mounted policeman had arrived, was attempting to restore order. Mikey was at the center of the mess signing autographs, kissing fans, smiling ear to ear. An anonymous hand snatched the baseball cap from his head; it vanished into the flagellating mass.

"Girls, girls," the big man shouted, began pulling the clutching adolescents away. "You can all have free passes to Mikey's show tonight at the University." He bravely waved a stack of free promotional passes over his head. More screams, a blur of greedy grasping hands. One last candid photo, the crowd melted away back to wherever they always came from. Sam's star was left clawed and tousled but otherwise unscathed (there had been instances where the kid had been picked almost naked by the clawing shrews).

"Just like I figured," the big man purred through a toothy car-salesman grin.

"Huh?" panted Mikey, sun-bronzed skin glistening in the sunlight. He ran a hand through his short bristly black hair, confirmed that his cap was missing. At least they hadn't ripped the gold hoops out of his ears.

"Great publicity, kid. Mikey spotted jogging in the Common. It's important for you to be seen by your adoring fans."

"Whatever." Mikey wiped the beads of dampness from his brow, traced the thin line of black hair that crept from his belly button up to where it spread out to lightly cover his chest. It was wet and shiny like a trickle of black oil.

"Come on, this is it, kid. You're a star now." He turned his whole enormous bulk and extended one arm toward a building on Beacon Street. "Can't beat that." There on one full side of a towering structure was Mikey, godlike and larger than life. The black and white image stared down into the park with dark eyes and a seductively boyish grin. He was bare-chested on the building, baggy jeans down low on his hips, baseball cap twisted around backward. The delicate sculpted contour of every muscle, every hair, was clear and crisp. And above his head in twenty-foot letters was a single word: MIKEY.

The young man just stared up at himself, not sure whether he should smile or turn away embarrassed.

"Not bad for a poor white kid from Boston. Nineteen and a star. What do you think of that?"

Mikey didn't say anything.

* * *

"What the hell were you thinking?" Sam screamed, flailed a fat cigar like a knife. He crushed the glossy magazine in his other hand, threw it out an open window. It flapped and tumbled twelve stories to the street like a broken bird.

"I wanted to do it," Mikey screamed back.

"Yeah? Well let me tell you something, bigshot, you don't do anything without me saying so. Got it? For Christ's sake, you can't *give* it away. How the hell do you think I sell you? Huh?" Sam's bloated face was red, slick with sweat. Droplets rained down as his cumbersome bulk shook.

"Yeah, well, it ain't no big deal, okay?"

"No? No? It is a big deal. It's a very big fucking deal. You're supposed to be seductive to these screaming twits. A dreamboy. That means leaving *something* to their horny little imaginations. The spreads in those crappy teen magazines are fine, but *Playgirl*? You're a teen idol for Christ's sake, not a frigging porn star. Do you know what kind of damage something like this can do to your image? And Christmas next month. Just what we need—shit right before the biggest goddamn shopping season of the year. Do you think parents are going to buy your CD and posters for their little girls if they see you in some magazine with your dick hanging out?"

"I didn't think about it. They called and I said okay. You were away. I thought that was the kind of stuff you wanted me to do." Mikey absently stared into the huge aquarium that nearly filled one wall of his spacious loft. The low steady murmur of billions of tiny bubbles hung like a curtain in the background.

"Well, it ain't," Sam wheezed. He slipped out of his cheap coat; the armpits of his tight shirt were soaked. "Jesus, I can't leave you for a goddamn minute. I take a couple days off to go fishing and you go and do skin pics."

"Okay," the young man gave in.

"Jesus, what a fucking mess," Sam panted, wiped a fat hand across his dripping forehead.

"Okay, okay. I wasn't thinking."

"You're goddamn right you weren't thinking."

The teen sat in silence, stared at the bubbling fish tank, at his reflection vague and ghostlike in the glass.

"You'll keep your dick in your pants from now on?" Sam bent to open the window, breathed deeply in.

"Yeah, I said okay," Mikey mumbled.

"Good," he finally smiled after a long moment of tense silence. It was a strong silence. It was a weak smile. "Good," he parroted himself. The red was beginning to wash out of his round face.

"Besides, I don't want to do all that undressing in public anymore." He remained transfixed on the tank, eyes empty, face expressionless. Several brilliant reef fish darted between chunks of coral; clown fish bobbed through waving anemone tentacles.

Sam stared blankly at him for a moment. "What? Why?"

Mikey wouldn't meet his fish-eyed gaze. "I don't know. I just don't," he squirmed.

"Yeah, well that body of yours is our meal ticket."

Silence, just the hypnotic murmur of billions of bubbles.

"Are you okay, kid? You don't look so good." He slapped a puffy hand to the kid's forehead. "Maybe I better call your doctor."

"No." He pushed the flabby hand away.

"You haven't worked out all week." He turned to the expensive gym equipment in one corner. Stark beams from track lights put it on display, made the bulky black machines more art than appliance.

"Yeah?"

"And you haven't shaved in days."

"So?"

"Well, so, you have to take care of yourself. That body of yours ain't going to stay pretty all by itself."

More silence. The kid blindly watched the mesmerizing dance of fish and bubbles. A starfish slid slowly across the glass.

"I'm calling the doctor." He shoved the crumbled cigar in his mouth and grabbed the phone, hand completely engulfing the receiver. Sausage fingers jabbed numbered buttons.

Mikey threw himself from the overstuffed chair, cut off the phone in mid-dial. "No. I don't need to see no doctor."

"Then are you in some sort of trouble? Did you knock up some girl?" He grabbed Mikey's arm.

"No." He pulled away.

"Then what the hell is it?"

"Listen, I just need a break, okay? A vacation."

"Yeah, well, we ain't got time for that. You have to be in New York on Friday. Then Rochester on Saturday, and Buffalo on Sunday," he counted on his fingers. "And then we go to Toronto on Monday and Tuesday. Monday and Tuesday, Mikey—two days in one town. Two fucking days. The fans want you and you ain't going to let them down."

"Just a few days. It's only Tuesday—I can still make New York this weekend."

"Where the hell you going to go in only two days?"

"I don't know, I thought I'd go up to Innsmouth."

"Innsmouth? What the hell you want to go to that shithole for?"

"I don't know."

"Why don't we just go to New York a few days early. You can take it easy there. Hang out, go to some of them fancy gyms, do whatever kind of shit you want."

"I can do all that here. I want to go somewhere small and quiet. Somewhere where no one knows my name."

"But Innsmouth?"

"I had relatives there a long time ago. Ma talked about them, and I just thought I'd like to go there. And see for myself."

"See what?"

Silence.

"Well, we ain't going to that shithole. At least not to stay. If you want we'll go up to Marblehead or Kingsport for a couple of days. We can drive out to Innsmouth from there, it's not much more than ten or fifteen miles. But we ain't staying in Innsmouth."

Mikey looked up at Sam, made eye contact for the first time. The corners of his mouth curled up into the sincerest smile Sam had ever seen on the kid. "Thanks," he almost sobbed.

"Christ, don't get all mushy on me. I'm still pissed about those skin pics. And I still think you should see the doc. But if taking a couple days off will put you right then that's what we'll do."

"Yeah, okay. Thanks, Sam," he folded his arms around the fat man's girth and squeezed.

Sam wriggled out of the hug, turned away. "Yeah, whatever. But," he rotated back, jabbed a stubby finger into the teen's chest, "if you ain't back to your old self after this trip you stop fucking around and see the doctor."

Mikey sighed agreement.

"After all, I got to take care of my star," he half-smiled, tousled the kid's short hair with a nervous hand.

* * *

The drive up the North Shore from Boston to Marblehead was a long thirteen miles. Mass. 1A North rambled and turned slowly through an assortment of quaint old New England towns with an assortment of annoying modern traffic lights. The late autumn sun hung low and sleepy in the darkening sky as they turned onto route 129 in Swampscott, headed into Marblehead. Thick drapes of heavy November clouds finally closed, banishing the day into darkness. Mikey quietly gazed out the car window as they made their way along the coastline. The ocean was black and still; a sharp sickle moon vainly struggled to cut through the thick night veil.

Route 129 became Atlantic Avenue, and they were in Marblehead. Sam turned his jet black Mercedes off Atlantic and onto Washington Street. The old New England town was dark and quiet. Globes of pale light hung from crook-necked posts above narrow twisting streets. Tall slim buildings sat on the brink of winding alleys, only thin pedestrian walks standing precariously between doors and street. There were few signs of life in the sleepy town beyond warmly lit windows and the occasional cat that crept through lifeless gardens, along cracked red brick drives.

"This is it," Sam nodded toward a large house, "58 Washington Street." He held a crumpled slip of paper in the dim greenish light of the car dashboard, read the cramped scratching. "Yep, 58." Welcoming light spilled from the building's many small-paned windows. A single lamp hung over the mahogany-hued door, flanked on either side by tall white columns. Mikey slid out of the car, stretched his legs. He inhaled deeply, clearing the cigar stench from his nose.

"Nice town." Wisps of steam ringed the kid's head as he spoke. He wrapped himself in his oversized jacket. A few early snowflakes danced on the cold night wind; bare-branched trees creaked and moaned in their sleep.

Sam ignored him, not knowing whether he was serious or joking. He opened the Mercedes' trunk, pulled out the bags. "Here, get your stuff," he puffed, then checked that the car doors were locked for the third time.

The fat man rang the house bell when he found the door locked. The door swung open almost immediately, a lovely woman stood there, hands clasped, motherly smile. "Mr. Kinney," she said more than asked, extended a delicate hand.

"Yeah, that's right." He stumbled into the entry hall.

"Come in, come in. It's rather nippy out tonight," she smiled.

Mikey squeezed in behind his agent, quietly slid the door closed. A comforting fire crackled in a hearth in the front parlor. Deep rich oriental rugs covered most of the mellow glowing wide board pine floor. Delicate paintings, antiques, and brasswork decorated the burgundy-hued room. Overhead hung a small brass chandelier, flamebulbs glowing brightly.

"And this handsome young man must be your . . . son?" The woman smiled at the teen.

"No," Mikey hurried, absently took a step away from the big man.

Sam shot the kid a look, raised an eyebrow, "Mikey . . . Michael's my nephew. I brought the kid up from Boston to do a little fishing."

"Really? How nice," she beamed. "I don't know how much fishing you'll get done, though. This time of year most of the tourist places are closed up. Most of the charters aren't running now."

"We're going up to Innsm—" Mikey started.

"We'll find something," Sam cut him off, gave him a venomous stare.

"Of course," she coughed, waved off a cloud of cigar smoke. "Well, if you'd care to sign in I'll show you gentlemen to your room."

Sam signed the inn's directory, waved a gold credit card in the woman's face. She snapped the plate through the credit card machine, gave the pair a key to the front door.

"Continental breakfast is included," the lovely innkeeper explained as she led them through the enormous 18th-century house and to their room on the third floor.

"Thanks," Sam closed the door. "Muffins and coffee. Swell," he grunted, tried to catch his breath from the climb up so many steep flights of stairs.

The accommodations were quite fine for a bed & breakfast. A large green-hued bedroom with a pair of canopied four-poster beds. A blaze glowed in the room's bedside fireplace. And more oriental carpets, pine flooring, finely tooled furnishings. Their private bath was completely mirrored on one wall, potted ferns ringed the large green-veined marble tub. The perfumed scent of potpourri struggled to mask the old-house-grandmother's-parlor-mustiness of the place.

"It's late. I want to catch a shower and then go to bed." Mikey unzipped one of his bags. Somewhere in the house a clock began to chime.

While the kid showered, Sam unpacked, poked through the room. *Pretty nice digs*, he thought and smiled. *Ain't no five star hotel, but it ain't half bad.*

The sound of running water stopped. Outside the wind whistled, the old house creaked.

After another half hour Sam knocked at the bathroom door. "Hey, you drown in there?" He swung the door open. Mikey stood naked in front of the mirrored wall, his face almost to the glass, studying his own reflection.

"Jesus, Sam!" The young man snapped a towel around his waist.

"Well, what the hell you doing in here, jerking off?" he blustered back. "You ain't got nothing I ain't already seen."

"I'll be out in a minute." He pushed the door closed on the round face.

The big man was already beneath his blankets when Mikey finally came out of the bathroom. The last glowing embers of the fire crackled in the hearth, bathed the room in a frail ruby light. Shadows stretched into elongated phantoms. The kid padded quietly to the other bed, threw back the heavy quilt. The sheets were icy against his bare skin. He lay there listening to the sounds of the house: the dying embers popping, a clock chiming, the wood floors creaking. And Sam's labored breathing, deep and steady like a hibernating bear. Outside the wind continued to whistle through bare tree branches, rattle the shutters.

"Sam?" Mikey whispered after he'd lain in the dark for what seemed like an hour. The last embers had crackled out, died.

The fat man snorted a reply, rolled onto his side.

"Sam," he repeated, suddenly noticed how his heart raced, his mouth was dry.

Another moan from the next bed.

"I think I'm changing." He gulped in breath, swallowed hard.

Sam groaned. And then the snoring began.

The kid stared up at the shroud-like canopy above his head. Outside, a branch knocked, a few dead leaves scratched at the glass. And the sharp lunar crescent peered through the small paned windows like a giant squinting eye.

* * *

The morning was a clear and crisp one. Lacy frost etchings decorated the windows of Sam's big car, slowly melted away in the just-warm rays of the November sun. There was real life in Marblehead this morning. Business people hustling to get to work in the city. Children heading for school. Old- timers walking their dogs, taking leisurely strolls through the twisting street. Everyone smiled and nodded to Sam and Mikey. A few stared. A few pointed.

Mikey was quiet all the way to Innsmouth, just stared out the car window at the passing towns. Salem. Beverly. Arkham. Kingsport Head rose in the distance, ringed with wispy morning fog.

"What's your problem today?" Sam finally coughed, mouth full of half-chewed blueberry muffin. He dusted crumbs from the black leather upholstery between his legs, onto the carpeted floor of the car. Two more home-baked muffins sat on the seat next to him, pirated from the inn along with a hastily swallowed black coffee. "I don't know what your big goddamn hurry is. We got two days here."

The teen just sighed in response.

More silence. Sam played with the car radio, tuned in a classic rock station out of Boston. Mick Jagger's voice cut through the thick silence.

"'Gimme, gimme shelter,'" the fat man crooned along with the radio, mouth still full of chewed muffin. "Hey, how about if I do some back-up on your next CD?" He flicked the brim of Mikey's baseball cap with a finger.

"Yeah, right." The teen finally cracked a smile, pulled the brim of his hat down over his eyes. "You sound like a pig in heat."

Sam laughed, mumbled some incoherent words in time with the song. "Jesus, what the fuck is Mick saying?"

Mikey shrugged.

"Never could understand that guy. How the hell did he get to be so goddamn famous? He can't even sing through them big fat lips."

Mikey laughed, sang some incoherent out-of-tune lyrics to the song.

"Is he saying 'just a kiss away' or 'just piss in my face'?" The fat man puffed out his lips, bulged out his eyes, got right in the kid's face.

Mikey held himself as he laughed, stomped his feet, threatened to piss his pants. Then he looked up, the laughter stopped. The expression washed out of his face, his eyes widened just a bit. There in front of them like a shadow was Innsmouth.

The old town spread out ahead of them, larger than the kid had expected it to be. The place was decayed and falling into ruin. Gambrel roofs drooped, completely collapsed in some houses. So many peaked gable windows were cracked, missing. Boards warped, were missing altogether from sides of buildings. And Mikey couldn't count the number of windows and doors that were boarded over, fading realtor signs standing blind guard on dead weedy lawns. The tired old structures huddled together under a shroud of mist from the frothing sea. There was some sign of recent construction. A dead McDonald's sign rose up in the distance, its yellow and red plastic busted and dark. Mikey recognized the signature architecture of another fast-food restaurant, also dark and boarded up. A gray melancholy hung over the place like the sea mist, the air thick with the smell of fish. A lone boat bobbed on the ocean, just off Innsmouth's sagging docks. Oddly, there were no gulls wheeling, squawking.

Sam auto-locked the car doors, steered down Federal Street and into the belly of Innsmouth. Smoke curled up from a few cracked chimneys, a few faceless pedestrians ambled between dark, twisting streets. They passed an old Masonic Temple, its facade cracked and weathered, sign above the door peeling and faded beyond recognition. Cracked, warped trees lined desolate streets, their last few leaves brown and withered. Overgrown lawns of dried weeds and gray grass trembled, snatched up bits of wind-blown litter and leaves. Mikey thought he saw dark furtive shapes peering from cracked windows as they slowly rode past.

"What a dump," Sam snorted.

They made their way to the downtown business district. More dark and deserted buildings, their wounds patched with fungus-sprouting boards. Finally Sam pulled up in front of a diner, only the word RESTAURANT still legible above the door. The place was obviously a converted residence, similar in architecture to their Marblehead inn, but in a state of decay. One pair of columns in the front was missing, only a rough stump left. The tall narrow small-paned windows were caked with grime or boarded over; the glassless lamp over the front door hung precariously by a few frayed wires. Across the unpaved street sat a large weathered building identified as The Gilman House Hotel. Things seemed slow at the hotel. Sam wondered if it was even still open for business.

The pair spent the day cautiously picking their way through narrow twisting streets, poking in the few remaining shops. Sam's head constantly swiveled to keep an eye on everything, everyone. Mikey took everything in, was mostly oblivious to his companion's unease. They wandered past great Georgian and Federalist mansions, many dark and closed up. Along unpaved, lampless alleys. Through overgrown, weed-choked greens. Down warped and rotting docks where the fish stench was almost sickening. All the time the townsfolk kept a cautious distance. They were an odd, unfriendly lot who kept mostly to themselves. Pedestrians crossed to the opposite side of the street. Merchants were reticent. Rust-eaten cars cruised by, their vague occupants peering, driving off.

Their last stop was the old Innsmouth burying ground. Shrouded skeletons capered and danced on thin gray stones. Weather-worn angels stared down, faces washed away into horrid grimaces. Generations of families crowded the ossuary; the roll stretched all the way back to the mid-1700's. Gilmans. Marshes. Eliots. Waites. All lines in silent stony neighborhoods. The big man squatted on a particularly firm stone, crossed his arms. Mikey passed among the markers, intently reading names and dates. Finally he stopped at one, stooped down. "This is it," his voice trembled slightly. "My great-great-grandfather." He ran his hand down the cold damp stone face.

"Is this why you dragged me to this shithole?" He glanced at his watch, up toward the deepening sky

The kid didn't reply. Said little all the way back to the car. Sam reluctantly suggested they get a sandwich and coffee at the diner before they headed back; his stomach growled its agreement. Mikey agreed in silence.

The restaurant was a dingy place, dirty and dank. The black and white checked flooring was yellowed and cracked. Paint peeled from walls, the ceiling. Once-fine woodworking was splintered, worm-eaten. A withered old hag perched in a corner booth, bony knees bent to her chest like a gargoyle. A pair of behemoth women sat in the center of the room, rolls of soft doughy flesh spilling over straining seats; long greasy hair framed puffy yellowed faces, rheumy eyes stared out from behind thick glasses. The weird sisters stared at Mikey and Sam, watched as they sat at a distant table. They smiled, thick tongues sliding side to side in wide gap-toothed mouths. Sam wrinkled his nose at the elephantine pair. They whispered, began to titter. High shrill tittering like enormous rodents.

The hag crawled stiffly off her perch, approached the table. "Yeah, what'll you have?" Her mouth was puckered, toothless. Mikey considered how the old woman looked like a Disney witch, with pointed chin and hooked nose.

"Coffee," Sam grunted back, "and a couple menus if it's not too much trouble."

The moon-faced woman sneered, looked down at the kid.

"Pepsi." He looked away.

"Ain't got that," she hissed.

"Just bring him coffee," Sam glared.

The fat jack-o-lantern-faced woman stared, giggled.

They ordered their food, sipped their coffee. And tried to ignore the other patrons. While they waited for their food a few others entered the establishment. They were an ugly lot, with stooped posture, wide mouths, bulging eyes. Their flesh had an unhealthy bluish tinge, their hair yellow and in sickly clumps. They were obviously town folk. Some sat at the counter, the rest took a table near the front windows. Like the behemoth sisters, the new patrons all kept an interested watch on Sam and Mikey.

"So you mind telling me finally why the hell we came to this craptown?" Sam stared into Mikey's dark eyes.

The kid turned away. "I wanted to see for myself," he said.

"What? See what? What a fucking dump it is? How ugly the locals are?"

"I think I'm changing," he finally said, gulping breath.

"Changing?"

The kid just looked at the fat man, eyes soft and sad.

"Are you trying to tell me you're queer?" he asked after a moment of uneasy silence.

"Jesus, Sam! No!"

"I mean, if you are, that's okay. No one has to know. It'll be our secret." He wiped his brow, nervously fished for a cigar.

The food arrived. The glowering crone slid the plates in front of them, refilled their coffee mugs, spilled it on the table.

"Shit, that's all you've eaten for weeks. You're going to turn into a fish," he gestured to the plate of steaming seafood in front of Mikey.

"No, Sam, I'm not gay," the teen whispered when the stick-legged woman limped away from the table.

"Then please explain this to me." He gestured with half his sandwich, slopped filling on the table.

"When I was little my ma used to tell me stories."

"Yeah?"

"Stories about my ancestors, and how they . . . ." He paused, surveyed the room, lowered his voice. "Changed."

Sam just stared, shrugged.

"They were from here. Innsmouth. Something to do with this town. Maybe the old plague. The people change. They change into something else. Monsters or something. It's in their genes." He glanced over his shoulder at the ugly men at the counter. "Whenever I was bad when I was a kid she'd tell me that I was going to change and the people from Innsmouth were going to come for me. They would come and take me out into the ocean."

"Monsters? You think you're turning into a monster? Come on, you're a smart kid—you don't believe that bullshit, do you? For Christ's sake, Mikey, your mother was a goddamn drunk."

"But it's started. See?" He stretched the collar of his T-shirt.

The agent leaned over the table. "What am I looking at?"

"The marks on my neck. The gills. They're starting."

"There ain't nothing there." He felt along the teen's throat. Nothing.

"Those people this morning noticed it."

"Who?"

"Back in Marblehead. You saw the way they stared at me and pointed."

"They stared and pointed because you're a fucking celebrity. Jesus, your face has been on magazine covers and shirts for months. And remember MTV? Videos? Oh, and what about your spread in *Playgirl*? Jesus, there with a fucking hard-on for all the world to see." He finally lit the cigar, inhaled more deeply than he could remember ever having inhaled. "Those people recognized you. That's why they stared and pointed. Shit, that happens wherever we go. You should be used to it by now."

"Well, what about this?" Mikey pulled a small cloth-wrapped bundle out of his coat pocket, handed it to Sam.

Beneath layers of yellowed cotton strips was a small lump of gold, smooth and maybe greasy-feeling. "Yeah?" Sam turned the thing over in his hand. "What is it?"

"Some kind of idol." He lowered his voice, huddled to the table. "Innsmouth gold. It was my great-great-grandfather's. Ma said it was one of the Innsmouth people's sea gods."

"Sea god? I don't see it. It's just a lump."

"There," he pointed, "can't you see the markings? The tentacles?" He traced his finger over the shapeless nugget.

"It's just a lump," Sam repeated, louder this time. The shrill tittering came again from behind them. And vague mumbling from the counter.

"Here, give it to me. I shouldn't have showed it here." Mikey grabbed the smooth chunk away from Sam, stuffed it back into his pocket.

"Okay, so let me get this straight. Because of some drunken ramblings of your crazy mother you think you're going to sprout gills or something and go off to live in the sea? And that little scrap of fool's gold is an ancient idol of some sea god? Please tell me you're shitting with me. This ain't nothing but a fairy tale. Just a line of bullshit she fed you to scare you when you were bad."

"No, I've seen it. I've seen the old photos. And now it's happening to me. It hurts. That's why I haven't been shaving. It hurt my skin. The changes. Just look at me."

"This is why you said you didn't want to take your shirt off in public anymore? Why you aren't taking care of yourself? Because you're turning into the fucking Creature from the Black fucking Lagoon?"

"Sam—" he started.

"No. Now that's enough. You're fine, for Christ's sake. I saw you in the john last night. I saw *all* of you, and there ain't a blemish on you. No gills. No scales. Nothing. Now knock off the shit and let's go. You have a show to do in New York and you're going to be ready for it, goddamn it. Come on." He stood, tossed money on the table. The weird sisters cracked jack-o-lantern smiles at him. "What the fuck you two looking at?" he growled. They just laughed their unnerving little laugh. Sam stared down the wide-faced folk at the counter, the miserable old hag. He pulled on his coat, yanked the kid out of his seat.

Mikey was quiet all the way back to Marblehead. Sam cooled off. He humored his star, offered to check the kid for malformities, blemishes. Said he'd have a doctor examine him. The kid declined. Sam suggested Mikey talk to a shrink. He only got mad, stormed out of the inn. When he finally came back he refused to speak. That night he spent almost two hours in the bathroom.

* * *

"This is it. No more goddamn kids," Sam grumbled to himself, slipped his key into the lock. "Come on, Mikey, we ain't got all day. Get your ass in gear," he bellowed as the heavy door swung in on the cavernous loft apartment. The place was dark, the blinds drawn tight. A tiny red light blinked near the door. The kid's answering machine, loaded with Sam's irate messages. "Mikey, where the hell are you?" he shouted up toward the bedroom loft.

Silence. Just the familiar steady hypnotic murmur from the living area.

"Fucking kid, I'm going to break his goddamn neck when I get hold of him." He slipped a cigar into his mouth. His face was getting red, he felt hot. He poked his head into the kitchen, the bathroom. No sign of Mikey. Tooth brush; razor; shaving cream: The kid hadn't even packed his toiletries yet. He cursed again, checked his watch. His face got redder. He climbed the spiral staircase to the loft bedroom. The bed hadn't been slept in. Suitcases sat in the bottom of the closet, untouched. "You little bastard, don't you fuck this up," he shouted, voice bouncing hollow in the high ceiling.

It wasn't until he leaned his cumbersome bulk over the loft railing that he found his star.

He squeezed down the spiral metal steps, legs unsteady, moisture beading on his puffed face. Mikey was in the big room, the living area. Sam didn't at first comprehend what he had seen from the bedroom loft. He stumbled into the big room, just stared, cigar falling out of his wide mouth.

A sickly greenish glow filled the living area, bathed everything in ghostly light. The steady murmur was louder here—closer—hung like a shroud over the room. The hardwood floor was spoiled with water, clothes strewn about in the puddle. The front of the wall-length fish tank was crusted with salt streaks. A chair stood there, out of place. And a shape hung in the water, floating, bobbing. A familiar shape.

Mikey stared at Sam from behind the glass, eyes wide and bulging, mouth yawning wide. His swarthy skin was tinged blue, made worse by the fluorescent lights. Colorful marine fish swam and danced around him. Skittering crustaceans nipped at his flesh, burrowed through his hair; starfish sluggishly moved across his naked body, through the stiff bristling hair. Crabs picked at his eyes, darted in and out of his mouth; anemones fastened themselves to his chest. He had no gills, no scales, although he was at one with his living reef microcosm. Mikey was a host. Habitat. Sustenance.

And at the bottom of the aquarium where his lifeless hand had dropped it was Mikey's small gold lump, glinting in the pale greenish light. Sam just stared, felt the air drain out of his lungs. He couldn't be sure, but he wondered if he didn't finally see the tentacles, the bulging eyes.

About "The Guardian of the Pit"

Talented son of *Weird Tales* author and Lovecraft correspondent Richard F. Searight (see the Necronomicon Press collections of his work, *The Brain in the Jar and Others*, 1992, and *The Sealed Casket and Others*, 1996), Franklyn Searight is working on a whole series of adventures of someone rather like himself—the son of a famous Mythos author, only the Mythos author is none other than Abdul Alhazred, and his descendant is skeptical reporter Alan Hasrad. One of his adventures, "The Innsmouth Head", appeared in *The Innsmouth Cycle*. Here is another.

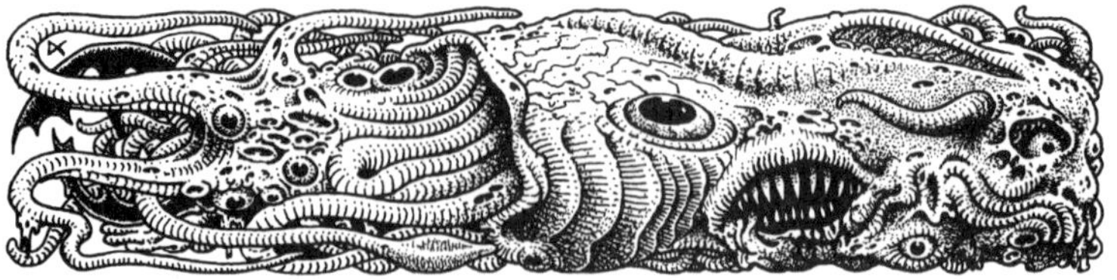

The Guardian of the Pit

by Franklyn Searight

When I had last been at Innsmouth, about three years ago, certain experiences had forced me to conclude that I should never, if it could be avoided, return. That is why I have since gone out of my way to stay clear of that decaying seaport town, why even the thought of visiting it makes me uneasy.

But recent events did, in fact, make it necessary for me to return. Sometimes one must assume duties one knows will be unpleasant even before they are begun. It is especially true in the newspaper business. My name is Alan Hasrad, and as a reporter for the Arkham *Advertiser*, I have had to cover assignments which I would greatly prefer had been given to someone else.

It was a bright, sunny day when Josh Prentice, assistant editor, came over and tried, unsuccessfully because of the rotundity of his bottom, to sit on the edge of my desk. His intent was to provide me with just such an assignment—one I would prefer to have avoided.

"Really, Josh," I said, trying to make him understand, as he slid off for the second time. "I've got too much to do now. How about that new fellow—Radley—taking it?"

"Nope." Josh wiped his perspiring face with an already damp handkerchief. He was a big man, an excessively tall and fat man, who always seemed to be sweating. "I want someone with experience to cover this."

"But I've just returned from an out-of-town—"

"Alan," he interrupted, his facial features becoming more stern, "this is the type of thing you're really best at—and you know it, even if you won't admit it." His voice became adamant. "I want you to take it."

We sparred about for another minute before I reluctantly gave in. "Okay," I agreed with a deep sigh, leaning back in my swivel chair. "Fill me in."

There was not a lot of information Josh could give in addition to what I already knew. During the past two weeks five bodies had been washed up along the coast near Arkham. This morning a sixth had been found. Perhaps more were to come. My job was to gather more details and attempt to answer the many inexplicable questions that were puzzling the authorities.

"Just look at these pictures," Josh exclaimed, shoving before me a portfolio of prints taken by the county medical examiner.

Six exhibits were there of the dead men in question. All had been so grotesquely mutilated the photos were used for interoffice purposes only; certainly, they could not be displayed in a newspaper.

"Study the features," he indicated, "the huge bulging eyes, the rough skin, those curious slits near the ears—"

"Yeah, yeah," I responded. "I know. All of them are from Innsmouth. They've all got the look."

The "look" they had was not at all pleasant, composed of facial and bodily characteristics that most of the people of Innsmouth, probably from many years of inbreeding, possessed to one degree or another. It is a . . . well . . . *fishy* look, and the older they get, the fishier they look. It is not at all difficult to spot an Innsmouth resident on the street, except for the very young ones.

All six of the photos were of men who possessed that characteristic look, which even a horrible mutilation could not efface!

"The authorities investigating this, including the state police, are really puzzled," Josh went on. "The police chief of Innsmouth—and my God, he's a queer one!—has been unable to come up with any information at all. He can't even identify them! Nobody seems to know who they are!"

"At least, nobody is talking," I contributed.

"Right. The Innsmouth police accept the returned bodies, but won't release any information they have—if they have any at all. I don't know if they do."

I nodded, puzzled, and drummed my fingers on the desk. "It's hard to believe they can't come up with something on this. It's a mystery all right. But why me? I'm no policeman. How can I tackle something like this?"

"Because you're a good investigative reporter, Alan. You're responsible and clearheaded, and you're not afraid to dig until you've got the facts. I don't know how you'll do it, but I know you will."

I pursed my lips. "I can try . . . I guess. You know where to send the flowers if I fail. Unlimited time and expenses?"

"Of course." Again he found it necessary to wipe his brow. "Stick with it until it's over, Alan. Let us know how you're coming and what we can do to back you up."

"Right."

"See you later."

He left, and I leaned back in my chair. It was a nasty job, but someone had to do it. Innsmouth! How I dreaded returning to that furtive, shadow-festering town about which so many dark rumors had been whispered.

I straightened up my desk, switched off the fan, and left for home.

Later, lounging in a comfortable easy chair and sipping a potent mixture of scotch and soda, I considered the job I had reluctantly agreed to undertake. It would not be easy. Certainly, it might be very dangerous. If I turned up missing after entering that decadent town, I would not be the first, but rather one of many who had ventured there to inquire into things they should have left alone.

Going there as a reporter would result in a fruitless mission—no one would talk to me—so I considered disguising myself, artificially acquiring the noted Innsmouth look to gain their acceptance. This, I concluded, would probably also be futile. With my deep olive complexion and large hooked nose that is by far the most prominent landmark on my face, I could never successfully acquire the look. Perhaps representing myself as something other than a reporter would be enough. It could work. I had no present contact with any Innsmouth people, and those I had met three years ago probably no longer remembered me.

To this end, temporarily changing my profession, I gave some serious thought, finally deciding that an itinerant book dealer would probably be as good a cover as any.

The following morning, dressed in a pair of faded slacks and a slightly moth-eaten sport coat, I dusted off a number of musty tomes that had rested undisturbed upon my shelves for some years and placed them in the back seat of my car, imagining myself attempting to sell them at one of the second-hand bookstores in Innsmouth. I hoped that, even though I had not read them in ages, nor for that matter hardly even noticed them, I would have no buyers. Along with the books I tossed a small grip containing extra clothes and toilet articles.

It was a pleasant day, not nearly as warm as the day before, and I enjoyed the ride that took me through the Massachusetts countryside, through rich farm lands and shadowed woods, from Arkham north to the depressing outskirts of Innsmouth. Approaching the town, I skirted the stagnant salt marshes and tidal creeks winding among rotted stumps, noting the gradual change of character in the sandy landscape as I passed old foundations and long-abandoned farms. It seemed as if I were passing from a sane normal world into one which was just the opposite, as I turned onto Federal Street and entered the town.

Innsmouth remained much as I had remembered it to be. On each side of the street, huge Georgian homes sprawled behind neglected lawns. They had been magnificent structures when built some two centuries ago but were now falling into a sad condition of decay and ruin. Many were boarded up and appeared to be totally deserted. Only a few showed indications of being lived in. Few people could be seen as I made my way toward the town square, and those who did come to view shambled along slowly, listlessly, looking from side to side with furtive glances.

It was shortly before noon when I maneuvered the car into the semicircular town square and saw on its western rim the looming facade of the cupola-topped Gilman House. It was here I anticipated spending the night. The edifice was in a deplorable state of dilapidation, with rotting boards sagging from its sides and no evidence of any recent painting or other restorative effort. It was a tall frame structure, uninviting and gloomy and foreboding. Unfortunately, it was the only hotel in town where I might be able to settle myself.

I parked in front of it, next to three other vehicles which had long ago seen their best days. My car, although now a bit dusty and no longer as shiny, stood out from its companions with their rusted bodies and cracked windows. I locked the doors and walked to where several steps led up to a long porch. One man, with a faint reptilian look, reclining in a chair reading a newspaper, gave me only a quick disinterested glance as I casually strolled toward the door.

Inside, I found it to be uncomfortably dim, little light penetrating the drawn shades. Several men lounged about the lobby engaged in a quiet conversation. Their sullen, guttural voices ceased as I walked across to the desk.

The clerk, a pale balding fellow of indeterminate age with a small flat nose, greeted me with a questioning frown.

"Yes?"

"A room for the night, please," I said, signing the fly-spotted register.

He continued to regard me . . . keenly . . . with deep-sunk, almost lidless eyes that never blinked but seemed to glower with mild suspicion. At last, with a thick clumsy hand ending in fingers that curled into the palm, he reached for a key.

"Room two fourteen—upstairs to your left. Three dollars in advance."

I nodded, handed him the required amount, and took the key. I vacated as soon as I could that dark lobby where I was becoming more uneasy at each passing moment, finding my way to the stairs and ascending to the second floor. Beneath me, the aging stairway creaked. I was appalled at the condition of the place as I saw walls from which large patches of paper had peeled and threadbare carpeting that should have been replaced many years ago. An odor permeated the whole place—a fishy smell that was faintly pervasive and somehow very annoying.

A minute later I had found my room and entered the most dreary and depressing chamber one could imagine. The floor was unswept and littered with paper, and the ceiling and corners were festooned with cobwebs. There was no inside lock, so I merely closed the door, tossed my grip on a chair that swayed on two broken legs, and crossed to throw up the shade and open the cracked and dirt-smeared window. Then I turned to inspect the bed, an old relic with iron posts. A shapeless mattress gave beneath my weight as the ancient springs sagged and creaked. It was covered by sheets, a bit torn but clean, that appeared to have been pressed with a cold iron.

I pulled a second chair, one able to support my weight, up to the window and gazed out upon the roofs of the nearby structures. Everything seemed to be in the last stages of decay, and a certain aura of menace struck me as I regarded the crumbling chimneys and poorly patched roofs. Off in the distance I could discern steeples and spires climbing and tottering above old churches.

My mind wandered over what I knew of Innsmouth, and although my knowledge was considerable, I found it hard to separate fact from fiction.

It had been, according to local history, a typical seaport founded more than three centuries ago—a quaint fishing settlement that nestled along the Atlantic coast, hardly distinguishable from others of its type. However, during the 1820's and '30's a sea captain named Obed Marsh had sailed the seas as a trader to foreign ports. The story is not clear, certainly not believable, but it seems that on one of those voyages he and his crew discovered a South Sea island where marine creatures of hideous aspect were being worshiped by the islanders. In return for certain sacrifices, the islanders were supplied with hand-worked golden jewelry by those aquatic entities—strange bracelets and necklaces and head pieces depicting a curious, alien, marine-like motif. This jewelry Obed Marsh traded for, offering in return gaudy trifles which were prized by the natives.

These scaly marine creatures were referred to as the Deep Ones, and were thought to be the earthly minions of Great Cthulhu who in his house at R'lyeh on the ocean floor waits dreaming away the eons. Between these entities and the islanders, unholy matings supposedly occurred.

In 1838 the islanders were destroyed and the supply of gold ended until Obed summoned the Deep Ones to Innsmouth, where he and his followers made sacrifices on their own in exchange for the desired jewelry. In 1846 the town was nearly wiped out by the marine creatures when the sacrifices had stopped for more than a month, and the result was a compact between them and the remaining residents that allowed those Deep Ones who so wished to inhabit the dark, unseen warrens of the town.

In the years that followed, strange children were born in Innsmouth—children who looked normal but were tainted by the fish-frog blood of one of their aquatic parents. Over the years their features gradually changed as they acquired the "Innsmouth look", and eventually, when the change had become complete, they took to the ocean to live almost forever, quasi-immortal, with the other Deep Ones. It did not take many generations of this particular inbreeding before much of the population of Innsmouth had been infected with the blood of these creatures. The problem then had been to hide this frightful condition from the world, and any step was regarded as being worth the risk to gain this end. Still, rumors did leak out, and although people in the neighboring towns suspected, they could not know for sure.

Obed became an immensely rich man, melting down the gold he secured in the form of jewelry from the Deep Ones into solid ingots which could be stored or sold. He, of course, was not subject to the "change", but his grandson Barnabas was. Barnabas, in later years known throughout the town as Old Man Marsh, was the offspring of Obed's son Onesipherus and one of those Deep Ones from the sea. He grew up looking quite normal, inherited the family wealth and, in later life, sometime in the 1920's after he had progressed in the change far enough, his hideously featured body had taken to the sea and had never been seen again.

All this had happened many years ago, but still had a profound effect upon the population. I did not believe the tale, I must admit, having never been presented with proof of any kind, although I suspected a few gems of incredible truth might be mingled with the general story. This was what I felt as I gazed out the window of the Gilman House.

The years had passed, the town had prospered, what with the abundance of gold and fantastically fine fishing that was then to be found off the coast. All had gone reasonably well—the dark secret had been protected—until the year of 1927 when one of the Marsh descendants, unaware he was one of *them*, exposed the seaport for the nightmare-cursed town that it was. The result was the entry of federal agents who burned many of the older homes, torpedoed the depths off Devil Reef, offshore from the town, and locked away strange-looking people, more fish-like than human, in institutions where none might see them.

All this was interesting speculation, and filled my mind as I peered at the shabby gables and gambrel roofs, sagging and half-caved in from ancient rot, of the homes spreading away before my view. The room to which I had been assigned smelled of dampness, age, and fish, and I was now anxious to leave. After surveying it for a minute and running a finger over a coating of dust on the dresser, I resolved to go to lunch and browse about the town.

The clerk greeted my descent to the lobby with an expressionless stare and tersely answered when I asked where I might find a good place to eat and where some used book stores were located. I subtly dropped the idea that I was a book collector in search of rare editions, but he made no comment to this and I do not know now whether or not he accepted it as my real purpose in town.

I decided to walk, rather than take the car, and made my way over the rickety iron-railed bridge spanning the Manuxet River far below to where the Fishman Restaurant was located at the intersection of Fall Street and Church Street. I entered, found the establishment to be nearly deserted, and hoped this was not caused by the quality of the meals served there.

Eating at this restaurant I found to be an unusual experience, although not an especially objectionable one. Two or three men were seated at the counter, all of them possessing the narrow heads, receding hairlines, and shriveled necks characteristic of the "Innsmouth look". They paid little attention to me as I passed them to occupy a seat near the end of the counter. Several minutes passed before a young woman with a most unhealthy pallor emerged from the back room to take my order. A soiled apron circled her unusually slim waist, and unclean, heavily veined hands rested on the counter as she took my order.

The food was not the best . . . but it was edible and did appease the appetite I had developed. The coffee I found to be even better, and actually indulged in a second cup.

Satisfied with my repast, I left the restaurant and followed a course that led me north along Fall Street to Martin, where I turned right and continued along toward Main. There I would find the first of two bookstores which I sought. I nonchalantly walked along, feeling the menace and hostility which infested this town as I passed the worm-eaten structures. At times I felt as if sharp eyes were directed at me from the upper cupolas of the blighted homes. But very few persons did I pass and they paid little or no attention to me. Many of the squalid buildings were boarded up, but I could not escape the absurd yet intense impression that it was from them especially that my movements were being watched.

Dirt and litter were everywhere in profuse abundance. Weeds and grass had established firm footholds in the cracked cement of the streets and walks; everywhere the air was laden with the noxious odor of fish, hardly relieved by the salty wind that swept in from the ocean—a decidedly unpleasant odor that did nothing to allay my apprehension.

After several blocks of leisurely walking I arrived at a low rundown building, with all its windows cracked, that bore a small dirt-smeared sign along its front indicating it to be Heimer's Bookstore.

I opened a creaking door and entered, setting astir a scurry of dust. Near the front was a small, cigarette-scarred desk behind which sat a man whom I presumed to be the owner. Otherwise, the eerie establishment was empty of people. He nodded and tentatively pushed his chair back. He was a man advanced in years, and I was relieved to see that he possessed none of the tainted Innsmouth features.

"Something I can help you with?" he asked in low, reedy voice.

"I hope so. I'm a book collector—looking for old volumes . . . first editions . . . and the like. You know."

He smiled. It was a tired smile that barely changed his gloomy countenance. "I'm afraid I can't help much. But you're welcome to look around."

I proceeded to the shelves where countless books were arrayed in haphazard disorder, stirring up more and more clouds of dust as I browsed about. Various titles attracted my attention, but nothing I really cared about; for the most part it was a cheap, poorly arranged accumulation of reading materials that had no appeal to me—nor had I really expected it to—so I returned and attempted to engage the ageing book dealer in conversation.

But no information was to be gathered from this source. He was interested in only one thing—books. Any attempt to divert him into other matters met with an abrupt defeat. I sensed that he had been conditioned over the years not to talk with strangers concerning any of the activities of Innsmouth. He clammed up and absolutely refused even to comment when I mentioned the bodies which had been washed up along the coast, nor would he respond to anything else after that. I suspected, as I left, that he was afraid to talk, and wondered how brave I myself would be if I were in the same situation.

From Heimer's store I made my way casually east toward the waterfront, finding the buildings to be in an even worse state of disrepair and neglect, if that were possible. Above me, peaked roofs reached upward and shuttered gables held behind them the prospect of unseen sinister eyes. I soon found myself on Water Street, along which stretched rotting warehouses from which occasionally came vague, slobbering noises and harsh croaking voices which I found to be of a disturbing nature and did not like because they could not be identified. Crossing the street I headed toward the wharves and soon found myself standing on a wooden platform raised on pilings which marched into the ocean.

An assortment of drying nets and crates stacked in a random manner added to the unkept appearance of the area. My eyes swept the contour of the natural harbor before me, followed the stone breakwater, and fastened momentarily on the ruins of an old lighthouse at its extremity. Beyond the harbor, a mile and a half out to sea, the low profile of Devil Reef brooded stark and barren against the horizon, marking the location of the ill-rumored sinister marine abyss.

At the far end of a nearby dock, an ancient warehouse making him invisible from the town, sat a lone figure, bent over a fishing pole, who remained motionless as I approached from behind to see if I might gain some information. As I walked along the weather-beaten planks, some of which sagged at crazy angles, the person ahead of me made no sign he was aware of my presence. I thought him to be asleep until I reached his side and looked down.

It was a boy, no more than fifteen years old, holding his face toward the water, looking at me from the corner of his eye.

"Hi!" I said, as pleasantly as possible.

Slowly he turned to face me and I saw then that he had been afraid. His facial muscles relaxed as he looked me over.

He nodded. "You're a stranger here," he decided.

"That's right. Catching anything?"

"Nope. Not yet. Caught a good-sized one yesterday, though."

Presumably he had sized me up and had concluded I presented no danger to him. He was certainly a talkative lad once he got started—probably very lonely. He had dirty brown hair that looked as if it had not been combed for a week, but a pleasant face, a bit grease-smeared, with none of the characteristic aberrations I had come to detest. I wondered what it was that had frightened him, then considered that I, too, if I had lived in this abhorrent town, would be apprehensive of someone approaching me from behind.

We talked for some minutes. I learned his name was Jeff and that he had been living here only a couple of months. His father owned the gas station on Federal Street and already was so disgusted with the town that he was trying to sell out and return to Marblehead from whence they originally came.

"Curious town," I remarked, as the conversation started to lag.

"I don't like it at all," he declared. "Can't wait to leave."

I nodded understandingly.

"That boat out there," I asked casually, "heading for the reef . . . what do you suppose the person in it is doing?"

Jeff glanced at me sharply and remained quiet for a spell, refusing, I thought, to answer. Certainly, his reactions suggested he was not totally ignorant of strange occurances concerning Innsmouth. At last he turned around, making sure no one was in sight, and spoke: "I probably shouldn't say. You learn to be careful in Innsmouth and keep quiet about certain things. Promise you won't repeat what I tell you?"

I agreed.

Jeff edged closer till he was right next to me. His voice was a near whisper. "They're looking for gold!"

"Gold?"

"Shh. Yes . . . gold. I think so. The people here don't talk with strangers, but they do talk among themselves and don't pay too much attention to youngsters like me."

"That I can understand."

"There's this rumor that there's gold on Devil Reef. They only recently found out about it. At least that's what I've overheard at the station. Seems Obed Marsh who ran this town more'n a hundred years ago had a gold refinery. He'd melt down gold jewelry and trinkets the sailors brought him from some island in the South Seas. His grandson, Old Man Marsh, continued the refinery when Obed died, and it's said that before he disappeared more'n fifty years ago he hid some of the jewelry that wasn't melted . . . hid it down in the pit on Devil Reef. I don't know just how they found out about the gold—some old papers that came to light, I think."

"The pit?"

"Yeah. There's this here pit on the reef. I've never been there to see it but they say it's like a huge shaft that sinks down until it connects with a passage leading through the reef to the ocean."

Jeff's voice sank even lower.

"Old Man Marsh hid the gold somewhere in that pit . . . more than fifty years ago!"

"I see. That boat then . . . the person in it . . . he's trying to get the gold. Do you see many go out there?"

He shook his head. "Not anymore. A while back, maybe once or twice a day someone would go out to look around."

I wondered. Maybe there was something here—perhaps some connection between the gold-seekers on Devil Reef and the bodies that had been washed up on shore. I steered our conversation toward other directions, so as not to let Jeff suspect the importance of the information he had imparted to me, then left shortly afterward.

Later, lying on my bed, listening to the occasional creak of the aging timbers of the Gilman House, I reflected upon what I knew had to be done. There was little more I could learn from the people of Innsmouth—what I had already discovered had been through fantastic luck. I would now have to become more aggressive in my investigation—take more initiative—and that meant visiting Devil Reef to judge for myself the situation. For it was there, I now strongly suspected, that this whole mystery had its beginning . . . and perhaps its end.

It was not a happy prospect—indeed, it was one to avoid if at all possible—but I knew it would have to be done. There would be little problem in getting to that bleak hunk of rock off the coast, I thought, remembering the rowboats I had seen pulled up along the waterfront, above the high tide mark. Surely, one could be fairly easily borrowed, without the owner's knowledge, as soon as it was dark enough. But my plans could not extend beyond getting to the reef, as I knew nothing of what was there. I would have to plan any further course of action based upon what I found.

The sun was setting as I left the Gilman House, painting the western horizon in a kaleidoscopic composition of reds and oranges and yellows. It was a pleasant view, but I felt uneasy knowing that later I would be setting foot upon that black tangle of rocks that seemed to float, far in the distance, in the swelling Atlantic Ocean.

I walked to the Fishman Restaurant and chose a seat at the counter. In attendance upon the few customers at this time was a large, lanky man who shambled from table to counter, his pale, hairless face, with deep-creased nose, an uncomforting sight for anyone to behold while eating. He watched me speculatively with cold watery eyes as I ordered, then retrieved the menu from me with rough, leathery hands.

Although the atmosphere of the dimly lit place was not pleasant, the meal was adequate, and I could not find fault with the waiter's service, other than that it was performed in a sulky, gloomy silence. Outside, darkness had descended by the time I had finished my dinner and a second cup of coffee. The time had arrived for me to embark upon the venture which I was resolved to undertake. Paying my bill, I slipped out into the shadows and began to stroll toward the waterfront.

The moon was hidden behind filmy clouds and few street lights were lit to chase away the darkness. The air was cooling quickly, providing some relief from the uncomfortable heat of the day. I made good time as I walked the darkening streets, passing the nearly deserted structures that seemed to leer gruesomely out of the darkness, seeing few people loitering about, but experiencing again that menacing sensation of being carefully watched from attic windows which I knew to be boarded up. Few of the buildings showed any signs of habitation, but some had dim lights aglow that spilled onto the street through sagging shutters drawn to conceal the interiors from any passerby. Sounds could be heard coming from within certain homes, but not from those showing signs of occupancy. They were strange sounds, of shuffling feet and croaking voices that reached my ears with eerie intonations and made me wonder what was behind those locked and boarded doors.

It took but a few minutes to reach the cluster of decadent docks that inched out into the dark water. Here I was surprised to find that I was not alone.

Ahead of me, silhouetted against the dark sky, was another adventurer who moved furtively about. I stood beside a crumbling shed, knowing I could not be seen, as I watched his secretive movements. Apparently, he was here for the same purpose as I, for he proceeded to untie one of the row boats, push it into the water, and settle himself into it. Moments later I could hear the soft pull of the oars and gentle splash of water as he glided away from the beach and headed out into the harbor.

At this point I began to have serious reservations about the wisdom of my proposed venture. To go to Devil Reef knowing I might not be free to explore it without interference seemed to border on folly. Besides, he who had just left might prove to be a dangerous adversary should an encounter result between the two of us. On the other hand, perhaps his presence—and for all I knew the presence of others—would be an aid to me in ferreting out the answers I sought.

I decided to take whatever risks were necessary and depart for Devil Reef. The man had about a five-minute start on me when I left my scanty hiding place and walked to the beach, where an assortment of boats were tethered. I chose one that had oars in it and seemed to be in better condition than the rest, pushed it into the water, and quietly lowered myself onto the bow seat. It took but a few moments to ship the oars and begin to navigate the shadowed, softly glistening harbor waters.

Ahead of me, some distance away, I could see a black smudge moving toward the reef, and was reasonably assured the unknown's destination and my own were the same. I set out in pursuit, rowing as quietly as was possible, matching the pace he had set.

Many minutes passed and I cleared the harbor and passed into the open Atlantic where broad, slow swells lifted the boat. Ahead, the dark outline of Devil Reef became more clearly defined. I had lost sight of the boat I had been following; it had seemed to blend right in with the reef, but I felt reasonably certain it was still ahead and had perhaps beached by now.

Eventually, the jagged rocks of my objective became more clear, and soon I was close enough to touch some of the black fangs that rose above the water's surface. Ahead of me, a small circular rock-bound cove came into view, and within it I made out the form of a small boat, gently rising and falling upon the crest of the water.

No one was about. I peered into the darkness, but was unable to perceive signs of any strange presence or motion. To be safe, I decided against sheltering my craft near the other and began to row along the line of rocks in search of another inlet. It was not long before one came to view, a miniature harbor ideal for my purpose, and I maneuvered the boat into it, jumped out upon the reef, and secured the rope to a nearby rock.

I looked about. Nothing was to be seen but black piles of tumbled rock and water that sparkled in the light of the moon which had now emerged from behind a bank of clouds. Behind me was the town of Innsmouth, with few lights here and there to indicate the presence of man.

Where had the stranger gone whom I was following? I wondered. He had a good start on me, but if I proceeded cautiously I could probably discover him and his activities without betraying my own presence. This was my intent, and I set forth accordingly, aiming toward what I believed to be the center of the evil-rumored reef.

Over black hummocks and craggy ridges I slipped and stumbled in the darkness on an upward-slanting course, not daring to use the flashlight I had brought, and soon found myself within view of a dark hole, many feet wide, which I believed must be the pit.

Cautiously, I went forward and gazed over the rim. Dim noises ascended from the depths and a soft splash, as though someone had lowered himself into the water, caught my attention. I saw that with care one might climb down the side of the pit, so I started down, careful to make no noise, feeling from rock to rock for hand-holds to ease my descent.

But I stopped at the sound of the scream that came erupting from below me—a hideous chilling scream that shrilled from rock to rock!

Looking down, there were only dim shadows to be seen.

But the blood-curdling shrieks continued, accompanied by a furious thrashing of water!

And then all was quiet.

The sudden silence disturbed me almost as much as the screams, but I knew I could not stop now and turn my back on whatever it was that had occurred below. I continued down, and presently reached the bottom of the pit, finding myself on a narrow ledge that overlooked a black pool of water perhaps thirty feet across. The faint moonlight that barely reached this eerie grotto was just enough for me to make out a shadowy form in the water. It was, I presumed, the man I had been following, floating on his back, splashing feebly.

I reached down, managed to secure a grip on his shirt, and pulled him out of the water onto the ledge. It was then, the scene before me now illuminated by the rays of my flashlight, that I saw that his throat had been nearly torn out and he had been nearly disemboweled, so savagely had he been attacked. Copious streams of blood flowed from his many wounds and I knew he would be dead within minutes. I marveled at the stamina which must have been his to maintain life in the body even now.

"For Dagon's sake!" he gasped, his voice a faint croak. "Don't go in the water . . . waiting . . don't try to get the gold . . . it's been guarding it for so long . . . won't let anyone touch it."

"What is it?" I cried, as the blood bubbled from his lacerated throat.

"It's . . . it's . . . it told me before ripping me apart! It can still speak!"

"What do you mean . . . ." I urged, seizing him by the arms. He was slipping fast. I had to know.

He told me, as his life's blood fouled the ledge upon which he lay and I knelt, then lapsed into silence. He ceased to move after a violent shudder and I laid him back upon the cold damp rock. His white sightless eyes remained open, staring at me, silently screaming of the horror they had witnessed.

I understood now. Those six who had been washed up on the shore had indeed trespassed upon the private domain of one who guarded the treasure. They had been ruthlessly destroyed in their futile attempts to wrest away the gold for themselves, and their bodies had drained out through the passage connecting this pit to the ocean, eventually reaching the open sea, to be washed ashore near Arkham.

A nearby splash aroused me from these reflections and, turning, I witnessed the sight of a Deep One—a sight I will try for the rest of my life to forget!

What I saw was a monstrous frog-like visage rising above the surface of the water near the middle of the pool. Cold, hideously bulging eyes regarded me with a savage look of utter malignancy, an abnormally large mouth hung partly opened, and huge gills palpitated menacingly. It was a hairless face, slightly green with mottled white, and bore no resemblance to any marine animal known to common man.

My God, I thought, the change that had taken place over the years! It had once been a man, but now this ichthyic horror bore no resemblance whatsoever toward mankind!

Powerful strokes of webbed hands and feet propelled it rapidly across the pool to the ledge, and had I not reacted immediately . . . instinctively . . . scrambling out of reach, clawing my way upward, I would have been its next victim. It heaved its grayish-green body out of the water and missed me by inches. I did not pause on my upward ascent to look back to see if it was following, but heard no sounds of pursuit and so assumed it had returned to the water. Two or three minutes later I scrambled over the edge of the pit and swayed on the black rock, utterly exhausted, and knowing that I was not yet safe.

Slipping and stumbling, I ran to where the boat still floated safely at its mooring in the sheltered waters, jumped in, and made my way as fast as my tired muscles would allow back to the mainland. At each stroke of the oars, I half expected to see that frightful creature in pursuit of me, but nothing was seen as I pulled steadily toward the shore.

When at last I did reach the shore and beach the boat, I scrambled out and made my way through the dark festering streets of Innsmouth, not running, but walking as fast as my tired legs would allow, past houses and stores that loomed ominously in the moonlight. Once at the Gilman House, I went straight to my car, roared it into life, and sped out of that infamous town of shadows as fast as I could.

I am now back in Arkham. I cannot sleep. I can only think over those experiences which will forever haunt my mind. I realize it will be impossible to write up the full story of these happenings for the newspaper, as much will have to be omitted; only the sketchiest of accounts can be given.

Surely, I cannot burden our world with the truth!

It was the truth I had learned from that man whom I had found so horribly mangled in the pit—the truth regarding that white-bellied Deep One who so fiercely guarded the treasure it had hidden over fifty years ago—the Deep One *who had once been Old Man Marsh.*

About "Trust Me"

The subtext of Lovecraft's "The Shadow over Innsmouth" was the depiction of repellent backwater decadence, together with the twin spectres of inbreeding and interbreeding. Here was Lovecraft's contempt for those who had fallen from the proper heights of civilized Novanglian society. Thus, at least for most of the story, the outsider's perspective is the sympathetic one. In the present tale, a light-hearted one, Stan Sargent realizes that Innsmouth can serve just as well to symbolize rough-hewn new England rustics when one views them sympathetically. "Trust Me" is on their side. It starts from a motif Lovecraft uses, *e.g.*, in "The Colour out of Space" and "The Dunwich Horror", the plight of humble townies who want only to be left alone but are made an object of jeering scrutiny by small-minded newspapers whose fancied sophistication is given the lie by their tabloid sensationalism. Here the rustics get their revenge at last. In the process we come to see something of the Innsmouthers' reasoning. What is there about the dry-land civilization that makes us think it is worth saving from conquest by the Deep Ones? Go take a walk through your local shopping mall and the question will come home to you with renewed force, I am sure.

Trust Me

by Stanley C. Sargent

A long white limo pulled slowly into town, its lack of speed emphasizing its importance, until it came to a halt near two grizzled old men who sat comfortably upon the fallen stone façade of what once had been a large hotel, the Gilman according to the broken sign. These men, both dressed in buttoned-up workshirts and bib overalls, casually glanced up from their whittling and "chawin'." Two well dressed men, one of whom was very short, stepped from the limousine and walked toward those seated in the ruins.

"Pardon me, gentlemen. This is the town of Innsmouth, is it not?" inquired the shorter of the two strangers, squinting to avoid the brilliance of the sun, which hung just between and behind the two whittlers.

"I'm a-wonderin' who'd be a-wantin' to knaow, ain't yer, Martin?" mumbled the larger of the two old whittlers, punctuating his remark by spitting an ugly glob of tobacco onto the ground only an inch from the questioner's expensive-looking shoes.

Jumping back in surprise, the little man volunteered, "Why, I'm Walter Wonshull." He stared at the inattentive whittlers expectantly, as if his name alone should bring instant recognition. When none was forthcoming, he added, "WALTER WONSHULL, the *Arkham Weekly Journal*'s most popular journalist!"

Wonshull hung motionless, still awaiting awed exclamations of praise and recognition that did not come. A moment later, the larger of the seated men spoke again, distractedly, to his companion. "Seems I heard Walter Winchell died 'bout twenty years er more ago, didn't yer, Jeb?"

His companion rubbed his chin and nodded. "I believe I recollect a report to that effect, Martin. So who'd ye 'spect this here fella might be? Don't look like he been dead twenty years to me. Ten maybe, but nowhar near twenty."

Neither man bothered to look up from his wood-working.

"No, no! Not Winchell, Wonshull! Walter Wonshull," the little stranger corrected. "Just trust me, okay? I'm a writer, let's just leave it at that. I'm here to write a story about Innsmouth and the horrors that still haunt it after all these years."

Receiving no response, Wonshull cursed quietly under his breath. He then turned to the other man from the limo, who was heavily loaded down with photographic equipment.

"I knew these inbred boonies were going to be a pain in the ass, Parker. It's obvious they know *exactly* who I am. They're just clamming up because they're afraid of what a famous writer like me might write about them," he added, sneering in the direction of the silent immobile whittlers. "Well, I don't need their cooperation; if there's anything 'fishy' going on around here, I'll find it. You can bank on that! I came here for a story and, by God, I'll get one!"

He abruptly turned his back on the two whittlers and strutted away indignantly as he extracted a small tape recorder from his coat pocket and began speaking into it.

"The reclusive, obviously half-witted descendants of those who miraculously survived the government's devastating assault on Innsmouth in 1928 can still be seen today," Wonshull dictated. "They appear as verminous forms squatting silently among the ruins, crouched in toadlike readiness as if awaiting an opportunity to spring upon the unwary. The amphibious taint upon their physical features readily suggests the FBI indeed had a greater justification for decimating the town than simple bootlegging." He obviously enjoyed his own venom.

* * *

Wonshull and Parker seemed to be everywhere over the next day and a half. It soon became obvious that, finding no real story in the crumbling harbor town, the writer intended to create one. Again and again he could be seen instructing Parker in the creation of suggestive, misleading images to be captured on film. He bullied and intimidated the town's residents whenever they objected to his misinterpretations and downright falsifications, always silencing dissenters with the same worthless assurance: "I'm a professional. I know exactly what I'm doing. Trust me, I-am-a-writer!"

* * *

Wherever the two strangers went around the town, the same two whittlers could be seen nearby, their knives silently gnawing away at their respective carvings, all thoughts kept strictly to themselves. Wonshull was too busy to notice them, apparently preoccupied with weaving one mystery after another out of thin air until, with the approach of evening, he and his partner would disappear into the limo that spirited them back to Arkham, only to return the following morning.

Even Wonshull seemed relieved that the third day was to be his last in the town. Early in the morning he had Parker scooping out circles in the bare earth near the docks. The two unseen old listeners overheard him remark that the circles would look good in the photos, lending support to the article's claim that secret tunnels still undermined the harbor area of Innsmouth.

It wasn't until early afternoon of the third day that Jeb and Martin observed the author haggling with old Ezekiah Morton over the cost of renting one of his rowboats for a few hours. Wonshull apparently felt anything over five dollars was excessive, considering he and Parker only wanted to row the craft out to Devil Reef and back. The old fisherman gave in, agreeing to the five dollar figure after the little man lambasted him for the third time with the idiotic pronouncement, "I know exactly what I'm doing. Trust me, I-am-a-writer!"

It occurred to Martin that the great man was being rather generous with the fee in this particular case, considering he had been willing to pay only nickels the previous day to children for posing for photos while holding their breath. Wonshull liked the puffy-cheeked, pop-eyed look "the little cretins" had gotten on their faces after holding their breaths for over a full minute.

Fifteen minutes later, Wonshull and Parker were about to launch the rowboat into the long-clogged harbor when Parker suddenly groaned aloud.

"Damn, Mr. Wonshull, I just realized I don't have enough film for an extended underwater shoot. Can we get away with just a dozen or so shots? It's not like there really are any ruins down there or anything; we'll just be shooting sections of reef we've lit to look weird."

Wonshull turned toward his partner, his face flushed with anger. "Every time I take you on assignment, Parker, I wonder how you dare to call yourself a photographer. No, I will not settle for a dozen or so shots, so you'd just better get yourself into Arkham and back here with LOTS of film. PRONTO!"

Throwing his hands into the air, Parker reminded his boss that the limo would not be back for hours.

"Parker, I don't care if you walk, but you'd better walk pretty goddamn fast, otherwise you might just as well stop off to file yourself a job application at the nearest quickie photomat!"

Without another word, Parker picked up his equipment and marched off, presumably to get more film. At least Wonshull seemed to think that was where he was going, although two less conspicuous presences harbored rather more severe doubts that Parker intended to return.

Standing there looking at the scuba equipment and the nearly empty camera piled in the aft of the small boat, Wonshull realized he had a problem. Exasperated, he turned to scan the dock and beach area for inspiration, finally spotting the only other signs of life, the two lonely figures in bib overalls.

An "Oh, Christ!" escaped Wonshull's lips before he forced himself to smile as he coolly sauntered over to the pair.

"How would you two gents like to make a few dollars this afternoon?" he queried.

He was not surprised at the total lack of acknowledgement he received. He would just have to try a different approach.

"Well, then, how would you like to do this fine town and its citizens a good turn?" He knew he was on the right track, though he still had not caught a reaction from either man.

"Okay, let's be honest, fellas. We all know there's nothing weird or special going on in Innsmouth, at least not these days. It's pretty obviously just a dying town with little chance of ever getting on its feet again." He was sure he detected a break in the rhythm of at least one of the whittler's endless efforts.

"But if I were to, say, write an article about Innsmouth, enhancing its haunting image and eerie history just a bit, why, it could breathe new life, and revenue, into the place. Think of the money thousands of tourists could bring to Innsmouth. Like the 'Witch House' in Salem, it's a gold mine. In no time at all your town would be a thriving community again. The going price of land would soar—people would pay a lot to live in the midst of all that eldritch atmosphere."

He had done it. The whittling had ceased abruptly; he knew he had them.

"Now if you gents would care to help bring all this about, it will only cost about an hour of your time—nothing more. As you can see, I'm alone at the moment, yet it's vital that my article be bolstered with a few photos of yonder offshore reef. I've got everything set to go, but I need someone to sit in the boat while I am under, just to keep an eye on the lifeline in the doubtful event that, due to some unforeseen occurrence, I might need a little help getting back to the boat. But don't worry, there's very little chance of anything like that happening.

"So what do you say, my friends? Do you feel up to performing a simple but worthwhile public service and all around good deed today?" Folding his arms over his chest, Wonshull tried to give the impression of honest, forthright sincerity.

After only a moment, the two old "yokels", which is how Wonshull thought of them now, stood and led the way to the boat. Without a word they climbed in and seated themselves, each taking up an oar. Delighted, the diminutive Wonshull ensconced himself among the equipment behind the self-appointed oarsmen and began changing into his diving gear.

It was nearly a mile to Devil Reef, but the old men displayed no signs of exhaustion upon arrival. They had maneuvered the wooden craft to the exact spot where the landward shelf suddenly ended, giving way to a seemingly bottomless, black expanse of ocean depth. It was here legend said one might find the deepwater entrance to long-lost Y'ha-nthlei, city of the monstrous Deep Ones who had worshiped the ancient, dread Dagon.

"This is perfect!" squealed their passenger. "I don't have much film, so I may have to go down a bit further than I'd like to for the best sites, but I don't expect to be long and can assure you I won't be taking any unnecessary risks. All you have to do is sit tight and watch the lifeline rope. I've made sure one end is securely tied around my waist, while the other end I've made fast to the boat."

The perpetual silence of the two old yokels was really getting on Wonshull's nerves, even giving him pause to consider that they might actually be morons without the faintest idea of what was going on around them. But it was too late now, so he would have to take his chances, though it was reassuring to know it was extremely unlikely that he would need the aid of the two old manikins.

He continued his instructions, speaking more slowly in case he actually was talking to a pair of mental cripples.

"If anything should go wrong, I will yank, very hard, on this line. That's your signal to pull me up. Whatever you do, don't untie the line as I will need it to find my way back to the boat in the dark water. Any questions?" He thought he detected a slight shake of the smaller man's head, which would have to suffice as their mutual answer.

Wonshull edged himself into position at the side of the boat and pushed off, easily rolling into the blue-green waters. He sensed the vivid beauty of the area immediately, but he addressed his attention to the craggy, twisted outcroppings of living reef barely visible in the darkening waters further below him.

On the surface above, the two men sat silently, stiff as statues except for their arms and hands, which whittled away with great enthusiasm once more.

* * *

The strange figures in the dark waters had been gathering in an enclosing circle around Wonshull for several minutes before he noticed them. It took only a quick glance at the bloated, bulbous-eyed features and the dark, squamous skin of the creatures surrounding him, however, to cast Wonshull into terrified panic. "Deep Ones! They're real!" he screamed into his mouthpiece, flailing his arms madly in an uncoordinated effort to propel himself upward.

Realizing he had to regain control of himself, Wonshull forced his mind to calm down. The creatures seemed in no hurry to approach him and had not made any threatening gestures yet. If he kept his head, all he had to do was follow the rope back to the safety of the boat. Everything was going to be fine, and the things probably wouldn't be able to catch him, especially with the added speed he would acquire once the old men began hauling him upward. He jerked several times on the lifeline, clutching it tightly as he swam upward, away from the leering abnormalities attending him. What an incredible story this would make! He could hardly ask for anything better!

* * *

Martin watched as Jeb reacted to the jerking rope. He felt compelled to ask his friend concerning those reactions when he saw Jeb raise his whittling knife to the rope.

"All I'm a-doin'," replied the larger man, "is makin' a small change to the climax of that fella's story, Martin. There's no need to worry yourself none."

Still unsure, Martin sputtered further doubts.

"Martin," Jeb responded, "I know exactly what I'm a-doin'. Trust me, I-am-a-editor!"

Both men suddenly howled with laughter, then Jeb sliced the rope in half and tossed the loose end into the waves far from the boat. They laughed so hard that, at one point during the row back to shore, Martin began to hyperventilate. Jeb was forced to rip open his friend's shirt collar and dangle him, head first, in the water off the side of the boat. *It's times like this,* he thought to himself as he pulled his aging partner's head from the water, *that make one appreciate his god-given gills.*

About "Just a Tad beyond Innsmouth"

Here is a tale of cracker barrel creatures of the Cthulhu Mythos, a story which zeroes in on a familiar but neglected detail of Lovecraftian stories including "The Dunwich Horror" and "The Horror in the Burying Ground", namely the presence, both ornamental and ominous, of store loungers in the haunted town. These are people who have somehow learned to make accommodation to the near presence of an elder, outer entity, something like residents of a chronic war zone like Beirut who have decided to stay put. What sort of rationalizations, justifications, compromises have such people had to negotiate in their own minds? With their own consciences? Have they accepted the Evil Powers as something like feudal lords, like neighborhood gangster-governments in Prohibition-era Chicago? Thus one fears to stop and ask them directions. One wonders whose side they are on, even if they appear to be normal.

Like the preceding story, "Trust Me" this one features a couple of continuing characters, a kind of Lovecraftian Bartles & James pair, refugees from a Horror Hee Haw. Are they Deep One hybrids? That's beside the point. Stan Sargent has grasped the fact that such fictive monster-men are thinly veiled analogues for a certain crusty New Englander type, even though their quarter of New England is one "you can't get to from here."

One last note: To appreciate this story fully, you might want to read August Derleth's "The Fisherman at Falcon Point".

Just a Tad beyond Innsmouth

by Stanley C. Sargent

A Chevy van pulled up to the curb before two old whittlers wearing faded bib overalls. Their busy hands didn't miss a single stroke as a young long-haired man dressed in neat work clothes exited the van and approached the intent carvers.

The stranger stopped directly before the aged pair, politely waiting for some sign that his presence had been noticed. A moment later, he shattered the silence.

"Afternoon!" he called to one, then the other. "Would you two gents mind directing me toward Falcon Point?"

The mention of Falcon Point brought a sudden but temporary halt to the whittling process, though neither of the old men glanced up at the stranger.

Jeb, the larger man, turned and addressed his companion. "I'm a-wonderin' who'd be a-wantin' to knaow 'baout Falcon Point, ain't yer, Martin?" he mumbled as he spit a chaw of tobacco that landed on the ground between himself and the stranger.

"Wonder no longer, sir," the stranger interrupted. "The name's Don Kitrell of the Commonwealth of Massachusetts Department of Land and Water." He smiled, stepped forward, and extended his right hand to the men. No hand was offered in return.

Martin, the smaller of the duo, spat a juice wad that landed exactly on top of the splat Jeb had made. He mumbled something to Jeb, then returned to his unabated woodcarving. It sounded to Kitrell as if Martin had a frog in his throat.

"Look, fellas, I'm trying to get to Falcon Point, specifically the old Enoch Conger place. I've never been in Innsmouth before, and I sure could use some friendly direction." Exasperation began to creep into the newcomer's voice. Though still ignored, Kitrell persisted. "The State has recently taken possession of the Conger land at Falcon Point in lieu of amassed back taxes, and I've been sent here to give the place a once-over. A surveyor will be out sometime next week, and we need some idea of what the land is like before plans can be drawn up to drain the marshes and ponds in the area. That way, as much of the land as possible can be reclaimed for sale. I know Falcon Point's south of Innsmouth, but I'm not too good at telling south from west."

Kitrell noted the sudden furrowing of his listeners' brows, but they still refused to speak or even look directly at him.

Kitrell felt his frustration give way to anger. "I'm just wasting my breath on you two buzzards, aren't I? I must have asked for directions six different times in this God-forsaken town, and not one person has so much as told me to go to hell. Well, I'll find my way to the Conger place and I'll do my job, in spite of you assholes!" He turned abruptly and started toward his van, had second thoughts, then returned to face the silent pair.

"I know what you're doing. You're playing 'spook the outsider', aren't you? You know everybody's heard stories about this place, and you figure if you act peculiar, then everyone will stay away." He paused and stared at the ground, growing angrier by the moment.

"Maybe you people have been alone for a little too long. Maybe your brothers and sisters got a little too friendly over the last few generations, so you're just too damn stupid now to understand English!" He paused for a reaction, but received none before delivering his parting shot. "You and this cemetery you call a town can suck brimstone in hell for all I care!"

This time when Kitrell turned, he kept moving until he reached the van, climbed in, and slammed the door. He blasted the vehicle's horn once as he pulled away from the curb and was pleased to see the two oldsters jump slightly in surprise.

Once the van was out of sight, Martin slowly turned to Jeb and noted, "Funny sort, that feller."

"Yep," Jeb replied ominously, "A real panic." He smiled to himself as he slashed deeply into the whittling wood.

* * *

Kitrell refused to stop and ask directions again, not that there were many people on the streets; "dreaded" Innsmouth struck him as more of a ghost town than a thriving port.

Looking at his watch, he saw it was already 2:30, which meant he'd wasted more than two hours driving around town in circles and getting snubbed by old people. If he didn't find the Conger place before dark, he'd have to wait until morning light to do his job, which meant sleeping in the van overnight. The idea held no appeal for him.

A few blocks later, on Federal Street, he spotted an open doorway out of the corner of his eye. Upon closer inspection, he read the faded letters of an overhead sign that identified the run-down storefront as a chain grocery.

He hadn't eaten since breakfast, and although the little grocery wasn't all that inviting, it was the only open store he'd seen. As he parked the van, he wondered if having money in hand would make the local yokels any friendlier. He saw no one else on the street, but he still locked the van.

It struck him as fairly dark within the store, and most of the wooden shelves were empty. It wasn't until he reached the rear of the store that Kitrell noticed a man reading a book behind the counter, the first young person Kitrell had encountered in Innsmouth. The young man sat with his book propped against the keys of an ancient cash register and seemed unconcerned that he had a customer.

Kitrell picked up a prepackaged sandwich and a pint of chocolate milk before approaching the reader. He dropped the items on the counter, then called out a cautious "howdy."

"Well, hello there, mister," came a surprised but friendly response. "How can I help you?"

Though Kitrell hadn't been prepared for open friendliness, he knew he'd better take advantage of it. He made a hesitant inquiry as to the way to Falcon Point and was amazed to receive an answer.

"You aren't from around here either, are you?" Kitrell asked the young clerk.

"No way! Home is back in Arkham. I just work summers here, sleeping in a room in the rear of the store. Working here helps pay my tuition to Miskatonic U. The name's Jim, by the way, Jim Gilbert."

Kitrell shook the clerk's hand, introduced himself, and explained why he was looking for Falcon Point. Upon mention of the State, Gilbert demonstrated unwarranted excitement.

"You're here to check out Falcon Point? Great! But there's no need to pretend with me; you're from the FBI, aren't you?" Gilbert stared expectantly at Kitrell.

"The FBI? Oh no, nothing like that," Kitrell assured Gilbert.

Gilbert obviously didn't accept the denial, suddenly lowering his voice and becoming secretive in his manner. "It's cool, man. I understand, low profile and all that. I'll bet you're here to follow up on Dr. Allen's disappearance, aren't you?"

"Doctor who?" asked the confused Kitrell.

"Well, now that you have asked me officially, I'll tell you everything I know. I want to cooperate with the investigation one hundred percent. Hell, I work here, and if something funny's going on—and I'm convinced there is—I want to know about it!"

Kitrell decided he'd listen to whatever followed, just for the heck of it. Gilbert was obviously a loony guy who relished the opportunity to talk to any outsider.

"Well," Gilbert began, "Dr. Allen came through here a little over a month ago. I'd seen him at school, but I didn't know him. He worked in the research lab but didn't teach any classes. Anyway, he was headed for Falcon Point, just like you. Some guy had sent Dr. Allen a frog he had found near Falcon Point and asked Dr. Allen to identify it. Dr. Allen was all excited because the frog was a mutation, some kind of sea frog that had adapted to living on land. He wanted to be the first to investigate it."

"So what'd he find out?" asked Kitrell, who despite himself was beginning to find the story interesting.

"That's rather hard to say. I told him the way to Falcon Point, but as far as I know he never came back. I spent the following weekend in Arkham with my folks, so I decided to drop in on Dr. Allen at the university lab. No one has seen or heard from him since the day he came in here."

The tale left Kitrell feeling a bit uneasy. If a doctor had really disappeared while at Falcon Point, that might explain the reaction of the locals to his mention of the place. "So what do you think became of this Dr. Allen?" he ventured of the student.

"I don't know, but I've been doing a lot of reading up on amphibians since then and, along with what Dr. Allen told me, I've come up with a couple ideas. Did you know that science has discovered all sorts of new antibiotics on the skin of frogs? Frogs have permeable skin—it's got to stay moist all the time they're away from water—and their warm and damp bodies provide ideal breeding grounds for all kinds of bacteria and viruses. They produce antibodies internally which are secreted through their skin to keep them from dying of bacterial and viral infection. That kind of protection from disease probably extends their life span quite a bit too."

"Go on," Kitrell said, curious to see how Gilbert would tie all of this in with his tale of the missing doctor.

"Well, while they were studying different species of toads and frogs in hopes of discovering new antibiotics, scientists noticed that lots of those species were becoming extinct. They figure the cause is probably either air pollution or ultraviolet rays passing through the diminished ozone layer. Frogs, because of their permeable skin, are very sensitive to those things. There's a species called the golden frog down in the South American rain forests, for instance; there used to be millions of them, yet none have been spotted in the last five years even though other species of frogs in the area seem to be doing just fine. Interesting, huh?"

Becoming a bit impatient at last, Kitrell decided to cut to the chase. "So what does all this have to do with Falcon Point and the doctor's theories?"

"That's the fascinating part. About the only way a species can deal with an environmental change is to adapt to it. Trouble is, today the changes are occurring too fast for any species to adapt normally, as it takes thousands of years; all the frogs would be dead long before that. Dr. Allen theorized that these sea frogs had found a short cut to adapting, evolving actually, to living their lives on land. All he needed was proof that they were now able to breed in fresh rather than salt water. If they could also breed in fresh water, that meant they had somehow accomplished an evolutionary leap within a time frame considered impossible by science. Pretty wild when you think about it, other species evolving at a rate a thousand times faster than mankind."

"But this Allen never proved this theory, did he?" added Kitrell.

Gilbert slowly shook his head from side to side, then glanced around the store nervously. When he spoke again, it was in a conspiratorial whisper.

"No, but all this got me thinking about Innsmouth and the half-human, half-frog things that are supposed to live out near Devil Reef. I'm not saying I believe in these Deep Ones as they are called, but you never know."

Kitrell nodded patiently.

"Well, suppose those stories were true. Then suppose the changes in the environment affect the Deep Ones too. They live in the same sea as Dr. Allen's sea frogs. What if they were able to adapt just like the sea frogs? Living on land, they would no longer be tied to a seaport, so they could spread out all across the country without any of us ever suspecting. Now think about that for a minute."

Kitrell thought about it for about half a minute, then decided the idea was too far-fetched for consideration. For one thing, he saw no reason to believe the Deep Ones had ever existed outside of folklore.

"So you think that's what's going on here?" he asked.

Gilbert hesitated a moment as if gathering his thoughts. "Well, no," he finally offered. "If the Deep Ones had succeeded, you'd expect Innsmouth to be overrun with young ones as they built up their numbers. You can see for yourself that isn't the case—but that doesn't mean it couldn't happen."

Kitrell remarked that the few people he had seen in Innsmouth all were elderly.

Gilbert perked up at the observation. "Everybody who lives here for long looks old, though I admit I've yet to see anyone who looks like a fish or a frog. I've got a theory about why there are no kids in Innsmouth, though, and it involves the local religion, the Esoteric Order of Dagon. They are so secretive that nobody else knows anything about them, though I'm beginning to think one of their tenets must be celibacy."

"Celibacy?" Kitrell repeated in surprise.

"I've been here for three summers now. The guy before me was here for over twenty years and we both agree on one thing: No one has been born in Innsmouth for at least twenty-three years. They must be some kind of closed society, like the Shakers, although they do recruit new members. They'd die out without converts or recruits."

The clerk leaned closer to Kitrell and lowered his voice even further. "Three years ago, right after I started, a load of teenage kids arrived in Innsmouth, about fifty of them. All fifty stayed out at Falcon Point for a couple months, then they moved into town. None of them spoke better than broken English, and when I asked one what nationality he was, he told me he was a Pole."

Kitrell laughed. "What? Are you sure you understood him right? It's kind of hard to imagine them shipping recruits in all the way from Poland! If they're going to go to that much trouble, they should have a Transylvanian membership drive! A few vampires would give this place some local color!" He shook his head, chuckling quietly. "You know, Gilbert, this is all starting to sound a little too crazy for me to accept at face value."

"It gets even weirder, man. All but five of those Polish immigrants were dead before I came back to work the following summer. I swear to God! When they all arrived, the oldest one couldn't have been over twenty years old. Yet three summers later, you'd swear that not one of the five survivors looks like he's less than sixty years old. I'll point them out to you if you don't believe me. So how can you explain something like that? It sure ain't normal!"

It was becoming very obvious to Kitrell that Gilbert had been in Innsmouth far too long for his own good. He decided it would be best to change the subject.

"So who runs things around here anyway?" he asked.

Gilbert didn't seem to notice he'd been maneuvered to a new topic. "Nobody these days. A guy named Hunt pretty much ran the town until about seven years ago, or so I hear. He was a real go-getter, organizing folks and getting the old Marsh refinery up and running. Folks started making a profit selling fish to surrounding towns, and there was talk that Hunt had negotiated some big deal with a Boston fish distributor. Of course, the big cave-in ended all that."

Realizing comment wasn't needed from him, Kitrell remained silent, knowing the talkative grocery man would continue without prompting.

"That must have been something! See, there was a big smuggling operation in Innsmouth during Prohibition, and they dug hundreds of subterranean tunnels so they could move the shipments of alcohol into town from the docks without being seen. Later on, folks forgot all about the tunnels until seven years ago when one of the tunnels started a cave-in down by the docks. Tons of sea water poured into the earthen tunnels, working its way inland by collapsing one tunnel after another. Everything on the surface was brought right down into the ground and washed away. More than a hundred lives were lost. Hunt disappeared when the whole damn refinery was sucked down below its foundations. It was a terrible mess, but there were no funerals as all the dead were whisked away by subterranean rivers. You've probably seen how tight-lipped this town can be so you can understand why no one outside Innsmouth ever heard anything about it."

"Jesus!" Kitrell moaned. "You're right, I've never heard anything about tunnels or cave-ins here!" He remained silent a moment, then asked, "So who took over once Hunt was gone?"

"There wasn't much to take over. The majority of the town's workers went down with the refinery, and without the refinery there was no need for volume fishing. Things just drifted further along into decay."

Kitrell glanced out the window and suddenly realized he was wasting too much time. He went over Gilbert's directions to Falcon Point again, then thanked the clerk and said goodbye. It would be twilight soon and he had to get moving to avoid spending the night in Innsmouth.

As he climbed into his van, he spotted two familiar figures in bib overalls seated on a wooden bench directly across the street from the grocery. Were the old coots keeping tabs on him?

* * *

Gilbert had told him that Falcon Point lay, as the locals put it, "just a tad beyond Innsmouth." Ten minutes later, Kitrell crossed the river on an ancient stone bridge that looked as if it had seen better days. A few blocks later, he was relieved to catch a glimpse of ocean in the distance. Now he needed only follow the fishy stench of the coastline south for a few miles until he spotted the rocky outcropping of Falcon Point. A fine mist was already spreading over the coastline, wetting everything in its path; even Kitrell knew sunset followed closely behind.

The first thing he noted about the Point was the ruin of a house, positioned near the spot where the finger of rock jutted out from the mainland; it could only be the abandoned home of the mysterious Enoch Conger, another person who had vanished from Falcon Point. Kitrell overcame the temptation to explore that decaying ruin, reminding himself that dusk was rapidly approaching and that his real interest lay in the two hundred or so acres of inland property directly ahead.

Kitrell had never exactly been enamored of the ocean, deeming it more or less a huge retaining tank for fish sewage and the decomposing corpses of the salty denizens of the deep. The mere smell of it could make him quite nauseated, but he took comfort in the knowledge that he was now traveling away from the sea with its sickening smell.

The only road inland proved to be a barely navigable dirt path that wound through ever-thickening vegetation. Five minutes later, the path ended abruptly before a grim-faced, elderly man in fisherman's clothes standing before the gate of a steel-railed fence that barred any further advance.

Kitrell stopped and climbed from the van, after making sure the man wasn't carrying a shotgun or any other obvious weapon. Every ounce of intuition alerted him that danger lay ahead.

"Yer the feller from the Commonwealth?" It was as much a statement as it was a question.

Kitrell realized the man had been expecting him. Apparently the old boys here communicated among themselves, if not to strangers.

He introduced himself and, to his surprise, the other man did the same. His name was Wogge, he said, but his friends called him "Bull."

Bull explained that he had taken it upon himself to act as caretaker of the Conger land for over three decades, warning off trespassers and generally keeping an eye on the property. The Wogge land bordered upon the Conger acreage, and Bull had clearly come to consider both parcels his own. Kitrell kept this in mind as he explained the plans for the drainage and disposal of the land and his part in relation to them.

Bull accepted the news with resignation, admitting he was well aware that he had no say in such matters. He ended the conversation by advising Kitrell to avoid any ground that oozed water lest he and/or his van become bogged down or trapped in the deep marsh mud.

As an afterthought to their parting, Bull mentioned that Kitrell might come across his teenage great-niece on the Conger property. Her name was Polly and she spoke little English, Bull told him; she was visiting him from her native Poland. Kitrell could only recall his recent conversation with Gilbert.

The old fisherman finally swung open the gate to allow the van to pass, and he waved as Kitrell drove into the darker woods. He only need take a quick drive around the property, he reminded himself, and he planned to remain in the van the entire time.

* * *

It would cost the Commonwealth a fortune to drain all of the lowland marsh and countless stagnant ponds on the property. Kitrell knew such a report would not be well received by his superiors, but he could only describe things as he saw them.

At first he kept an eye out for skulking figures concealed behind trees, but once he'd covered the better part of the acreage, his paranoia began to taper off. He felt a definite sense of relief as he maneuvered the van back in the direction of the entrance gate.

The dirt path ran parallel to a small stream which flowed for several yards before dispersing into a fairly large standing body of water. Something caught Kitrell's eye at the very spot where the stream met the stagnant pool. A grouping of trees threw a dark shadow over the area, blocking the twilight illumination. Kitrell felt uncomfortable about getting out of the van, but he stopped to get a better look through his binoculars.

It looked as if dirty suds had collected where the stream joined the stagnant water. The gray foam and slime had mounded up, covering even the tops of cattails that rose several feet above the pond's surface. The rays of the setting sun created a glare on the water that obscured any details, but it didn't look good. Kitrell would have to recommend the waters be tested for pollutants coming from upstream. The size and stability of the bubbles made him wish he'd brought a sample jar with him.

Fifty or so yards further along, he spotted something big splashing in the pond. He used the binoculars to get a better look in the dim light. He saw a girl of about sixteen standing waist deep in the stagnant water about twenty feet from the bank. She wasn't dressed for swimming. Whatever she was doing, she seemed to be enjoying herself, acting at times as if she taunted some invisible playmate with her splashing.

Kitrell drove as close to the pool as possible, noting the spongy feel of the ground beneath the wheels. He honked the horn and waved his arm out the window, trying to call the girl to the shoreline. He was sure she was Wogge's great-niece, but the polluted water was an unsafe playground for her. He did get her attention, but she had no idea who he was, so she ignored his summons. He resigned himself to leaving the van long enough to speak to her directly, then recalled she spoke little or no English.

He tested the ground as he stepped from the van, deciding it wasn't too soggy as long as his shoes didn't sink too far into the mud. He tiptoed to the grassy bank of the pond. Once there, he called out and made gestures until his frustration got to him; he walked right into the water, trying not to lose his balance on the muddy bottom. As he waded toward the girl, he wondered if she understood any of the expletives escaping his mouth.

Polly showed no fear of the approaching stranger; she greeted him with a smile as he neared her. He talked to her in gentle tones, but she displayed no hint of comprehension until he spoke her name. Convinced her smile was an indication that she trusted him, he resorted to the only avenue available to him—he scooped her up in his arms with the intention of carrying her out of the pond. She allowed the advance without objection but wordlessly refused his attempt to transport her. With a wink, she straightened both arms, extending them over her head, then arched her back like a child who refuses to be held. Her form slipped free of his grip, as she propelled herself away from him to plunge head first into the waters.

The move had caught Kitrell completely off guard so that he found himself standing, frozen in surprise, and staring at the squirming thing she'd left lying in his still upraised arms. His confusion slowly turned to revulsion as his mind identified the slowly undulating object before him. It was a yard-long, gray and speckled *tail*. The wiggling movement of the discarded appendage diminished as Kitrell stared in disbelief. A full minute passed and the thing still remained in his slime covered hands as the words "Polly Wogge" ran through his mind over and over again.

The horror of sudden comprehension struck him fully in the pit of his stomach, and he flung the unnatural thing away from him in disgust. He saw the girlish head surface a few yards away from him; she still smiled broadly at him as she brought herself to a standing position.

"Get the hell away from me!" he groaned. He felt himself automatically backing away from her leering smile. He realized he was distancing himself from the safety of the earthen bank. He halted his retreat, raising his arms as if to stave off the horror. "Stay back, you mutant . . . polliwog!" he warned in trembling tones.

His foot slid on something slippery in the mud beneath him, and Kitrell fell back, splashing down and beneath the surface of the now-dark waters. Panicking, he struggled to pull himself back into the evening air only to be confronted by an unbroken line of large, glaring eyes which peered at him continuously from just above the surface of the water. He was surrounded, but by what?

A slight movement on shore to the left caught Kitrell's eye. A ray of hope surged through his being as he detected the shadowy outline of a man, no, two men, standing on the bank not so very far from shore. He lunged forward in awkward desperation, defying the stubborn pull of the mud beneath him. He waved his arms and screamed frantically for the men to help him in return. He stood perfectly still despite his terror, trying to hear the man's words over the settling noise of the disturbed pond water. Innumerable eyes still calmly observed his every move from the ring they'd formed all around him.

He could hardly believe it when the voice of the man finally reached him. The voice wasn't familiar as he'd never heard it before, but as the two forms stepped forward from shadow into light, he recognized the bib-overalled pair.

"We're stupid, 'member?" a deep voice called out. "Too damn stupid to understand English!"

"Yeah!" the second voice chimed in, "We're so damn stupid we don't even knaow that yer a-callin' fer help!"

A round of raucous guffawing followed, mockingly spanning the waters to reach Kitrell's ears and leaving him dumbstruck. He could only watch as the two old men paraded around the water's edge, then carefully snapped open a pair of folding chairs on which they sat, intently staring at him as if anticipating some impending thrill.

As the sun's glaring rays fell below the horizon, so fell the smile on Polly's face. Kitrell could only watch as her slender, girlish throat suddenly exploded appallingly outward into a hideous distended bubble of thinly stretched skin. The high-pitched froggish croak that followed tore at his ears, forcing him to cover them with his cupped hands. The paper-thin balloon below Polly's chin deflated slowly into a withered wattle before the skin eventually smoothed itself back into the semblance of a normal throat.

At this signal, the circle of terrible, unblinking eyes rose up in unison around Kitrell. None of the fifty encroaching beings appeared completely human. Some bore a hunching, batrachian cast, while others displayed miniature, half-developed limbs that dangled uselessly from their shoulders. They all began croaking and screeching in varied tones as they waddled inward, relentlessly closing the circle upon their helpless victim. The water heaved with waves created by the semihuman monstrosities. The air became a torment of ear-rending clangor that rose to a diapason of hellish noise, effectively drowning out Kitrell's pathetic screams.

The mob of ravenous polliwogs leapt as one upon their victim, overwhelming him in the splashy by-product of their feeding frenzy.

The toothless tadpoles fought to set their greedy mouths upon Kitrell's flesh, the fierce suction of their slimy lips eventually perforating the skin, that all might feed. Soon only the sound of bodies and tails, furiously slapping in the water, echoed across the scarlet ripples of the muddied pond.

* * *

The two onlookers, Jeb and Martin, nodded in satisfaction at the scene before them.

Martin squirmed delightedly in his seat. "This here second batch looks to be lots heartier than the fu'st. This evolvin' may be the redempshun o' th' Deep Uns yet! Afore ye know's it, we'll be a-spreadin' out coast ta coast, a-takin' o'er aught we want!"

A less enthusiastic Jeb responded, "Don't be a-judgin' any too soon naow. Yer remember how the first bunch went an' aged later on. Good thing we got lots more eggs a-sittin' upstream, ready fer hatchin'."

"Well, I got high hopes, Jeb. So leave me to my pleasure fer the nonce."

The two sat in silence until their night vision assured them all the ripples had vanished from the pond's surface.

"Well, now that the young uns has been fed, guess we can go on home," Martin volunteered.

"Yeah," Jeb answered, "but I was just a-thinkin'. Don't sumthin' 'baout this whole affair strike yer as a-being a bit bass ackwards?" Jeb wondered aloud.

"Whatcher mean, Jeb?"

The large man was slow in replying. "Well sir, the way I al'ays heard tell, a girl weren't supposed to let 'er date get a piece o' tail 'til *after* he fed her."

Martin squinted in thought before breaking into an uncontrollable fit of laughter, bending almost double. When he calmed down, finally able to stand erect again, he saw Jeb move quickly away from him while pointing at the expanding wet stain on the crotch of Martin's overalls.

"Now yer done it!" Jeb scolded. "Stay right where ye air, ye ol' toad in the hole! Last time ye peed yer damn pants, yer gave warts to ever'body comin' inside o' ten feet of yer, and I jest ain't in the mood."

As Jeb led the way back to town, the embarrassed Martin made sure he maintained at least ten feet between Jeb and himself.

About "The Deep End"

Greg Luce's crisp style and headlong narrative pace are reminiscent of the great old days of the pulps . . . and of something else: good old time *monster movies*! Greg is no stranger to them, being the mastermind of the phenomenally popular mail-order video cassette service Sinister Cinema. If Quentin Tarantino learned to create "pulp fiction" from working in a video store, so did Greg Luce! You may forget momentarily whether you're in the middle of a movie or a short story!

Greg Luce's fiction has appeared previously in magazines including *Cthulhu Codex*, but "The Deep End" appears here for the first time, another brand-spanking-new Innsmouth hatchling.

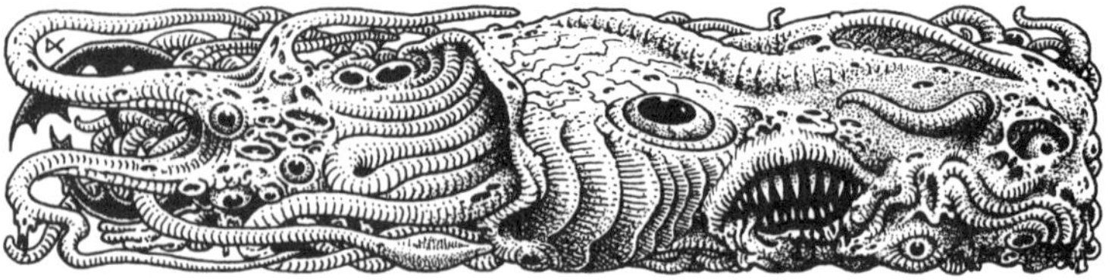

The Deep End

by Gregory Luce

They pulled the boy from the pool screaming. He was kicking and thrashing about wildly in the deep end. Everything had been peaceful just moments before, then suddenly the eight-year-old's head had broken the surface of the water and turned a typical summer day at Greybill's pool into a nightmare—screams like you couldn't imagine. Horrified looks of surprise came over everyone's faces. A couple of high school kids paddled over and tried to help the shrieking youngster to the side of the pool, but it wasn't until the new female lifeguard dove in from her rickety 10-foot platform chair that they were able to get the boy to safety.

I was lying on the ancient wooden deck that surrounded the pool, almost asleep, when the commotion broke out. *What in the sam hill?* I jerked up to find out what was happening. The sound of splashing and screams reverberated over the surface of the pool, almost drowning out the Dave Clark Five song playing in the background over the pool's loudspeaker system.

I looked over at Parker—he *was* asleep.

"Connie . . . wake up!" I reached over and shook him. He woke up with a start.

"Jesus, who's dyin'?" he asked as he sat up. We both looked over just in time to see them drag the boy—kicking and screaming—out of the pool.

"What the hell's his problem?" I said.

Connie just shook his head and got a weird look on his face. We both got up and started moving toward the frenzied youngster. There was already a crowd gathering around him, including a couple of other lifeguards and a number of older adults. The boy had stopped screaming by now but was still babbling hysterically. He kept repeating the same thing over and over.

"It grabbed my leg! It grabbed my leg!"

I looked over at Connie: The look on his face got even weirder. As we tried to move in closer, a crouched figure suddenly straightened up and turned toward us. "Please stand back," she said.

It was the new female lifeguard.

At that moment I got my first real good look at her; I felt a mild rush of physical attraction. *Hmm. Not bad.* She was probably about my age—20 or 21. A two-piece not-quite-a-bikini swimsuit helped show off her trim, very attractive physique, and a mane of long, sleek, wet black hair touched the top of her shoulder blades. Her face was somewhat thin—a perfect contrast to those beautiful almond-shaped brown eyes. I couldn't tell if she was naturally dark or just had a good tan that summer, but it looked as though she might have some kind of foreign blood in her, like a Hawaiian native or some other South Sea islander.

"What's wrong with the kid?" Connie asked her.

"He's just hysterical," she replied. "Some punk probably grabbed his foot and held him under too long. He probably panicked." She looked back at the huddle: The boy seemed to be calming down a little. "I think he's going to be okay. Why don't you just stand back and let us take care of him."

She motioned the rest of the throng of onlookers to back up as well. A minute or two later, the boy was carried out by a husky-looking lifeguard, accompanied by a couple of other pool employees. As quickly as it had started, it was suddenly over. Swimmers began hopping back in the pool and resuming their sunbathing positions on the pool deck. Connie and I lay back down on our towels to catch a few more rays.

"That was weird, man," he said.

"No big deal. Just a screamin' kid."

"Gimme a break, Kirby. That kid went bonkers. It even gave *me* the creeps. Somethin' scared him bad . . . real bad."

I didn't say anything. I just raised my head and glanced over toward the deep end. The Hire's Root Beer thermometer on the fence by the high-dive read 97 degrees. The new female lifeguard had climbed back atop her rickety observation chair and was just sitting there, motionless, peering over that end of the pool. The sun was hanging behind her and made her look like a big black silhouette with sunglasses.

I leaned over and nudged Connie in the ribs. "Listen . . . maybe you're right," I said, half smiling. "Maybe there's something down there that scared the crap out of that kid . . . something on the bottom . . . ," I raised my eyebrows and widened my eyes, " . . . something . . . *inhuman*."

Connie glanced up and got that weird look on his face again.

"Come on," I continued, "let's dive in and see what's down there."

"Forget it, man. I'm practically dry."

I got up anyway and hopped into the shallow end. The aroma of chlorine was strong. I dodged my way around a group of rowdy Wa-High kids having a major splash fight and slowly waded down toward the deeper end of the pool. Greybill's was basically an old, dilapidated facility built around the turn of the century, but it was well known by local swimmers for having the deepest deep end in town, bottoming out at nearly 13 feet. There was a buoyed plastic rope that separated the main body of the pool from the deep end; it ran across the width of the pool, bobbing up and down in the choppy water. I paused on the shallow side, then took a deep breath and dove under the rope. As I kicked down toward the bottom, I could feel the pressure rising in my ears like a couple of big hands were trying to squeeze my brains out. I started feeling around on the bottom with my fingers—the cement was cold and slimy.

Then I noticed it.

In one corner there appeared to be a dark, circular area, a couple of feet wide with something protruding out of it. After heading to the surface and grabbing another breath, I shot back down for a closer look. I was surprised to discover what appeared to be some type of round, rubber-sealed door, or portal, a few feet away from the main drain. It was made out of metal—probably iron—and had a handle on one side of it. I gave it a good rap with my knuckles; it sounded solid. Then I grabbed the handle to give it a tug. Right as I began to pull, a hand suddenly reached in and grabbed my wrist. *What the hell!* I practically had a heart attack; my head jerked around—

It was the lifeguard.

I lost my breath and kicked back suddenly. She was just hovering there near the bottom, staring at me with those almond eyes, shaking her head and pointing a finger. My lungs were ready to burst, so I shot back to the top, gasping for air as I broke through the surface. I swam over and hung on to the side of the pool, trying to catch my breath. She broke through the water next to me and looked at me apologetically.

"Sorry if I scared you."

"For cryin' out loud, man. I almost peed in your pool."

She tried to suppress a smile. "That's exactly what I thought you were going to do there for a second or two."

"Why did you grab my arm?"

Her eyes glanced downward. "Nobody's supposed to fool around with the old drainage gate on the bottom."

"Drainage gate?"

"Yeah. The one that leads over to Jacob's Pond on the other side of the hill. That's how they used to empty the pool . . . years ago."

"I'll remember that next time."

"Thanks. Please do." .

She flashed an attractive smile that helped me get over my momentary fright. I once again felt that mild rush of physical attraction that I had felt earlier.

"You're new here, aren't you?" I asked.

"Just since the beginning of July. You a regular?"

"Only this season. I'm a senior over at Marcus, and I'm usually in Tacoma during the summer months. This year I decided to stick around for summer school."

"Steep tuition," she commented.

"You can say that again. I work part-time as a board-op over at TV-26, too."

"What's a board-op?"

"Uh . . . somebody who sits behind a control console and makes sure that everything goes on the air that's supposed to. You know . . . network feeds, local commercials . . . that kind of thing."

"Sounds interesting." She looked me over with those almond eyes for the next few seconds, then said, "Well . . . gotta get back to my chair." She smiled again and climbed out of the pool.

I just hung there on the side . . . watching, ogling. She was a beautiful young woman. If you're a 21-year-old male with a high testosterone level, there's nothing quite like having a shapely female figure slide up out of the water next to you. I could see her wet, beautiful tan skin glistening in the sunlight, the moisture beading up on the back of her long, lovely legs. When you're that close and you stare hard enough, it's almost as though you can see *through* the swimsuit.

I stared hard—*real* hard.

She sensed it, too. She stood above me for several seconds, wringing out her hair. As she started climbing back up into her rickety chair, I called out to her: "Hey . . . what's your name?"

She stopped in mid-climb and stared down at me before answering.

"Carrie . . . Carrie Marshfield," she replied, that attractive smile slowly creasing her mouth again.

I watched her slide back into the chair before I climbed out of the pool. As I walked back over toward Connie, I thought I saw her steal a glance in my direction. When I got back to my towel, Connie was sound asleep. I poked him softly in the ribs with my big toe.

"Connie, wake up."

His head tilted up slightly. "What is it, man?"

"What do you know about the new female lifeguard?"

"I don't know anything," he replied, glancing in her direction. "She ain't no dog, though . . . that's for sure. You interested?"

"Oh . . . I'm not sure. Maybe."

"Ask Hawkins about her, he'll know." Connie nodded toward the snack stand at the opposite side of the pool where an old, white-haired concessionaire was busy pulling sodas and selling candy.

"I'll catch him when we leave," I said as I lay back down.

A little later Connie and I stopped at the concession stand on the way out of the pool. Hawkins was a real Walla Walla old-timer and loved to talk. He didn't know much about Carrie Marshfield except that she seemed to be a little on the quiet side and always walked to work. He too was impressed with her physical attributes.

"Nice ass and nice legs," he said, raising his bushy eyebrows up and down.

"She was telling me something about an old drainage flume on the bottom of the pool that leads over to some pond," I said.

"Jacob's Pond." Hawkins nodded and pointed over his shoulder. "Just over that rocky rise behind the back side of the pool . . . couple a' hundred yards or so."

Connie's eyebrow's raised. "Jacob's Pond . . . gawd, that's where all those kids drowned back in the '50's. I used to go swimming there myself . . . before they closed it off. That's where *all* the kids went that didn't have pool money. I got chased outa there plenty a' times."

The crusty old concessionaire rolled his eyes from side to side as he reached back into his aging memory banks. "Ten years ago to be exact . . . summer of '55. Three kids in three months . . . ," Hawkins' voice lowered a bit, " . . . but who said they drowned?"

Connie looked perplexed. "What do you mean?"

"I mean they never found any of the bodies."

For the third time that afternoon, Connie got a weird look on his face. "Why in hell do you say that?"

Hawkins shifted the Yankees baseball cap back on his head and wiped his brow with a paper napkin. "Well . . . I'm not a geologist, so I don't know how to explain it from a scientific point of view, but as I understand it, Jacob's Pond ain't got no bottom . . . it ain't no regular pond. If you've been there you know what I'm talkin' about. Nothing but a bunch a' rock slabs with water sittin' on top of 'em. Peculiar thing is, though, once you get out into the center of the pond, it drops off . . . some kind of a big hole . . . goes straight down hundreds a' feet. That's why they never found those kids' bodies. If they did drown, they're still churnin' around down there somewhere. I remember the Army Corps of Engineers sent some divers down not long after the last kid disappeared. Couldn't find nothin' except more water. They did come up with some kinda cockeyed theory, though."

"What was that?" Connie asked.

"They said the pond was being fed water by some deep, deep underground stream. God only knows where they thought that came from. They fenced the pond off not long after that. There's barbed wire and 'no trespassing' signs all around the place."

"Why did they quit using the old drainage flume?" I asked.

"Used to give 'em back-up problems whenever we had wet summers," Hawkins answered. "You see, the level of the pond is normally a bit lower than the level of the pool. But during rainy summers . . . especially after a hard winter . . . the pond level got too high and backed up dirty water into the pool. Caused all kind a' problems." Hawkins got a hesitant look on his face. He seemed to be having second thoughts about what he was going to say next. Finally, he continued, "Another thing, too. . . . "

"What's that?" I asked.

"The last couple a' years before they shut off that drain, the water from the pond changed."

Connie look at him quizzically. "Changed? What do you mean? How?"

Hawkins leaned forward and grimaced. "Stunk to high hell. You could really smell it when it backed up into the pool, too. They shut us down a few times because of it. That was back in '57. You can still smell it comin' over the rise now and then . . . 'specially when there's a southeasterly breeze. Almost makes you wanna puke." Hawkins paused and lowered his voice again.

"Bad place . . . Jacob's Pond."

Connie and I just looked at each other. By this time we *both* had weird looks on our faces.

* * *

The 11 o'clock news was just starting. I hit the audio cart that started the show's intro: *And now . . . the Inland Empire's most comprehensive newscast . . . Action News at 11, with anchorman, Dick Hoover . . .*

Connie punched in camera one; his finger cued Hoover.

"Good evening. In our headline story tonight, another young man has turned up missing in the Walla Walla area."

I was startled by Hoover's lead-in and looked up in surprise. Hoover must have seen my jaw drop, because he stumbled over his next word or two before continuing with his disturbing story.

"Twenty-two-year-old Arthur Benefield was officially listed as a missing person by the Walla Walla Police Department today after his employers reported his disappearance Wednesday afternoon. Benefield's vehicle was found earlier today, parked on the south edge of town. Neighborhood residents say the abandoned 1963 Ford Ranchero had been sitting in the same spot since at least last Monday evening, almost two days before Benefield's employers reported him missing."

This was the fourth guy to turn up missing in less than two months. No trace of any of the others had been found by local authorities, either. I looked over at Connie: A familiar expression was coming across his face. I leaned toward him and whispered.

"Can you believe this? That's four since June."

Connie shook his head. "Heads are gonna roll downtown if the cops can't figure this thing out soon."

We sat and listened to the rest of the story. Benefield's deserted pickup had been found out on School Avenue just outside the city limits. There was no blood, no vandalism—no signs of violence of any kind, not a clue.

"How much you wanna bet that pickup was parked there by somebody else?" I whispered.

Connie looked at me quizzically.

"Just a hunch," I said.

Connie whispered back, "Well, whoever it is, it's gotta be more than one person. I mean, these are all young guys that are disappearing . . . probably not a bunch a' wimps, either. A lone kidnapper's gonna have a hell of a time handling all four of these guys without any trouble."

"Yeah . . . unless he's got a knife in their ribs or a gun to their heads. Besides, what makes you think these are all kidnappings? I mean nobody's found any ransom notes so far. Hell, I don't think they've even found any actual clues, yet . . . have they?"

"Not that I've heard of."

"So what gives?"

Connie didn't answer, he just shook his head and shrugged his shoulders.

The rest of the newscast flowed smoothly. After the end of the show I fired up the National Anthem tape and signed the station off the air. A few minutes later I was punching my timecard and heading down the stairs to the front door of the station. It was fast approaching midnight.

My car was parked up Main Street about a block away. As I walked in that direction I noticed another car parked alongside the curb just up from the Liberty Theater. The Liberty was a beautiful old movie palace built back in the '40's. There were double features every evening that usually got out around the time we shut the station down for the night. The car parked in front was a '56 Chevy Bel Air with its hood up. Standing in front of the vehicle in the shadow of the raised hood was a darkened figure.

I slowed my pace a little as I approached. Whoever it was hadn't heard my footsteps. The person was bending over, looking over the engine with a flashlight. I came to a complete stop as the person came into full view. I cleared my throat and spoke softly.

"Need a lift?"

There was a momentary look of surprise on her face as she looked up at me, then a slow smile of recognition crossed her face.

"Why sure," Carrie Marshfield replied. "Thanks very much."

* * *

I went crazy over Carrie Marshfield.

It started out with an innocent lunch date at the A&W the day after her car trouble—a Mama Burger, a Papa Burger, two root beer floats, and some easy chit chat in my '59 Fairlane. Two days later we had dinner and a movie. By the end of the week there was another date and things were already starting to get steamy.

"You meet all the qualifications," she'd tell me with a smile.

She started spending occasional nights at my apartment, some really memorable nights, too—the kind of stuff bachelor pipe dreams are made of. I was swept off my feet by her unpretentious disposition and sexual magnetism. In a matter of days she had me completely infatuated; by the end of the second week I was already pondering marriage. I mentioned it to Connie one night at the station.

"You gotta have rocks in your head," he told me. "Marriage?"

I shrugged my shoulders and gave him a goofy smile.

Connie shook his head, laughing under his breath. "C'mon, Kirby. I mean . . . granted . . . she's a babe . . . but this is crazy. Are you really gonna hang it up for this broad? Permanently?"

I shrugged my shoulders again. Connie lectured for another minute or two, but I wasn't really listening. All I could think about was that gorgeous, sleek body inside that skimpy, dripping, not-quite-a-bikini swimsuit.

"You're hopeless," he finally told me, looking down at the control console.

One evening, about a week later, Carrie dropped by unexpectedly and asked me out on a double date.

"Why would I want to share you with a couple of other people?" I asked.

"Cause I've got something up my sleeve," she replied, leveling a hard, knowing smile at me. "And you're gonna like it."

"Like it? Like what?"

"It's a secret."

I rolled my eyes from side to side. "Secret?"

"Uh-huh. And you can't tell anybody we're going out. I've got something special planned and nobody else can know about it . . . okay?"

"Are you kidding? A *secret* date?" I folded my hands behind my head and leaned back in the chair. "I've never been on a *secret* date before. What did you have in mind . . . an orgy in Pioneer Park or something?"

She winked. "Be good and you'll find out Saturday night. Come by late."

"How late?"

"Make it around 11 o'clock. It'll be you and me and Helen."

"Who's coming with Helen?" I asked, referring to Carrie's younger sister.

"Nobody you know. You'll find out Saturday." She leaned forward and pecked a quick kiss on my cheek. "Oh, by the way . . . "

"Yeah?"

" . . . be sure to bring your swim trunks."

Carrie turned and dashed out the door, leaving me wondering about what she had planned for the coming weekend.

That Saturday evening I cruised out toward the Marshfield house in my green '59 Fairlane. The house was just outside the city limits, a couple of hundred yards down Kendle Road from Greybill's pool, which explained what Hawkins had meant about Carrie always walking to work. Carrie and Helen lived there with their invalid father, Homer Marshfield.

Homer had been severely crippled for a number of years, some type of grisly cannery accident involving a conveyer belt—very unpretty. He was confined to a wheelchair and never left the house that I knew of. In fact, according to Carrie he rarely came out of his bedroom. I used to see him occasionally peering out of his bedroom window on the third floor. One day as I drove up I saw his bushy face staring down at me. He rolled back into the shadows when he saw me look up and wave. Another time I heard his voice echoing down the stairwell near the end of the foyer. It had an odd sound, similar to the froglike croaks of someone who's had his larynx removed. I was quietly glad we never met.

I made the turn onto Kendle Road and passed by Greybill's pool. I could see the moonlight shimmering off the smooth surface of the water. Just up ahead was the Marshfield place. The house itself was a crumbling old three-story affair with gabled windows protruding through the roof on the third floor. A pair of large sycamore trees obscured much of the structure from view. I had only been in it a few times and then only in the main parlor, Carrie and I having spent most of our time over at my apartment or out on dates. As I pulled into the driveway, I saw Carrie sitting on the front porch swing, waving to me in the brilliant light of the full moon that blanketed the countryside.

I killed the motor. Carrie called out to me playfully, "Get a horse!"

My hands went up on the steering wheel and gripped it tightly. "Take me as I am, baby."

"You're such a retard," she laughed back, "but you do meet all the qualifications." She waved me toward the porch.

Sitting next to Carrie were Helen and her date, a bodybuilder-type named Vince Locatti. Locatti was a blue-collar stud who practically broke my hand as he rose to meet me.

"Glad to know you, Kirby," he said with a smirk, squeezing my metacarpals as hard as he could.

Helen was fairly attractive, but not nearly so much as Carrie. She was somewhat quieter, too, and didn't smile much, her personality being hidden behind a mane of exceptionally long black hair that usually covered half her face. She had a funny way of tilting her head sometimes when she spoke to you.

"Nice to see you again, Kirby," she said with that odd crook in her neck.

Carrie walked past her and embraced me. "Bring your trunks?" she asked.

I held up a pair of ragged cut-offs. "These'll have to do."

The four of us soon wandered across the open field between the Marshfield house and Greybill's pool. Carrie used her employee's key to open the main entrance and the doors to the men's and women's locker rooms.

"Don't turn on any lights except for the overhead in the locker room while you're changing, and be sure to keep the door closed," she told Vince and me. "Can't chance being seen by somebody driving by. The Sheriff's Department loves to prowl up and down these country roads in the middle of the night."

Vince and I stepped into the men's locker room. It had the usual locker room aroma: a mixture of chlorine and human body odors. We flipped on a dull yellow light that hung from the ancient wooden rafters and started to change. Locatti peeled off his shirt revealing a muscle-rippled physique. It made me feel a little inhibited taking my clothes off.

"Where in town do you live?" I asked him.

Locatti shook his head. "Not from around here . . . from Kennewick. Been over here weekends on a construction job. Just finished up today."

"How long have you known Helen?"

"Haven't," he said, pulling his trunks up over his jock strap. "I camp out at the Marcus Hotel when I'm in town. The company pays for it all . . . you know. Anyway, I met her in the hotel lounge last Saturday. Had a couple a' drinks and talked for awhile." He got a big, shit-eating grin on his face. "Said she wanted to see me again this weekend."

* * *

It was a midnight swim under the brightest full moon you could imagine. Greybill's pool took on an entirely different persona in the warm lunar glow. It was a soft ambiance of ashen beauty. The aged, rickety wooden buildings looked somehow newer, the softness of light hiding the defects and scars of age. Even the peeling painted image of an old-time bathing beauty on the side of the main building looked fresh and new.

The water was amazingly warm for this time of night, especially considering Greybill's was a non-heated pool. Vince and Helen were the first to dive in. They splashed around the deep end, hopping in and out and laughing and screaming like a couple of grade school kids. Carrie and I stayed mainly toward the shallow end, holding each other in long wet embraces.

The distorted, dancing images of the full moon reflected in my eyes off the surface of the choppy water.

"Beautiful night," I commented.

"Glad you're enjoying it," she responded warmly.

"Glad to be here."

She kissed me softly on the mouth.

Before long we climbed out of the pool and stretched out on the wooden deck, snuggling under a huge beach towel and holding each other close. Carrie lay on top of me and nibbled at my ears and neck. Presently she sat up, still on top of me, and shook the limp hair out of her face, the beach towel falling from her shoulders onto my lower legs. I had never seen her so beautiful. The warm moonlight gave her an unusual, pallid beauty.

I laid my hands behind my head and said, "So this was your big secret."

"Well . . . I wasn't sure how my boss would react if he knew one of his lifeguards was throwing a private midnight pool party."

"Just how long have you been a lifeguard, anyway?"

"For a few years." Carrie rolled off and sat up. "Since high school."

I leaned up on an elbow. "So where did you learn to swim so well?"

Carrie stared at me blankly before answering. "Innsmouth."

"In what?"

"Innsmouth . . . it's a town. I used to live there when I was younger. We moved here about ten years ago."

"Never been there," I said, shaking my head. "Never even heard of it."

"I'm not surprised. It's a little village on the coast of Massachusetts." She hesitated and gave me an odd expression, then said, "I'll take you there someday."

I raised my eyebrows. "*Will* you, now?"

Carrie leaned over and gave me a half-smile. "Sooner than you think."

A curious remark, I thought. I was about to respond when something caught my attention from the other end of the pool. Helen and Vince had been laughing and splashing around in the deep end for several minutes. All at once I heard Vince cry out with surprise.

"My foot! There's someth—" His voice gurgled out, cut off as though he had been dunked under water in mid-sentence. I glanced over. Vince was nowhere in sight. All I could see was Helen treading water in the deep end. She was still laughing a little, but after a few seconds she grew quiet—just treading water, saying nothing, staring right back at me, that funny tilt in her head even in the water.

It struck me as queer, so I rolled over and called out to her, "Helen . . . where's Vince? Everything all right?"

She didn't say a word.

I stared out over the pool for the next few seconds, waiting for Vince to resurface. He didn't. I called out again, "What happened to Vince . . . where is he?"

Helen just continued to tread water in the moonlight, still staring in my direction. There was no expression on her face of any kind that I could see. I didn't know what to think. *This had better be some kind of a joke.* A wave of uneasiness rolled up my spine and suddenly I wasn't feeling romantic anymore. Something wasn't right. I started to get up, then I saw Helen kick up a little and dive under the surface. I looked down at Carrie: She was sitting there cross-legged, staring at me blankly—exactly like Helen. The strangest expression was on her face.

"Carrie . . . what's goin—"

Before I could finish I was cut off by the sound of splashing at the other end of the pool. I looked over: It was Vince. He was back up again, yelling at the top of his lungs.

"Carrie! Kirby! Help! Something's trying to pull me down!"

Before he could say anything else he was yanked under again. I broke toward the pool, but before I could dive in he resurfaced. This time he appeared to have broken free of whatever it was that had grabbed him and was swimming as fast as he could in my direction, toward the shallow end. I hopped down the pool stairs and started wading quickly toward him. He had covered about 30 yards and was well past the middle of the pool, only a few yards away. Suddenly his speed slowed. My arms reached out—I was practically touching him. What happened next made me freeze with sudden, intense fright.

Locatti started moving backward.

He was still swimming toward me as hard as he could, but his movement was in the opposite direction, like a car with no chains, spinning its wheels madly as it slides down an icy hill in the dead of winter. The warm summer evening air suddenly seemed cold and I began to tremble as I realized what was happening—

Something was dragging him down from under the surface—backward, back toward the deep end.

Locatti's arms flailed frantically, but to no avail. His face rose out of the water and looked up at me in a contorted, pleading look of absolute horror.

"For God's sake, Kirby, help me! They're comin' out of a hole in the bottom of the pool! Help me . . . quick! *Help m—*" His voice cut out again as he slid under the surface.

"Vince! *Vince!*" I yelled frantically. I looked back in Carrie's direction. She was standing at the top of the stairs now, motionless, like a picturesque statue radiating with a warm moonglow. The look on her face was like a statue's, too—cold, almost blank. I was suddenly very pissed at her.

"Carrie . . . you're a lifeguard, dammit! Get in here and help! Come on!"

I turned and splashed toward the middle of the pool, but a dim flicker of movement beneath the surface brought me to a dead stop. My eyes locked in on the body of water in front of me.

Most people go through their lives without ever knowing what it means to be really horrified, scared so bad you can take your own pulse without fingering for it, your ears being able to feel that pumping, pounding high-pressure rhythm all up and down your body. On that warm summer night under a beautiful full moon I felt that kind of cold, raw terror for the first time. As I stood there in the middle of Greybill's pool at midnight staring toward the deep end, I could see four shadowy figures, all under water, swimming rapidly in my direction. They were all converging on the very spot I was standing, moving quickly—very quickly. I turned my head and screamed.

"Holy shit!"

I whirled around and started splashing as rapidly as I could back toward the pool steps. It was then I saw Carrie descending the stairs toward me. I waved my arms frantically.

"Get back! Something's after me!"

There was no concern on her face, though. She waded into the shallow end, moving smoothly and quietly toward me in the glimmering moonlight, that cold look still on her face, those almond eyes staring blankly, straight into mine.

She intercepted me a few yards from the bottom of the stairs. I almost fell headfirst into the shallow water between us as I charged toward her, but she reached out and grabbed me by the shoulders. The coldness suddenly disappeared from her face and she smiled. A big smile, a wide smile—it was probably the widest smile I had ever seen on her face. Not a smile of warmth and affection, though, it was a smile of someone who's committed a treacherous act—a smile of betrayal.

"You meet all the qualifications," she said.

Her words froze me in my tracks. This wasn't the same girl that had been kissing me passionately minutes before. She was different now . . . *changed*. Carrie's arms reached up and wrapped around my neck. "I have something to share with you, Kirby . . . some secrets to tell." The moonlight fell across her beautiful face as she moved forward to kiss me. Something was wrong, though, horribly wrong.

So I punched her in the stomach.

She gasped and bent over, her face almost slapping into the water. The ridges of her vertebrae glistened in the moonlight. She hadn't expected me to do anything like that. Neither had I for that matter. This was the woman I loved. My thoughts were chaotic.

Are you crazy!?

Then the woman I loved looked up and gave me the most God-awful expression of animalistic rage you could ever imagine. No more smiles, no more affection in those almond eyes—there was no way to describe it.

So I punched her again.

This time she crumpled completely and sunk down into the water, her head dipping below the surface. I rushed past her toward the pool stairway. As I reached the top stair I looked over my shoulder and saw the four underwater figures streak past her just as she was straightening up again. She turned and pointed a stiff arm in my direction.

"Get him!"

I didn't wait around to see who was supposed to get me. I scrambled out of the pool area as fast as I could. Behind me I could hear the noise of someone—or some thing—splashing up out of the pool. I flew into the men's locker room at full speed, slipped, and fell on my ass. In the dim light from overhead I could see a sign on the wall staring back at me.

NO RUNNING

I hopped up and snagged my Converse low-tops off the wooden dressing bench and bolted for the entrance. I got outside and slammed the door behind me, pausing just long enough to slip my shoes on. The sound of wet footsteps approaching from the other side of the door made my eyes grow wide. There were voices, too—gurgling, barking sounds that were unintelligible to me. I streaked across the parking lot and cut back through the open field toward the Marshfield house. I had to get to my Fairlane. I had to get the hell out of there.

As I scurried up the rise near the north side of the house, I slowed up a little and looked over my shoulder. At a distance of about forty yards I could see four figures loping in pursuit. I couldn't really see them clearly, but they were running in an odd manner that reminded me of how an ape might run, not at a fast gait, but at a quick, steady shuffle; and although I was sure they were losing ground on me, I continued running as hard as I could. I lost sight of them as I sped over the rise and down the slope toward the house. Right at the Marshfield property line, a field mouse scampered in front of me and nearly gave me a heart attack; I practically fell head over heals trying to dodge it. I regained my balance and moved in toward the back side of the house where there was a large, overgrown hedge lining the upper end of the driveway. My nostrils suddenly flared—an incredibly foul stench was in the air. I crept up behind the hedge. Here the stench was even stronger. My Fairlane was only a few yards away, though, just on the other side. Then it hit me.

My pants—and car keys—were still hanging back in the locker room.

"Dammit!" I cursed under my breath.

I peered over the top of the bushes. In front of me was something that made me suddenly forget about my keys. The Fairlane was sitting about twenty yards down the driveway, but standing around it were three figures; this time I got a good look at them and cringed in horror. Before me were three utterly inhuman creatures that appeared to be guarding my car. They were all fishlike in appearance: sloped, apish heads, protruding mouths, webbed hands and feet, and scaly green skin, except for a bloated, white belly. They looked like they had literally stepped off the set of *The Creature from the Black Lagoon* (which Carrie and I had seen on TV just a few nights earlier—her favorite movie).

I was completely winded so my breathing was heavy and loud, and I was afraid the creatures on the other side of the hedge would hear me. Ever try to breath quietly when you're completely out of breath? Forget it. It's nearly impossible without fainting for lack of oxygen, but I tried anyway, backing slowly away from the hedge, hoping the fish-men around my beloved Fairlane wouldn't hear me. In the distance I could hear the barking and baying sounds of the other creatures approaching from the far side of the rise.

I had to get moving again.

The fish-men near my car were standing roughly between me and Kendle Road—no escape that way—so I turned and sprinted across the open field to the east. Prospect Drive was a few hundred yards in that direction. I'd find a house and call the cops. I ran quietly toward a clump of chestnut trees that lay behind the Marshfield house. My lungs were screaming for oxygen by this time. It felt like high school track and the 200-yard dash all over again. When I came into the trees I slowed my pace. It was darker than hell. Very little light crept through the twisted branches above and I was afraid of tripping and falling on my ass again. Cold, unfriendly moonlight washed over me once again as I stepped out of the trees.

Lying in front of me was Jacob's Pond.

I could see it fairly clearly. On the other side of the barbed wire fence around the edge of the pond must have been a dozen or more of the scaly fish-men. Some of them were diving into the pond; some of them were climbing out—monsters' night at the old swimming hole. My nose twitched again as more of the foul smell drifted into my nostrils, the same smell as the driveway. Then a slimy hand grabbed my shoulder and spun me around.

I was nose to nose with a fish-man.

I screamed and stumbled backward as it went for my throat. My legs faltered, but I dodged haphazardly to the side and ended up on the ground as the creature lunged past me. It made an unholy baying noise as it whirled around. The earth beneath my hands was dry and loose so I scooped up a handful and aimed at its face as it came for me again. It bayed a guttural scream and doubled up in obvious pain as the dirt sliced into its eyes. While it was leaning over, I saw my chance. I jumped to my feet and kicked it on the side of the head as hard as I could. It grunted and tottered for a moment, just long enough for me to kick it again. It tumbled to the ground and I sprinted off as fast as I could. I didn't know if it was still after me or not, I just kept running. My lungs were wheezing; the adrenaline was pumping; and I kept running and running, the dry summer soil crunching beneath my feet.

I finally took a moment to look back as I went over a slight crest in the field. There didn't appear to be anyone following me, so I turned and ran on. There was an old wooden fence up ahead. I cleared it in one flying leap and landed in the soft dirt beyond. It was a plowed field. I trudged forward, but I was spent, all in. Sweat dripped off me and my head throbbed with distress.

Carrie . . . Carrie . . . what the hell were you up to? What were you trying to do to me?

I almost felt like crying. My feet sank into the soft, plowed earth as I plodded ahead. It was like running in a nightmare—pumping hard, getting nowhere. I was moving south now, parallel to Kendle Road, away from Greybill's—away from town. Up on my right I noticed the driveway light of a farmhouse. It was on the far side of Kendle Road. I had a sudden feeling of hope.

A telephone.

I angled off in that direction, crossed the road, and scurried up the porch. I slammed my fist repeatedly on the door.

Even though it was after midnight, there was a dim light inside. I thought I could hear the muffled sound of a television so I kept pounding on the door, looking around every few seconds to see if I had been pursued. Presently I heard the sound of approaching footsteps. A porchlight went on overhead. Then a muffled male voice sounded through the door.

"What d'ya want?"

"I need help. I'm from town. I—I need to call the police."

There was no response.

"Please . . . you can make the call for me. I'll stand out here on the porch."

A few more seconds went by, then I got my answer.

"Ain't got no telephone."

"Uh . . . well . . . can you let me in? I'm in trouble . . . I really need help."

"What kind of trouble?"

"I'm being chased."

"Who's chasin' ya?"

What a predicament. There was no way he'd open the door if I told him the truth. I could just hear it. "Hey buddy, I've got four scaly monsters trying to kick my ass and take me for a late night swim in Jacob's Pond."

Right. Even if he did open the door I'd probably have a shotgun zeroed in on the middle of my nose, ready to turn my skull into a cranial sinkhole. Then again he might have a baseball bat, which would be even better: "Louisiana Slugger" emblazoned across my forehead—no thanks.

So I lied.

"There's some guys chasing me. They—they jumped me . . . and my girlfriend . . . down by the pool. I think they're still after me . . . but I—I'm not really sure . . . I just need your help . . . *please*."

A key turned in the latch; the door swung open; and a man stepped out onto the porch. He was big—well over six feet and at least 200 pounds. Fortyish. There was a lot of hard work in his face, like so many other farmers in the area. He had a Pacific Trails windbreaker on and his right hand was in one of the pockets—a pistol, I figured. He looked me over with eyes permanently squinted by too much field dust.

He pulled his hand out of his pocket: In it was a set of car keys. "Got a pickup in the driveway. C'mon."

We hurried down the steps and climbed into a dirty, dusty vehicle. It was a '64 Chevy pickup with a V-8 engine and automatic transmission. We pulled out onto the roadway a few moments later. He hit the gas pedal hard and we jetted down the road toward town. A pair of fuzzy white dice dangled flimsily from the rearview mirror. A little plastic man was mounted in the middle of the dashboard; his free-floating head bobbed up and down with each noticeable vibration.

The farmer glanced over and nodded his head at me. "I'm Henry . . . Henry Stockstead." He took his right hand off the wheel and held it toward me.

I reached for his hand. "Name's Kirby—" I started to reply, but Stockstead gasped and hit the brakes before I could finish my sentence.

A fish-man was standing in the middle of the road.

The tires screeched and the creature raised its arms. A split second before impact the creature hurtled to one side, but it was too late. The right fender caught it hard. There was a loud smacking noise and its body went spinning to the side. The pickup skidded to a stop a few yards down the road. Stockstead looked at me in astonishment.

"What in the name of God almighty was that thing?"

"It's been chasing me," I replied in a trembling voice. "I didn't think you'd help me if I told you the truth back at your door. I—I don't know what to tell you . . . but there's a bunch of 'em after me. Don't ask me what they are. All I know is they came up out of Greybill's pool and they've been chasing me all over the damn countryside. They already got another guy. He's dead . . . I think. My damn girlfriend's mixed up in this somehow . . . but I really don't know what the hell's going on." I stared Stockstead straight in the eye. "These are monsters . . . I mean *real* monsters. I think they came up out of Jacob's Pond." I glanced down the road and nodded my head. "And we better get out of here before more of them find us."

Stockstead looked like a happily married man who had just been served divorce papers in a busy office. "I gotta see this for myself." He popped open the glove compartment and pulled out a flashlight.

"Come on," he said. We climbed out of the pickup. Stockstead grabbed a crowbar from under the driver's seat and we trotted back to the body. The overpowering stench stopped us a few feet away. Stockstead's face contorted with a look of nausea. "Gawd . . . that thing stinks to high heaven!"

We moved in closer and kneeled down beside it. Stockstead scanned it with his flashlight: no breathing, no twitching—there was no movement of any kind.

"I think it's dead," I said, my voice shivering.

Stockstead looked awestruck. "Hell's bells . . . look at that thing will ya." He glanced up at me and shook his head. "We gotta be dreamin' . . . this can't be real." He poked it in the ribs with the end of the crowbar.

It was then that everything really hit me. Stockstead, too, I think. This was a monster at our feet. A real, true-to-life monster. Not a dime novel, not a cheap horror movie, but a real, honest to goodness, slimy, grotesque, fishlike monster.

Stockstead looked at me contemplatingly. "They'll never believe us in town." He went back to the truck and grabbed an old blanket out of the back. "C'mon. Help me get this thing in the back of the pickup."

I cringed at the thought of touching it, but we wrapped the creature in the blanket and tossed it over the gate. We hopped back in and continued toward town. On the way down the road I started telling Stockstead about what had happened. We were almost to Greybill's when he pumped the brakes and slowed us to a crawl. "Good God!" he exclaimed. He flicked on his brights; I looked down the road in the waning distance of the beams.

Marching up the road was a bevy of lumbering fish-men.

"Turn around now! Get us the hell out of here!" I yelled. Then Henry Stockstead did something that scared the crap out of me.

He punched it.

We went flying, straight down the road, straight for the approaching band of monsters. I scooted down in the seat and closed my eyes almost all the way. Henry had the Chevy up to about 50 when we zoomed into them. They went flying in all different directions. We didn't hit any of them, but we certainly sent them running for cover.

"Now *that's* how you play chicken!" Henry trumpeted loudly. He gave a war-whoop and hit off several blasts on the horn. I looked at him in disbelief.

"Gawd, Henry!"

He took a hand off the wheel and shook his index finger. "That'll teach those goons to—"

An eruption of shattering glass cut off Stockstead in mid-sentence as the back window of the pickup exploded. A scaly hand shot through and wrapped itself over his mouth. The pickup swerved violently; I thought we were going to end up in the ditch. I leaned over and grabbed the wheel, trying to straighten us out. Suddenly a scaly hand clamped around my face, too. The stench was overpowering. I jerked forward violently and escaped its grasp but tumbled to the floorboard. Knowing we would crash at any second, I reached over and slammed on the brake pedal as hard as I could with both hands. Stockstead's feet were thrashing about wildly and almost kicked me in the head. I kept pressing down hard on the brake pedal; the pickup slowed to a stop.

I looked up and half-screamed.

The creature from the back of the pickup had revived and had both hands around Stockstead's face, pulling his head back toward the jagged opening of the broken window. I could hear Stockstead's muffled screams blurting out between the webbed fingers of those scaly, monstrous hands. It looked as though his neck were about to snap. I glanced above Stockstead's head: There was a gun rack above the window—a shotgun lay across it.

I scrambled off the floor and went for the gun. As I grabbed the butt of it, one of the creature's hands came loose and smacked me hard across the face. I pitched backward—along with the gun—and ended up back on the floorboard. The side of my head hit the radio, which came blaring to life. A rollicking country tune by Tex Ritter roared in at full volume, filling the cab with an outlandish sense of gaiety. Stockstead was still thrashing wildly about. The top of his head was being pulled into the jagged glass; blood trickled through his hair. I could see the creature's face just inches behind Stockstead's.

I raised the shotgun and aimed it through the broken window.

If Henry Stockstead had been frightened by the hideous monster that was yanking at his head from behind, he was suddenly pale as the moon at the sight of a single-gauge shotgun aiming inches past the side of his face. Only one of Henry's eyes was visible, and it went wide with terror.

I pulled the trigger.

A burst of buckshot went screaming past Stockstead's right ear, blasting straight into the creature's face. The impact sent it toppling backward onto the bed of the pickup. It lay flat on its back, completely motionless. This time it was dead for sure.

I looked at Stockstead and shouted, "Are you okay!?"

For a moment Stockstead didn't say anything. He was holding the right side of his face where a few pellets of buckshot had grazed him. Blood trickled through his fingers and he grimaced widely in pain.

"Hell's bells, buddy! What are you trying to do . . . blow my damn head off? Gawd!"

"Sorry, Henry."

We got out of the pickup and climbed into the back. The creature lay utterly still, its face completely blown off. I couldn't tell in the moonlight what color its blood was, but it looked as though it might be some dark shade of brown. I poked it in the ribs with the barrel of the shotgun—there was no reaction. I looked over at Stockstead.

"Got it for sure this time," I said.

It was then that I noticed Stockstead was bleeding badly. Not only had the buckshot grazed him, but the creature's claw-like fingers had deeply punctured his skin in several places along the left side of his face and neck. There was also a considerable amount of blood oozing from the glass cuts on top of his head. In short, he was a bloody mess.

He started to stagger so I grabbed him by the arm. "Gotta get you to a doctor."

I helped him climb down and into the passenger side of the pickup. I hopped behind the wheel, started the motor, and gunned it. We flew down the road toward the center of town. The police department was nearer than the hospital, so I headed in that direction. As we pulled up in front of the station I slammed on the brakes and laid on the horn. Two officers came running out a side door.

Stockstead managed to climb out of the pickup, but he was getting groggy from the loss of blood. He took a few staggering steps toward the approaching officers, then fell to the ground. Even though I had the catch of the century in the back of the pickup, my immediate thoughts were of Henry's wounds. I helped the officers carry him into an infirmary inside the station where a police medic began working on him.

"You're gonna be all right, Henry," I said encouragingly.

I was pulled to the side by a couple of officers. They walked me down a hallway and into an office where they started to interrogate me. After a couple of minutes, a burly-looking, cigar-chomping sergeant named Riley burst through the door, demanding to know what had happened.

"What the hell's goin' on?" he trumpeted in a loud, demanding voice.

One of the officers pointed his finger at me. Riley moved in behind his desk, shooing a younger officer out of his chair. There was a noticeable creaking sound of wood being strained by too much weight as Riley settled his heavy frame into the chair. Then the interrogation started all over again.

"Let me get this straight," said Riley. He tipped his hat back, tapped his cigar, and pointed his pencil at the notes he had been scribbling, then in a skeptical tone he said, "You're telling me your girlfriend . . . this, this Carrie Marshfield . . . along with her sister and a bunch of these . . . 'fish-men' . . . as you've described them . . . attacked you and another guy out at Greybill's pool tonight. Is that right?"

"That's right."

"So . . . this Carrie and these fish-men chased after you . . . but you got away. Then you met up with this Stockstead fella who gave you a lift into town. On the way in you ran down one of these things and killed it . . . only it wasn't really dead . . . just faking or something. Then it smashed through the back window of the pickup and tried to kill Stockstead."

"That's right. That's when I shot it in the face."

Riley looked skeptically at the other officers in the room.

"With Stockstead's shotgun?" he asked.

"It's still lying in the back of the pickup out front."

"The shotgun?"

"No . . . the fish man. Wanna see him?"

Riley looked at both officers and chomped on his cigar. "I can hardly wait."

We marched out of the station and gathered around the back end of the pickup. I thought Riley's eyes were going to pop out of his head. The cigar fell out of his mouth and two of the other officers staggered back several feet in horrified astonishment. I cringed myself and looked the other way.

"Jesus H. Christ!" Riley exploded. "What in God's name is that thing?"

The sight and stench of the dead creature were so overpowering that one of the officers turned away and threw up in the gutter. Riley looked at me in amazement; there was no longer any sense of doubt in his stare.

"Got a picture of this Carrie girl . . . in your wallet maybe?" he asked.

"No . . . but I've got one over at the apartment."

"Good. We'll pick it up on the way over to the pool."

Not long after, I was in a squad car racing over to my apartment. Riley drove; two other officers accompanied us. Behind us was another squad car with four more officers.

"Are you sure you don't have a picture of the sister?" Riley asked me.

"No . . . just Carrie. I took it through my front window when she was walking up to my door the other day . . . a Polaroid. I don't even think she saw me take it."

"Good. We'll pass it around to the rest of the boys for identification purposes. After that we'll head over to Greybill's and see what's happening there . . . then we'll check out the Marshfield house. I want you to stay put in your apartment for the time being. Barton here's gonna keep you company while we're gone. I want him to take a full report . . . don't leave anything out. We'll pick him up on the way back in." Riley looked over his shoulder at me, a stubby cigar hanging out of the side of his mouth. "This is the damnedest thing I've ever heard of."

We pulled up in front of my apartment a few minutes later, an old duplex over on Newell Street. It was 2 a.m. Riley waved for the officers in the other car to come inside as well. We all marched into my apartment. Turning the lights on, I motioned the officers into my living room.

"Wait here and I'll get the picture."

Riley followed me down the short hallway.

"Gawd, Kirby . . . you better change your clothes. They stink to high heaven." Riley commented.

We opened the bedroom door and walked in. The stench seemed even greater as we stepped into the darkened room. I switched on the light.

"I missed you, Kirby."

Carrie stood against the back wall, still dressed in her wet swimsuit.

Riley pulled the cigar out of his mouth and pointed. "Is this her?"

Before I could answer, a powerful blow to the side of Riley's head sent him careening sideways into the wall. He collapsed in a heap next to my bed, unconscious. I whirled around and saw two fish-men standing behind me on either side. I started to cry out but was struck by a hard blow from the one nearest me, its slimy hand catching me flush on the temple. I crumpled to the floor, stunned. My head was spinning, but I tried to raise myself up. An instant later the things were all over me. In the other room police officers were screaming; there was the sound of a violent struggle. I heard one gunshot. Suddenly a hand pulled the hair on the back of my head and a cloth of foul-smelling stuff was muzzled over my face. I blacked out completely.

* * *

I don't know how much time had passed, but when I woke up I was lying on a marble table, cold as ice, in a very dimly lit room. I could feel a wet, sticky substance running down the side of my cheek and a vile taste was in my mouth. Carrie was standing over me, holding a small glass of reddish solution that had been used to revive me.

"I'm glad you came out of it so quickly, Kirby. We haven't much time."

I didn't say anything at first. I was groggy, like when you first start to wake up in the morning—your eyes are still closed, you're still technically asleep, yet you have a conscious knowledge that you're still asleep; you can hear voices in the next room, even choose if you want to drift back into full sleep or wake up completely. That's how I felt on that cold marble slab. The only difference was that my eyes were wide open.

"Carrie . . . " I started to sit up but couldn't move. I raised my head up and saw the straps that were holding me down. I was so groggy it probably wouldn't have mattered.

I looked around. There was a window at the end of the room and a lamp on an old wooden stand near the wall. Another marble table lay parallel to me a few feet away. It was about eight feet long and had a wooden frame and wooden legs. Lying on the floor in between was something more ominous: a long, black oblong container—about the size of a coffin. I couldn't tell what it was made of, but it appeared to be quite solid. There was a seam about a foot above the floor that ran the length of it. Some type of mist appeared to be seeping out of it. In the middle, an inch or two above the seam, was a handle.

I spoke in a slurred manner, "Carrie, what in God's name is going on?"

She put her finger to my lips. "Quiet, my love."

My eyes rolled in my sockets as my head lowered back onto the table. "What happened to Vince? Where's Helen?" I asked groggily.

"Vince is fine. Helen will be with us soon."

"But what happened?" My voice rose a little as I raised my head and shoulders up again. "What were those damn things chasing me?"

"Shhh!" Carrie scolded me softly. She pushed gently and lowered my head and shoulders back down.

I had to be dreaming. It was like a dream, yet I knew it wasn't.

Carrie stroked her hand on my cheek. "You were special to me, Kirby . . . not like the others. The others were needed for the ritual of the flesh . . . the metamorphosis that allows our continued crossover into the surface world. It's something Helen and I must go through every ten years. Our mother was. . . . " She hesitated for a moment, as though changing her mind about telling me anything further.

"You murdered Vince," I said

"You're wrong, Kirby. Vince is alive. He and the others will soon take their place as helots for the great master . . . the great master from below the sea. But you—" The slightest trace of a smile crossed her face. "You'll be with me. I'm allowed it."

"You're completely nuts," I garbled. "The police . . . they know about you."

"The ones at your apartment are dead or unconscious. We'll be long gone before they recover or others discover what's happened to them."

"Gone . . . where?"

"Your contact with the police means time is short. We'll be leaving soon . . . returning to. . . . " She hesitated and looked away, then said, "You'll be coming with us."

"Coming where?"

Before she could answer, I heard a door open. Walking into the room was a tall older man whom I recognized as Carrie's father—so much for grisly cannery accidents. He was dressed completely in black and his face was hidden by a scraggly beard and mustache. A stench followed him into the room. I looked up and saw four fish-men straggle in behind him. Even in my grogginess I started to tremble. My eyes widened as they followed the misshapen creatures across the room.

Homer Marshfield stopped at the end of the long black container. He signaled to the fish-men and spoke in a strange tongue. All four of them shambled over to the container. One of them grabbed the handle and pulled up. The container opened up at the seam, just like a coffin. Within it was a strange mold made out of some type of opaque stone.

The mold was in the shape of a man.

I could see a waft of mist rising from within. The fish-men positioned themselves in pairs at either end. Then they stooped over and grabbed something from within and began to lift. It appeared to be another fish-man, only this one was dripping with some type of horrendous ectoplasm that fell to the floor in large, quivering droplets. They carried him over and placed him on the other marble table. When they moved away I got a good look at him as he lay motionless on the table.

Then I started to scream.

I screamed long and loud. I kept on screaming. Carrie rushed over and tried to calm me. I screamed even louder. A look of disdain came over the face of Homer Marshfield. He barked another command in that strange tongue and the four fish-men began moving toward me. I went silent, staring up at the approaching figures in utter horror. They positioned themselves around me, each one grabbing an arm or leg.

Homer Marshfield then began untying my straps.

Even in my dizzy state I tried to struggle. I rigged my arms and legs as much as I could, but it was hopeless. The fish-men held on tight.

So I started screaming again.

Carrie was standing next to me the whole time, trying to calm me. I felt the straps slide off as the fish-men began to lift me up. I started kicking again, harder than before. My screams were ear-piercing. My mind was reeling in a frenzy of total panic. Then through the wave of my own screams came a sound in the distance.

It was a gunshot.

Carrie and her father glanced up, expressions of surprised concern on their faces. Homer Marshfield barked another command and the fish-men laid me back on the table. The sound of a violent commotion erupted from somewhere downstairs. The police had obviously arrived sooner than expected. Numerous gunshots followed and I could hear glass breaking and wood splintering. Yelling and screaming echoed through the floorboards along with that awful baying sound emitted from the throats of fish-men below.

Homer Marshfield looked down at me, a look of rage on his face. He turned and walked briskly from the room, the four fish-men sauntering apishly after him, two of them carrying the fish-man from the table. Carrie remained in the room with me. She stared down at me with a look of strange intensity on her face.

"Kirby . . . you'll never know the wonder of it. Another world . . . another life." I thought I saw tears welling up in her eyes. Then she did something I'll never forget.

She bent over and kissed me.

I was repulsed, yet strangely taken by it. For a moment we were back at my apartment. The passionate nights . . . the memories of her touch. She pulled away and looked at me one last time. Then she was gone.

I was alone in the room.

I must have lain there for at least a minute or two. I tried sitting up, but my head began to swim so I lay back down. Finally, I flopped my legs over the side of the table. I managed to pull myself to my feet and struggle to the window. The stench in that oppressed room was almost overpowering. I turned the latch and swung the window outward. Fresh air poured in rich and sweet and helped revive me a little. I looked outward. I was on the third floor, looking toward the east. As I gazed over the illuminated countryside, I could make out the vague outline of the Blue Mountains in the distance. The slopes were dotted with the pinpoint lights of farmhouses and cars moving along the various roads that criss-crossed the countryside. Nearest to me I could see the large clump of chestnut trees that I had hidden in earlier. Beyond that I could see the light of the moon reflecting off of Jacob's Pond. There were still a number of fish-men around it; they appeared to be diving in, one by one.

The commotion had gotten louder downstairs; gunshots continued to ring out above the din of yelling and screaming. Some of the noise came from, I thought, outside the house, maybe from the driveway area or perhaps from around front. I even thought I heard the sound of gunshots coming from the direction of Greybill's pool, but I couldn't be certain. Then I saw a figure emerge from the far side of the clump of chestnut trees.

It was Carrie.

Even in the pale moonlight I couldn't mistake her. She ran straight for Jacob's Pond. I saw her sleek figure duck under the barbed wire fence and trot up to the edge of the water. Then for just a moment she turned and gazed back toward the house. I'll never be certain, but I could swear she was looking back at me as I hung out of the upper window of that awful house—staring at me with those almond eyes. A moment later she turned and dove into the dark water. She did not re-emerge.

The nature of my thoughts was weary, confused, and groggy as I hung out that window gazing into the half-darkness. There were flashlights now, emerging from the far side of the trees as the police chased a number of straggling fish-men toward the pond. Presently I detected sounds behind me—voices and footsteps. My ears were assailed by the sound of splintering wood, then the door burst open and five gun-wielding policemen rushed into the room. Two of them leveled their guns directly at me.

"Hit the deck . . . now!"

I dropped to the floor—probably the easiest thing I had done all night—and muttered a few words into the floorboards, telling them who I was. I could hear guns sliding back into their holsters and suddenly I was being helped up and led out of the room. As they took me downstairs I saw the bodies of fish-men strewn everywhere. There were wounded policemen, too, being tended to by other officers. Some of them were weeping from agony, some from fright. They got me outside and walked me slowly out to the roadway where a number of patrol cars were parked.

Then I did the conventional thing and fainted.

I woke up the next day in a hospital bed, recovering from the effects of the strange drug I had been subjected to. I was on my feet later in the evening and released the next day. I spent most of my time over the next few days with the local police and the FBI.

I never found out what happened to Carrie's sister and father, or, for that matter, what they did with all the bodies of the fish-men that had been killed. I did hear that Riley and most of the other officers had survived the ambush at my apartment. They had been subjected to the same drug that was used on me and were out for hours. None of them were the worse for wear other than a few side effects—nausea and prolonged vomiting. Henry Stockstead, too, made it through with flying colors. I still see Henry occasionally, but we seldom speak of our incident. We're not allowed to. The FBI made sure of that. Oh, sure, they paid us a lot of money for our silence and cooperation—can't have the country go into a tizzy over the greatest, most horrifying scientific discovery of modern times. So we bite our tongues and keep the whole thing to ourselves. I don't understand how they managed to keep it so quiet with all the police officers involved—but that's the FBI for you.

They never did reopen Greybill's pool. Some story was leaked about it not meeting local health and safety standards. The dressing rooms and concession stand were torn down long ago, but most of the pool is still there. You can see it to this day, lying behind a wooden fence at the corner of Reiser and Kendle Roads just outside the Walla Walla city limits. Jacob's Pond was drained, as best they could, and a short time later was covered with a huge cement slab, courtesy of the Army Corps of Engineers.

Is Carrie Marshfield still alive? Was she even human? I don't know—I don't want to know, because I know what it was that Carrie and her "family" had in store for me that night. In fact, I know the horrible truth about all the other young men who disappeared mysteriously over that long, terrible summer. You see, we were all bachelors with little or no family. No one to check up on us. No one to miss us. During that ghastly night as I lay helpless inside the upper floor of the Marshfield house, I saw the horrible truth lying on the marble table next to me. I shudder at the memory of it. As I lay there in a groggy haze, I screamed at the sight of the fish-man lying on that marble slab just inches away from me; but it wasn't the sight of a fish-man that had frightened me, but rather, the sight of *this* fish-man. He lay staring at me in all his hideous repulsiveness: webbed, claw-like fingers, scaly dark green skin, a bloated white belly, and a slimy putrescence over his entire carcass. But none of that had made me scream. What shook me to the inner depth of my soul was his pitiful face and those terrified, saddened eyes. For staring at me wasn't the face of a horrendous monster . . .

. . . but the agonized face of Vince Locatti.

About "It Was the Day of the Deep One"

Peter Cannon is the master of fun-poking, or, in the present case, frog-gigging. He skewers both the conventions and the venerable authors of weird fiction, with a few barbs thrown in the direction of colleagues and fan editors to boot. The present endeavor is aimed right between the lines. It works as a story even if you don't get the in-jokes, but you'd rather be in with the in-crowd (in this case, the "Inn[smouth]-crowd"), wouldn't you? In that case, here's that scorecard without which you wouldn't be able to tell the players. The astute reader will know Halpin Chalmers as the ill-fated delver who meets his doom in "The Hounds of Tindalos", while Fred Carstairs is derived from the intrepid hero of *John Carstairs-Space Detective*. Both are creations of Frank Belknap Long. In this story, Frank Carstairs is, of course, Frank Long himself, while Halpin Chalmers stands for H. P. Lovecraft. Carstairs'eccentric wife Ida is a clone of Lyda, Frank Long's wife, and the shenanigans of the pair at the Chalmers Centennial perfectly mirror those of the real couple at the 1990 Lovecraft Centennial at Brown University. Peter, who selflessly saw to the needs of Frank and Lyda Long in their declining days, walked many a second mile for them, and it is a mark of his irrepressible exuberance that he can now look back on those sometimes trying days with such a sparkle of genial good humor.

Partridgeville is, of course, the site of Long's "The Space Eaters." As for "It Was the Day of the Deep One", it is a tip of the hat to Long's novel *It Was the Day of the Robot*. The narrator is a thinly veiled analogue of fan editor Perry Grayson, chief keeper of the Belknapian flame. He edits a Long fanzine called *Yawning Vortex*. Father Iwanicki is a character occurring offstage in Lovecraft's "The Dreams in the Witch House" as well as in the discarded draft version of "The Shadow over Innsmouth."

As in Cannon's "Nautical-looking Negroes" *(Lore* #5, Summer 1996), the theological satire flies fast and thick! And the internecine squabbles of Lovecraft scholarship are no less amenable to the jibes than actual mainstream religion. "It Was the Day of the Deep One" first appeared in *Midnight Shambler #5*, Eastertide 1997.

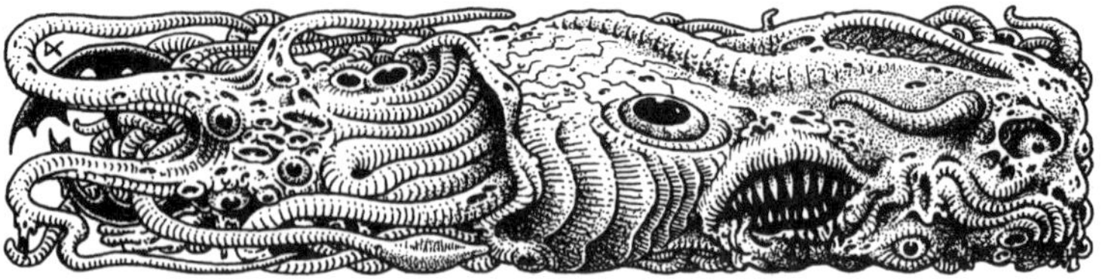

It Was the Day of the Deep One

by Peter H. Cannon

I. *The Legacy in Green*

Life is full of funny connections, coincidences you might say. As a practicing accountant and *Skeptical Inquirer* subscriber, I take a jaundiced view of what Jung calls synchronicity or what surrealists prefer to think of as "objective chance", yet I am convinced that the laws of probability can produce highly unusual results more frequently than is commonly assumed. Take the matter of an unexpected legacy—from, on the face of it, a most unlikely family source. It is no exaggeration to claim that I owe my present philosophical outlook to what amounts to an offhand gift of fate.

My knowledge of the thing began in 1983 with the death of my grand-uncle, John C. Dunn, chaplain emeritus at Mercy Hill Hospital, Brichester, Ohio. An ardent advocate of Irish independence in his youth, this relative, then a plumber by trade, was convicted of treason for refusing to register for the draft in World War I and served two years of a twenty-year sentence in Atlanta Federal Prison, so his passing at the age of ninety-four may be recalled by at most a few other ancient Fenian fanatics. In his dotage he was an unapologetic supporter of the I.R.A. and proudly displayed a "Brits Out of Eire" bumper sticker on his '67 Pontiac GTO.

I was by no means my grand-uncle's only heir, for his survivors included dozens of nephews and nieces, the children of those of his late brothers and sisters who elected not to take holy orders, as well as hundreds of their offspring, who promise to keep the Dunn line increasing exponentially for at least another generation. In his last years, though, I was his closest kin, both geographically and emotionally. Soon after I entered college at nearby Oberlin, my mother urged me to call on "Uncle Johnnie", then the most venerable member of our clan, at the home for retired priests where he had a room. I did so, via the intercity Brichester bus line, and was delighted to discover that we shared a common interest—not in religion or politics, mind you, but in amateur journalism.

In his mid-twenties my grand-uncle had been active in the Partridgeville Amateur Press Club, whose ranks happened to include the future occult authors Halpin Chalmers and Fred Carstairs. Father Dunn (the name by which I addressed him) had no taste for genre fiction, though he was aware in his own way of the modern reputations of these two illustrious Partridgeville natives. Having devoured their works in my early teens, I was amazed at my good fortune to find a blood link to my literary heroes. At our first meeting I was able to coax my relative into telling me all he could remember of the pair—which admittedly wasn't a whole lot after more than six decades. Still, I gathered enough material to fill one issue of my fanzine, *Drowsing Cortex*, for the Order of the Secret Watcher, the a.p.a. devoted to Halpin Chalmers and his circle.

Thereafter I visited Father Dunn on average once a semester, since without a car I had to rely on not-always-convenient public transportation while he avoided all highway driving. We kept in touch through a correspondence largely concerned with superstition and the supernatural. ("I have never actually seen a ghost or had what is commonly referred to as an 'occult experience,'" he wrote when I prodded him on his beliefs, "though I suspect there is something behind the old legends of the 'wee folk.'") An unobservant Catholic, I was deliberately vague where I stood on religion. On the other hand, my relative made it clear that he'd never suffered any doubts about the faith of our forefathers. As for his time in the "big house", I gathered he'd found his fellow cons less contentious, more open to a gentlemanly exchange of views, than his colleagues in the Partridgeville Amateur Press Club.

At what was to prove our last meeting, the spring of my senior year, Father Dunn started off by denouncing the occupation of Northern Ireland with his usual vehemence, then settled down to hear me recount my latest exploits in the amateur press world, as had become our custom. At parting I gave him a copy of the current *Drowsing Cortex*, which he said he looked forward to reading. Alas, I'll never know what he thought of the issue, with its rare reprints of some early Carstairs poems. A week later the charwoman discovered my grand-uncle slumped over his desk, where lay a half-completed letter to the *Brichester Herald* attacking the Irish policies of the Thatcher government. A true son of Erin to the finish!

After the memorial service, attended by some half-dozen inmates from the retirement home, the presiding priest drew me aside as the sole relative present. Father Dunn's only asset, the Pontiac GTO, would soon go on the auction block, the man confided, and the proceeds per his final wishes donated to the Tommy Sands defense fund. In the meantime his meager personal effects were mine to dispose of as I pleased.

Back in my late grand-uncle's room there was little enough to sort through. Above his desk was a bookshelf, whose predictable contents had never piqued my curiosity—a couple of Bibles, several biblical commentaries, a life of St. Patrick, a biography of Michael Collins, an illustrated history of the "Emerald Isle." These I now removed from the shelf and examined for the first time. All were indeed entirely ordinary books, except for one slim volume. With its plain green cover it had appeared to be another work of Irish interest. It wasn't, being some sort of diary written in a hand not my relative's. Tucked inside was a typed note on paper so fragile that it tore along the crease when I unfolded it. At the top was the seal of the U.S. Navy Department, with the inscription "Chaplain, R.C.: Portsmouth Naval Station." This was what I read:

> My dear Father:—
>
> Among the belongings of those seized in the February raids was the enclosed. I don't know what became of its author, but I think you'll agree after reading that his is (was?) a first-class mind, despite his heretical notions. I was reminded of certain matters you and I used to discuss in seminary. Don't hesitate to correct me (as if my old roomie wouldn't!) should you think otherwise.
>
> No rush to return.
>
> Yrs in Christ,
>
> Fr. Iwanicki
>
> P.S. Unlike in your case, the feds aren't apt to release any of the prisoners here *ever*. Rest assured, their reasons for this precaution are excellent. The ways of the Lord are merciful.

The letter was undated, but I guessed from the age of the paper and the art decoish-looking Navy seal that it was pre-World War II vintage. Here, if I was to have any keepsake of my grand-uncle, was the obvious souvenir to take home. While I might have been able to sell some of the other books, especially the oversized illustrated history of Ireland, I decided none of them was worth lugging with me. The diary fit snugly into my jacket pocket.

On the bus back to Oberlin I inspected the diary page by page. Printed in bold blue letters inside the front cover were the words "Property of Percy

Babcock, E.O.D., Innsmouth, Mass." The body of the text, written in a cramped cursive script, was not so easy to decipher, though it seemed to be mainly concerned with spiritual matters, the record of its author's sometimes rocky progress toward enlightenment. The total wordage was not great. The first entry dated to 1924, the last to 1927.

Why my grand-uncle had never bothered to return this odd volume to his friend, why he had hung on to it for so long, was unclear. Perhaps he was moved by Babcock's fervor, despite the diarist's patently alien faith. Or maybe he merely liked how it looked on his shelf, with its "emerald"-colored cover. The more I reflected on its contents, however, as well as on its physical form, the more certain I became that the modest volume I struggled to read as the bus bumped along the highway represented a mystery beyond any ultimate understanding. Was it even authentic? Might it be a hoax, I wondered, a practical joke left behind by my deceptively simple relative to puzzle posterity?

Certain anomalies troubled me. First, I had the feeling the diary was transcribed from an earlier, cruder state. The handwriting was too neat, too regular, with no crossing out of words, to be spontaneous, although, to give him credit, Babcock may have written as naturally and fluidly as he spoke—but in a language other than English. Some sixth sense told me this was a *translation*. On returning to my dorm room, I performed an experiment with a variety of pens, pencils, and markers, to confirm or deny another aspect of the diary that struck me as very peculiar. Binding and pages had a waxy, almost plastic sheen, like a deck of expensive playing cards. Neither ink nor graphite left an impression. After further trial in the men's shower that evening I could only conclude—the diary was waterproof!

II. *Extracts from the Diary of Deacon Babcock*

1924

Sept. 15: Took the Fourth Oath of Dagon before Rev. Eliot and congregation at ten o'clock baptismal service off breakwater—can now assume full duties of deacon. Glorious day! Father Dagon be praised! Hail Mother Hydra!

Oct. 19: Rev. Eliot reassuring on the Trinity—Great Cthulhu of course supreme, with Father Dagon on His right facial feelers and Mother Hydra on His left. These two equal but not always so. Worship of Mother Hydra a relatively modern development.

Nov. 1: Ring cracked chimes calling the faithful from Devil Reef. An honor in my new role. Spectacular sight under midnight moon!

Nov. 20: Point out to Rev. Eliot resemblance of Elder Sign to symbol of upstart political party in Germany much in news. He says not to worry—NSDAP swastika clockwise, Elder Sign counterclockwise.

Dec. 10: Ponder basic EOD commandments—not obvious why Old Ones should be banished for practicing "black magic." But belief in their ultimate return unshaken.

1925

Jan. 4: Agree to teach fellowship course on Elder Gods. Problem of lack of materials. Only Nodens named. Why? Must ask Rev. Eliot.

Jan. 7: Rev. Eliot reminds me that certain sacred doctrines are not for "self-blinded earth-gazers" to question. Cites Epistle of F'rness.

Jan. 22: In sermon Rev. Eliot preaches against Manicheism. Elder Gods rebel only under sufferance of Old Ones. Hence they rarely stir forth from the Great Abyss at or near Betelgeuse.

Mar. 1: Awakened by slight earthquake tremor from fantastic dreams. Elated, as if on verge of new revelation.

Mar. 24: Very bizarre dreams last night. Maybe vision of submarine city R'lyeh. Feel feverish. Am I "psychically hypersensitive" or just "queer?"

Mar. 28: Dreams persist. Broad impressions of vast angles and stone surfaces. Cyclopean architecture?

Apr. 2: He is risen! He is risen! Hallelujah! Hallelujah! The stars are right! *Iä, Iä, Cthulhu fhtagn!*

Apr. 3: For the first night in what seems like strange aeons sleep without dreaming. Feel reborn. Need time to think, to absorb His revelations.

May 1: Am reluctant to accept the call—why should I, of all His myriads of minions, be chosen to serve as His avatar on earth? Stupendous implications.

May 30: After teens transition class, raise issue of "elementals" with Rev. Eliot. While I don't put it in these terms, I suggest that the notion of Great Cthulhu as a "water elemental" is a bunch of blarney. He only happens to be trapped under the sea, I point out, having originally filtered down from the stars where H_2O is scarce, to say the least. Rev. Eliot patiently explains that our Lord has spent millions of years submersed—plenty of time to assume characteristics of ocean floor. Analogy—after a mere two or three centuries, some Yankees feel they typify soil of New England. Hence Great Cthulhu is the *genius loci* of sunken R'lyeh, etc. Remain unconvinced.

Aug. 19: Summer doldrums. Many parishioners on vacation in Y'ha-nthlei. Again take opportunity to challenge dogma. Can accept Nyarlathotep in role of messenger as "earth elemental", but Cthugha as "fire elemental?" On whose authority is this hierarchy decreed? Hint darkly that EOD has strayed from true path, like so many lost young of Shub-Niggurath. Rev. Eliot not amused.

Sept. 3: Stern lecture from Rev. Eliot on my recent "blasphemous" notions. Says I'll never be allowed to take Fifth Oath if I continue to challenge authority. Decide to lie low for a while, not make waves. Better perhaps to work quietly from within.

Oct. 31: Demoted to mere acolyte in this year's Devil Reef ceremony. Despite efforts to dissemble, fear permanent loss of Rev. Eliot's trust.

Dec. 2: Establish secret coven of converts, headquartered at old firehouse. We are but three or four (I'll name no names), those open-minded enough to discard a naïve evil vs. good world view and accept instead a more sophisticated faith. Promote what I term a "cosmic" perspective.

Dec. 26: Interdenominational singles supper with Kingsport brethren a roaring success. Doctrinal differences forgotten thanks to Yule spirit and case of bootleg liquor.

1926

Jan. 3: At firehouse gang debates efficacy of Elder Sign. No one willing, however, to take risk of putting to real test, so issue remains unresolved.

Feb. 10: Distinguish between "pessimism" and "indifferentism" at secret coven, now grown to six. Put to rest one member's concern that to take a detached view of the universe amounts to emotional denial.

Apr. 18: We are now ten. Call ourselves Church of the Starry Wisdom, after defunct sect in Partridgeville. Discuss significance of Shining Trapezohedron legend, as revealed in the *Book of Dzyan*.

May 1: Rev. Eliot informs me that as part of exchange program I'll be spending the summer in Dunwich. Reluctant to go, distance from sea, etc., but don't dare protest overly much.

May 3: Great Cthulhu speaks in a dream—gives go-ahead for Dunwich sojourn.

Jun. 18: Bus trip through some pretty weird countryside. Stone altars atop nearly every dome-shaped hill.

Jun. 20: Dunwich EOD in sad shape. Handful of regular worshipers at most. Fear taint of general indolence and apathy.

Jun. 22: Board with family in semirenovated farmhouse outside town. A dump. Makes Innsmouth waterfront look like model community. But price is right.

Jun. 25: My hosts a fascinating case study in rural degeneracy. Half-crazed Old Whateley, twisted albino daughter, Lavinia, and uncouth gargoyle grandson, Wilbur—who I sense has Messianic ambitions of his own. Since most of firetrap of a house unusable, must share ground-floor room with Wilbur.

Jun. 30: Attempt to make Wilbur see the light futile. Egregious example of religious fanaticism.

Jul. 5: Pervasive and revolting tarry odor getting to me as the days become hotter. Tempers short. Discreet criticism of housekeeping leads to blow-up with Lavina. She accuses *me* of stinking up the joint—"like a week-old mackerel!"

Jul. 14: Complain of loud noises at night from boarded-up upper floors. Old Whateley says giant squirrels in woodwork impossible to get rid of. Lame excuse if ever I heard one.

Jul. 20: Hillside ramble with Wilbur spoiled by pack of dogs, who chase us up tree where we spend several hours before local rustic comes to rescue. (Hard to believe a kid seven feet tall is such a chicken.) Truly have sense of trial in the wilderness. The ways of Great Cthulhu are devious.

Jul. 27: Am counting the days before I can leave here.

Aug. 25: Return to Innsmouth to find I've not only been stripped of my diaconate but excommunicated from the EOD! During absence Rev. Eliot assailed me from the pulpit as an apostate. As fronts for EOD, Congregational and Baptist churches provide no refuge. Nothing to do.

Aug. 28: Discover others in secret coven gone, now permanent residents of Y'ha-nthlei. Am close to despair. How can Great Cthulhu have forsaken me, His avatar?

Sept. 15: Consult *Necronomicon* at Miskatonic U. Find some consolation in the mad Arab's double entendres, though they're not easy to sort out from his superstitious misconceptions.

Oct. 20: Decline Whateleys' illiterate invitation to return for "Sabaoth" [*sic*] festival. What short memories some entities have. As if I'd ever consider setting foot in that pest zone again!

Nov. 1: Resume His work while most everybody at sea. This time I'll be even more careful.

Dec. 15: Old firehouse no longer possible as site to meet, so new coven gathers in abandoned railroad cut toward Rowley.

1927

Jan. 22: Less hierarchical, more inclusive approach gaining larger following than before. Original sin precludes no one from joining the saved.

Jan. 31: Revelation—any sincere male believer in Great Cthulhu can become a priest, or even a wizard-priest.

Feb. 15: Formally declare New Church of the Starry Wisdom. We are nearly a score strong. Select "safe" upside-down variation of Elder Sign as our symbol.

Mar. 1: Write Old Whateley and Wilbur a brief condolence note. According to their latest communication, there's little hope after all these months that Lavinia will ever be seen again.

Mar. 10: Suspect Rev. Eliot may have gotten wind of our activities. But we'll soon be too powerful for him and EOD to oppose.

Apr. 4: Rev. Eliot stigmatizes females for choosing to be masters (mistresses?) of own bodies. Grave offense to Mother Hydra, etc. We of the NCSW pride ourselves, quite justifiably, on right to choose whether or not to remain half-human.

Apr. 14: Females eligible for the priesthood? So Great Cthulhu has decreed in His wisdom, I reveal to flock. Could the wizard-priesthood be far behind?

May 21: Size of NCSW doubled in last month or so since revelations sanctioning female priesthood. Many propose we go public. As leader urge caution, but promise day will soon be at hand when we may do so.

Jun. 9: Newest revelation—divorced Deep Ones may remarry within NCSW. Brethren greet with enthusiasm.

Jun. 15: In vision Great Cthulhu puts His tentacle of approval on right to mate with Fungi from Yuggoth. Decide it best to withhold this revelation for time being. Must introduce slowly idea of intergalactic miscegenation.

Jun. 20: Agree time has come to proclaim His message in the open. Select New Church Green, opposite the Order of Dagon Hall, for late night rally. Can fix date later.

Jun. 22: Plaster every rotting pier and crumbling store front with NCSW posters—"safe" Elder Sign prominently displayed.

Jun. 23: EOD thugs, no doubt on Rev. Eliot's orders, tear down or otherwise deface NCSW posters.

Jul. 2: Run off new posters, with rally date below Elder Sign. Advise church not to shrink from confrontation, verbal or physical, if our opponents make further trouble. Innsmouth awake!

Jul. 8: Scuffle with EODers on Fish St.

Jul. 11: Plans now set irretrievably in motion. Entire population invited, both on shore and off. Nothing can stop His avatar now!

Jul. 16: Disaster. Early this morning, just as folk are beginning to gather in force on New Church Green, word arrives that every able-bodied Deep One has to join hunt for visiting outsider to ensure he doesn't leave town. Am certain a ruse on Rev. Eliot's part to disrupt rally, but can't convince crowd. Circumstances force me to participate. Lead search party down abandoned railroad cut toward Rowley, where (no surprise) we find nothing. Can't say we look all that hard.

Jul. 19: Town full of rumors. Some persist in believing there really was someone staying at Gilman House, that he made a miraculous escape, etc. I object. What person would be fool enough to spend the night in Innsmouth? How did he get away so easily? Such is how legends or myths get started, with no real basis in fact.

Jul. 21: Some in NCSW think this outsider heralds a Second Coming or dawn of a New Age. Do best to disabuse.

Jul. 30: Great Cthulhu silent. General loss of confidence.

Aug. 3: Plans to reschedule rally postponed to fall.

Aug. 15: Revelation regarding mating with Fungi from Yuggoth hooted down by congregation.

Sept. 21: New sect, consisting of malcontents from both EOD and NCSW, takes over Congregational church. Mysterious transcendent visitor proclaimed their savior. Too depressing.

Sept. 28: Rally postponed indefinitely.

Oct. 14: Baptist church now in transcendent visitor fold.

Nov. 3: What if, just what if, it's all a delusion? What if there are other, even higher, "gods" who are exploiting Cthulhu *et al.* as dupes and ill-fated stooges? The mind reels, the spirit sags.

Nov. 10: Infinite regress. The end?

III. *Peril in Partridgeville*

Probably the most intriguing reference in Deacon Babcock's account was to Partridgeville, the hometown of Halpin Chalmers and Fred Carstairs. In the next issue of *Drowsing Cortex* I duly noted this connection, with passing mention of the diary as a legacy from my late grand-uncle. Judging from later mailing comments, or lack thereof, my fellow Secret Watchers weren't terribly impressed. At any rate, around this time my activity all but stopped, what with graduate study and eventual placement with an accounting firm on the West Coast. Only after my professional career was firmly on track, circa 1987, did I resume serious pursuit of Chalmers and Carstairs.

Or perhaps I should say Carstairs and Chalmers. The truth is, after a period of being out of the field, I returned to it free of the received wisdom that Halpin Chalmers was the superior writer of the two. Far from being a mere moth basking in the glow of his friend's flame of fame, Fred Carstairs was a behemoth of the occult in his own erratic flight/divine right—as I poetically put it in "Fred Carstairs: Moth or Behemoth?", the lead article in the first issue of the revived *Drowsing Cortex*. That not everyone in the order agreed with my reevaluation came as no surprise. Championing the unjustly neglected can be a lonely job.

One self-appointed task was unearthing the mountains of unreprinted Carstairs material from the tons of pulp magazines that proliferated in the first half of this century. The same dozen and a half tales from his classic *My Dog Tindalos* had been reprinted endlessly in various editions, mostly cheap paperbacks, and I was sure many gems and kernels if not outright nuggets awaited the diligent fan-collector-prospector's pick ax. (Please excuse the poetic metaphors, but at times it's all I can do to resist lapsing into the master's rhapsodic style.) I haunted garage sales, scouted secondhand book shops, scoured occult catalogues—in short, conducted a treasure hunt on a scale never before attempted in the annals of Carstairs research. Collecting these brittle, flaking, yellowed souvenirs of a bygone era's popular entertainment was, I'll admit, for the most part more exciting than reading their contents. Then one day at an estate sale near my home in West Hills, I picked up a ratty copy of an obscure 1940's pulp called *Amazingly Ignorant Planet Stories* (later shortened to *Ignorant Planets*). One tale immediately caught my eye on the contents page—"It Was the Day of the Deep One", by Dana Autosteps—a name I'd come to recognize from my delvings as my hero's preferred pseudonym.

The title was a tip-off that it was set in Innsmouth, and in this respect my hunch proved correct when I settled into my Barcalounger back at my bungalow with my new find. What I soon realized, however, was that this was truly a far more "amazing" (if not astounding or astonishing) tale than I suspect Mr. "Autosteps" let on to the unsuspecting editors of *AIPS*. "It Was the Day of the Deep One" features a protagonist who undergoes a series of spiritual trials uncannily similar to those suffered by the author of the emerald diary I'd inherited from Father Dunn! Coincidence? Synchronicity? "Objective chance?" Sorry, none of the above. No, I could cite page after page of parallel passages, as Martin Gardner has so devastatingly if pedantically done in his recent exposé of that monument to human vanity, the *Urantia Book*—but suffice to say that the main character is named "Perry Babson", who becomes "assistant curate" of the "EOG" (Esoteric Order of *Gorgo*), lives briefly with a family of half-wits in a hick burg called "Dulwich", and so on and so forth. You get the idea. The only important difference is that instead of just petering out like the deacon's diary, "It Was the Day of the Deep One" ends with a *deus ex machina* twist—"supermortals" rescue Babson from the concentration camp where federal agents have illegally imprisoned him and his followers.

If on first reading I felt Carstairs had barely disguised his models, later I wasn't so sure. Just suppose my initial assumption was wrong. What if, just what if, instead of the diary being the source for the story, the story was the source for the diary! As noted earlier, there was something fishy, pardon the pun, about Babcock's account. Carstairs could have written "Day of the Deep One" (an abbreviation I'll use from here on) years before it was published in 1940. The hoaxer, possibly this Father Iwanicki, could have concocted the diary after reading the tale in manuscript. Or, in a somewhat less contrived scenario, he simply cribbed from the magazine appearance. I doubted Father Iwanicki was still alive, if indeed he'd ever existed, but if Poles are at all as fecund as us Irish I had reason to hope I could track down surviving relatives.

But then fate intervened in my favor. I learned that Fred Carstairs was still alive! Yes, as incredible as it may seem, I had been ignorant of this most basic of biographical facts regarding my demigod of occult fiction. He'd been born in Partridgeville in 1893, or 1894, had been the last person to see Halpin Chalmers alive before his brutal murder in 1928, and had married for the first time circa 1960—so much was part of the public record but little else. It just so happened that one member of the Order of the Secret Watcher, who was helping organize the Halpin Chalmers Centennial Conference and was pretty certain the news of his death would have reached at least one of us in the O.S.W., decided to try inviting him to Brooklyn as a special guest of honor. Finally, after many months and much networking, the venerable occultist was located—in Partridgeville!

Diffidence kept me from writing the man immediately, though I refrained in part because rumor had it Carstairs had long ceased answering fan mail, evidently one big reason for his fall into total obscurity. In addition, he appeared to have no phone. In the end, with the Halpin Chalmers Centennial Conference only a few months away, I wrote him a ten-page single-spaced letter in which, almost as an afterthought, I asked about the background to the composition of the "Day of the Deep One." In closing I said I was looking forward to chatting with him in Brooklyn. I had not, by the way, shared my extraordinary discovery with others in the O.S.W., since I had resolved to get the scoop from Carstairs himself before making any announcement. I wanted to avoid any premature speculation.

Receiving, as expected, no response, I decided as a tribute to "Li'l Frednik" (Halpin Chalmers' nickname for his friend in their correspondence) to prepare a special all-Carstairs issue of *Drowsing Cortex*, including a reprint of "Day of the Deep One" along with salient entries from Babcock's emerald diary. In my commentary I drew no conclusions. I signed and numbered each issue by hand. I anticipated presenting copy number one to my idol at the Centennial gathering, now only a week away, but in the moment of creation I was too proud of the finished product to wait. The next morning I dispatched the zine via express mail to Partridgeville, suitably inscribed.

The following day at my office I accepted a collect call from none other than the living legend himself!

"Where in tarnation did you dig up that diary?" shrieked a thin piping voice over the line. "You damned fool! No, I'm the damned fool for having written that story in the first place. Iwanicki was a fool, too, and he paid the price. . . . At the time I needed the money, you see. I was broke. Do not, I tell you, do not republish it! I forbid it—it's too dangerous! *It's not allowed!*"

How characteristically modest of the man, I mused. His protests notwithstanding, I took the opportunity to query him on "Day of the Deep One." Did he borrow from the deacon's account, or did the deacon (or Father Iwanicki) borrow from the appearance in *Amazingly Ignorant Planet Stories*—or perhaps even from the manuscript itself?

"Babcock, er, I mean Babson, stole the idea from me—I swear it! Iwanicki gave your uncle that diary, you say? My God, never trust a priest. My reputation will be ruined, ruined I tell you, if the least hint of any of this gets out. Even though I'm innocent. As if I didn't have enough troubles already. I've never been under such pressure. My wife. . . . "

It was fascinating to listen to Fred Carstairs speak at such length about his current projects—further exclusive material for *Drowsing Cortex*!—but finally I had to ring off, pleading a need to return to my actuarial tables.

"See here, young man, I'm not a plagiarist. I repeat, I'm not a plagiarist!" he said, returning at the last to the subject that had prompted his call in the first place. "And if you have any more copies of that rag you sent me, destroy them, destroy them all! *I beg of you, if not for the sake of an old man on death's doorstep then for your own safety!*"

I ended by saying it would be an honor to meet him in person at the conference. I couldn't take his admonition against reprintng "Day of the Deep One" too seriously, not that I told him that. After all, *Drowsing Cortex* was only a fanzine (though I confess I was hoping to graduate soon to semi-pro status), and I'd put a lot of extra effort into producing this special Carstairs number.

* * *

For all of us who attended the Halpin Chalmers Centennial Conference that fall weekend in Brooklyn, it was an event never to be forgotten. Every notable in the world of Chalmers studies—not to mention Carstairs studies—was present. The highlight of the festivities came Saturday evening with Fred's one-man salute at the Brooklyn Academy of Music, before dozens of adoring fans. During the question and answer period, I perked up when he said that around 1917-18, at meetings of the Partridgeville Amateur Press Club, he remembered his old friend used to enjoy sparring with some Irish plumber over U.S. support of the Allies. I stood up, ready to reveal the identity of Chalmers' long-ago antagonist as my grand-uncle, but before I could be recognized Fred's dynamic wife Ida saw fit to add her two cents to this discussion. With her pet parrot perched on her shoulder, she clambered onto the stage, where she promptly seized the microphone from her open-mouthed husband and started to vilify various occult authors and agents, several of whom were in the audience. Then the bird chimed in, drowning her tirade with its squawks.

I was later disappointed to hear that both Fred and Ida had been whisked back to Partridgeville shortly after this episode by their chauffeur, for I'd been biding my time for the chance to grab a minute or two alone with Carstairs. In particular, I'd been hoping to pin him down on *when* he wrote "Day of the Deep One." As if to make up for this loss in some fashion, I unburdened myself Sunday morning to a reporter who was covering the conference for the *Partridgeville Gazette*, Doug Linnet. To him I explained the whole business about the diary and my theory about who was the originator and who was the imitator. In a show of sympathy, Linnet promised to try to work this into his article. In gratitude I let him have a complimentary copy of the Carstairs issue of *Drowsing Cortex*.

A few months later I received advance tear sheets from the *Partridgeville Gazette*, with the byline Doug Linnet. I scanned the write-up of the Centennial fête for references to myself, to no avail, until I noticed a sidebar with the title "Literary Mystery." "Amateur Carstairs buff believes Halpin Chalmers' unsung sidekick may have resorted to forbidden source for his celebrated occult yarn, 'Daze of the Deep Ones,'" began the piece. It went on to give a more or less accurate account of my researches into the matter, with sample quotations (clearly courtesy of *Drowsing Cortex*) from both the Carstairs story and the Babcock diary. I felt flattered, to say the least, to be cited in a mainstream venue.

Sad to say, not everyone involved was thrilled with such exposure. A couple of days after the tear sheets arrived I took another collect call at my office from Fred. To report that Partridgeville's most esteemed living author was beside himself would be an understatement. Much of his high-pitched whine was unintelligible, but the gist was plain enough—since the publication of Linnet's article all manner of people had been knocking at their door, from curiosity seekers to con men. As eager as he and his wife (and their parrot) were for visitors, this was far more than they could handle at their age. Would I please put a stop to it? I said I'd see what I could do.

Well, as the whole world knows, there was nothing I could do at that point to prevent things from snowballing. Some Woodward and Bernstein wannabes based in Washington got hold of Linnet's article, took advantage of the Freedom of Information Act, and, in a series of investigative reports, in print as well as on TV, blew the lid off the government cover-up of the secret Innsmouth raids during the winter of 1927-28. In due course a bipartisan Congressional committee looked into the affair. A few implicated nonagenarians testified, though not Fred Carstairs—he'd gone into the hospital as soon as the hearings had begun and was deemed too ill even to give a deposition. The headlines said it all: "Ethnic Cleansing in Innsmouth"; "Aquatic Citizens' Religious Rights Violated"; "Shameful Precedent for Internment of Japanese-Americans in World War II." Perhaps the most sensational revelation was that the federal government was still operating a "concentration camp" as an adjunct to its naval base in Portsmouth, New Hampshire. While some conservative fundamentalist types opposed the action, President Clinton issued an executive order in January of '94 authorizing the immediate release of all remaining prisoners. Cynics accused him of playing politics, of throwing a sop to liberals after his betrayal of gays in the military, but I don't think he would have invited the survivors unless he was sincere. (A pity Father Dunn died before the Clinton era—he would have been green with pride to witness this son of the old sod promote peace in Ireland.)

Through it all, to my annoyance, the literary niceties were overlooked. Despite my offers to talk, no reporter bothered to call me for more than an exploratory interview. Nobody outside the occult field seemed to care whether Fred Carstairs had written "Day of the Deep One" based on the Babcock diary or not. (Even within the field, despite all the national publicity, few were that interested in resolving the question.) Happily, some tantalizing clues did come out in the Congressional hearings. One Father Iwanicki had in fact served as R.C. chaplain at the time of the raids, which experience led him to open a mission in Innsmouth later that year. Unfortunately, within a week of arriving in the rumor-shadowed seaport he'd drowned after falling off a rotten wharf. This explains why my granduncle never returned the diary. As for Fred Carstairs, at a date shortly after Halpin Chalmers' murder (a tragedy that must have shaken him a great deal), he had taken a janitorial job at the Portsmouth concentration camp, a position in which, it struck me, he could have easily mingled with the prisoners. Perhaps as a writer he carefully recorded the conversations he overheard for possible future fictional use!

At last I felt as if I were on the verge of some final answers. I even started to plan another trip east, whose central purpose would be to speak with Fred in the hospital, assuming he was still *compos*. No one in the O.S.W. was quite sure of his current state of health. Then, a week after the presidential pardon, I opened a letter from Doug Linnet and saw the obituary: "Local Occult Author Dead at 100." I was too late. I immediately wrote the widow a condolence letter in which I specifically asked if she could shed any light on her late husband's composition of "Day of the Deep One."

Not long afterward I was awakened before dawn by a collect call from someone whose name I didn't catch but in my fog accepted anyway. In the next second a shrill female voice, with no introduction, barreled through the line. I heard a bird screech in the background and I realized I was talking to Ida Carstairs:

"Thank God, thank God, deliverance has come! My poor little Fredela is free at last! And one of his oldest and best friends has been here to help me through my time of grief. Oh, thank God, thank God. And what a gentleman, too, not like those awful occult fans. Bah! Not one of them ever visited Fred in the hospital, not one! Let me tell you. . . . " I listened patiently until she returned to what seemed to be her main point. " . . . yes, he was the only one. Came all the way from Portsmouth or Innsmouth, some coastal town up north. Fred took one look at his old friend and his mouth dropped a foot. I was there! I saw it! He was so touched by his only visitor besides me, his devoted Idasha, he couldn't stand it! He went into convulsions. It was the end. But do you know what? His old friend was a clergyman! It was perfect—he performed the last rites at his bedside—in Latin! Anyhow, it wasn't English. Can you imagine?" As eager as I was to hear the details of Fred's final moments, I was beginning to wonder what on earth all this had to do with me. "He took me home, dealt with the arrangements, went through Fred's papers. When I showed him your letter he got very excited. He was sure you had some book that used to belong to him. Couldn't wait to call you—had to fly out last night to L.A. His name? Babson, Babcock, something like that. He said just to call him *Deacon*."

I was now sufficiently awake to realize I was soon to meet the answer to my prayers.

About Robert M. Price

Robert M. Price has edited *Crypt of Cthulhu* for seventeen years. His essays on Lovecraft have appeared in *Lovecraft Studies*, *The Lovecrafter*, *Cerebretron*, *Dagon*, *Étude Lovecraftienne*, *Mater Tenebrarum*, and in *An Epicure in the Terrible* and *Twentieth Century Literary Criticism*. His horror fiction has appeared in *Nyctalops*, *Eldritch Tales*, *Etchings & Odysseys*, *Grue*, *Footsteps*, *Deathrealm*, *Weirdbook*, *Fantasy Book*, *Vollmond*, and elsewhere. He has edited *Tales of the Lovecraft Mythos* and *The New Lovecraft Circle* for Fedogan & Bremer, as well as *The Horror of It All* and *Black Forbidden Things* for Starmont House. His books include *H. P. Lovecraft and the Cthulhu Mythos* (Borgo Press) and *Lin Carter: A Look behind His Imaginary Worlds* (Starmont).

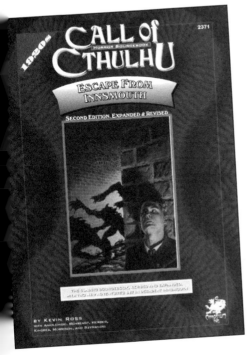